Touched

Touched

CORRINE JACKSON

KENSINGTON PUBLISHING CORP.

www.kensingtonbooks.com

To my Mom—
You gave me my first dictionary, first typewriter,
   and first book. That's pretty much everything.
All my love,
Me

CHAPTER ONE

Okay. This is going to hurt like hell.

Taking a deep breath, I stepped into the room, my movements piercing the alcoholic haze insulating Dean. He straightened to his full six-foot-three when he noticed me, his eye twitching when I stared back unblinking. Maybe he suspected I was a freak and it scared him. Maybe he was scared of himself, of what he wanted from me. I figured that's why he mostly hit my mother when I wasn't around.

Unknotting my hands from white knuckled fists, I hoped to defuse the tension before it exploded.

"You're home early," he said, his heavy-lidded stare straying over me without meeting my eyes.

Tall and plain, I was skinny with no curves, but that didn't matter. My skin crawled when his pale blue eyes tracked me through a room. I went out of my way to stay away when he was alone in the apartment, but sometimes he managed to corner me in the shadows of our dim hallway. Sick in ways I couldn't cure, he'd crowd me with his hulking body and laugh when I'd lurch away to avoid his touch.

The funny thing was that Dean looked like the grown version of that charming, innocent boy all the girls crushed on in high school. He had soft, blond curls and a friendly, open face that charmed the unaware. Perhaps that's what had attracted Anna to him in the first place.

"Maybe I should call ahead next time?" I mused. "That way you could plan to finish beating my mother by 9:05, I can arrange to have the ambulance here by 9:10, and we can all be in bed by midnight."

My flat voice held no sarcasm, only bitter resignation. Dean's hands tightened into fists that could feel like steel. I'd stayed too long, trying to protect my mother, but Anna loved Dean more than anything. More than me. Dean loved how my father's child support checks kept him drinking down to the worm at the bottom of his tequila bottles.

He stepped closer. "Gonna stop me, princess?"

My indifferent act never fooled him. After seeing Anna's unconscious body on the floor, I wished I could kill him. I shuddered in anticipation of the brutality to come and the moment I would touch Anna. Never taking my eyes from him, I slid sideways to keep the threadbare couch and scarred coffee table between us. Anna moaned, and Dean's gaze flicked to her, his lip curled in disgust.

"You think you're a man because you beat up women?" I taunted to distract him.

His smile raised the hair on my arms. It was a smile of warning—a smile to predict the weather by because hell was sure to rain down on its recipient. "You think you're better than me, kid, but you're gonna respect me." He whipped his belt from the loops of his dirty jeans. The buckle glinted in the light when he wrapped the black leather around his fist—a bright, shiny weapon.

Hate speared through me, along with paralyzing fear. *Better to make him angry,* I decided. Then, maybe, it would end faster. I sneered while sidling closer to Anna.

"Respect you? You're barely human. A pathetic coward. You want to hit me, don't you, Dean? Go ahead."

I'd never ridiculed him before and, within two feet of Anna's limp body, my courage faltered. *Stupid. Stupid. He'll kill us both.* At least the ghoulish waiting game would be over. He'd come close enough to touch me when I whispered, "I dare you to try."

He charged and pulled back his arm to hit me as I stepped in front of Anna. His fist landed in my stomach, and I tripped over her. My head bounced off the wall with a dull thud. Dean's hand clamped around my throat, stalling my fall to the ground as he pinned me, and I inhaled the stale mix of sweat and tobacco wafting from him. Cutting off my breath, he smiled and squeezed his fingers until the pain weakened my knees.

Anna rolled at my feet and screamed, "No!" She jumped on Dean, trying to drag him off me, her red fingernails biting into his forearm. Desperate for air, I clamped one hand on his arm and clutched my mother with the other.

My eyes squeezed shut. *I'm dying,* I thought. Then my ability to think fractured. The mental wall barricading my power collapsed and, without the defense, Anna's pain thundered through me, allowing me to see inside her body. I noted two broken ribs, a concussion, black eye, and bruises scattered all over her body. Dots of color popped against my closed lids in a spectacular fireworks show. My lungs constricted, and I embraced Anna's aches, healing them and grafting her pain to my own.

Dean's grip loosened as he stumbled beneath Anna's attack, and he yanked her hair to toss her away. She sobbed, and the storm inside me doubled and tripled in size. I had failed to protect her. Filled with rage, I imagined all my pain striking Dean down like fiery lightning.

Violent red light sizzled between my hand and his arm. His face froze in horror as his body jerked and convulsed. A loud crack splintered the air—his ribs breaking or mine—and I passed out.

★ ★ ★

I woke to a soft hand brushing the hair from my face and the scent of musky perfume. *Anna.* Fear cut through the hazy edges of sleep, and I sat up too fast. Ignoring my aching stomach muscles, I searched for Dean, but only Anna sat with me. Weak sunlight shone through the single window, and the scratchy sheets screamed hospital. *So I didn't die.*

My throat burned as I tamped down tears.

Anna watched me, and I assessed her injuries. There'd been no time to finish healing her with Dean's hand wrapped around my neck, and she would have hidden her injuries from the doctors. I seized her arm, ignoring her attempt to pull away in undisguised revulsion. My internal body scan revealed some older wounds she'd hidden since I'd healed her a few weeks ago. A sharp pinch of regret stung me, and then my emotions flew away as I opened my mind to absorb her injuries.

Anna winced, but I ignored this, too, helping her deeper bruises to heal. Her broken ribs I'd taken on already, but I couldn't heal her concussion. Head wounds did the most damage to me and were the most difficult for me to heal. My mother would have a pounding headache, but she'd survive to be beaten down another day. Finished, I sighed in relief. Soft, familiar blue sparks trailed from my fingertips down her arm as I released her.

She shrank back and started to cry. Frigid cold replaced the heat of energy that went hand in hand with the healing, and I shivered. She knew what I could do. How could she not know with the number of times I'd healed her since I'd discovered my ability at twelve? She hated my power and pretended it didn't exist, even while bruises sprouted on my skin, twins of those disappearing from hers.

"Where's Dean?" The rasp of my voice startled me, and

I wondered if the damage caused by strangulation could be permanent.

"He's here, too. He . . . he was hurt . . . when he fell. His ribs are broken. The doctor says he'll be okay."

Her tone said she'd already convinced herself that the impossible had not happened. She touched my hand in a rare gesture. "Listen, baby. The cops . . . They have a lot of questions about what happened. I told them it was all a misunderstanding."

That explained why she sat with me instead of Dean. She'd wanted to ensure I'd lie for her. I rolled away so I wouldn't have to look at her, and she brushed a tentative hand through my hair. She would tell me I shouldn't anger Dean. If I would just behave . . . I'd heard this all a thousand times before. It was never Dean's fault when his fist cuffed her in the head. It was her fault for not getting him his beer fast enough. It couldn't be his fault he ground his lit cigarette into my arm. I should have handed over my paycheck from the video store.

Sure enough, she started talking about how things would be different when we got home. We had to try harder to be a family. Her words sickened me, and I covered my ears with a pillow, shouting *Shut up! Shut up!* in my head.

I must have slept after she left because the room had darkened, and my father had arrived.

Ben O'Malley had been MIA most of my life. Once, years ago, I'd called him, thinking he would come riding in like a knight in shining armor to save me. His secretary had told me he'd been too busy to come to the phone and promised to give him a message. He'd never called back. After that, I refused to talk to him when he made the obligatory birthday and holiday calls, until eventually, he'd stopped calling altogether.

Ben noticed I'd awakened and stood over me. "Remy? How do you feel?"

My eyes raked his tall frame, studying him for the first time in years. Any stranger could see I was his daughter. I had his height and wavy, thick hair that walked the border between curls and frizz, though his was a peppered black to my dirty blond.

"Remy?"

"What are you doing here?"

My father filled a cup with water from a pink pitcher sitting on the bedside table. Dropping a straw in the cup, he tilted it toward me. I wanted nothing more than to refuse that sip of water, but my throat burned. After drawing on the straw for a moment, I leaned back, and it occurred to me that my injuries should have healed by now. Whatever had happened with Dean had short-circuited my ability to heal myself, though I'd healed Anna without a problem.

My father's voice cut into my thoughts, and I frowned. "The police called to notify me that my daughter had been admitted to the hospital," Ben said. "They suspected her mother's husband was responsible for her injuries, although Anna denied that."

The cops hadn't believed her lies. "So?" I croaked.

Ben's black brows drew together over navy eyes like mine. "What do you mean 'so'?"

"I mean, so what are you doing here?"

"I told you. They said you were hurt," he repeated, confused.

My rusty laugh sounded like an ancient engine turning over. "Where were you the last eight times this happened?"

His shock sliced deeply because he hadn't cared enough to know what happened to me. Ben sucked in a breath, his tan face ashen, and his voice tight with anger. "Why didn't you tell me? I would've helped you. Remy, I would've . . ."

Shaking my head, I laughed again. He blamed me.

"Right. You would've. Why don't you go back to your wife and your perfect family? You can remind yourself what a good father you are when you sign your next child support check."

I shut him out by closing my eyes, like I had with Anna. It was too much. My father's appearance, my mother and Dean, my erratic ability . . . And the gnawing fear about how Dean would punish me for hurting him.

Then my father said, "You're coming to live with me."

Two days later, the March wind cut through my thin coat and whipped my hair out of its band as I sneaked out of my father's house. I headed for the deserted beach near the marina at the end of the street. Melting snow mingled with the sand and dirt to create puddles of watery mud. Rocks and broken clamshells littered the beach, and I picked my way over to a weathered log to sink down and watch a lone sailboat fly across the water. The water didn't work itself up to waves, but lapped the shore like a lazy tongue.

The forest with its naked ladies shivering without their autumn dresses, the blue water of the harbor, and the immense morning sky soothed my anger. My father had grown a conscience. Anna had cried when Ben told her he was taking me and to hell with the custody agreement. He did not ask if I wanted to go, but threw his weight around until I found myself on a plane to Nowhere-Frickin'-Maine.

Nobody cared what I wanted. It had been so long since I'd thought beyond surviving Dean, I wasn't sure how I would have answered. Three options lay before me. I could give up and let Dean win. Let him convince me I was worth nothing. Or I could run and try to make it on my own. My savings would get me a week of freedom in a cheap motel, but that was about it. Last option, I could accept my father's help. Maybe I could convince Ben to sign emancipation papers.

I'd have to keep my freak ability a secret if I stayed. That meant leaving my injuries alone because people would notice if the bruises disappeared from one moment to the next. Yet, I needed to know if my power to heal myself had returned. Crowds could kill if the stranger next to me carried a disease or illness I couldn't cure. Sometimes, their pain could reach out and grab me, no matter how hard I concentrated on blocking them.

To safeguard my secret, I'd have to pick a hidden injury, one of my taped broken ribs. Like I'd done a dozen times before, I pictured the broken bone and imagined it mending. A sharp stab speared my side as the bone fused, and I gasped even as the pain faded and my breathing flowed easier. I tipped my face to the sun in relief.

In the distance, a camera shutter clicked.

A boy about my age stood some yards away holding one of those large professional-looking cameras with all the mysterious attachments. My heart skittered as my attention shifted from object to boy.

Striking. If I'd had to pick one word to describe him, that would have been it. Tall and lean, he moved with ease, at home in his skin and sure of his footing. He'd tower over me, I noted with odd pleasure. Deep-chocolate brown hair fell in long waves to his neck. Sharp planes and angles defined his tanned face. Full, sensual lips and a square, shadowed jaw completed the rugged picture marred by a two-inch white scar that slashed through one eyebrow to the top of one high cheekbone.

And his eyes. I sucked in a breath. Even from twenty feet away, their dark green color reminded me of the woods that hugged the marina. The intent expression in those deep-set eyes held a trace of surprise as if he hadn't expected company on the beach. An all too recognizable air of resigned loneliness hung about him, prompting a pang of kinship.

One of his thick brows rose, and I realized I'd been returning his stare for some time.

Sudden, wild embarrassment sent my gaze flicking back to the view of the harbor. *Stupid, Remy. He was probably taking pictures of the scenery.* I wondered if he would try to talk to me. Perhaps he'd say, "Do I know you?" Except it would not be a pickup line. Gangly and boyishly slim, I wasn't the kind of girl boys hit on. I was the girl who went to a high school for two years and managed not to have a single friend.

It didn't matter, anyway. He walked toward the water with long strides. At the edge of the shore he twisted from the view of the bay as if to determine his next shot of the backdrop of sky and forest behind me.

I peeked over at him, only to look away when I found him staring back. My heart stuttered until the meaning of that raised eyebrow penetrated. *It's the bruises,* I realized. This morning, the bathroom mirror had revealed a black eye and a grisly necklace ringing my throat, the mottled blend of purple and indigo betraying the impression of five fingers. My battered face had sparked the stranger's curiosity. Feeling like an idiot, I returned his stare with open defiance.

He didn't pretend he'd been watching anything other than me. As he gripped his camera in both hands, his stare traveled over my face and unkempt hair, and I tried to ignore him by studying the view.

Soon, the town yawned and began to wake, and the odd intimacy of the isolated beach faded as cars and people created a buzz of activity. A restaurant at the marina must have opened for business. The smell of brewing coffee and greasy diner food nearly doubled me over. My last meal had been a packet of peanuts on the plane the night before. My joints had stiffened in the brisk air, and it hurt to stand as I braced myself for the walk to Ben's home.

A shutter clicked for the second time, and I turned to see the boy aiming his camera at me. Pictures snapped in quick succession, and I was his subject. Not a person, but an object to be studied and captured on film.

Perhaps the boy thought I'd be flattered. I felt violated.

I moved without premeditation. He continued shooting pictures at my approach, adjusting the lens as I stalked closer. Maybe he was taller and more muscular, but the outrage vibrating through me evened the odds. An arm's length away, I stretched up to grab the camera. The boy shifted away and gave a surprised laugh.

Furious, I tried to grab it again, careful not to touch him. When he sidestepped me again, I slipped on the stones and landed on my back in the snow and mud. My body ached with the jolt, and I focused on the act of breathing.

I expected him to laugh again, but he crouched down on his heels at my side. "Are you okay?"

The anger disappeared, replaced by mortification when he leaned close, his worried eyes capturing mine. My thoughts splintered. I'd been wrong about the scar. It wasn't an imperfection. Every one of his features had been chosen with care by a master.

"I didn't mean to make you fall. I was protecting my camera."

He stretched one arm toward me, and panic had me twisting away until I gained my hands and knees. The remaining broken rib protested, and I breathed in harsh gasps. Bracing an arm around my middle, I looked up into the boy's startled face, his hand still frozen in midair. He'd been offering to help me up, unaware that any illness he carried could flatten me.

He didn't know what to make of my actions, and I

couldn't blame him because I'd acted crazy. An unexpected laugh bubbled out of my lips as I kneeled in the muck with an arm wrapped around my ribs and wet sand caking my jeans. The boy's lips twitched. When I lifted one hand to swipe my hair back, I realized that mud covered it and laughed again.

My raised arm caused his eyes to drop to my neck, and I sobered in an instant as his eyes narrowed on the bruises my blouse didn't cover. I bared my teeth in a polite smile and stood without his help. He rose, too, and the lithe movement hinted at a power leashed by tight control. This wasn't the first time some stranger had studied me after one of Dean's beatings, and I hated to be pitied.

Up close, I could see that the camera wasn't digital. Who used film anymore? I held out one dirty hand and asked, "Do you mind?" At his puzzled look, I added, "The film, please."

"Why?"

My irritation resurfaced. "You should've asked before you took my picture."

One side of his mouth tilted up in the smallest suggestion of a smile. "You're on a public beach."

I couldn't place his accent, and it occurred to me he could be a tourist. His rough voice had the clipped precision of the British, but the tone sounded a little flat, like an American. Maybe I looked like a local to him.

"You still should've asked." I said.

One elegant shoulder lifted in a shrug.

He had no intention of giving me the film. Those pictures of me would end up out in the world to be viewed by complete strangers. People like him could never understand what it felt like to be reduced to a defenseless animal.

No more wasting energy on lost causes, Remy. Without another word, I walked away.

His low voice followed me. "That's it? You're going to give up that easy?"

"Yes," I called over my shoulder.

"You're not going to ask why I took your picture?"

I wanted to, but I wouldn't give him the satisfaction. Instead, I shouted, "No."

The boy walked at my side and I hadn't heard him move, though my steps crunched in the grit of crushed shells and rocks. Startled, I tripped over a piece of driftwood. He threw out a hand to steady me, but I jumped out of reach.

"I'm not going to hurt you."

"I never thought you would."

"Then, stop overreacting." His voice gentled as if he reasoned with a child.

"Go to hell."

We glared at each other until the wind worried my blouse. I forced my hand to be still at my side instead of hiding the marks like I wanted.

"Who did that to you?" He indicated my neck with a tilt of his head.

Years of living with Dean had taught me to lie about my injuries and my ability to heal. I'd developed a talent for spinning stories because no one would believe the truth. Most people didn't care enough to ask questions and, if they did, they believed any explanation offered because they didn't want to get involved.

"I ran into a door," I said. Not one of my better lies, but what did it matter?

"When did you run into this . . . door?"

I sighed. "Three days ago. Are you always this nosy?"

His eyes took on a speculative gleam as a breeze ruffled his hair.

My body stilled, and I wondered if he suspected what I could do. What I was. A freak. It wasn't likely, but I hurried my pace. I didn't know what would happen if people found out about me, but every instinct I had shouted bad things. Very bad things.

I looked toward the parking lot nearest the beach and saw Ben's silver Mercedes pull up. He'd discovered me gone and had come looking for me. When he got out of the car and stood with one hand on the roof, I waved to catch his attention.

"Here."

The boy's smooth voice stopped me, and I turned to see the roll of film he held out in one palm.

"Take it," he said, when I hesitated.

I don't know why I did it. I'd never tried to scan a person without touching them. My ability had always required a physical connection to work. Yet I lowered my mental wall and opened my senses, letting the energy flood through me before pushing it out toward him.

The boy frowned, and his eyes widened. His dark head tilted to one side as if he could *feel* me scanning him. I tried to break the connection. Usually I thought it and it happened. Now, a fiery wave of energy poured back at me from him. The boy hadn't moved, but his forehead wrinkled in concentration.

This had never happened.

It wasn't how my healing worked. Pain I expected when I touched someone for the first time, not knowing what their injuries and illnesses were. But always after the aches followed a . . . *humming*. A hum of electricity flowed through me, and I could direct the current of energy to scan a person. That's how I knew what their injuries were and how I healed the diseases, the broken bones and bruises I found. It felt like a thousand pins and needles rippling under my skin like my entire body was one large limb gone to sleep. It was always a relief to break contact with a person after healing when the humming would fizzle out. That's when whatever ailment I'd healed would settle into my body, and the real pain hit.

It all began with a touch.

This boy and I weren't touching, but my entire body hummed with energy like I was healing stage-four cancer. Except I wasn't focusing the power. The heat of his energy surrounded me in an unbreakable embrace, and my heart skipped because I had no idea how to stop him.

A green spark passed between us.

My father called, "Remy?"

The boy's focus broke. The electric current dissipated, and I threw up the mental barrier I kept in place when walking through crowds. Ben still stood at his car, and I noticed with relief that he couldn't have seen the sparks with my body blocking them.

I waved again before turning back to the boy. He hadn't moved an inch and stared at me with hunger. His energy felt like a lit keg of explosives, and I sensed it coming at me again. The boy's face twisted in something like pain and frustration when my defenses held. I wasn't sure what he'd done, but I knew I'd never been this terrified, even when Dean stood over me with both fists raised.

I took several steps toward Ben, and, when I was brave enough to turn my back on the boy, ran the distance to my father's car. Not caring that my wet, sandy jeans ruined the gray leather, I slid into the passenger seat. Safe inside the car, I chanced a look at the beach. My retreat had taken maybe twenty seconds, but the shore was empty.

The boy had disappeared.

CHAPTER TWO

*S*itting across from Ben in a maroon vinyl booth at the Seaside Café, I waited for him to yell at me for sneaking out my first morning under his roof or for ruining his leather seat with my muddy clothes. His continued silence made me uncomfortable, but the scene on the beach had left me shaken.

"Hey, Ben. What can I get you?"

A server—Dana, according to her plastic name tag—arrived to take our order, and she eyed me with curiosity.

Ben asked me, "Are you hungry?"

My stomach gave an embarrassing growl. Ben must have been a café regular because Dana took my order for a veggie scramble and coffee and left without taking his order.

The café butted up against the bay with huge windows offering sweeping views of the harbor, filled with everything from working boats with their tangle of nets to expensive sailboats rocking against their wooden berths. I studied my father in the bright morning light. A lot of women would consider Ben attractive in his jeans and cable-knit sweater. He examined me, too, his gaze roving over my face. I grimaced when I realized my black blouse mirrored the exact shade of his sweater—no one could deny I was his. Except he had, time and again, when birthdays and holidays passed without a call or a stupid Hallmark greeting card.

"You look like me. I don't see your mother in you at all. Except the hair and freckles."

"I'm not like either of you," I answered in a flat voice.

With a frown, he started to speak, but Dana returned with our coffee. Ben watched me dump three packets of sugar and four thimble-sized containers of creamer into my mug. "You're too young to drink coffee."

Taking a sip, I eyed him over the ceramic edge of my cup. The time had passed for him to tell me what to do.

He almost smiled, and some of his edginess disappeared. When he shook his head and laughed, it vanished entirely. "I see what you mean. Your mother would never have your nerve."

I thought he laughed at me, and I scowled. He spread his hands wide, palms up on the table as if to apologize. His eyes flicked to the bruises on my face, but Dana interrupted again by bringing our food. It smelled incredible, but I felt too self-conscious to dig in while he watched. Ben seemed to understand because he waved for me to start eating and excused himself to make a call.

I'd finished my eggs and was playing with a piece of toast when he slid back into the booth. He eyed my empty coffee mug and the crumbs on my plate, but I didn't make excuses. The food at the hospital had sucked.

"You called Laura?"

We'd arrived in Blackwell Falls so late I hadn't met his wife or daughter yet.

He smiled. "I didn't want her to worry. We thought you'd run back to New York."

"Oh." After tossing the toast on my plate, I wiped my fingers on a napkin.

"Remy?" Concerned eyes met mine. "At the hospital,

you asked me where I was the other eight times you were hurt. Will you tell me what happened?"

Shredding my napkin, I shook my head. Some things I couldn't talk about.

Ben's brows drew together in frustration. "Your mother called last night. She asked if you were okay."

His eyes scanned my face, inspecting the bruises that would match those that had covered Anna's face. My least favorite part of healing was that it always came at a cost.

"Well?" he asked.

"Well, what?"

The edgy tone returned as he grew impatient. "Are you okay?"

Watching a local refill his coffee cup from the server's station, I wished I could do the same with my empty mug.

Ben slapped both hands on the table, causing me to jump. "Talk to me, Remy, because I don't know what you need."

Of course he didn't know what I needed. He didn't know *me*. I shrugged. "I'm fine. I can handle a few bruises." Then, to make my intention clear, I added, "I'm not going back to New York."

Without hesitation, he nodded. "Where does that leave us?"

The edge of the booth cut into my thighs as I slid forward. "I want to be emancipated. I turn eighteen in a few months anyway."

My eager answer surprised him, and he leaned away to study me. "What do you need from me, then?"

He didn't seem against the idea, and I rushed on. "I need a place to stay until I get on my feet. I'll pay rent, of course."

I tapped my fingers on the table until Ben's hand stopped me. My guard was up after what happened on the beach. No blue sparks. Warm brown skin blended with mine. The brief touch revealed he had an irregular heartbeat before I yanked my hand away.

He waited for me to look up. "What kind of job will you get without a high school diploma? Where will you live? What about college? Have you thought this through?"

"Yes," I hissed. "I'm not stupid. I intend to finish high school, and I have money put away for college." It wasn't much, but he didn't need to know that.

"The little you saved working at the video store? I don't think so."

How did he know that? "I'm not going back," I repeated.

With an encouraging smile, he pushed his coffee mug toward me as if he knew how badly I yearned for another cup. "Of course not. There's another option. The one we've already set in motion. Live with me."

I shook my head before he finished. I wasn't prepared for how tempted I was to take him up on it, but I'd learned the hard way not to count on anyone.

"Think about it," I said. "You don't want me. I would get in the way of your perfect life. Have *you* really thought this through? Imagine having to tell your friends about your seventeen-year-old mistake. You couldn't even bring yourself to introduce me to Dana, who obviously knows you." Bitterness crept into my tone. "What about your wife and daughter? You think they'd be happy if I stay?"

His expression didn't change, so I exchanged logic for persuasion. "Look, just sign emancipation papers and let me go. It'll be like I never came here." I didn't know how I'd keep that promise considering my savings, but I would.

Ben said nothing, and I hated him for stringing this out. *We both know you want me gone.*

He signaled the waitress for the check. When she came to our table, he smiled and said, "Dana, I'd like you to meet my daughter. Remy moved to town this week to live with my family."

I stared at Ben in shock, ignoring Dana's greeting. She wandered away, and I said, "That's not funny. What do you think you're doing?"

He stood and threw money on the table to pay for the check. "I'm not signing any papers. You're coming home with me. No job and no rent."

Simmering, I followed Ben when he walked away. He had to be toying with me. He held open the café door for me, and then the car door. The mud that speckled the passenger seat went unmentioned.

"Why?" I demanded when he sat next to me.

"You need me."

At my stormy expression, he said, "Okay, maybe you don't *need* me, but you shouldn't have to go it alone. I won't let you. I'm going to be there for you this time."

A new emotion overwhelmed me. Hope. Irrational, unreliable hope. Ben put a hand under my chin, touching me for the second time. Blue sparks shot from my skin through his fingers, and I noted again his heart arrhythmia. The condition didn't seem harmful, but my body worked to heal him.

He didn't seem to notice the flash of light. "You don't believe me."

I didn't deny it, and he let me go to start the car. "It's okay, Remy. I wouldn't believe me if I was you, either. But I am your father, and I'm going to start acting like it."

"You're not my father, Ben. It's too late."

Grimacing at my use of his first name, he nodded in reluctant acceptance. "Okay. That's fair. Then I'll be your friend as long as you let me."

I shrugged this off as one of the lies adults told kids when they thought it was what we wanted to hear. "Why the about-face? For seventeen years you've acted like I didn't exist."

Shame and guilt twisted his features. "I've wanted you in my life a long time. Your mother convinced me it was better for you if I stayed away. I *let* her convince me because it was easier for me that way." His eyes turned fiercely to the road. "I won't be that selfish with you again. I'd like to get to know you if you'll give me a chance."

My arms crossed in stubborn refusal as we turned onto his street.

"Give me one month," he entreated. "If it doesn't work out, I'll help you go out on your own. Deal?"

Hope tried to emerge again, but I wouldn't let it. A person didn't change from one heartbeat to the next. *And yet . . .* My heart skipped in an irregular rhythm while his now beat a steady tempo. He almost didn't hear me when I whispered, "Deal."

Laura met us at the door when we arrived home. *Home. This isn't your home, Remy. Don't forget that!* I could handle being unwanted, and Ben's wife and daughter would not hurt me when they rejected me, as they were sure to do. Squaring my shoulders, I reminded myself this was temporary as I faced his family.

Laura, a petite woman with a heart-shaped face and short red curls, had a mouth ready to tip into a smile at any moment. The top of her head just reached my shoulder, making me a giant next to her.

"Hi," I said.

"Remy, you're okay!"

Her arms surrounded me, as she enveloped me in a cloud of floral perfume. Another scan and diagnosis: *Healthy.* I sighed in relief. During the short car ride I'd realized how drained I felt, both emotionally and physically.

Another sick person might be the end of me. When I didn't return the embrace, her arms loosened and she stepped back, dropping her hands to her side. Dark circles underscored her soft brown eyes, and I was certain I was responsible for them.

"Thanks, Laura," I said, licking my chapped lips. "I'm sorry if I worried you. I went for a walk and lost track of time."

She beamed, but she didn't touch me when she gestured for me to enter the oversized white "cottage" I'd only seen the likes of in pictures of Cape Cod or the Hamptons. My surroundings surprised me as I looked at the interior for the first time in the light of day. The wild outdoors trailed inside like the ocean had crashed through the house, leaving behind bits of coastline. Sea glass hung from invisible threads in the windows, setting off a colorful display of light on the walls and ceiling. A stone fireplace blazed with a welcoming fire, and the furniture and decorations mimicked the sea and sand in shades of blues and tans. Better yet, the wide windows offered an unobstructed view of the harbor and the beach I'd walked earlier.

Also reflected in the window were Laura and Ben sharing an intimate look behind me. He gave her an encouraging smile, and she reached for his hand, their love for one another obvious. What would it have been like to be raised by them? My throat ached: It did no good to wish things were different. Reality sucked, but you couldn't escape it.

Laura smiled when I shifted and cleared my throat. "Are you hungry, Remy?"

"No, thank you. I had breakfast at the café."

"Oh, of course. Okay, then."

An uncomfortable silence ruled the room, and none of us knew what to do next. I decided to retreat. "Ben, would you mind if I rested for a while? I'm pretty tired."

He'd mentioned going to the hospital again on the drive here, but I'd refused. Instead of picking up the thread of that argument, he said, "Sure. You remember where your room is?"

I nodded and left them to walk up the stairs to a huge second-floor landing with two doors on either side opening to bedrooms. I headed to the right and shoved the door open with my foot. My new bedroom was larger than both mine and Anna's together in Brooklyn and decorated with furniture that cost more than our savings account had ever seen. The view from the window drew me.

My breath iced the glass. It was snowing outside now, and white powder dusted the sea grass that crept from the beach toward a tangle of leafless maples. The scent of wet earth and sea permeated everything, cloying and clinging with each breath. It should have been depressing for a girl used to miles of concrete and steel. Instead, the untamed beauty of the landscape fascinated me.

As I had been by the boy from the beach.

Perhaps I'd imagined the whole thing. I wasn't suffering the normal aftereffects of a healing, and my aches weren't new. Yet, he'd sensed when my guard had come down and turned the flow of energy back on me before I could scan him. Was that what it felt like to be on the receiving end of my power? A raw buzz of energy had poured through my body. When I did the scanning, there was *humming* and pain. It hurt Anna when I healed broken bones, but no worse than what a doctor caused when setting the same bone. Sharp pain followed by intense relief, as I knew from experience.

Could he heal people, too? Maybe he'd been trying to heal my injuries. If so, being on the receiving end of my ability was scarier than I'd imagined.

No . . . his energy had been different. Hungrier. More

terrifying. Plus, he'd had that scar on his brow and should have been able to heal himself. Maybe he had other powers. . . . I felt a surge of excitement. He was the first person like me I'd encountered. More than anything, I wanted to learn everything about him, but instinct warned me away.

Good instincts had kept me alive this long, and they said the boy was dangerous. If I ever saw him again, I'd walk the other way. The slight twinge of regret I felt could be ignored.

I stared down at the dramatic scenery. An urge to be out there in the storm, to feel the snow melting on my skin, seized me. If I stayed long enough, I could explore those woods in the fall when they exploded into reds and molten gold. Bells sounded in my head clamoring *"danger, danger"* when I thought of the future.

What the hell, I decided, and rested my forehead against the cold glass. One month wasn't so long.

As soon as my head hit the pillow, I fell asleep. I started awake in a darkened room in the middle of a nightmare in which Dean had cornered me in a hallway without doors. It took me a moment to remember where I was when I heard the bedroom door open and the soft murmur of unfamiliar voices. It wasn't Dean watching me from the shadows, but Ben and Laura checking on me. I pretended to be asleep, and they left without disturbing me.

The nightmare made it impossible to fall asleep again. Sweating, uncomfortable, and aware of every gloomy silhouette, I waited until the house itself seemed to sleep. Then I climbed out of bed and crept to the kitchen, where I hunted for and found the knives in the third drawer from the left. Five months ago I'd started sleeping with a steak knife, and I wanted the small amount of security it offered. Back in the guest room, I slipped it under my pillow and ran my finger along the serrated edge. I didn't know if I'd be able to use it, but I felt safer with it nearby. Exhausted, I closed my eyes on the shadows.

Drifting in a dreamless sleep, I woke again when someone bounced on my bed.

My eyes cracked opened enough to spy a girl about my age staring at me. Lucy had Laura's heart-shaped face and brown eyes, but Ben's black hair that looped in tight curls instead of indecisive waves like mine. I pulled a pillow over my head to shut her and a twinge of envy out. It was too early in the morning to deal with my new family. Then it hit me. *Morning.* I'd slept a day and night away.

My voice came out muffled and grumpy when I asked, "What time is it?"

She sounded cheery and bright when she answered, "Seven. We were starting to wonder if you were ever going to wake up. Dad sent me to act as an alarm. He said to tell you we're enrolling you at the high school with me tomorrow, if you feel up to it."

Groaning, I tossed the pillow aside. The girl hadn't moved and wasn't planning on leaving. I guessed she must be a year or so younger than me since I was Ben's firstborn.

"I'm Remy."

Your sister. Her knee brushed my calf when she shifted. Out of habit, I focused my attention on her enough to make sure she wasn't carrying a hidden disease capable of flattening me. *Nothing. Healthy, except for her irritating morning cheer.*

She nodded. "I know. I've been waiting for you to wake up."

"Sorry about that. It's been a long week."

Serious brown eyes studied me. "Dad told us what happened. Want to talk about it?"

"Uh, no." Seriously, what was with this family's need to talk everything out?

Lucy smiled and wound a curl around her finger. "That's okay. We're glad you're here. By the way, I'm Lucy. We're sisters."

She didn't sound upset. In fact, she sounded downright chipper, a fact which surprised me. Lucy rose when I stood, and I towered over her like I had Laura. I'd have to thank Ben for passing on the genes that made me an Amazon next to most women. I escaped to the bathroom that connected to my room, half expecting her to follow. A door on the opposite side of the shower opened onto another room that had to be her bedroom.

The bathroom door muffled her voice. "You're not a morning person, are you? Neither is Dad. He says I can't talk his ear off until he has his first cup of coffee."

Good rule. I opened the door a few minutes later to find her going through my few belongings.

"Hey!"

She didn't even act guilty. She held up one of the few shirts Anna had packed for me, an old, hand-me-down tee with the color faded to an ugly puce from too many washings. "You can't wear this. They'll eat you alive at school. Where're all your clothes?"

I grabbed the tee from her and shoved it back in the dresser. "You're looking at them." Anna and I'd never had money since Dean tended to drink through it faster than we could earn it. I'd learned not to care *much* that my clothes had been used and ill-fitting, but my face flushed at her obvious disbelief.

Lucy didn't notice my embarrassment. She reached back into the dresser for the tee before I could stop her and held it between two fingers in disgust. "Why would you wear this? It's way too big. You'd swim in it." She studied my figure with a critical eye. "You're too skinny, you know. My mom intends to fatten you up."

Gee, thanks. I moved to take the tee again, but she strolled through our adjoined bathroom to her bedroom. It was a duplicate of mine, except posters of rock bands plastered every wall. Her bedspread was a frightening shade of fuchsia, like spilled nail polish. She disappeared into a walk-in closet with my shirt and resurfaced a moment later with a turquoise silk blouse. I'd never owned anything so luscious and wanted it as soon as I saw it.

Lucy surprised me when she handed me the blouse. "I think this will fit you. I think I have a scarf, too, to hide those bruises around your neck so you can avoid all the questions. Mom'll want to take you shopping later. By the way, Crimson Chaos is playing at the Underground tonight. I thought maybe you'd like to meet a few of my friends before you start school tomorrow."

Nobody was this nice.

She saw my suspicious expression and laughed. "You better get dressed before Mom and Dad barge in to check on you. I'll find that scarf for you."

Walking toward the bathroom, I stopped in the doorway. "Thank you, Lucy. For the shirt." *And the welcome.* She laughed again and waved me away, and I rushed to get dressed.

Chapter Three

That evening Lucy drove us to the Underground in her white hybrid Toyota. The Underground turned out to be a tiny club with red brick walls, worn pool tables, and a few tables surrounding a stage where tarted-up rockers were sound checking their gear. The room was packed with teenagers taking advantage of the club's under-twenty-one night.

"Come on."

Lucy shoved through the crowd. Lagging behind slightly, I already regretted coming.

I hated crowds, and I really hated meeting new people. For too long I'd kept to the shadows to hide what I could do. Before that, I'd learned to hide evidence of Dean's abuse. Going unnoticed had been easy in Brooklyn when I was one of 4,000 kids at my school. That wouldn't work here at a school with "only 452 students total including grades eight through twelve," according to Lucy.

From my spot at the door, I watched her greet a group of her friends across the room. She waved at me with a huge smile, and I waved back, abandoning my plan to duck out the entrance. Three sets of curious eyes stared at me when I stood next to her.

Feeling like a complete moron, I muttered, "Hi," and wished I hadn't let Lucy railroad me into this. I didn't particularly care if I fit in, but it seemed important to her that I meet her friends, so I'd agreed to come.

I knew what her friends saw—the fragile bone structure of my cheeks and jaw, the dark blue eyes too large for my face, and the unruly hair in need of a trim. Even with the aid of Lucy's cabinet of makeup, I hadn't been able to hide the bruises or the black eye. I looked . . . damaged.

"This is my sister, Remy. Remy, this is everyone. You can forget their names later."

She laughed and tossed her black curls in a way that would look ridiculous if I tried it. A girl and boy sat at the table, and she shoved the boy until he made room for us. As we settled in, one of the musicians sauntered up to the table and stole a chair from a nearby table to join us. He was a slice of Brooklyn among Lucy's clean-cut crew, with his inked arms, spiky hair, and pierced ears.

The pretty brunette with glasses introduced herself. "Hi, Remy. I'm Susan Reynolds. Great shirt," she said, lightly brushing her fingers down the sleeve.

I smiled and tried to shove away the shyness tying my stomach into a snarl of knots, like the mysterious clump the cheap necklaces in my jewelry box formed when I wasn't looking.

Susan gestured to the tattooed boy on her left. "This is Brandon Green. His family owns this place."

I nodded hello and he acknowledged my new throaty smoker's tone with a "kickass voice, new girl."

Last, but not least, was the tall, muscular blond. I would have bet all the spare pennies at the bottom of my purse that Greg De Luca played football, but it turned out he preferred playing chess to first downs and yearbook to touchdowns.

When I noticed Greg and Susan eyeing my discolored face, I rolled my eyes, despising the way people treated me with pity and fear. As if Dean's brutality was my fault or, better yet, as if it was something contagious they could catch on contact.

"You think I look bad, you should see the other guy."

My tone cut off any discussion about the bruises, and they looked away quickly.

"Remy, you're from New York, right?"

Susan's question sparked an inquisition about my life in Brooklyn. My sister's friends surprised me with how welcoming they were, and she quizzed me along with the rest until I grimaced at her. She caught on and grinned. I couldn't blame her for being curious about me since I shared her bathroom. My own curiosity about her startled me, when she'd scarcely registered on my radar before coming here. I'd never expected to meet her, let alone hang out in a club with her and her friends.

The conversation died when Brandon rose and joined the band onstage. I was the only one left sitting at the table when he manipulated the first grinding note out of his guitar. Arms and legs flailed to the primal beat on every inch of the dance floor. Watching Brandon sway with closed eyes, I felt a spark of envy for his ability to lose himself in the music.

Tapping my fingers on my leg in time to the song, my gaze strayed to the far side of the room. Forest-green eyes stared at me with familiar intensity.

I inhaled to steady my suddenly jangling nerves. The boy from the beach sprawled in a chair, with his long denim-covered legs stretched out under the table. In the dim light his disheveled brown hair looked black. The shadow had disappeared from his wide jaw, but he didn't look any less dangerous. Even with the stage between us, I could see the scar cutting through his right eyebrow. His broad shoulders slouched as he played with the wrapper from a straw.

I hadn't realized how perfect his posture was at the

beach until seeing him relaxed like this. Relaxed didn't look . . . right on him. Despite his lazy demeanor, his potent gaze had the power to make my pulse sprint. He watched me with a curiosity that mirrored my own, and I couldn't look away.

Lucy sounded anxious when she appeared next to me. "Oh, no, you don't. Don't even think about it."

Her words enabled me to break the spell cast by those wicked green eyes. One song had faded into another while I'd been staring at the boy, and I hadn't even realized it. I turned to her in confusion. "What?"

She nodded her head in the boy's direction. "Asher Blackwell. He's your classic bad boy, black motorcycle and all." She leaned close to shout over the music. "Dad would have a frickin' heart attack."

Asher Blackwell, I thought, glad to have a name to go with the face.

I forced a smile for Lucy's benefit, trying to appear normal. "Ooh, a motorcycle. That's bad, right?"

An impish playfulness colored her grin. "It's our job to worry Dad, not kill him."

Asher no longer studied me when I turned, but spoke to a boy and girl I hadn't noticed sitting at his table.

"Is that Blackwell as in Blackwell Falls?" I asked.

"Got it in one. His ancestors founded the town in the 1800s. That group is the latest descendents and heir to the estate."

I set aside the pictures that the word "estate" brought to mind. "Who's that with him?"

Lucy tossed a glance at the table, but she needn't have worried about being surreptitious. None of the table's occupants paid us any attention. "The girl is his sister, Charlotte, and the really hot one is Gabriel Blackwell, their brother. He's their guardian. Their parents died last year in a car accident right before they moved to town. Apparently, they didn't know they owned property in town until they read the will."

The Blackwells shared the same angled bone structure and dark brown hair; although Gabriel wore his cropped shorter than Asher's. Charlotte shouldn't have been pretty with the sharp features of the two boys, but somehow it worked on her. Her scarlet lips and bobbed hair made her look like some 1920s gangster's jailbait girlfriend.

Gabriel appeared a couple years older than Asher. He seemed larger and more muscular than Asher and was breathtaking. Gabriel's eyes flicked up as if he sensed my stare. They were the same green as his brother's, and I couldn't help being awestruck by his beauty. The air in my lungs disappeared until Gabriel dismissed me by looking away.

I glanced sideways, and Asher glared at me as if he knew my thoughts. As if he wasn't happy his brother's appearance impressed me. His arrogance irritated me, and I raised an eyebrow. A scowl darkened his features, and fear skittered up my spine. Just in case, I strengthened my mental brick wall.

He looked away first, and I smiled, feeling I'd won my first skirmish with him. A silly idea since we weren't at war.

Lucy breathed, "Whoa."

"What?"

She shook her head with a grimace. "Remy, Asher is the worst kind of player. When he targets a girl, she can kiss her brain good-bye. And every girl who's gotten serious about him has had her heart broken when he walked away." She spoke in a rush as the music ended and the others returned to the table. "It would be a really bad idea to hook up with him."

My initial impression of him had been right. Lucy didn't have to worry. I had no intention of messing with him for reasons she couldn't understand.

Susan overheard her last comment. "You're talking about Asher Blackwell, right?" She didn't wait for Lucy's confirmation. Her eyebrows wiggled above her glasses as she grinned, and I guessed she was the gossip of the group. There always had to be one. "Hot, right?"

Lucy's breath hissed out, and I had the urge to laugh.

"A talented photographer and the best center our hockey team has ever had. Lucy's right, though," Susan continued. "The Blackwell boys are serial daters. My older sister went out with Gabriel last year before she left for college. She was a wreck when he broke it off."

Greg nodded. "They lived all over the world before they moved here. They're grotesquely wealthy. Even more than Brand's family. Some kind of inheritance their parents left them. Lucky bastards."

Brandon shoved Greg. "Dude, jealousy is an ugly emotion. Just remember. You'll always have a job cleaning my pool when you need it."

"Hey, man. Anything that gets me closer to your mom. You know she's in love with me, right?"

They started bickering, and the others joined in. Asher's accent made sudden sense. It wasn't American or British. Maybe some weird mix of the two, plus other places he'd lived. Exotic, like him. I glanced over at the Blackwell table, but Asher had left when I wasn't paying attention.

Lucy touched my arm when I rose several minutes later. Contact with her grew more familiar with each brush of her hand, but I didn't mind.

"Seriously, Remy. Be careful." Her eyes flicked to the table where the Blackwells were sitting. I guessed she thought I was planning to look for Asher, and her next words confirmed my suspicion. "Asher and Gabriel bought sailboats from Dad last summer to race in the festival." Ben ran a shipbuilding company in town, building the sailboats and racing ships used in the Sail Master's Regatta. "They crashed them racing each other. They're a little . . . reckless."

To acknowledge her concern, I nodded. She was more right than she knew. Asher, at least, was dangerous. Maybe good instincts ran in the family.

"Is there somewhere I can go to get some air?"

"Try the patio."

Following her directions, I headed to a side door that opened onto a deserted patio, sheltered from the snow by a large awning. I picked a table in the shadows, rubbing my arms to keep warm. Everyone with half a brain stayed inside, but the press of bodies exhausted me. Alone in the dark, I could relax my mental walls without fear of someone bumping into me.

Chatter filled the night air as the door swung open again behind me, and a couple headed to a corner of the patio to smoke. They didn't notice me in the darkness, and I closed my eyes listening to their quiet conversation and the constant roar of the ocean in the distance. There was something peaceful about this town.

"It's beautiful here, isn't it?"

The low voice rasped over my nerves. With a small sigh, I firmed my mental barricade again and looked up. Asher sat at the table next to mine. He must have been sitting there before I came on to the patio because I hadn't heard him arrive. Up close, he was more handsome, more attractive, simply more than I remembered. The scar slashing through one brow was highlighted by his high cheekbones and the long hair swept off his forehead. The imperfection reminded me he could be bad for my health. That and the small hint of anger I glimpsed in his gaze

His eyes lit with a challenge when he said, "I'm Asher Blackwell."

He introduced himself as if we'd never met. It took me a minute to realize he held a hand out for me to shake. I didn't shake hands. Ever. It left me open to pain, even with my barricades. After what had happened on the beach, I wouldn't be touching him anytime soon. I nodded in his direction and ignored his outstretched hand.

He smirked as if he'd won this battle.

As I returned to watching the couple, I caught him studying me from the corner of my eye. The deep curiosity I sensed beneath the scrutiny unsettled me. He wasn't like me—able to heal. He was something else that used energy like I could. My guard stayed up as I pretended to ignore him.

"And you are?" Watching the smokers take furtive puffs, he made polite conversation without looking at me.

"Remy O'Malley." My voice sounded huskier than usual.

That caught his attention, and he turned those amazing eyes to mine with rapt attention. Trapped, I couldn't have glanced away even if I wanted to. And I didn't want to.

One dark brow rose again. "Lucy's sister?"

I shifted in my seat, uneasy answering questions about myself. "We have the same father, so I suppose she is."

He mistook my discomfort for another emotion. "You don't like her?"

"Sure, I like her. What I know about her."

He waited for me to continue, leaning forward as if to pull the words out of me. When my silence continued, he snapped his fingers. "That's right. You're new to the Falls. You're the other daughter."

The other daughter. Great. I'd been labeled. I shrugged and the noncommittal gesture seemed to irritate him as much as his shrug at the beach had me.

"Do the marks on your neck have anything to do with your move?"

The blood drained from my face. His angry tone had been too low for others to overhear, but I checked to see if the couple had heard him anyway. The girl tossed a curious glance our way, but her boyfriend paid us no attention.

I looked at Asher, trying to understand his motive for asking the question. His enigmatic face remained composed, and I wondered if he'd ask louder if I didn't respond. What answer would satisfy him? The truth wasn't an option. I should have stuck with my decision to ignore him.

"Do you always ask so many questions?"

Asher's eyebrow rose again, and I returned the look with one of my own. *Mind your own damn business.* He grinned and I scowled, turning back to the couple to end the conversation. Asher didn't seem disturbed as he sat beside me in the dark. I felt his gaze land on me a couple of times, and I resisted the urge to stare back.

The music started inside with Brandon's distinctive guitar riff, and I hesitated, giving Asher a chance to leave first to avoid any accidental touches. The smokers stamped out their cigarette butts and hurried inside, letting the door slam shut behind them. I watched Asher's shoes, noticing the expensive leather boots, and waited for them to shift as he got to his feet. Except they didn't. The charged, heated air swirled between us as neither of us moved.

It was another challenge, I realized. My breath hissed out in frustration as I stood to leave. He rose at the same time, crowding me between the two tables and knocking me off balance. I stepped back to avoid his touch and tripped over the table leg. My mental wall dropped. Strong hands grasped my waist to pull me upright, hitching my blouse up at the ribs a little as he caught me, and his hand slipped to skim bare skin.

The sparks of heat kindled where his fingers touched my waist and spread in little licks of green fire. Without my shield, the hot wave of energy crashed in on me, his energy flow like a heat-seeking missile.

The pain of that ambush scorched my skin, beginning where he touched me and radiating over my body like a fiery breeze. Inside, the opposite of fire stripped away my defenses, and I gasped as ice shards rushed straight to my heart, causing it to beat in a sluggish rhythm. A black fog descended when it froze, and my focus narrowed to Asher's face.

For the second time in a week, my body took over. It gathered all my pain and shoved it outward. Red flames shot from my skin to his.

Asher yanked his arms back as if he'd been burned by the inferno. The current of energy coming from him cut off.

I doubled over and grabbed hold of the nearest chair as my heart started pounding in double time. My glare took in the pallor of his tanned face and the sweat dotting his forehead, as I raised my mental defenses. Too little, too late. He stood ramrod straight, his expression pained. He hurt, I realized. I'd done that. My angry smile turned fierce with pride.

A waiter stepped on to the patio, and I tried to blend once more into the crowd. When I was sure I could move without falling, I turned my back on Asher and walked into the club.

The door didn't open behind me, and I assessed my body. The pain had dissipated, but I remained weak. Not as bad as after I'd hurt Dean, but then this pain had been different. I hadn't absorbed another's injuries in the process of . . . What? I wasn't sure what I'd done, except that my body could now cause pain in addition to taking it away. Two times the freak.

And now Asher knew, too.

He'd think twice before he touched me again.

CHAPTER FOUR

*M*y first week at school was uneventful.

A weathered, red brick building, Blackwell Falls High perched at the top of a hill in the midst of modest homes and groupings of sugar maples and oak trees. Ben drove me to campus to sign me up for classes the first day. He was pleased to find out I was a complete nerd and, through sheer grit and sweat, a straight-A student. Perhaps I was more motivated than others by the necessity of escaping hell as soon as possible. It hadn't hurt that hanging at the library meant time spent out of the apartment away from Dean.

My time among the books meant I had very little catchup to do in my classes. This was lucky since my concentration lasted about thirty seconds before thoughts of Asher crept in.

I'd worried I'd be fighting off repeat attacks in the hallways at school. One blast of his energy scared me worse than watching Dean's fist fly at me, but at least I could defend myself now. My new power left me conflicted. I was proud I could take care of myself, where before I'd been an animal scrambling for a hole to hide in, and scared I'd injure someone accidentally. This developing ability seemed the opposite of who I thought I was—a healer.

Part of me celebrated my first day at school when Asher

spared me no more than a glance in English, the single class we had together, before turning to flirt with the petite girl next to him. I didn't understand why I also felt frustrated. The loneliness I'd sensed in him at the beach didn't fit with reality. At lunch, he sat with his sister and their friends in the cafeteria, while I sat with Lucy. I should have been happy he ignored me, but the whole situation left me in a foul mood that didn't go unnoticed at home during the week. Pensive looks passed between Ben and Laura, and we acted like the strangers we were, skirting each other. I spent a lot of time alone in my room.

Without help from me, Lucy and Laura planned a shopping trip to the mall in South Portland for the weekend. They acted like they didn't detect my lack of enthusiasm. I couldn't help it. A bigger city meant more crowds. It wasn't their fault I was a freak. They'd done their best to make me feel part of the family, so I gritted my teeth and agreed to all their plans.

By the end of my first week, tension had me squirming in my seat until I noticed Asher was missing from his table. Charlotte seemed unaware of what had happened between me and her brother. At least, she didn't acknowledge my existence, as she held court over a group of well-dressed girls. If we'd been in New York, I would have guessed they were Fifth Avenue private school groupies. The Blackwells—or better yet, the Blackwell fortune—attracted them like yuppie, suburban moms to a Starbucks.

As Lucy had said, cliques ruled at Blackwell Falls High and having a town, let alone a school, named after you increased your popularity tenfold. It didn't hurt that Asher played center on our hockey team. I'd surmised from the others' gossip that Charlotte was a sophomore, younger than me. At sixteen, she had confidence the rest of us lacked, and I couldn't imagine her with acne or worrying about her weight.

With Asher gone, I relaxed and listened to Lucy's friends make plans for that evening. Temperatures had dropped low enough that the town's waterfall had frozen over. A bunch of students had decided to go see it, and the trip was quickly becoming an impromptu party.

Susan asked if I'd go, and Lucy cajoled, "Come on, Remy. Let's go. It'll be fun." She ended on a singsong tone.

I returned her smile. She really was nice to the core, and I was dying to get out of the house. "Sure. Sounds like fun."

That evening, Lucy worked miracles with my makeup, an easier task since the bruises had faded to a pale yellow. I'd helped them along a little, anxious to skip the phase of healing when the bluish bruises morphed into a revolting green. With a little assistance, mine had gone from blue to almost nonexistent.

My remaining broken rib no longer required taping, either, since I'd healed it the day before. My voice remained throaty despite my best efforts. Whatever Dean had done, the damage appeared permanent. Since I wasn't planning on a career as a singer and it no longer hurt, I'd decided not to stress about it.

Later, I laughed with Lucy as we headed down the stairs to meet Brandon, who'd arrived to pick us up. Ben and Laura grinned at us, and I wished I didn't like it that we gave the appearance of a happy family.

Raucous noise filled Brandon's van. He had picked up Greg and Susan on the way to our house, and we set off. When we arrived at a steep cliff at the edge of the woods, we piled out of the van and followed a worn path downhill toward the small roar of about sixty kids letting loose.

Someone had cleared away mounds of snow to get a fire started. A huge pile of wood from broken crates, pallets, and fallen trees blazed in the dark, the fire illuminating some faces, while others remained hidden in darkness. The effect was kind of creepy, and I huddled my shoulders in my jacket.

As we neared the fire, Susan wandered off with Greg, dating or on the verge of it. Brandon headed for the keg. I looked over at Lucy and watched as her eyes locked on a stranger who wasn't handsome so much as boyishly cute with his auburn curls and dimples.

Shoving an elbow in her side, I teased, "Someone's been holding out." When Lucy blushed, I grinned.

"That's Tim," she said. "He graduated last year."

"An older man? And you gave me hell for merely looking at the town Romeo?"

She flushed in embarrassment and muttered, "Shut up, Remy" without any heat, her eyes returning to the boy. He'd spotted her, too, and strode through the sand to meet us.

"That's my cue to make myself scarce."

Lucy spared me a grateful glance. "Thanks. You going to be okay?"

I smiled to reassure her. "You forget. I'm used to it. I'll catch up with you later."

Moving closer to the fire, I shivered and experienced a fleeting relief that we were shopping for a warmer coat this weekend, because I'd freeze to death in the dumb excuse for a jacket I had. It had been thin when new three years ago. I moved as close as I dared to the large blaze, seating myself on a log. The spectacle before me was worth every frozen inch of my backside. Rushing water had frozen as it tumbled toward the small creek below it, so that it looked like some demented artist had carved a floating sculpture. My hands slid into my pockets as I stared up at the obsidian sky speckled with dots of light. The heat curled into me and my eyelids drooped.

"You shouldn't fall asleep so close to the fire."

My body came triple-espresso awake. Asher sat next to me just out of touching distance.

"I wasn't asleep." I checked my walls to ensure there were no chinks, since he didn't seem able to hurt me when they were in place. Common sense told me to walk away, but that could be interpreted as fear or weakness.

"Of course, you weren't," Asher said. "You always snore when you're awake."

My vow of silence was forgotten as I studied his dark eyes. It really wasn't fair that such a jerk should be so appealing. I didn't understand my desire to touch the scar that glowed in the firelight and shoved my hands deeper in my pockets to fight the urge.

"I don't snore."

White teeth gleamed when he smiled. He liked getting a rise out of me, but his smile had a hesitant quality I hadn't noticed before.

Good, the new powerful me thought. *He should be cautious.*

As if to gauge my mood, he studied my face. His gaze dropped to my neck, and he frowned. "Your bruises are gone."

"That's what happens to bruises when they heal." My casual tone hid my anxiety that he'd noticed when no one ever had.

He smiled as if he knew a secret. "It's only been a little over a week. Shouldn't it take longer?"

I suppressed an urge to bite my lip. Maybe I shouldn't have healed the marks, but I'd been sick of people looking and wanting to ask about them. I shrugged.

His eyes narrowed, and I remembered he didn't like it when I shrugged by way of response. More questions lingered in his eyes, and I didn't want to answer them. I started to rise.

"Wait."

He didn't put out a hand to stop me, but his voice had the same effect: I froze.

"What?"

"I wanted to apologize," he said, his low voice serious. "For what happened. On the patio."

The nervous stops and starts sounded odd coming from him in his clipped enunciation. I had the inappropriate urge to smile and clamped down on the impulse.

"I didn't know that would happen. I thought I could control myself when I touched you, but . . ." At a loss for words, he stared into the fire. "I've never met anyone who could do what you do."

That makes two of us.

"What is it you think I can do?" I asked.

Those eyes swung back to mine and flicked to the shadows. "You want me to say it here? Where others might hear?"

I'd forgotten we sat in the middle of a crowd. My entire attention had focused on him, with my body inclined toward him, as he leaned toward me. Our physical proximity and my obliviousness to it scared me. My vow to keep my distance had lasted about a minute.

"Forget it."

I stumbled to my feet to get away from him. I didn't know if he realized he'd reached out to delay my retreat, but we both reacted to it. He jerked his hand away with a frustrated, tight expression as I stepped back, slamming into a blond boy I didn't recognize. Too drunk to save himself, the boy fell toward the fire, his light eyes blurry and unaware.

Both of my hands tangled in the scratchy wool of his letterman's jacket as I scrambled to steady him, stepping so close my vision was filled with his pale face and the mole nestled next to his large nose. When his leaden weight began to topple us both, Asher's hands were there, reaching around me to pull us both upright. His arms pressed into my side, his warmth registering through layers of clothing. The shock of his body against mine from back to thigh overwhelmed me, and I braced myself for the heat wave. And yet . . . Asher didn't attack.

The stranger staggered against me, and a log shifted in the fire beyond his shoulder. The burning piece of drift-wood wedged at the top of the wood stack tumbled on a collision course with his head when its support collapsed. Asher's right hand whipped out to knock the burning wood into the bonfire. As the chunk of driftwood flew backwards, it sent sparks up into the starry night.

Seconds later, Asher stepped back, yanking the boy and me to safety.

The blond stumbled again—this time away from the fire—and leered at my chest. "Thanks," he slurred. "I'm flattered, but I have a girlfriend." Then, he shuffled off, yelling at a group of his equally drunk friends, "Shit, did you guys see that? The new chick wants me."

I stared after him, unsure if I should be pissed or amused. The idiot hadn't even realized he'd been in dan-ger. I turned to face Asher, but he didn't look at me, his face impassive. Instead, he tucked his hands in his jacket pockets and stalked away, as if he hadn't saved a seriously inebriated idiot—and myself—from third-degree burns.

I stood frozen, stunned at the abrupt change in him. The party continued around me, and I wondered if he blamed me for bumping into the boy. The scene replayed in my head and an alarm went off. His bare hand had pushed away a burning log.

My brain shut off, and I acted on instinct, running to-ward where I'd last seen him. The back of his navy blue peacoat disappeared as he rushed up the path toward the top of the cliff, and I worried I wouldn't catch him if he entered the tree line.

"Asher!"

His body froze long enough for me to catch up with him at the edge of the woods. He didn't turn around or take his hands out of his pockets, so I circled around until I could see his unfocused eyes. His tanned face had turned ashen with pain and shock.

Yearning to help him, my hand automatically stretched to touch him. It hung in midair when he twisted his shoulders out of my reach. The waxy expression of pain dissolved into the fury I'd seen simmering below the surface every time we talked. "Don't!"

"I can help you."

Asher's bleak eyes shut me out. "You can't! Don't you get it? I don't think I could stop myself from hurting you, and I'm not sure why I should even care." Every word was forced through gritted teeth.

That he understood what I could do should have sent shivers of fear down my back, but it didn't. Better yet, his words sounded like a threat. A threat that the blond bimbo always ignored before the killer chopped her to pieces in the woods. I shivered, wondering why the hell I didn't run for the nearest crowd. The answer was easy. When it came to healing, I got by on pure intuition. Who to heal, how to heal: I didn't ponder these questions when someone was hurt. Besides, I would turn and fight before I let some wimp stalk me through a forest in a mask. Eager to get this over with, I felt calmer than I'd ever been near Asher.

My jaw set. "You were hurt saving that boy from the fire. Let me help you."

Raw, humorless laughter cut through the air. "Who will save you from me if I let you?"

Without waiting for my answer, he stepped around me

and off the path until his body was one more shadow among the trees.

I plunged in after him. "Asher, stop!"

"Go back, Remy!"

In seconds, he would be out of my sight, and I wouldn't be able to keep up. Maybe he would attack me. He'd done it twice already, and I had no idea what would happen if he lost control. I remembered how hungry his energy felt and knew he could hurt me. *Had* hurt me. I should let him go. He could go to a doctor, and we could pretend this had never happened. I could walk out of the forest with a clean conscience.

But my feet wouldn't take that first step to the beach. My instincts hadn't let me down before. That didn't mean I wanted to chase him through the woods. I dropped my mental barricade and a current of energy spiraled inside me. I sent it unwinding toward Asher and knew the instant he felt it. It was a repeat of the first time I dropped my defenses to scan him at the beach. A wave of my energy sparked something in him, and his body went rigid. I held my breath and waited for his attack. When it didn't come, I moved to his side.

Asher refused to look at me, and he shook. In a hoarse voice, he asked, "Remy, what are you doing?"

"Helping you whether you like it or not."

Circling around him for the second time, I wasn't prepared for the hunger on his face. My heart stuttered, and I sucked air from malfunctioning lungs. Seeing my expression, his eyes squeezed shut, and he inhaled several deep breaths of his own. He remained in control, but just.

Acting as if it were a normal thing to do, I ordered, "Give me your hand."

Green eyes opened to dangerous slits and his control slipped. Powerful energy unfurled toward me as if he would try to hold me hostage again.

My eyes narrowed in warning. "Go ahead and test me. Imagine the pain you're feeling doubled and tripled back on you."

He must have been in agony, because his energy turned off with startling abruptness. He grimaced, and I thought he muttered, "It might be worth it."

I ignored that and demanded, "Just give me your damn hand, already."

The corners of his mouth curved in a small, edgy smile, and he gave up. He pulled his right hand out of his pocket and held it out to me.

When I saw the damage, I couldn't contain my gasp. The tender skin on the meaty flesh of his palm had blistered red and white and was charred black. Blood oozed in some spots where the burns were the worst. The wasted flesh smelled worse than it looked. I'd healed burns before, but never one this bad.

My stomach flipped over, and I thought I'd be sick for a moment. I took another deep, calming breath through my mouth. My defenses would have to be down to heal him, and I couldn't think too long about the fact that his wound would be mine because I didn't know if I'd have the courage to continue.

I eased my right hand on top of his burned palm, and the *humming* began. I listened to it start in my body, deep in my chest where my heart beat, and let it flow outward through my limbs and down my arm. It traveled through my palm and into his. He jerked and stilled as he gritted his teeth to contain his desire to push back at me, to hold me hostage again.

Scanning him took longer than I'd thought it would.

His body was different in ways I couldn't begin to explain. The muscles, organs, and bones were all as they should be—healthy and working. Yet, they worked faster and harder than others I'd scanned, and he gave off more heat. The internal machinery *felt* human, but the gears were more efficient and fine-tuned. It was the difference between a performance BMW and a seventies clunker. I began to understand why his reflexes were so smooth and why he moved with confidence. I wondered if the differences were to do with his talents or for some other reason. The one thing I was sure about was that, at least on the inside, he was not like me.

My discoveries were cast aside as my entire being became absorbed with healing his flesh and on soothing away the redness and hurt. Green sparks arced between our palms. Drained, my hand fell from his.

The pain dropped me to my knees.

I needed to heal my body, make the throbbing stop, but I couldn't concentrate with the shrieking in my head. Incoherent screams threatened to slip out, and I bit my lip.

"Remy?" The sound came from a long distance. "Remy, are you okay?"

The voice anchored me. Whimpering, I said, "Give me a minute."

The continuous ribbon of syllables soothed me until I could gather enough of my mind together to concentrate. It wasn't possible to heal the burn in my weakened state, but I could numb it. I shivered with cold and distress. What I did could be likened to cauterizing the tips of the wailing nerves so they couldn't tell my brain about the excruciating pain.

It worked. My body sank to the wet ground, and I curled in a ball in the snow, sweating and exhausted. A long time later awareness returned, and I felt a rough hand stroking my hair from my face. Heat fired where the hand touched my skin, but it didn't hurt like it had that time on the patio. The warmth felt pleasant when a wintry breeze chilled my wet forehead. This wasn't the best time to let my brick walls crumble. I was weak now, while Asher was strong. I wouldn't be able to fight him off.

He seemed to sense my anxiety, and his hand disappeared from my face as he backed away. A mental wall was up—his, not mine—and I blinked. He had a defense, too. My wall reined my power in, like a dam keeping my energy from spilling out to heal random strangers—or to keep someone like him from holding it hostage. I wondered how his worked because, for the first time, his touch hadn't hurt me. His color should have been better, but his tanned face glowed white. Distracted, I frowned. *Tell me I didn't do that to myself for nothing.*

"You okay?"

His deep laugh sounded shaky. "You're asking me?"

I nodded.

The clipped tones returned. "I'm perfectly fine. It's you I'm worried about. What happened?"

So he didn't know the truth. Only partial truth. He knew I could heal, but not what it did to me. I decided it would be better to keep that Achilles' heel to myself but had to give him some answer.

Shuddering, I sat up and told a half-truth. "Healing takes a lot of energy, that's all."

He didn't believe me and shook his head while shrugging off his jacket. "You're lying. You were in pain. You shouldn't have been. That's not how it's supposed to work."

The coat slipped around my shoulders, and I savored the banked fire from his body. I tucked my nose under the collar and breathed in his woodsy scent as I warmed at last.

He was inflexible and wouldn't give in until he knew the whole truth. Despite our momentary truce, telling him my secrets was unthinkable. I was curious if his mental wall worked like mine to block energy, but questions could reveal more about me than I wanted to share.

Using the nearest tree trunk, I used my left hand to struggle to my feet, hoping he didn't notice how I favored my right hand. I couldn't risk him telling anyone what he knew about me. The little knowledge he had could ruin me, but I also had information about him that I doubted he'd want others to learn. Doctors and scientists would love to test his streamlined internal system, his over-efficient heart that pumped blood at twice the normal rate, as much as they'd want to test my ability to heal.

In the distance, Lucy called my name, sounding worried as if she'd been searching awhile.

"I'm okay, Lucy," I shouted. "I'll be right there."

She called back in relief.

Sighing, I faced Asher, whose expression hadn't changed. "I have to go."

Not one muscle moved, but I sensed his opposition. I wasn't going anywhere until he allowed it. That sounded silly in my head, so I took a step away to test the theory, which he immediately matched with one of his own.

The lethargy that followed a difficult healing settled into my limbs. I needed a bed quickly before I collapsed. Desperate, I pleaded, "Asher."

His face softened when I said his name, and his tense shoulders lowered a millimeter. There was another blur of movement, and he lifted me, cradling me against his chest as he walked toward the path. I should have been too heavy at my height, but he didn't breathe harder with the effort of carrying me. I fought my body's desire to relax into the heat, to put my head against his shoulder and sleep. I sensed that his wall remained up, but I wasn't safe.

"Why doesn't it hurt when you touch me now?"

He shook his head and didn't answer. We didn't speak

until we saw the light of the bonfire bouncing off the trees.

"Put me down, please. I don't want to worry Lucy. I'm fine, really."

Asher set me on my feet as if I was fragile cargo, and I kept my right palm curled away from him. We stared at each other, neither of us wanting to spoil the peace with questions. His eyes traveled over my face taking in my exhaustion, and those full lips of his curled in a slight smile. "Go ahead and go. We'll talk another time, Healer."

Knowing we would not talk again, I nodded and handed him his jacket.

Perhaps that would have been the end of it if Lucy hadn't called my name again from mere feet away where a grouping of trees hid her from view. The light from the bonfire flickered over my burnt hand when I turned toward her voice.

Asher's breath rushed out in an angry hiss, and I knew I was busted.

I didn't hesitate to shoot through an opening in the trees and into Lucy's arms before his hand could close on my shoulder.

Lucy eyes rounded in surprise when I ran into her, and then shock when Asher stepped from the woods right after me. Her arm wrapped protectively around me. I figured Asher wouldn't want to give away my secret—our secret—in front of everyone. We were each safer keeping our mouths shut—a stalemate of sorts.

I chattered to Lucy with forced cheer. "Hey, Luce. You mind if we go now? I'm exhausted, and it's freezing out here." My momentum forced her to move at my side when I started walking.

Lucy gave me a suspicious look. "Sure. Everyone's ready to go. We were waiting for you."

She bit back an incredulous laugh when I babbled on

about how excited I was to go shopping the next day. We would be playing a game of twenty questions later, but that was better than playing games with Asher I feared I couldn't win.

With Lucy at my side, I felt secure enough to toss a smug, "'Night, Asher" over my shoulder. He stood where we'd left him, his expression black.

I distinctly heard him growl with frustration.

Lucy heard it, too. She tensed with shock until she felt my shoulders shaking with suppressed laughter. "What was that about?"

"I turned down an offer to ride his motorcycle. Dad's heart, you know."

I bit my lip to keep a smile from surfacing, but Lucy saw it anyway.

We grinned at each other. Then, we both laughed, and the sound echoed through the night air.

CHAPTER FIVE

*A*t home, I climbed the stairs with Lucy on my heels. My sister had kept the conversational ball rolling on the ride home to stall questions about what I'd been doing in the woods with Asher Blackwell. Lucy was quickly growing on me.

I didn't fight her when she pulled me into her room. She sat on the bed with her legs crisscrossed, and I lounged next to her. Her eyebrows rose and she eyed me like a stern parent.

"Okay. Spill."

"About what?" It felt odd to tease someone, to be this close to another person. I liked it, even while my secrets weighed me down.

One pink fingernail poked me in the chest and then picked a stray leaf out of my tangled hair. "Remy O'Malley, don't even think you're getting out of this. Sisters tell each other everything. You were in the woods tonight. With Asher Blackwell. Alone."

"And?" I smiled.

She shrieked. "Oh. My. God. You're. Dating. Asher. Blackwell. Dad is going to flip."

That sobered me, and I shook my head. "No, Luce. I was teasing. I swear I'm not dating Asher."

Her eyes squinted in suspicion. "Then, what were you

doing in the woods with him? And someone said the two of you were looking pretty serious together down by the bonfire."

Someone had interpreted our intense behavior as attraction. I would have to keep my guard up around Asher in the future. "They were wrong. We were talking. I decided to go for a walk and got lost. Asher heard me calling out and helped me back to the path. The end."

I tried to stifle my guilt. That last bit was true at least.

"Do you like him?" Lucy didn't sound happy about the idea.

Her question made me pause. Tonight, I'd seen another side of him. He'd helped save another, after he'd apologized to me. Later, when I had lowered my defenses to heal him, he hadn't taken advantage of me. His abilities intrigued me, and it was far too tempting to spend time with someone that I didn't have to hide from. He'd called me "Healer" like it was a title, not like he was talking about my power.

And then there was his touch. I remembered his hands on me when he carried me. Even now, I could almost feel the fire dancing under my skin.

Lucy giggled. "Your eyes went all blurry when you were thinking about him. I'd say it's a safe bet you like him."

I grunted. My eyes went blurry? I decided to test her theory. "What about you? Do you like . . . Tim?"

The room was silent for a long time as she pondered my question. When her eyes went blurry, I laughed.

She shoved me. "Shut up, Remy."

Later, when the house slept, I slipped out of my bed and closed the door that led to the bathroom between my room and Lucy's. It was time to get down to business while everyone slept. Asher thought my hand was damaged like his, but it had been dark, and I'd moved out of his line of sight as fast as I'd been able. If I could heal my hand before I saw him again, perhaps I could convince him it had been a trick of the light. Besides, I wouldn't be able to hide the injury while shopping with Laura and Lucy.

Seated in the center of my bed, I concentrated until exhaustion made me dizzy. As I had with Asher, I let the current of energy curl through me and spiral down my right arm to my damaged hand. It took a full hour, but soon the blisters smoothed and the angry colors faded. The skin on my palm looked shiny and new.

Relieved, I collapsed back into my pillows and slept.

Ben woke me the next morning when he knocked and opened my bedroom door. He entered when he saw I had one eye open and trained on him.

"Time to get up."

With a huge stretch, I sat up. "Is it time to go shopping?"

He had a mug in one hand and passed it to me. His fingers brushed mine, and I noticed his heart arrhythmia had returned. Absently, I wondered at its cause and continual return even after I'd healed him, but nothing seemed to ail him that I could find.

"Lucy and Laura are champing at the bit. I don't think I can hold them back much longer. I saved a cup of coffee to give you strength."

Apparently, Ben and I had the same view about shopping. "I'll be right down."

We shared a small smile, and he turned to leave.

"Ben?"

He paused and looked back over his shoulder.

"Thank you for—" For what? Acting like my friend? For my sister who was becoming the best friend I'd ever had? For a safe home? For a kind stepmother who cared about my needs? My verbal dismount was as awkward as

my beginning as I gestured to the coffee. "Well, for everything."

My father's voice sounded rough. "You're welcome,
Remy. Anytime."

Shopping with Laura and Lucy was nothing like the
loathsome task I'd expected. I let them go crazy picking
out my new clothing, but I drew the line at exchanging
my jeans for skirts. I had no objection to skirts, but no way
would I wear anything that exposed my bare legs to icy
temperatures. Later, Laura surprised me with a haircut and
manicure.

On the way home, I sat in the backseat of Laura's Lexus
SUV listening to her and Lucy talk. As we pulled into the
driveway, I noticed a classic black motorcycle parked next
to Ben's car.

Lucy stirred in the front seat. "Uh, Remy. I think you
have a guest."

Asher walked to the car to meet us, and it impressed me
he'd waited an entire day to come calling for answers.

To stall for time, I headed to the back of Laura's SUV to
gather shopping bags. A pair of masculine hands startled
me by scooping up the bags before I could.

Asher's polite voice held an undercurrent of tension.
"Allow me. Do you think you should be doing that, considering your hand?"

Laura came around the back of the car and eyed Asher
with suspicion before turning to me. "Remy? Is something wrong with your hand?"

My easy smile reassured her. "No, Laura. Although, I
think I smudged the nail polish already."

"No worries. Is your friend staying for dinner?"

I gave a casual wave. "No. I'll be along in a couple of
minutes. Asher is in my English class and needs help on an
assignment. Asher, this is Laura O'Malley."

Asher nodded in her direction. Laura remained uncertain, but Lucy steered her toward the house. Behind Asher's back, my sister mouthed, *Liar.* Then she was gone, shutting the front door behind her. It took me a moment to realize she meant about my involvement with Asher. I flushed and met Asher's gaze head-on. Better to get this over with.

"What's up?"

His lip curled. "Your hand. Let me see it."

It was childish, but I held out my left hand, knowing it would provoke him.

"Your right hand, Remy. It's not wise to mess with me."

I widened my eyes in innocence. "Wouldn't dream of it."

My right hand went up this time. He stared in disbelief at my unblemished flesh for what felt like an eternity. To lighten the mood, I wiggled the fingers at him and he scowled. Then, he looked relieved and leveled a considering look at me.

"Your palm was burned last night. Like mine."

It wasn't a question, so I said nothing.

"You absorb the injuries you heal."

I didn't confirm or deny his guess.

"I don't get you." He moved close enough to touch me. "Why won't you talk to me?"

I raised one brow as if to say, *Really? You have to ask?* Shifting my weight from foot to foot, I sighed. "This . . . us . . . it's too complicated."

He nodded once as if he'd come to the same conclusion.

Glancing over his shoulder, I glimpsed Lucy ducking out of sight in the front window. When I reached to take the bags from him, he let them go without a fight. I stepped around him and was at the front door before he spoke.

"Remy? I know more about you than you think.

Maybe more than you do. If you decide you want answers, I'm here. It doesn't have to be anything more than that."

We both knew that wasn't true. I walked in the house and didn't look back. A moment later his motorcycle gave a guttural roar as it sped away. The sound of that bike summed up all the temptation and danger of the boy himself. It would be so easy to cave in and tell him all my secrets, but I'd be risking everything.

Ben, Laura, Lucy, and the small amount of peace I'd found in Blackwell Falls. Was I willing to give that all up? Because that was what could happen if I trusted Asher Blackwell and he betrayed me.

I didn't even have to think about the answer when I entered the kitchen and saw Lucy, Laura, and Ben arguing over dinner like they hadn't been watching me from the window and discussing the boy on the motorcycle.

No way am I giving this up.

CHAPTER SIX

I dressed for school in dark brown knee-high boots over a new pair of skinny jeans paired with a deep green satin blouse I pretended didn't remind me of anyone's eyes. As had become our habit, Lucy and I rode to school together in her car with her talking my ear off the whole way. I refused to be nervous about seeing Asher again and was determined to stay away from him for my own good.

The first temptation of the day occurred as soon as we pulled into the parking lot. Asher lingered a few spaces over, leaning against his black motorcycle—a vintage Indian according to an envious Ben. The black helmet he held in one hand had tousled his long, wavy hair. All lean muscle, he stood in a rare beam of sunlight and for once, a flirting hussy wasn't attached to his side. His eyes glowed hotter than the weak sun as he stared at me, daring me to walk to him. Giant monarch butterflies flitted about in my stomach.

Lucy whispered, "Down, girl. Put your tongue back in your mouth."

The distraction worked, though it hurt to tear my eyes from him. Looking up at the cloudy sky, I said, "Okay. I can do this."

It didn't sound convincing, even to my own ears. Lucy shook her head in pity. "Are you sure you want to?"

She didn't know why I'd decided to avoid Asher, only that I had. That was reason enough for her. Glad of the support, I hooked my arm through hers, and we strolled past Asher. I felt his eyes follow me, but I didn't look back. "Oh, ye of little faith. We O'Malleys are made of sterner stuff than that. A pretty face and a gorgeous, perfect, out-of-this-world body will not break us."

She looked doubtful, and I supposed I'd tossed in one too many accolades about Asher's body.

I didn't see him again until lunch. Unlike that morning, he didn't acknowledge my existence as a small brunette curled into his side and made cow eyes at him. Despite my mission to ignore him, his dismissal smarted. *All's fair.*

I returned my attention to my new friends. They were making plans to go sailing for the weekend and appeared shocked when I admitted I didn't know how to swim. That surprise was nothing compared to the look they gave me when talk turned to cars, and they found out I couldn't drive. A car had been way beyond our keep-Dean-in-beer budget.

Glancing away from their horrified expressions, I looked right into Asher's eyes. He studied me from his table, ignoring the brunette who'd finally given up on burrowing her way into his side.

Lucy shoved my arm to get my attention again. "Have you taken driver's ed?"

"Yes, and I have my learner's permit, but I need practice."

"Well, for God's sake, make sure Dad takes you. I thought I'd kill Mom when I was learning. She's a nervous passenger."

"You know, Remy," Brandon said. "You are seriously damaging all my fantasies about city girls."

Greg smacked him in the back of the head, and Brandon grunted. "Nobody drives in New York, dumbass."

They moved on to insulting each other, my deficiencies shelved for the moment.

I laughed along with everyone else and ignored the empty spot in the pit of my stomach when I noticed Asher had left the cafeteria.

Lucy's friends were regulars at the Clover Café after school. We'd hit the coffeehouse to drown in espresso, accomplishing equal amounts of homework and intake of gossip. The Blackwells showed up from time to time, including the older brother, Gabriel, who did not deign to socialize with the high school crowd. Usually, he brought a companion—dubbed Sorori-toys by our group since they appeared to be a variety of particularly clueless sorority girls—to keep him entertained. I wondered how it was possible that some judge had given him guardianship of his younger siblings.

If I'd assumed Asher would strike up a conversation with me once we were alone, he proved me wrong. About a week after he showed up at my house, I found him sitting alone at a table reading a book. My friends had yet to arrive, and I hesitated. Things had been uneventful, though, so I took a seat at our regular table next to him, and he acknowledged my arrival with an impersonal nod.

After ordering a large café mocha, I picked up my copy of *The Picture of Dorian Gray* and pretended to read. Despite his distant behavior, I felt Asher's gaze on me often. At one point, I could have sworn I sensed his energy cresting toward me. It arrived with a slow roll and very little power behind it. Rather than the tidal wave he'd sent my way twice before, this was more of a . . . prod. I strengthened my mental barricade, and the current bounced away without causing any harm.

Asher's eyes widened in mock innocence when I swiveled my head to glare at him.

Lucy and the others arrived, and I turned to greet them, unsure of his game.

Several minutes later, as I listened to Greg complain about our math teacher, the next wave of energy hit. Like before, it was the mental equivalent of having someone poke me in the side. Exasperating, but not painful. My walls held, and this current bounced away, too.

I didn't give him the satisfaction of acknowledging him.

From the corner of my eye, I glimpsed his full lips tilting in a smile.

Another hour played out the same way. Every so often I would feel one of those mental pokes. He made it impossible to ignore him. Around the fourth time, I realized his goal—to make it impossible for me to ignore him.

My smile turned grim. *Two can play that game, jerk.*

Later, as my friends gathered their things to head home, I guessed he planned to touch me to throw me off guard like he had at the Underground. I kept my expression relaxed, waiting for the others to clear out so I could follow them.

Then, I let my mental guard crash down, remembering how he'd reacted before.

Asher knew instantly. His body tensed as he seemed to struggle for control. His eyes flashed, and I wondered if he was fighting a desire to attack me. Whatever he was up to, he wasn't trying to hurt me. It was like he wanted me to keep my guard up around him, and those prods were warnings. Reminders that my unguarded energy looked like a chocolate sundae to him.

While he sat surprised, I rose to my feet and walked away. By the time he recovered, my mental barricade was once more entrenched. At the door, I gave him a haughty smile.

The staggered look left his eyes. He glared and I could almost hear him reprimanding me for playing dirty. Shrugging, because I knew it irritated him, I stalked away and heard his laugh follow me out of the café.

The next few weeks passed the same way, except Asher's mental prodding wasn't restricted to the café. It was before school, in English, at lunch, in the hallways between classes. All fair game.

I'd be walking along talking to Lucy or Greg, and a wave of energy would sneak up. There'd be scant seconds to reinforce my shield before it hit me. Always, Asher stood nearby, watching me with studied casualness and barely hidden delight. When I'd scowl, he'd toss an arrogant, satisfied smile my way to show he knew he'd gotten under my skin.

After the first week, I didn't bother relaxing my guard, except in classes I didn't share with Asher, and then only because I needed the short respite. Staying on high alert exhausted me, but the fatigue was worth it the day he realized his game wasn't working anymore. The prods had become easier to ignore with all the opportunities he'd provided for practice.

In English, he'd made it a point to always sit next to me in class and then ignored me while he flirted with our female classmates. All the while, unbeknownst to them, he tested my defenses for fractures. One day, I grew fed up with the game.

When I felt a wave of energy coming at me while Mrs. Welles took attendance, I turned on him. "Seriously, do you mind?"

Mrs. Welles glanced up from her computer when she heard my fierce whisper. She looked like every English teacher I'd ever had—part librarian and part frustrated artist. A brave pencil speared a lopsided, haphazard bun to her head. Her clothing was persistently colorful, in a blinding kind of way, and mismatched as if she dressed in the dark.

She turned back to her computer, and I faced Asher. He looked as if it had finally occurred to him that he no longer took me by surprise. The impulse to touch me to force a reaction rested there in the long, tense fingertips that tapped his desk with impatience.

I lowered my walls all the way for a brief second to remind Asher he wasn't the only one with power. He tensed as he always did when he sensed my vulnerability, as if he fought an internal battle to stomp down his need to attack—his conscience or whatever held him at bay had become my ally.

"Tease," he whispered.

I smiled with grim satisfaction and mouthed, *Bite me*.

His wide grin gleamed perfect and content. He'd gotten to me again and knew it.

Disgruntled, I stared straight ahead.

The weekends brought a welcome respite.

Brandon, a lifeguard during the summer, had agreed to give me swimming lessons at the community pool after Lucy bullied me into it. A ton of kids shared the shallow end with us, and Brandon acted like a professional, both gentle and firm as he taught me how to hold my breath underwater, and then supported me while I learned to float.

I grew impressed by his restraint from cracking jokes at my expense and relieved to find another of my new friends healthy. One by one, I'd tested them and hadn't detected any illnesses. The knowledge had enabled me to relax with them. As for the group, they followed Lucy's example and touched me frequently with small hugs or an arm looped through mine as we walked through the halls. I didn't mind as much as I'd thought I would.

When Brandon and I clambered out of the pool to dry off, he reverted to his regular self. His gaze dropped to the top of my bikini and, as Greg always did, I smacked him in the back of the head. His coffee-brown eyes crinkled in amusement, and he chuckled.

"You're such a guy, Brand." My tone had less disgust than resignation as I mock-scowled at him.

He threw a tattooed arm around my shoulder. "I wouldn't have it any other way, babe."

He gasped when I elbowed him in the ribs. He laughed again, and I couldn't help but smile back, surprised to have found a good friend in him.

Later, Laura drove me to the BMV to transfer my learner's permit, and Ben took me for my first driving lesson in his Mercedes that evening. When I almost steered the car into a large tree to one side of the yard, his foot sought an imaginary brake. I stopped at the last possible second, slamming us both forward against our seatbelts.

Ben's sigh of relief turned into a chuckle, his head thrown back against the seat as he stared at the tree trunk less than a foot from the front bumper of his very expensive car. I would have quit right then and there, vowing to take the bus for the rest of my life, if Ben hadn't insisted in a calmer voice that I reverse the car out of the front yard so he could teach me how to parallel park.

Later, we gained a long stretch of Highway 9, and I stepped on the gas. For the first time, sitting in the driver's seat became a pleasure.

"You're going to get a speeding ticket before the year is out," Ben predicted. Strangely, he sounded more proud than upset.

By the end of the lesson, I felt far more confident and

had earned the affectionate nickname "Lead-Foot O'Malley."

When we arrived home, Laura had just finished making dinner. At the table, he proceeded to tell Lucy and Laura what a talented driver I was already, leaving out the episode with the tree. That's when it hit me.

I was falling in love with them.

Lucy, Laura, Ben.

My family.

My life with them was the opposite of the one I'd lived in Brooklyn with Dean and Anna, and it hurt to think about what I'd left my mother to survive alone. I hadn't slept with the knife under my pillow since a week ago when Laura had discovered it while changing my sheets. She'd replaced it where she'd found it, and I wouldn't have known if not for the freshly washed sheets. That night, the knife returned to its kitchen drawer.

Loving them would make it ten times, a hundred times, harder to leave if they discovered my secrets and sent me away. I resolved to guard my heart even closer, and my throat ached with unshed tears.

On Sunday, Lucy and I decided to hit the ice rink to watch our hockey team "beat the crap out of our rivals." Brandon had convinced me to go with his fighting words, but it hadn't taken a huge amount of effort when I knew Asher would play. We left the house, and a new Ford Mustang GT sat in the driveway. Candy-apple red with gleaming chrome, it stole my breath away. I could imagine driving with the windows down and my hair blowing in the breeze.

Busy coveting the car, I didn't hear Ben call my name right away.

Distracted, I turned in time to catch the key ring he tossed my way and glanced at it in confusion. Laura and

Lucy stood beaming behind Ben. I looked at the car, at Ben, at the car again. My head swiveled back to my father, and he grinned, nodding.

Shrieking, I jumped up and down like a maniac. I ran to Ben and wrapped my arms around his waist in a tight, brief hug. I bounced away, saying, "Thank you, thank you, thank you," before I realized what I'd done. I'd never voluntarily touched my father, and he looked as stunned as I did. We froze and eyed each other with awkward embarrassment, until Lucy grabbed my hand and dragged me to the car. We both pretended Ben didn't have to clear his throat before he launched into a list of the car's features.

"This car isn't practical, Remy, what with the icy roads around here," he said.

Lucy laughed. "But it's his dream car."

Despite myself, I was moved that he would choose his favorite car for me. He cleared his throat again. "Yes, well, I couldn't think of a better car for Lead-Foot O'Malley, Jr."

When we grinned at each other shamelessly, Laura admonished Ben not to encourage me with his bad habits, or I'd end up with three speeding tickets by eighteen just like him.

The only downside was that the Mustang—*my* Mustang—had a manual transmission. Ben insisted it was the only way to experience a sports car and promised to help me practice for my driver's exam. With a last look of adoration for the car, I followed Lucy to her Prius.

At the game, Brandon offered to give me a driving lesson. His shoulders touched mine as we sat side by side in the bleachers directly behind our team's players' bench, and he laughed as I repeated the stats Ben had told me about the 300-horsepower V8 engine.

Flushed with exhilaration, I didn't think to reinforce my defenses. When I glanced sideways, Asher stood not ten feet away in the team box, suited in full hockey gear minus the helmet, his brown hair gleaming with sweat from the warm up. Only a sheet of Plexiglas separated us as he leaned against the boards, and his eyes crinkled at the corners in amusement. He must have known my walls were down the entire time he stood there.

I grinned, including him in my delight, and nodded my thanks for not killing my buzz.

His lips tilted at the corners as he nodded back to acknowledge my gratitude.

My eyes caught on his scar, and I wondered what it would feel like to trace my fingers across it. My thoughts spun out in a dozen different possibilities.

"Remy!"

I looked around in confusion. Judging by the stares my friends gave me, Lucy had called my name more than once.

Susan shot a glance at Asher's back as he jumped the wall and hit the ice skating. "What was that, Remy?"

"Nothing. Just saying hi."

Greg's deep laugh boomed out. "That smile didn't say hi. It said *hello.*"

I rolled my eyes while the others laughed.

Brandon snorted. "Yeah, you never smile like that when you say hi to me."

I gave him a clownish grin. "How's that?"

"Give it up, Sis. Greg started a wager on how much longer the two of you will keep pretending to ignore each other," Lucy said.

My head whipped around to stare at Greg. "You idiot. Who would bet on something like that?"

Everyone had a sudden preoccupation with looking anywhere but at me.

"Lucy!" I accused.

She laughed without apology. "If you cave by the end

of the night, I win twenty bucks. I don't suppose you'd want to split a twenty with your favorite sister?"

Greg shoved her arm. "Hey, no fixing the odds."

"Put me down for ten for never," I said, with more confidence than I felt.

Susan wagged a finger at me. "Never bet money on a losing game. I'd say your days are numbered."

I shook my head in mute denial.

Four heads nodded back at me.

"Oh, shut up," I muttered and stalked off to get a hot chocolate with their chuckles ringing in my ears.

CHAPTER SEVEN

*A*sher had arrived at the same conclusion as my friends.

After watching our team demolish our opponents with a humiliating 8-0 spread, my friends and I headed to Rosy's, a retro fifties diner, for a celebratory meal. Returning to our table after placing an order at the walk-up counter, I felt a tug on the end of the crimson and pink-striped knit scarf wrapped around my neck. Asher walked away with my scarf wrapped around his hand, and I rushed after him to avoid strangulation. Admiring the muscles shifting in his back as he towed me to an empty table and pulled out a plastic chair for me was a bonus. His stubborn expression made it clear I could sit or be seated, but I paused as long as I dared before complying.

He sat across from me, not his usual superior and amused self. In the last couple weeks, I'd learned he could be charming—a favorite with the puck bunnies and the teachers. I'd thought Asher basked in their adoration, but lately I was convinced there was more to him. For all his admirers, he seemed lonely. This speechless Asher was new.

A waitress slammed a soda and a basket containing my cheeseburger and fries on the table. I popped a fry in my mouth while I stared, fascinated, and waiting to see what Asher would do next.

One hand shoved through his hair, and he said, "So, here's the thing . . ."

I wondered if his frustration meant his control could slip. My own ability felt tied to my emotions at times, so I reinforced my mental barricade to be safe.

With a groan, he rolled his eyes, his hair a gorgeous mess from his impatient hand. "Could you stop that, please?"

"Stop what?" I asked, in confusion.

"The wall thing. It's distracting the way you're always raising and lowering it. Keep it up, and we'll both be okay."

"Shh!" I looked both ways to ensure our conversation remained private. "Keep your voice down, okay?"

Despite my irritation, I couldn't deny any longer that I was drawn to him. I yearned to know what he knew about my abilities and why he didn't seem to think me a freak for having them. And then there were his talents and my desire to know more about why he was constantly testing my walls.

"We need to talk. I wish we had more privacy, but . . ." He indicated someone behind me.

When I shifted in my seat to see whom he'd gestured to, five sets of inquisitive eyes stared at me, waiting for me to call their bet. I waved at Lucy and nodded once in answer to her silent question. She punched a fist in the air and turned to a disgruntled Greg with her palm up and a smug smile. Susan gave a loud *whoop* as he pulled out his wallet to pay off the bet.

Asher watched the whole thing with bemusement, while I dumped ketchup on my fries.

"You owe me ten bucks." I chewed a fry with slow deliberation. "Although, to be fair, Lucy did offer to split the pot with me."

Dark eyebrows rose. "What was that about?" he asked.

"Trust me. You don't want to know." I brushed salt off my hands with a napkin. "You were saying?"

Instead of answering, Asher swiped my cheeseburger and took a huge bite.

I eyed him as I sipped my soda. "You're playing with fire, Blackwell." When he reached for a fry, he barely missed getting stabbed by my fork. "I'm hungry."

Asher grinned and returned my cheeseburger. "So am I. I saw you when I walked in and forgot to order dinner." His expression sobered. "You can't keep ignoring this." He waved a hand between us, daring me to deny the truth.

Having come to the same realization, I nodded in reluctant acceptance.

Asher studied me for a moment, his gaze tracing over my face and neck. "You remember the day we met on the beach?"

My response came hesitantly as I wondered where this was going. "Yes."

"You never asked why I took your picture."

"I figured it was obvious." I gestured to where bruises had colored my face that day.

His angry frown didn't mar his good looks in the least. "You thought I was taking pictures of your bruises?"

"What else?"

"Remy, that's ridiculous."

"Right. It must've been my astounding beauty in all its glorious high-def clarity that caught your attention."

Asher leaned forward and slid a hand across the table until his hand almost touched mine. Heat zinged from his fingertips.

"Remy." He waited for me to look up. "Don't you know? You take my breath away."

Solemn eyes focused on mine without a hint of the teasing I'd expected. Feeling exposed, I tucked my hands in my lap out of his reach.

Asher pulled back, too, giving me space. "I can't believe you'd think I was that low. I didn't even notice the bruises, at first. I went out there to get shots of the clouds moving in. It's wild when it storms over the harbor." He smiled, remembering. "I stepped on that beach, and there you were with your hair blowing about and your wise, sad eyes. I had to take your picture to prove you existed somewhere other than my imagination."

The handsome, sculpted face and gentle voice mesmerized me. I'd connected to him when I'd sensed his loneliness. Asher reached for me, and my heart thudded into my rib cage. His powerful gaze dared me to back away. I didn't move, and he slipped a hand in my hair, his fingers combing through the long strands near my cheek. It felt like a touch, though the movement barely stirred the air.

"Hey, Asher. Great game."

The deep voice shredded the intimate moment. I wished the visitor would go away when Asher's expression hardened and his hand dropped. With some distance between us, I remembered how to form complete sentences and twisted to see who had joined us. His brother, Gabriel, stared at me with green eyes like Asher's.

"Gabe." Asher's clipped tone was unfriendly.

Gabe's gaze didn't stray from my face. Seeing his features up close, I was captivated, though my appreciative perusal was impersonal. Almost too beautiful to be real, his appearance left me cold. Gazing upon Gabe, you had to admire the artistry of the creator who could mold such perfection.

He reinforced the illusion when he smiled. I couldn't find a flaw anywhere, and that made me nervous. For some inexplicable reason he reminded me of a predatory shark who'd sensed blood and circled in for the kill. He had to be only a couple of years older than me, but that age gap could have been ten years for all I cared. Still, that didn't stop me from admiring perfection in its purest form.

A throat cleared and I shifted to find Asher scowling at me. On anyone else that expression would have been jealousy, but it made no sense. Even if he'd had grounds for jealousy, it wouldn't have been fair. His brother was a work of art, and Asher couldn't blame me for looking. When Asher continued to glare, I rolled one shoulder in a shrug.

Forest-green eyes narrowed and I blinked. *Whoa. I guess he can blame me for looking.*

Gabe missed the exchange as he stared into my eyes with soulful intent. "Asher, introduce me to your friend," he demanded.

Asher remained silent, and I introduced myself. "Remy O'Malley. But you can call me Jailbait."

"Hi, Remy O'Malley. I'm Gabe. My brother didn't mention you had a sense of humor."

His voice had the same proper accent as Asher's, but with none of the sandpaper roughness that caused goose bumps to form on my arms. I detected a hint of competiveness in Gabe's smile as he leaned forward with one hand on the table and the other on the back of my seat. He was too cocky; too sure I'd be putty in his hands if he deigned to notice me. I'd thought Asher arrogant, but his brother owned it.

I decided I didn't like Gabe.

It also occurred to me that Asher's abilities might run in the family. Distaste filled me at the idea of Gabe's energy mingling with mine, and I shored my mental walls up five stories higher and ten miles wider.

Out of the corner of my eye, I noticed Asher's satisfied smile.

Gabe continued to invade my space, and I scooted my

chair toward Asher until he had to let go or fall. Gabe
didn't seem to notice my evasion. He stood over me, leaving me with the distinct impression that he was hunting me.

"I heard your dad bought you a new car. My own car
is a manual transmission, and I'd be glad to come to the aid
of a damsel in distress."

Who said things like that? He smiled, turning the full
force of his charm on me, and I bet his technique had
worked in the past, if the string of his Sorori-toys were
anything to judge by. I thought, *Shark!* I grinned up at
Gabe showing all my teeth in my best impression of the
carnivorous animal he channeled. He frowned as if I'd
frustrated him.

"Thanks for the offer, Gabe, but—"

"But Remy already asked me." Asher gave his brother a
warning look.

Gabe's shrugged. "Didn't hurt to try, bro." He winked
at me before leaving, and his rich voice threatened, "See
you later, Remy."

I watched him stride away—really, he was a lovely
shark—until Asher's tapping fingers threatened to bore a
hole in the tabletop. Twisting about, I observed how close
we sat. My face was inches from his, and his breath fanned
my cheek. I scooted my chair back so I could think without the spicy scent of him filling my head. I wondered
what he was so upset about. *It's not like we're dating.*

Asher's smile turned grim. "Go ahead and shrug,
Remy."

I'd been about to do just that, but the dare implicit in
his voice had me rolling my shoulders as if my intent had
been to ease tight muscles in my back.

"So, when's my first lesson, Teach?" I asked.

The tension in Asher's body lessened as he blew out a

breath, ruffling the hair on his forehead. I fought the urge to run my fingers through it. "Sorry about that. Gabe wanted to get under my skin, and it worked."

"No! Really? And here I thought two of the hottest guys I've ever seen were going to throw down over me." There was no missing the sarcasm in my voice.

"You think I'm hot?" he said, with a laugh.

He looked pleased by the idea, and I rolled my eyes. "Like you don't know you're good looking."

"I don't care about that kind of thing, but I'm absurdly glad you think so."

This fact seemed to annoy him. He stared into the distance, frowning, and I decided to change the subject. "Do you and your brother not get along?"

"We do, actually. From time to time, we happen to disagree on some things."

Curious, I asked, "Like what?"

"Like you."

My voice reached a high-pitched squeak. "Me? Your brother never even noticed me before today."

Asher stole my soda and took a long sip. "Remind me to show you those pictures from the beach." Before I could process that he'd developed the photos and kept them, he added, "Gabe noticed you about five minutes after I noticed you. He's biding his time."

"For what?" Asher didn't respond, and a second later the answer occurred to me. My nose wrinkled. "Did you call dibs on me?"

"I wouldn't put it quite like that, but yes. I told him to stay away from you."

I wasn't angry in the least. I should have been, but I felt a warm glow of pleasure instead. "Why would you do that?"

One strong hand slid close to mine where it rested on the table until I could feel the heat from the tips of his fingers. A scarred brow arched as he eyed me with cool arrogance.

"Oh." My traitorous hand tingled, and I sat on it to stop the sensation.

A knowing smile curved his mouth. "Yeah. Oh."

"So, what was today about? Have you decided to make your move?"

Green flames burned from his eyes. "Is that what you want?"

Every nerve screamed, *Yes!* and I shifted in my seat. My heart galloped around the track in my chest, but I hesitated, remembering how he'd tested my defenses. "Are you sure that's a good idea?"

He sighed. "I'm not sure of anything. Except that I could hurt you."

"Back at you," I answered without hesitation.

Asher looked frustrated. "Remy, don't be foolish. You have no idea what you're dealing with. Who you're dealing with."

I snorted. "And you know everything there is to know about me?"

He bowed his head in agreement. "Not everything, but enough. Certainly, more than you."

That sounded like a taunt, and my temper flared.

Asher's soft voice stopped me when I started to rise. "That wasn't fair of me."

My curiosity overcame my pride, and I sank back into my seat. "Explain something to me. What happens when I let my barricade down?" A desire to know more about his power, about what would happen if I let my defenses down all the way, became harder to disregard every minute I spent with him.

Instead of answering my question, he smiled. "You call it a barricade? That doesn't sound adequate. It feels more like running headfirst into a brick fortress."

The description made me feel a little smug. My barricade *had* been getting stronger since I'd met him. His wall had been a tiny, white picket fence in comparison.

Asher chuckled at my expression.

Fascinated, I asked, "If it's like running into a brick fortress, why do you keep trying?"

He leaned away, and I couldn't interpret the misery I read in his face. "You don't know anything."

"I know what I felt on the beach, and what I've felt since. You have powers. You attacked me."

His expression flattened, the emotion gone in an instant. "Don't ask questions I can't answer. It'll be better for both of us that way."

I didn't know what would happen if he succeeded in attacking me, but I'd never been afraid of what I couldn't see. The boogeyman didn't frighten me because I'd had a real monster living down the hall. If Asher wanted me to be afraid of him, he'd have to give me good reason because from where I sat, he didn't seem to want to hurt me.

He must have read my decision on my face because he sighed, resigned, and stood to go. "You're not getting it. This was a mistake. Do me a favor and stay away from my family, okay?"

He'd sought me out today, and then he told me to back off. The way he ran hot and cold pissed me off. Sick to death of men and their head games, I rose and told him, "I don't know, Asher. I've always had a thing for older men. Maybe one Blackwell brother is as good as another."

I ignored the black scowl that darkened his features and walked away to join my friends. Hooking my arm through Brandon's, I smiled when they ribbed me for fixing the bet so Lucy would win.

Asher's gaze scorched my back until I was out of sight.

CHAPTER EIGHT

The next day I skipped English to avoid Asher and raced home at the first opportunity.

After dinner, Laura drove me to the pool for my swimming lesson. Brandon already waited in the shallows when I left the locker room in my suit and walked down the pool steps to join him.

"You know, if the other guys ever figure out you have legs, we'll have to find another place to practice."

I splashed water in his face, and he laughed.

We spent the next hour practicing the breaststroke. Brandon made me proud when he only smirked once at saying "breast." He cut through the water in a smooth line, swimming lap after lap beside me, the contracting muscles in his arms making the ink on his arms ripple. Soon, we noticed the pool had emptied out, and it was close to closing time.

Brandon climbed out of the deeper end of the pool instead of using the stairs. Leaning down, he offered to help me out, and I grasped his hand. He exerted too much force yanking me up to his side. My body fell into his, and he reacted by wrapping both arms around me tightly enough to steal my breath. He stumbled from the impact, and his hand dipped below my waist.

The logical part of me knew it was an accident. Brandon treated me with kindness and respect. He didn't know that Dean had held me like this last year when I stepped between him and Anna during a brutal fight. He'd wrapped his arms around me as if to apologize for slapping me. Then, he'd squeezed me until I'd passed out and bruises covered my ribs.

My body ignored logic and reacted to Brandon's embrace with pure instinct.

My head shot up and butted him in the chin. His head snapped back with the blow, and his large body fell sideways, the back of his head hitting the cement siding. With a loud splash, he toppled into the water.

Reason returned as drops of water sprayed me. Brandon didn't surface, and my fear shifted into something darker as I saw him unconscious and sinking. A brief glance around the room found it empty.

"Help! Somebody help!" I screamed with frantic desperation. Nobody answered my yell for help, and I knew I was on my own.

"Oh, God, help me please," I whispered and dove in after Brandon.

He rested at the bottom of the deep end, his eyes closed and limp arms floating. I kicked as hard as I could until I could grab him.

When I wrapped a hand around his arm, blue sparks shot from my skin to his as my body attempted to heal him. I'd forgotten how instantaneous my body's reaction could be to injuries and hadn't bothered to shield myself. Brandon was drowning and now, I was, too, because I couldn't separate his wounds from my own. His lungs filled with water. My mouth was tightly closed, but still I felt heaviness invading as the water began to fill my own chest. Lights gleamed a few short feet above my head, but they might have been the stars, so far were they out of my reach.

I wouldn't let Brandon drown without trying to save him, and I couldn't pull him up on my own.

We would both die.

Defeated, my lungs ached as my air ran out. Seconds away from opening my mouth to breathe in, I glimpsed a body diving through the water above me. *Asher.* His eyes narrowed as he kicked his way toward me faster than should have been physically possible. I sensed his wall go up before he wrapped an arm around my shoulders and another around Brandon's. Placing both feet on the bottom of the pool, he shoved off and sent all three of us rocketing upward.

My head cleared the surface, and I choked up chlorinated water as Asher dragged both Brandon and me to the edge of the pool. He knocked my hand from Brandon's arm with an almost violent move in the process. Just like that, I could think again.

Hank, the pool superintendent, who closed the community center every night—a kind man in his sixties—helped pull Brandon over the lip of the pool onto the concrete floor as Asher lifted him. Then, Asher launched himself out in one lithe movement and reached back to haul me out. Unlike the effort Brandon had required, Asher placed his hands under my arms and picked me up as if I were a child instead of a gangly girl two inches shy of six feet.

He didn't put me down, either.

He cradled me against him with his arms wrapped around my back and my feet dangling in the air. We were both dripping wet, but my chilled body warmed wherever he touched me. Red-hot fire spread when one of Asher's large hands slipped into my hair to press my face into his shoulder, and I welcomed the heat.

We might have stayed that way forever if Brandon's coughing hadn't pulled me back to awareness. I pushed

against Asher's shoulders until he set me down. We moved
to where Hank had turned Brandon on his side. Semi-
conscious, Brandon was choking up a gallon of chlorinated water, and blood stained the puddle of water by his
head. Hank told us to stay with Brandon while he ran to
the office to call an ambulance.

Asher clasped my hand in an unbreakable grip when I
reached out to touch Brandon. I peered up into his grim
eyes; he looked scared and unmovable as he shook his
head at me.

Hoping it looked believable, I smiled to reassure him.
"Let me go."

"Your guard will be down. What if I . . ."

"Go if you have to, but don't try to stop me."

Asher didn't respond. I tugged on my hand, and a long
moment later, he released me. I sensed him reinforcing the
barrier in his mind. "Make sure Hank doesn't see," I whispered.

Touching Brandon's shoulder lit a current of energy that
poured through me to him. The healing that had begun
six feet underwater continued as if it hadn't been interrupted by our near drowning. His lungs would be okay:
He'd thrown up most of the water and breathed in rough
gasps. His chin sported a red bruise from my blow, and a
small cut bled on the back of his head from hitting the lip
of the pool. These wounds healed with ease, but his concussion worried me.

I'd never done well with Anna's head injuries. They
hurt like hell and created such mental confusion and distress, I often couldn't heal myself for hours afterward.
Gritting my teeth, I strained to relax. Closing my eyes, I
pictured the wound and then imagined the swelling dissipating. From a distance, I heard Hank returning and Asher
shifting to hide me from his view.

Having done all I could, my hand fell from Brandon

and my eyes opened to see the familiar blue sparks. They'd faded when Brandon opened his eyes. My sigh of relief was palpable when he focused on me. I struggled to appear normal as my vision clouded, and my brain threatened to explode out of my skull. He blinked at me with concern and said, "Remy? What happened? You okay?"

Leaning forward, I rested my aching forehead against my friend's and shivered with the aftermath of the healing. "Sure, Brand. The next time you want to drown, though, you better make sure there's a good swimmer around. Asher had to pull us both out."

Brandon rubbed a gentle hand on my arm to chafe some warmth into me. "What happened? I was helping you out of the pool and . . ."

"It was my fault. I took a trip down memory lane and panicked." His eyes widened in comprehension. He'd seen the bruises on my face my first week in town. Lucy had to have told him something about why I'd moved to Blackwell Falls, but he'd never questioned me. I felt another surge of affection for this boy I'd almost killed with my loss of control. Ashamed, I squeezed my eyes closed against the humiliation. "I'm so sorry, Brandon."

I'd been kidding myself to think I could fit in, could be accepted.

He shocked me when he sat up and hugged me, carefully placing his hands high on my back. "For what? You're always smacking me upside the head for being an idiot. I'm sure you owed me for all the times I've checked you out in that bikini when you weren't paying attention." To prove it, he leered at me.

With a tiny laugh, I returned his hug.

Then, the EMTs were running in to check him over, and I reassured them I was fine. When I stood, the pain radiating from my head made me stagger like Dean on a drunken tear, and my stomach roiled with nausea. Asher said something to the group, and his voice came from a long distance. He steered me to the locker room, staying at my back to shield me from the EMTs, while my body shuddered uncontrollably. As soon as I entered the locker room, I ran to a bathroom stall to empty my stomach in the toilet.

I sank back on my heels to wait for the pain to ease to a manageable level. Asher had propped me up with an arm around my shoulder and held my hair away from my face.

"Remy, your head's bleeding."

My fingers came away red when I touched the throbbing spot at the back of my head. Disoriented, I stared at the blood and thought, *Damn, that hurts.*

Asher's laugh sounded shaky. "Do you feel sick still? Can you stand up?"

I winced. "I think so. You mind getting my bag out of my locker while I rinse out my mouth?"

After helping me to my feet, he retrieved my bag and waited outside the stall while I changed into street clothing. He left once to check on Brandon at my request and returned in a dry set of clothes someone had loaned him. The EMTs couldn't find anything wrong with Brandon since he didn't even have a bruise to show for his fall. They'd called his parents, but it didn't look like a trip to the hospital would be necessary. Asher had told Brandon I'd call him tomorrow.

Asher helped me rinse the worst of the blood out of my hair and dried the long strands with a towel as best he could. I couldn't bear to pull my knit cap on, even if my wet hair would be exposed to the frigid night air. Asher watched with concern as I arranged my hair in a loose braid and helped me into my coat. Exhausted now, it occurred to me that Laura should have arrived by now to pick me up.

"I don't have a ride," I said, stumbling to a stop.

Asher steered me to the door. "I called Lucy earlier and asked her to let Laura know I'd drive you home."

The idea of getting on his motorcycle now sounded like pure, unholy torture. I pictured us hitting a bump and the jolt of pain that movement would set off in my body.

"I have my car. This way."

We walked out of the community center into the cold, and my trembling worsened. He rushed to open the passenger door of a sleek, navy sedan and helped ease me in. I sank into the seat and closed my eyes while he started the car, turning the heater up full blast. We drove in silence to my house where he parked on the street in the halo of a streetlamp. He cut the headlights, but left the engine running so the heat continued to pour through the vents.

Asher reached for my hand, twisting his fingers through mine. "Why are you shivering so badly?"

"H-h-heat leaves body. W-w-worse with head injuries." The full aftereffects of a complex healing had set in, and shudders wracked my body. Experience told me nothing could be done but try to stay warm and wait them out.

Asher's shadowed face was impossible to read in the dim light of the car. Without warning, he shoved his seat back and lifted me across the console onto his lap. Something warm—his coat—wrapped around me as he cradled me. His hand spread over the back of my neck, and my cold nose pressed into his scratchy wool sweater. He smelled like Blackwell Falls, a natural mixture of salty air and the woods, and his heart beat double-time beneath my ear.

"Relax," he breathed, as if I had the strength to fight him. "We're calling a truce until you get warm."

His heat felt delicious, and after several long minutes my shivering tapered off. The last hour had drained me physically and mentally. My defenses had been stripped since before he'd shown up to save me, but he'd kept his raised.

I pulled back to study his square jaw, shadowed with dark whiskers. It felt nice not to have to be the responsible one for the moment. *I wouldn't be able to stop him if he did attack me now, anyways.*

He groaned and dragged a hand over his face. "Geez, Remy. I'm not a saint."

Still disoriented, I asked, "What are you talking about?"

He froze and dropped his hand, refusing to look at me. "Never mind."

He appeared so upset that I let it go. "Asher, what were you doing at the pool?"

"I planned to warn you off my brother, even though I know you made that comment to provoke me. But the truth is I was jealous."

Even in the shadows his expression looked hard, and I believed him. The darkness wound around us, inviting us to share our secrets.

"Of Gabe?" I asked. "You're right. I said he interested me to irritate you. I don't have any intention of going near your brother."

"I know. I meant Brandon."

Surprised, I tilted my chin to see his face better. "Why would you be jealous of Brandon?"

"After I got over being angry at you for taunting me with Gabriel—thanks for that, by the way—it occurred to me that maybe there was someone else. I asked around and found out you've been spending a lot of time with Brandon here at the pool. You seem . . . close."

Green eyes gleamed when he finally looked down at me. He *was* jealous. My heart thudded against my ribs. "Oh. He's my friend. A good friend."

The clipped edge to his voice betrayed his anger. "I got that distinct impression when you were willing to die for him. What were you thinking, Remy?"

He'd returned to insulting me. My voice sounded thick as I tried to put some space between us. "I was thinking my friend would drown if I didn't try to save him."

"Why didn't you let go of him when you realized you couldn't pull him up?"

"I couldn't—"

One hand slammed the steering wheel, and he glared at me. "Of all the stupid, reckless actions . . ."

"If you'd shut up, I'll explain."

The dark muttering halted, and I continued, "When I touched him to pull him out of the water, his wounds jumped out and grabbed me. It was like I was drowning, too, and I couldn't save myself."

His hollowed cheekbones worked as his jaw clenched. "Has that happened before?"

"Not that bad," I whispered. "I've never been in a situation where someone else's injuries could put my life in jeopardy before I could heal myself."

It was odd talking about this, especially while resting in his arms. These were my deepest secrets that not even my mother knew.

"You take on whatever illness or injury you heal?" He sounded horrified to have his theory confirmed.

I rolled my head away to stare out the windshield. "But you already guessed that."

"And the pain? Do you take that as well?"

"Yes," I admitted.

Asher remained silent for a full minute taking that in. Then he sucked in a shaky breath, and I knew comprehension had dawned when he shook me lightly. His voice burned with raw emotion. "My hand. You healed my hand. I would never . . . I would *never* have asked. . . . What were you thin— Why would you do that, Remy? Why?"

"You were hurt."

He laughed with disbelief. "I was hurt? Are you crazy? You let your guard down, knowing you would take on that pain, and I let you do it. And then, I thanked you for it by attacking you."

I needed distance to think. When I pushed against his chest, he seemed to understand and helped shift me back into the passenger seat. The cold returned without the warmth of his body against me, until he tucked his jacket around me again. I almost regretted moving. Dangerous or not, Asher was the first person to take care of me after a healing.

His jaw tensed, and his eyes took on a flinty look.

I hadn't answered him and didn't know what to say.

In a flat tone, he said, "Did it ever occur to you that I'm not like you? That, in fact, I'm the opposite of you? You feel too much. Your power even works by feeling—by touching."

"And yours doesn't?"

"Remy, I can't *feel* anything. This car, the water in that pool, my wet hair, the air coming out of that vent."

My body stilled. "I don't understand. You were in pain when you burned your hand. You can't deny that."

"I'm not denying it."

Frustration sharpened my tone. "You're not making any sense. Either you feel things or you don't. When you're touching me, you . . ."

I remembered how he'd looked on the beach. How he looked at school. Laughing and surrounded by people, he somehow managed to look alone. Detached. Unreachable.

Until I lowered my defenses and sent my energy arcing at him. Until he touched me.

Then he looked in pain.

I shifted in my seat until I faced Asher.

He reacted with a humorless laugh as if he could see my expression in the shadows. "Got it in one. I don't feel anything, *except* when you're near me."

"How can that be?" I whispered.

As if he spoke to himself, his voice lowered. "I'm walking on the beach, and you appear out of nowhere looking so damned fragile. I wanted to know who had hurt you, to tear them apart. When I took your picture, I hoped you would look up and speak to me. Instead, you came after my camera, and I realized how wrong I'd been. You may have been covered in bruises, but I would never call you frail. You're a warrior, Remy, and I had to know you."

"But something changed. I felt you change."

"You're right. Until that moment when you dropped your defenses, and I felt your power, I didn't know what you were. I could've killed you. You're my enemy."

He used the present tense. He still considered me an enemy, after everything that had happened. "You started this," I snapped. "Why keep coming after me? Why follow me here tonight if I'm from the dark side?"

"Curiosity? You're not like other Healers."

He shrugged, and I wanted to punch him. My emotions had been stuck in a spin cycle, and he'd simply been curious about my abilities. "Really? Then, why jump in the pool after me? That's taking curiosity to an extreme, don't you think?"

His eyes dropped. "I reacted without thinking. When you're near, I feel too much. I didn't want to give that up, but it has to stop now. You're affecting my judgment, and I can't have that. I'm not the only one involved here."

His family, he meant. He wanted to protect his family. I couldn't blame him since my priorities were the same.

"So what now?" I asked. "We tried ignoring each other. That worked out really well." I waved a hand around to encompass the both of us sitting in his car, our hair still wet from the pool.

"I'll make it work. We have no choice."

"We have a choice," I said. Neither of us was willing to risk our families, though, to choose differently.

He turned, and I sucked in a breath at the rage I saw staring back at me. "Don't you get it, Healer? I still could kill you."

"What the hell are you talking about?" The shivering started again, but it had nothing to do with being cold. Enemies and killing. The entire conversation sounded bizarre to my ears.

"Didn't you feel it on the beach when I tried to give you the film? I needed you to trust me because I intended to save you from whoever had left those marks on you. Then I *felt* it. Your power was there between us, and my body *hurt*. I experienced the first physical sensation I'd felt in years, and I couldn't stop myself from grabbing hold of you to make it last. I don't trust myself to keep my walls up."

Finally, an explanation. My voice came out a husky whisper. "If I hurt you, why try to be near me? Why would you want the pain to continue?"

"When you've gone without sensation for as long as I have, it can make you desperate. Any feeling is better than none. Even pain. Do you see why I'm a danger to you? Why I warned you to keep your walls up? You must have sensed I was different. Remy, the longer I'm near you, the more I *feel* again. When you're near me, I stop caring what could happen to you."

"How do you know about me when I know nothing about you? Why are we enemies?" There were others like me. Still others like him. The knowledge should have terrified me, but it seemed too big. Too impossible to take in.

He sighed. "You're a Healer—your energy . . . It's like a temporary stimulant for my kind; it makes us feel alive again. Everything about you is designed to give, to sacrifice, but I'm not like you. If I lost control . . . took too much . . . you would die."

He could kill me, his enemy. What was he that my power to heal people would make him my enemy?

In silence, I contemplated all the times I'd felt his energy zinging toward me. After that first meeting on the beach when my ability had surprised him, he'd treated me with caution—like I had a "Danger" sign painted on my forehead. Even the weeks of testing my defenses had lacked menace. His mental prods *had* been warnings. As if he sought to keep me on my toes with my shield up against possible danger. Against him. And tonight he'd saved my life. Even now, it was his mental wall that protected us both from what he could do to me.

I knew what danger felt like, what it felt like to be hated. Asher wanted to harness my energy to feel human again, but he would not sacrifice me to do so. His own actions belied him. He couldn't be my enemy.

"I don't believe you." Still cuddled in his jacket, I inhaled his scent.

"What do you mean you don't believe me?"

It was my turn to laugh. "You heard me."

I was certain I was right. *Asher's protecting me. He'll never hurt me.*

Asher groaned, his expression bleak. "Damn you, Remy, for making me do this."

One hand curved to my cheek. At once, his wall dropped, and his energy blasted me. It didn't build up like mine, unfurling a little at a time. It arrived without warning, overwhelming me until I couldn't breathe. The icy sludge flowed through my veins, and like before, my heart beat faster in distress and then slowed until I thought it would stop altogether. With my senses wide open and my defenses down, I felt everything. And it hurt.

Unconsciousness loomed, and the pain worsened, more intense than healing Anna and ten times more intense than healing his burned hand or Brandon's head. Everything blackened, and a droning sound filled my ears that I realized was the sluggish rhythm of my heart. With my last shred of awareness, I focused on it. I concentrated on each beat, each measured thump in my chest until one corner of my mind cleared.

The pain didn't ease, but I struggled to get my barricade in place to block the onslaught of energy still pouring from Asher. He reached inside me with his power, as if he scanned me. Only he wasn't healing me. *This* was the danger he'd warned me of. As he stretched his senses through my limbs, his energy grew and expanded, while mine weakened. I understood, then, what he'd tried to tell me.

He didn't just hold my energy hostage, he could *steal* it. He was a thief.

Rage consumed me. My body grew weaker by the instant as he strengthened, and I couldn't stop him.

Even as this realization struck, his energy receded from me. I sensed the tight rein he had on his power as he pulled his hand from me and resurrected his mental barrier. The pain disappeared along with his touch. Control of my limbs returned, and I recoiled into the passenger-side door.

Asher flipped on the interior light. He twisted to face me with a ferocious hunger glowing in his eyes. He looked dangerous. And full of self-loathing.

I'd let myself trust him. Stupid, stupid girl.

Through his teeth, he said, "Do you understand now? Stay the hell away from me." He glanced away. "I can't be the one to hurt you."

I said nothing. He'd reminded me of a lesson I'd learned

early in life, one that I'd forgotten since coming to Black-well Falls. A string of memories played through my mind. Dean striking Anna in the face, and then knocking a twelve-year-old version of me into the kitchen counter when I tried to stop him. He'd broken my arm that time. And later, Anna's horrified expression when I healed her by accident for the first time, and her pleading voice when she begged me to keep it a secret. Then, I was a defiant fourteen-year-old, and Dean crushed his cigarette into my arm, furious because he couldn't make me cry. Last, Asher sent that energy wave barreling at me when I'd decided I could trust him.

Everyone you care about betrays you in the end.

Asher put out a hand to touch me. "Remy, please."

I wasn't sure what he asked, and I didn't wait to find out. Tossing his jacket away, I reached behind me for the handle to open the car door and scrambled out, almost falling to the ground. I looked back once into Asher's pained expression. Then I ran into the house as fast as I could.

CHAPTER NINE

*I*n my room, I crawled under my down comforter, not caring that my wet hair smelled like chlorine, and curled into a ball.

Tonight had been a good lesson. I'd forgotten what happened when you trusted people. At the pool, I'd allowed my past to sneak up and harm someone I cared about. My mistake had been getting involved. Luckily, the mistake could be corrected.

My dry eyes burned. Things couldn't continue on like this. I needed to start cutting the ties that bound me to this place. I'd let Brandon know my swimming lessons were over to keep him safe from me. As for the rest of my new friends . . . I'd find a new place to have lunch.

Without question, I would avoid Asher. His actions tonight had proved how dangerous he could be. It burned that I'd been stupid enough to develop feelings for him. He knew about my power and could betray me to others at any time. Already, he'd intimated that his family knew about me. Gabe's interest in me made frightening sense, and I'd bet my new car he had power similar to Asher's.

What to do, then? I'd have to be on my guard around the Blackwells until I could leave town. *And Asher?* I thought, as I focused on healing my injuries. I couldn't be weak again. I would not be.

★ ★ ★

I woke when a hand shook my shoulder, and I scanned the owner of the limb before my eyes opened. *Ben.*

"Remy, wake up, hon."

He sounded upset. Sitting up, I shoved my hair out of my eyes. Ben turned on my light and eased down next to me on the bed. He couldn't look at me. Laura hovered in the doorway with her tired eyes pinched with concern. They both wore robes as if they'd come from bed. They hadn't appeared so distressed since I'd arrived in Blackwell Falls.

"Hon, it's your mom. Anna's in the hospital."

I heard the words, but they didn't penetrate right away.

"The manager at your apartment came to collect the rent and found her. Apparently, she suffered a head wound in the last week that went untreated. She collapsed today and is in a coma."

He squeezed my hand, but I pulled away. I'd known it was a matter of time before Dean hurt her, and I'd left her behind. In a cold voice, I asked "Will she be okay?"

His expression turned bleak, and I had my answer.

"How did you find out?"

"The hospital. Anna listed me as her emergency contact for some reason."

That made perfect sense. I was too young, and she would never have chosen Dean. Not when he was the reason she needed help in the first place. If something happened to her, she would have wanted Ben to know for my sake.

Ben and Laura stared at me, most likely concerned with my unnatural composure. They didn't know how I needed to lose myself in the details so I wouldn't crack apart inside. I didn't try to reassure them. Their worry took a backseat to Anna's pain.

"You have to take me to her."

Ben stood. "Of course. I've already called the airport. You and I are on the eight a.m. flight out of Portland."

They left me alone to dress when I nodded.

That afternoon, Ben and I took a taxi to the hospital, the reverse of the trip we'd taken a month ago. Such a small amount of time, but my life had changed in a radical way.

My thoughts focused on Anna. I wondered when Dean had hurt her and if the police knew who to blame. I'd guess not since Anna had been such a good liar when it came to her husband, and I'd aided and abetted her by limiting the number of trips we'd made to the ER.

We were directed to the Intensive Care Unit when we arrived at the hospital. A doctor told us Anna's condition hadn't changed. Untreated, the swelling in her brain had increased, and she'd lapsed into a coma. They didn't know if she would wake up.

They let me in Anna's room first. A nurse cautioned me to stay no longer than the allotted fifteen minutes and left in cushioned shoes. The only sounds in the room came from the machines that monitored Anna's vital signs.

I was glad to be alone with her. The reckless action I contemplated would not bear witnesses. If I managed to heal Anna, I could end up in a coma my body couldn't heal. And for what? For a mother who'd let her husband use me as a punching bag.

At her bedside, I scrutinized her faded features. Her brown hair had been smoothed from her face, and her fair skin was pale. Deep black half-moons rested under her closed eyes like upside-down eyebrows. Week-old green and yellow bruises colored her jaw.

Taking a deep breath, I laid a tentative hand on her forearm. I had thirteen minutes left according to the clock on the wall. I let the energy build within before sending it spiraling outward into her. First, I healed the visible bruises on her jaw because I couldn't stand seeing Dean's mark on her. Then, I moved on to the head injury, expecting it to be difficult to heal, but it was impossible. Her unconscious mind had become a snarl of black nothing that I couldn't penetrate. The injury was invisible, and what I couldn't see, I couldn't heal. This had never happened before. Panicked, I aimed a wave of energy at her head in a random burst of blue sparks. Exhausted, I held on to the railing of her bed with my free hand to stay upright.

Her eyes flickered open.

I stepped back reeling in shock, but she grasped my hand.

"Remy." She closed her eyes for a moment and swallowed. I tried to pull free to get a nurse, and she held on tighter.

"Mom?"

I scanned her again, to see if my last-ditch effort had wrought a miracle, but her head proved impenetrable. She wasn't healed.

Her brown eyes focused on me, and she started crying. "He'll come after you."

She sounded terrified. It didn't come as a surprise to find Dean meant me harm. On top of an oversized ego, he had a vicious streak that would demand vengeance for hurting him. I held tighter to her hand with both of mine and whispered, "It's okay, Mom. Let's concentrate on getting you out of here. Then we'll worry about Dean."

That made her cry harder. I started to pull my hand free again to get someone to help, but the strength of her grip shocked me. "He knows. All my fault. The journal."

"Mom, what journal?"

Lost in her memories, she seemed far away when she continued, "Tells truth. About you."

Her cryptic response made no sense. Was she admitting to knowing about me? "What truth?"

Wrinkles formed as her brow furrowed. "Danger. Find it, baby."

"What are you talking about?"

No response came from the bed. I wondered if the pain had clouded her reason. This was the first I'd heard of her keeping a journal. Her words made no sense.

She needed a doctor. I forced her hand loose from mine, and her eyes fluttered closed. The instant I freed my hand the machines in the room beeped a shrill warning. Anna's heart skittered and stopped beating.

"Mom?" Panic streaked through me as I leaned close to listen for her breathing.

No answer.

A group of nurses and doctors rushed into the room. Impersonal hands shoved me out of the way as they set to work, ripping the bedding from my mother and shoving her gown open. Paddles were charged like I'd seen in movies.

"Mom! Please let me . . ." If I could touch her . . .

A doctor with brown hair, the one who'd explained my mother's injuries in the hall, glared at an unknown person behind me. He shouted, "Get her out of here!"

Someone pushed me from the room. I registered the new set of hands that gripped my shoulders to stop me from running back in. Ben pulled me into his chest and wrapped an arm around me. We stared in joint horror as my mother's body leaped into the air as the paddles sent volts of electricity into her chest. Then the door closed, cutting off our view.

It didn't take long for the doctor who'd shouted to come out of the room. His defeated expression told me what I already knew. She was dead. My mother was dead.

She had been weak and cold and broke my heart a thousand times. I shouldn't have loved her.

The emotions roiling through me threatened to send me to the floor in a heap of twisted grief and rage and guilt. Like I had done with the nerves in my burned hand, I cauterized my heart to blunt the pain. I couldn't stop the flood of obscure details pressing themselves into my memories as I watched the doctor walk up to where Ben and I sat in matching plastic chairs.

"Mr. O'Malley? There wasn't a lot we could do. The injury was too severe. We knew there was a possibility she wouldn't regain consciousness."

They didn't know. They had no idea she'd woken up and spoken to me, and I couldn't tell them because of the questions they would ask. I felt the doctor's eyes on me and wondered if he'd noticed the absence of bruises on Anna or the similar ones on my jaw, but he only said, "I'm sorry for your loss."

He nodded at Ben and turned to stride down the hall.

Ben reached for my elbow, but I stood and called, "Wait!"

The doctor hesitated and looked back. "Yes?"

My voice strengthened as I took a step toward him. "My stepfather. Dean Whitfield. Have the police arrested him?"

He shook his head. "Your mother was alone when she was brought to the hospital."

"This happened because of him. He killed her. Dean killed her." His name tasted like poison in my mouth. "He hurt her so many times, and we came here for help. You should've stopped him. Why didn't you stop him?"

My voice sounded harsh with unshed tears. The doctor didn't respond, and I knew he didn't have an answer. It wasn't his fault. He'd never met Anna before. I should have protected my mother, but I'd abandoned her.

The doctor said again, "I'm sorry." He walked away, and I let him go this time.

Ben tried to embrace me, but I shoved his arms away. I would shatter if he comforted me. "I can't, Ben. I won't cry."

My words upset him, but he allowed me to put space between us. "Tell me what you need, Remy," he said.

It was an echo of something he'd said when I moved to Blackwell Falls.

"Help me plan the funeral."

CHAPTER TEN

*T*wo days later, we had the funeral in a small Brooklyn cemetery.

A rare bit of April heat baked the white roses on my mother's grave, browning the edges of the drooping petals. The pastor said one last prayer, and the ceremony ended. Two men in overalls waited respectfully for the mourners—Ben and me—to leave so they could fill in the grave with the dirt hidden beneath a strip of Astroturf.

Dean had not come to the funeral, and I had no way of knowing if someone had told him about my mother's death. It was left to Ben to shake hands with the pastor. Then he shepherded me into our rental car for the ride to my old apartment. We planned to catch the last flight out to Portland, and I sensed his desperate desire to return home. He'd been tense these last few days. He waited for me to break down, and I think he hoped for it.

He got behind the steering wheel and didn't start the car right away. After a full minute, he said, "It's okay to cry, Remy. She was your mother."

As if I didn't know. As if I didn't feel the grief smothering me. "I'm fine."

He seemed ready to argue, and I urged, "Please, let's go. We have a lot to do before our flight."

With a sigh of resignation, he started the car. Apparently, Dean had skipped out of town. Since rent hadn't been paid on the apartment I'd shared with Dean and Anna, Ben had made arrangements with the manager to pack up the contents for storage.

We used my key to enter our fourth-floor walk-up apartment. Ben crossed the threshold on my heels and told me to stay near the entry while he checked every room to ensure we were alone. I ignored the tug on my heart at his protectiveness as he paced through the windowless rooms. Eventually, Ben went to meet the movers outside, leaving with a grimace when sirens echoed off the thin walls. Violence wasn't uncommon in our neighborhood, and Dean hadn't always been the most dangerous person in the vicinity—just the most dangerous between these walls.

Alone, I stood in the living room and turned a full circle, taking in my surroundings. The place was worse than I'd remembered with its shoddy, threadbare furnishings and stale air. The cheap wood coffee table featured water stains and black scuff marks from Dean's boots resting on it. The once white walls were a sickly yellow from the nicotine that swirled in the air from his cigarettes. A flat screen TV, Dean's prized possession, sat in a cheap entertainment case—bought with my father's child support checks. Nothing of me or Anna lived in this room, except the faint whisper of blood and tears. It had been Dean's domain, and there was nothing here that I wanted.

I moved to the kitchen doorway, expecting to see Anna huddling at the round dining table where she often sat alone, in between waiting on Dean and doing her crossword puzzles. It smelled of leftover Chinese takeout—very few meals had been cooked here. Mostly this room had been Anna's refuge. One of her crossword puzzle books was lying facedown on the worn plastic tablecloth as if waiting for her to finish it. I picked up the book and hugged it to my chest as I roamed looking for a journal.

I headed down the hallway to her bedroom. I hadn't been in this room since we'd moved here, and I felt like I was trespassing as I searched the drawers and closet without any luck.

My last destination was my bedroom. There wasn't much in the way of comfort in the sparse prison of a room with its twin bed, used dresser, and makeshift desk forged from plywood and concrete blocks.

The few things I wanted to keep went into a duffel Ben had given me. Most of my clothes and personal things had already been sent to Blackwell Falls by Anna. Little of me remained. On top of the pile went the iPod Anna had surprised me with on my birthday a few months before. We didn't have a computer, and I'd wondered at the extravagant gift I had no way to use. I'd never taken it out of the box, but it seemed Anna had used it since I'd moved to Blackwell Falls. If Dean had known about the iPod, he would have tried to sell it. Last into the bag went her crossword puzzle book and a picture of a younger, more carefree Anna taken pre-Dean. Next, I checked the bed where I'd hidden some money under my mattress. This was gone, as I'd expected. Dean would have found the cash right away.

Noise sounded from the living room when Ben returned with the movers, and I went to meet him, duffel bag in hand. It took very little time for the movers to load up the contents of the apartment. Soon the rooms stood bare as if they'd never been inhabited, as if the walls hadn't witnessed our pain. All traces of Anna and the girl I'd been were erased.

Ben followed the movers out to return the apartment key to the manager. Only the kitchen chairs and the furniture in the living room remained, and the movers would take care of those items in short order. As I did one last walk through the empty, still rooms, my steps sounded an eerie echo. One last thing waited to be retrieved, and history had taught me to keep its hiding place a secret. Old habits were hard to break.

In my bedroom, I moved to the bare closet and felt along the wall until I discovered the small hole I'd made at the very bottom of the drywall. It would have been impossible to find if you hadn't known it existed, if you hadn't been locked inside the small space on more than one occasion. Reaching into the hole, I rescued the small nest egg I'd saved working at the video store. This money had been my hope for a new start.

I counted it. Fifteen hundred, ninety-eight dollars. I wouldn't have gotten very far.

"So that's where you hid it."

Dean lounged against the doorjamb, inspecting me with his pale eyes while he flicked a lighter open and closed.

He nodded to the money I crushed in my hand. "I knew the forty under your mattress wasn't all you'd stashed."

His large body straightened, and he took a step forward, his blond curls askew. False sympathy resonated in a voice that sounded rougher than I remembered—as if a hand had wrapped around his throat to choke him. I'd done that to him. "I'm sorry about your mom. I was on a job in Springfield when I heard. Just got back today."

So that was his story. There would be people who would corroborate, too, if the police asked questions. He almost sounded sincere, and I had to give him credit. Dean was stupid, but he had a rat's instinct for survival.

My situation was precarious. I was alone in the apartment with my stepfather, and he had me cornered in the bedroom. I didn't know how long Ben had been gone, or when he would return. What if he'd already returned and Dean had hurt him? My gut clenched. *Oh, God, please no.*

Dean read my thoughts with his uncanny ability to sniff out fear. He sneered as he flicked the lighter to life again in a threat he knew had terrified me since he'd first burned me with his lit cigarette. "It was real nice of you and your daddy to pack up my things. I slashed the tires on your daddy's rental car to return the favor. It'll be a while before he comes looking for you, princess."

A surge of relief flooded through me to know Ben was safe, followed by a tidal wave of panic. I would have to save myself.

Dean took another step and said, "What's the matter, Remy? Cat got your tongue?"

Rather than cringe as he expected, I moved toward him with confidence. Showing fear to Dean was inviting death, so my smile exuded calm. His advance halted, and he appeared wary for the first time. Was he recalling the pain I'd caused him the last night I lived here?

In a conversational tone, I advised, "Remember what happened the last time you touched me? Two broken ribs, right?"

One lip curled in a snarl, but he stopped advancing.

He didn't know I couldn't hurt him without an injured Anna nearby to transfer wounds from. I would have to run for the door as soon as I could and hope he didn't find out. "Do you know I've gotten even better at it? I've been practicing in case we met up again. Where is my mother's journal, Dean?"

My head spun with dizzy relief when he retreated from the bedroom, and I stalked him through the dark hallway. In the living room, he regained his composure and smirked. "She didn't tell you? I learned a few things from it. Like how you're powerless if you can't touch me."

Shock and sorrow blasted me. Anna had betrayed me once more by telling him the one thing that could have saved my life. The journal was gone. He had to have it because, while it was possible he'd figured how my abilities worked, it wasn't probable. Hopelessness overwhelmed me.

Dean flexed his arm, and I knew he was finished talking.

He cracked his knuckles, and I forced steel into my backbone. I would not be easy prey. He wouldn't walk away from this fight uninjured. Balancing on the balls of my feet, I waited for his next move.

It didn't take long.

He rushed me like a linebacker, and I waited until the last possible moment to sidestep him. His body moved past me, stumbled into the wall, and crumpled, sprawling on the floor. His momentary confusion allowed me to make a run for the front door.

My retreat wasn't fast enough. One of his hands closed around my ankle and he yanked my foot out from under me with a vicious twist. I tripped and threw out my hands to break my fall, unable to stop my face from colliding with the edge of the coffee table. My lip split open, and my shoulder tore as I slammed to the floor on my left side.

Before I could register the pain, Dean dragged my body across the carpet toward him. I rolled over, ignoring the jolt in my shoulder. His face was mottled red with fury, and his blue eyes lit with malice. I used my free foot to kick him in the face as hard as I could. Blood spurted from his nose and I hoped I'd broken it as I stunned him into loosening his hold.

Scrambling onto all fours, I scuttled away. Gaining my feet, I ran the few feet to the door. Panicked, I heard him rise and felt the change in the air as he rushed me. The doorknob twisted in my sweaty hand and opened two inches—my freedom so close—when his flat palm slammed it shut again. My forehead dropped against the hollow wood as he locked the door and crowded me against it. Hot breath fanned my neck, smelling of the beer and stale cigarettes from my nightmares.

Taking a deep breath, I pulled back my right elbow and shoved it in his gut as hard as I could.

Doubling over, he grunted, and I twisted away, running for my bedroom. Maybe I could lock myself in until help came. Until Ben could come for me.

I'd gone a few short feet when Dean gave me a brutal shove. My body flew over the couch and slammed into the entryway table. A new explosion of pain rippled from my hip to my back as I collided with the large mirror that hung on the wall, and it crashed down on me, shattering into tiny shards that sliced my arms and back. Stunned, I slid off the table and crumpled to the floor.

Dean stood over me and shoved me on my back with his foot. I was too weak to run, and the triumph flaring in his eyes said he knew he'd won. He would kick me, and it would be over then. I wouldn't be able to fight.

Energy gathered in me like a snake coiling to strike. He drew his foot back.

The front door shook as someone battered it.

Dean glanced away for one brief moment, and I had my chance. I grabbed his leg and let the current sizzle through me to him in a violent lash of red electricity. My pain barreled into him before he could react. He grabbed one shoulder as it dislocated and his lip split, the blood mingling with that from his broken nose. New blood appeared in a dozen tiny cuts on his arms as he shrieked and collapsed on the floor, moaning. I rolled to my side, grabbed a larger piece of broken glass, and held it over his throat. His eyes locked on mine in terror, and I experienced a rush of primal satisfaction.

There was a *crack* of wood splintering, and the door fell off its hinges as Ben kicked it in.

My father rushed into the room and froze in shock. A male police officer filled the doorway behind him and moved to stand over Dean with a gun while Ben knelt at my side.

"Drop the glass, miss. You're safe now," the officer said, in a calm voice.

I did as he asked, and Ben lifted me from the floor without hesitation. He carried me to the kitchen like a child and sat in one of the hard-backed chairs with me cradled in his lap. His tight grasp hurt my shoulder, but I didn't protest. Whatever he saw in my face, my father started crying. I wondered if he'd hurt himself breaking down the door. Under the guise of reassuring him, I patted his cheek to scan for possible injuries. "It's okay, Ben. I'm safe."

He was healthy, unharmed, aside from the uneven beat of his heart, which could only mean he cried for me. "I'm safe now," I repeated.

When a female officer walked into the kitchen, Ben's expression turned fierce and he said, "You better believe we're pressing charges."

Ben refused to leave my side at the hospital, even to talk to the police.

He told the two officers what he knew about my situation, including why I'd come to live with him and what he suspected about Anna's death. He didn't have to tell them about this latest confrontation since Officer Gonzalez had walked in on the scene with him. It turned out someone had seen Dean slashing the tires on Ben's rental car while we'd been busy packing and had called the police. They'd come to investigate some hours later while my father was returning the key to the manager, and that was when he realized I might be in danger.

Officer Gonzalez questioned me about the abuse, and I told the skeleton truth. Yes, Dean had been abusing us for years, starting with Anna and then me. Yes, the police had been notified by neighbors and hospital staff. No, charges had never been filed. Anna always lied to protect him, and

I'd lied right along with her, afraid I'd be sent away. Each word that came out of my mouth seemed to cut Ben, so I kept the details to a bare minimum. I didn't tell the police everything, but said enough to give them the picture while a nurse cleaned my split lip and the dozen cuts on my arms and back.

The officers had heard stories like mine before. They nodded and asked more questions whenever I paused. The emergency room doctor told the men to step out so he could inspect my hip and side where I'd slammed into the entry table. Officer Kazinski—a policewoman whose face was locked in a permanent grimace—stayed behind to document my injuries. She took loads of pictures, and I resigned myself to another set of injuries I wouldn't be able to heal for fear of discovery.

The men stepped back in, and Officer Gonzalez continued questioning me while making notes in a small notepad. At last, they left to question Dean, who'd been admitted to another area of the ER. According to Kazinski, he would be transferred to jail when the doctors finished checking him out and a temporary restraining order would be put in place. Ben could file for a more permanent restraining order when we returned to Maine. For my part, I felt confident they would diagnose Dean as crazy if he tried to tell them what he knew about my ability to heal. No sane person would profess to believe in the abilities I had.

Ben said nothing while I spoke to the officers. His tension grew as the doctor tallied my injuries. X-rays showed no new broken bones, but I'd sliced my palm with the glass I'd used to threaten Dean. Also, aside from the cuts and split lip, I had a deep bruise the size of a football spreading from my left hip to my back in a brilliant, livid blue and a dislocated shoulder. They assumed the pale bruises on my face from healing Anna were also from Dean.

Even Kazinski had gasped when the doctor uncovered the deep, circular scar on the tender flesh on the underside of my upper arm. When I was fourteen Dean had noticed I healed more rapidly than normal, and he'd tested his theory by putting out his cigarette in the same spot night after night. That was when I realized he fed off my tears, and I'd refused to ever cry another drop for him, even if I had to bite my lip bloody to do it. Eventually, I'd stopped healing the burn so he'd leave me alone, and the grotesque scar served as an ugly reminder of what could happen if I wasn't careful about who discovered my ability.

Ben's face turned a frightening shade of gray when the doctor reset my dislocated shoulder. My scream was stifled as I worried my father would snap. My vision blackened, but I managed to stay conscious by focusing on the smear of blood drying on Ben's shirt where I'd brushed my hand or lip. I couldn't remember which.

The doctor slipped my arm into a sling and stepped back with a look of admiration for his handiwork. "That should do it, kid. You'll be wearing this a few days, but you'll be good as new before you know it."

I rose to my feet with as much haste as my abused body allowed. "Can I leave now? We have a flight to catch to Maine."

Ben finally spoke. "No, Remy. We'll stay in New York tonight. You're not in any shape to fly."

"I'm perfectly fine to fly." When he would have argued, I added, "Look, I'm going to be in a lot of pain tomorrow, and I'd rather be at home. Please. I don't feel safe here."

Guilt surfaced in his eyes. He blamed himself for not protecting me again, and I'd used it to manipulate him. I couldn't be sorry because I didn't want to stay in New York one more minute than was necessary. This place had become my waking nightmare.

His jaw tightened, and he nodded with grim acceptance.

It was decided. We were going home.

CHAPTER ELEVEN

*L*aura met us at the airport, her pretty face tensed with worry. She started to cry when she saw my face and embraced me. It felt like a homecoming, and I hugged her a little harder than I'd intended.

In the car, I fell asleep from the painkillers Ben had compelled me to take, and my lids didn't flutter open until he lifted me from the backseat. Lucy's concerned whisper mixed with his husky reassurance in the icy darkness. He carried me up the stairs and tucked me between my familiar lavender-scented sheets like a child. Lips brushed my forehead, cool fingers skimmed my hair from my face, and I surrendered to nothingness.

When I opened my eyes to morning light, I experienced a vague sense of *déjà vu* to discover Lucy sitting cross-legged on the bed staring at me. Her red-rimmed eyes swept over my face and caught on my split lip.

"Think you have enough makeup to cover my lip for school?"

With a shaky laugh, she said, "I don't think the cosmetics counter at Macy's has enough makeup for that miracle."

I laughed, too, and then grimaced when my entire body rebelled. "Oh, frick."

That made us snicker harder until I shuddered and

shifted my stiff arm, held immobile in the sling. "Oh, man, that hurts. Why are we laughing?"

She sobered. "I'm so relieved you're okay. Dad told me what happened. Feel like talking?"

Trying to soften my rejection, I shook my head. "Not now. Maybe sometime, okay?" I wouldn't have known where to begin since I didn't want to lie to Lucy any more than I already had.

Her solemn gaze scanned my face. "You okay, Sis?"

Clearly, she wasn't asking about my injuries. No, I wasn't okay. I felt guilty, angry, and sad. The release that tears offered sat out of reach when I yearned to howl with grief, but I'd turned off that spigot at thirteen, causing it to rust shut with disuse. My sister worried about me, though, so I lied.

"Yeah, Luce. I will be now that I'm home." I switched to a lighter tone. "Except for my desperate need for a bathroom."

Every muscle in my body revolted in pain when I tried to rise. Apparently, I wasn't going anywhere without help. I grimaced with distaste. "Lucy, you better call Ben."

She ran to the doorway and shouted, "Dad!"

He appeared immediately, while I scowled at Lucy. "Way to go, slick. You scared him."

With a careless shrug, she responded. "You said you were desperate."

Later, Ben put me back in bed with a pillow to prop my sling, and I realized with disgust that the activity had exhausted me. Ben told me to rest, Lucy handed me my iPod from my duffel at my request, and they both left.

Alone, I thought of my mother. I'd known that Dean would attack her more often if I wasn't there to step in, and there'd always been a chance he would kill her if things went too far. I'd been so angry at her for protecting him, I'd left anyway. Now, remembering her lying in the hospital bed, I felt sick.

Wanting to forget, I put the earbuds in and turned the iPod on, curious about what my mother had been listening to. There wasn't much on the player, just one playlist that contained a few untitled tracks, and I picked one at random expecting to hear my mother's favorite type of country song about a man who'd gone and done his woman wrong.

Shock had my mouth dropping open when I heard my mother's voice.

What was I saying? Oh, yes. My mother, your grandmother. She was a Healer like y—

Her throaty voice—earned from smoking too many cigarettes—washed over me, and I missed the rest of what she'd said. My attention caught on one detail: My mother had called me a Healer in her most casual tone. She'd known all along what I could do. I'd wanted nothing more than her acceptance while she lived, and she hadn't given me even this small acknowledgment. Instead of talking to me, she'd recorded a one-way conversation on my iPod. What possible reason could she have had for doing this?

I scrolled through the menu back to the first track. The menu showed the playlist had been added the week before. I hit play again, and she spoke, sounding like her usual, tentative self.

Remy. Hi, baby. You probably wondered why you got an iPod for your birthday. No computer, and you got a gift we couldn't afford and you couldn't use.

That was precisely what I'd thought. I'd have considered selling it myself for more getaway money if it wouldn't have hurt her. She'd acted so excited when I opened it.

I had my reasons. The day was coming when I'd have to tell you the truth about us. About who you are and what you can do. You and I . . . We don't talk, and it's my fault. I don't know how to fix things, baby. I don't—

She broke off. I could hear her breathing, so I waited. It sounded like she moved around the apartment from the way her voice echoed when she laughed with a trace of her signature bitterness.

Enough. This isn't an apology. I've made mistakes. You know it. I know it. That's not why I'm keeping this journal. On to the important stuff. There are things you need to know if you're going out on your own. Remy, you're a Healer.

I snorted. Like I didn't know that already. This was her idea of a journal?

I know what you're thinking. Hold the phone, right? Let me see if I can get this right. You noticed you were different when you were about twelve. Your cuts and scrapes healed faster than those on other kids your age, and you stopped getting sick. Better yet, you knew when others were injured and sensed you could fix them when you touched them. Am I right?

She nailed it. I'd been so frightened by what was happening to my body, and I'd wanted my mother to comfort me. Except when I healed her by accident that first time, she'd shrunk away in fear.

Anna's cheap high heels tapped on the kitchen linoleum, and I imagined her pacing through the room as she talked, the plastic cherries on her favorite shoes swinging with each step. Where had Dean been when she'd recorded this?

*Of course, I'm right. My mother told me the story of how
it happened for her, so I could tell my own children one
day. See, the power you have . . . it's in our blood. The
women in our bloodline have been Healers as far back as
we can trace our lineage.*

*I have to confess I didn't listen to my mother as well as
I should have. The power skipped me. I was disappoint-
ingly normal, while your grandmother had this amazing
talent.*

My grandmother had been like me. Dozens—maybe
hundreds—of women had been like me. I wasn't the only
one. Asher had told me so, but I hadn't truly believed him
until now. Turning my face against my pillow, I muffled a
scream of pure rage. For five years my mother had let me
think myself a freak, and she'd held the answers to my
questions all along.

*I hated what she could do because it took her away from
me. When she was murdered because of what she was,
I swore I'd never have children. I didn't want to chance
having a daughter who'd live in constant danger.*

A chair scraped across the floor, followed by the snick
of a lighter and her deep inhalation. She would be sitting
at the kitchen table with smoke swirling around her head
and her crossword puzzle book half done in front of her.
I pulled the covers over my head.

*Let me back up and tell you about my family. Our family.
You wondered why I never talked about them. Your
grandparents were good people. They grew up neighbors,
and their families always knew they would end up
together. They dated through high school, married at
twenty, and had me by twenty-two.*

My dad knew about my mother's power almost before she did. He was the first one she healed when they were eleven, and he broke his arm falling out of a tree. He used to say that he fell out of the tree and straight into love with her. Her being a Healer made things difficult for them, but he never cared. We lived quietly, moving around a lot, and they did odd jobs. Mom was a housekeeper, and Dad a handyman. They tried to make things as normal as possible for me, but it was necessary for us to stay "off the grid," according to Dad. I didn't mind as a child. We never had much, but it was enough.

My throat ached at the affectionate nostalgia in Anna's voice. She hadn't sounded that happy since way before my stepfather. *What happened to you, Mom?* Ice clinked in a glass—I'd guess she was drinking vodka and tonic since Dean wasn't around to berate her for stealing more than her share—and she sighed.

My parents warned me people existed who would hurt us if they found out what my mother could do, but I didn't believe them. I grew up feeling so safe and loved I didn't think anything could hurt us. The truth is I didn't think beyond my own selfish desires.
I told someone our secret, and that mistake is the second biggest regret of my life.

I shut off the iPod, unsure I wanted to hear any more. If my mother had told someone the secret and my grandmother died because of it, would I want to know that? I hadn't told Asher what I could do, but he knew. My greatest fear had been that his knowing could drive my family away from me. I hadn't considered that it could cause them harm. If my mother confirmed that possibility as her second biggest regret, what was her first? Having me? Feeling it and suspecting it was one thing, but it would be something else to hear her say it out loud.

A longing to forget I'd ever heard this recording flowed through me, but I'd been a coward before and ended up abandoning her.

I hit play.

We were living in some tiny town in New Hampshire—the thirteenth town I'd lived in in ten years. At sixteen, I was an awkward loner, trying not to call attention to myself. Different town, same drill.

Except, that town had a clever, handsome boy named Tom. Tom was popular and confident and everything I wasn't. I thought I would die from loving him, and he never even noticed I was alive.

So when a car accident threatened to ruin his chance at a football scholarship, I grabbed hold of my chance. I told him about my mother, and he broke my heart when he laughed in my face. It never occurred to me he wouldn't believe me because I'd grown up believing in the impossible. That should've been the end of it, but Tom told his friends about everything, and those friends told others. Nothing but a joke, but rumors spread like wildfire in our small town. It was just a matter of time before the Protectors heard them and hunted us.

The only pleasure I can get out of what happened next is that Tom lost that scholarship when his injuries didn't heal right. Last I heard he still lived in that town working as a used car salesman.

My mother had always had rotten taste in men, aside from my father. She'd made one wrong choice after another, even at sixteen. I tried to imagine her as she'd been, innocent and in love. There'd been no pictures in our home of her parents or her as a young girl. Her mistake had been trusting the wrong boy. What if I was like her?

I was scared to confess what I'd done, sure my parents would move us again. A couple of weeks later, I couldn't take the guilt any longer. I decided when I got home from school I'd tell my parents everything. I'd come clean, let them ground me, and maybe they'd see my side of things for once.

I never got the chance to tell them the truth.

"Remy?"

I shrieked when a hand touched me through my bedspread. It took me a moment to realize it wasn't my mother's ghost. I hit stop and pulled the covers from my head. Laura stood over me with a tray of food in her hands. She saw the iPod and smiled.

"I thought you might be hungry. I brought you lunch and another pain pill." She set the tray on the nightstand. "You look like hell, sweetheart."

Laura had never cursed around me, and it took me by surprise. She stepped forward and put a smooth hand on my forehead. The burn in my throat now affected my eyes.

"If you need anything, I'm here. It's not the same, I know. I'm not your moth—" She lifted one hand. "Well, I'm here."

I nodded, unable to speak. She left, and I tugged the covers over my head again. The smell of the vegetable soup wafting from the tray made my mouth water, but I couldn't swallow food now. I started the iPod again. Anna couldn't quite hide the grief in her voice.

My father came to school and pulled me from class with blood on his shirt. He told me to get in the car and shut

*up. He was a gentle man—doted on me, even—but that
day I thought my father would hit me. I thought he'd
found out what I'd done, and we headed home to pack up
and leave town. Then, when we neared our neighborhood,
I saw the cloud of black smoke. I had one brief glimpse
of our sweet house in flames before Dad steered the car
past our street and out of town. My mother died because
of me.*

*We drove for three days. We had nothing because our
belongings burned in the fire. We slept in the car at rest
stops and didn't speak until the third day when my father
told me what'd happened. Two men—Protectors—had come
to our home because of rumors they'd heard. They suspected
my mother was a Healer and hurt my father to force her to
choose between betraying her secret and watching him die.
When she healed him, they murdered her and would've
killed my father, if he hadn't managed to escape.*

The Protectors sounded evil, like Dean. He'd forced a
similar decision on me: heal my mother or watch her die.
Except I hadn't been able to heal her. It had been too late.
I shuddered, thinking of the house burning down around
my grandmother, a woman I'd never met but had more in
common with than my own mother.

*My father did what Mom would've wanted him to. He
saved me and made sure we stayed hidden, but he never
looked at me the same way. I think he hated me.*

And she'd learned to hate herself. The sad resignation in
her voice said it all. She'd stayed with Dean and let him
tear her down a little more every day because she hadn't
believed she deserved any better. There was a long pause
filled with the sound of her deep inhale and exhale as she
smoked.

The day I turned eighteen I ran away. I moved to New York, got a job as a waitress, and tried to get lost in the city. I thought I'd put the past behind me but, if I've learned one thing, it's that you can never outrun the past.

She sighed, and I guessed what she'd say next.

I met your father, and he was like nobody I'd ever met in my life. He was fireworks and moonlit walks and flowers for no reason. My entire world revolved around him. Despite the fact that I knew we'd never work out, I fell in love with him. Then I got pregnant, and I knew in my gut you were a girl. I broke up with Ben the day I took the pregnancy test. He's a good man and wanted to marry me, but I couldn't put him in that kind of danger. It was your destiny to be a Healer, and your destiny goes hand in hand with death, no matter how you try to escape it.

My fist went in my mouth to stifle the cry of pain. She'd known having me would end in her death, and she'd been right. She'd given up her chance at love to keep my father safe. Grief lit a fire in my belly, and my eyes burned.

I have a confession, Remy. Okay, two confessions.

Her voice sounded thick with guilt, and I held my breath waiting to hear her tell me how having me became the biggest regret of her life.

First, it's my fault your father was never part of your life. He probably hasn't told you that, or at least not all of it. He wouldn't say anything bad about me to you. Did I tell you he's a good man? He wanted to help raise you, but I refused. He called once when you were older, and I made sure he knew he wasn't welcome and went so far as to tell

him you wanted nothing to do with him. I was too afraid of
what would happen when he found out the truth about you.

Had that call been in response to my one desperate plea
for help? Bitter rage surged through me, even though I
understood why she'd turned him away. She'd kept us
apart because she'd been afraid of rejection, or worse, that
he'd trust the wrong person with our secret and end up
hurt. A small inner voice reminded me I had the same
fears. Still, I'd often wondered what it would have been
like to have been raised by Ben. I hadn't realized it had
once been a possibility in his mind.

So, now that you're good and angry at me, I'll make my
second confession.

My mouth twisted in a sour smile. She knew me better
than I'd thought. Glass skittered across a surface, and I
guessed my mother had crushed out her cigarette in the
glass ashtray she kept on the kitchen table, often overflow-
ing with gray ashes and cigarette butts.

I know you think I didn't want you. That's just not true.
I acted selfishly because I wanted you from the instant I
found out I was pregnant. It scared me how much I
wanted you. From the moment I held you in my arms,
the thought of losing you terrified me. And when you
healed me the first time, my worst nightmare came true.
I wanted to pretend you weren't a Healer, and I made
you keep a secret you shouldn't have had to bear alone.
I can't ever make that up to you, baby.

It sounded like Anna was crying. She'd never been one
for apologies, and this confession was the closest she'd ever
come. There was no mention of how she'd let Dean ruin

both of our lives. Raw grief replaced my anger because I would have forgiven her in a heartbeat if I'd been given the chance.

Okay. Enough of that mushy crap. Let's talk about the Protectors.

I hit stop. For once, I wished my ability to heal worked on emotions. I didn't want to feel the maelstrom of sorrow, anger, and hurt Anna inspired. Craving the forgetfulness of sleep, I took the pain medication Laura had laid out on the tray with a glass of water.

Night had fallen while I'd slept. My bruised hip ached from lying on it. Cotton filled my head from the medication, and the growing intensity of the pain must have wakened me. I sat up and hissed in frustration because circumstances dictated I couldn't heal the visible wounds. I hadn't appreciated how easy it had been to heal myself when I was invisible.

After a slow-going trip to the bathroom, I felt relieved that I wouldn't need help from Ben again in that arena. Entering my room, I couldn't bring myself to crawl back into bed. Grabbing the iPod, I curled up in the chair by the window. A chill permeated the air, and I wrapped a blanket around my legs before hitting play.

Okay. Enough of that mushy crap. Let's talk about the Protectors.
Way back in the beginning, the Protectors and Healers were allies. Protectors have been around as long as there have been Healers. I can't say when the first Protector and Healer showed up—or why they showed up—but my mother assured me they'd been around for centuries. There are those in the Protector bloodlines with no powers.

*Some have forgotten the old ways, unaware this world
exists, while others like me can't escape it.*

*As you know, Healers have zero defenses after a
healing when their energy is lowest. The Protectors
watched over our kind, protected us, if you will, when we
were at our weakest. Protectors had certain gifts of their
own—more strength, speed, and agility than the average
human—that made them good allies. In exchange for their
service, the Protectors gained immunity to most illnesses
just by being near the Healers.*

At least that's the way my mother told it.

Protectors were superhuman. Like me but with their
own set of crazy powers. That explained a lot about Asher.

*Sounds insane, huh? But then, so does the idea of a
person who can manipulate energy and heal with the
touch of their hands. It's amazing what you can do, Remy.
And dangerous. You have to be careful. You won't always
choose who you heal. My mother told us how she hated
touching strangers because she couldn't stop her body from
healing them. I've noticed how you steer clear of crowds
yourself.*

Unlike me, my grandmother hadn't learned how to
shield herself. With my guard up, I could touch people. Of
course, Anna didn't know I'd had a defense because she'd
never asked.

*So, what happened, you ask? The Healers and the
Protectors are great allies and become very, very powerful.
Around the 1850s, the Healers began to sell their abilities
to the highest bidders, and they chose not to share the
profits with the Protectors, who were dying in service to
the Healers. Before you know it, war has broken out*

*between them, and as I mentioned before, the Protectors
are gifted with massive strength and speed, while the
Healers . . . aren't.*

I sucked in a breath. It must have been a slaughter. Anna
got into the story now, pacing around the kitchen again,
her footsteps tapping on the linoleum floor. She spoke
faster and breathier.

*The Healers almost became extinct. There were
thousands of us alive at the time, but only a handful
survived the war. Oh, and that's not the worst of it. . . .
    You see, the Healer-Protector relationship has always
been a mystery. We know that as the daughters become
Healers in certain bloodlines, so do the daughters and sons
in other bloodlines become Protectors. My mother said
that sometimes a female Healer would form a bond with
a male Protector. Not romantic bonding, since it was
unheard of for a Healer and Protector to be together that
way. Rather a mental bonding that made each of them
more powerful. Unfortunately, neither party had a choice
in who they bonded with.*

Okay. That gave me the creeps. Wrapping a hand
around my cold feet, I studied the shadows on my bedroom wall.

*Bonding is all about energy. Every Healer has a unique
kind of energy. Think blue sparks like yours, while my
mother's looked purple.*

My mother had pretended not to notice the blue sparks
that happened when I healed her. I experienced another
sting of betrayal that she hadn't told me any of this when
I healed her the first time. I continued listening to her excited voice.

Healers are a conduit for energy. It's how she heals since she is able to control the flow of that energy into another's body. A Protector, though, is more like a sponge. He or she absorbs the energy flow and converts it into strength, speed, agility. When a Healer and Protector bond, it's like he can absorb her particular brand of energy. I'm not sure what the actual bonding was like, except that there's a lot of heat and pain involved. As far as we know, it hasn't happened since before the war. Crazy, right?

Yeah, crazy. A sudden, awful feeling made itself known in the hollow of my stomach. I gripped the iPod tighter in my hand and squeezed my eyes shut.

Well, things get crazier.
Protectors found the key to immortality. If they killed a Healer, they absorbed her energy and became immortal. Her energy cured them of any possible sickness, including the greatest disease—aging. See, the war was never really about money. Oh, yeah, the Protectors were greedy, too, but what they wanted was eternal youth.

My breathing came faster. I knew. I knew what was coming. Anna's voice sounded ripe with satisfaction.

But nothing comes for free. Oh, the Protectors got their immortality, but it cost them. When they stole a Healer's energy, they got more than they counted on. The surge of energy shorted out their systems, and the Protectors lost the use of most of their senses. Touch, taste, smell—all gone in the blink of an eye.
Can you imagine living forever and never being able to feel another person's touch?

I couldn't imagine it, but I knew someone who could.

It's ironic, isn't it? The Protectors are in a living hell of their own making, and the Healers are the only ones who can cure them.

Anna laughed, and I understood. The Protectors had killed her mother. She felt no pity for them.

Since the Protectors discovered what they'd done, they've been hunting the few Healers that remain. Those Healers caught have a single fate: death. It's your energy, see? It's like radiation for cancer patients: A full dose kills what makes them human while a small dose is therapeutic. It makes them feel alive again. They take their time to draw it out, keep a Healer like a pet to feel a little at a time, until the Healer is all used up. Dead. The sensations never last long, though, so they are always on the hunt for another Healer to feed on.

But some time ago, we made a discovery of our own. It's another reason why I kept you hidden all these years. Because of what you can do. You're not like other Healers.

Oh, Remy, you have the power to make them mortal again.

Anna's words continued, but I heard nothing else. The puzzle I'd been working out these last weeks had been impossible to solve without all the pieces.

Asher.

I'd seen for myself how different his body's internal workings were when I'd healed him. When no one else would have been able to react with such speed and amazing reflexes, he'd saved that boy from landing in the bonfire. Stronger than anyone I knew, he'd pulled both me and Brandon from the pool, and he carried me as if I were a featherweight when my father struggled with the task.

Asher knew about me because I wasn't the first Healer he'd met.

And by his own admission, he could feel nothing except when near me. He felt pain. If my energy was like radiation to him, then I was poison to him when our walls were down.

When he told me we were enemies, he'd meant it. He was a Protector, and I was a Healer. His kind had been killing off my kind for over a century. *He* was an immortal and, according to Anna, that wasn't possible unless he'd murdered a Healer.

I shivered and could sit no longer. Rising, nervous energy had me pacing in front of the fogged window.

Several things didn't make sense.

Anna thought Healers had no defenses, but I did. Plus, I wasn't just a conduit for energy. Like a mirror, I reflected pain onto those who hurt me. Surely, I wasn't the only Healer with these abilities?

And what of the pain that came with the healing and the coldness afterward? Anna had mentioned the weakness I felt, but not that I absorbed the injuries and pain of others. She had to have guessed, as I'd taken on too many of her injuries over the years. Except Asher hadn't known I would take on his pain along with healing his burned hand. I remembered how distraught he'd looked when I'd admitted the truth.

And that brought me to the biggest discrepancy of all. Asher had warned me away because he didn't want to risk hurting me. If Protectors were out to kill Healers, Asher broke the mold. He knew what I was and didn't want to harm me.

Anna said that Healers and Protectors hadn't bonded since the war. If I guessed right, Asher and I proved the exception to this rule. What other explanation could there be? Since I'd met him, my powers had strengthened, in-

cluding my skill for shielding myself. I was dying to confirm my suspicions because it would mean he'd changed,
too.

Picking up the iPod, I smoothed a finger around the
wheel to rewind to where I'd left off and hit play again. I
stared out the window into the forest below. Morning approached, and the black night faded into dove-grays and
soft purples. The mass of snow-covered woods below separated into individual trees sprouting their first green
leaves.

*Oh, Remy, you have the power to make them mortal
again.*
*It's what they want more than anything, and they'll
kill you to get it. If you think they've found you, run.
Because if they catch you—Don't. Get. Caught.*
*Now, the third track will tell you how to find your
grandfather. I should've taken you to him long ago, but I
couldn't . . . I ignored my instincts and we ended up . . .
You're better than I am, kid.*

My mother's voice softened with worry and regret.
Worry for leaving me on my own. Regret for choosing
Dean. I noticed a movement down below. Asher. It didn't
surprise me to find him standing in the wooded park at
the edge of our yard.

Trust your instincts.

The track ended, and my finger hit stop. He stared up
at me through the window with a tormented expression—
caught between regret and yearning. Perhaps I was making the biggest mistake of my life, but my choice had been
made.

I wasn't going to run.

CHAPTER TWELVE

I slipped a coat on over my sling and hurried down the stairs as fast as I dared in the ratty tee and sweats I'd slept in. I scribbled a quick note to my family to let them know I'd gone for a walk in case they woke before I returned and stuck it to the fridge with a magnet before leaving through the back door.

Asher had disappeared, but I knew he hadn't left. A labyrinth of short paths divided the wooded nature reserve of Townsend Park. Only a block wide, the miniature park was a favorite for birdwatchers and bored teenagers wanting to lose a few hours in the maze. Some trails took you to a haven in the center, and I headed toward the entrance where I'd last seen Asher. Inside, snow smothered every surface, and the overhead arch of branches dimmed the foggy morning light. I'd halted, unsure of which direction to go, when I heard his low voice.

"Remy, what are you doing out here?"

He chided me for walking out in the cold alone to meet him. Focusing on his voice grew easier as my eyes adjusted to the light, and I stepped into a circular clearing. He stood with his back to me.

"I couldn't sleep. The pain pills wore off."

My husky sleep-filled words got his attention. He twisted about and reached my side in an instant. The color faded from his face when he spied the sling, split lip, and new bruises. My bulky clothing hid the cuts on my arms and back and the deeper bruises banding my hip and back where I'd hit the entry table.

His eyes slipped to my hip with a shimmer of danger, and I wondered for an insane moment if I'd betrayed the painful injuries in some way. Then, those melancholy eyes were back on mine, and a fresh emotion distracted me: I'd missed him.

"How bad is it?"

He didn't look surprised to see me hurt. "How did you hear about it?"

Asher's expression turned bleak. "You're all anyone's been talking about at school. I tried calling Lucy, but she wouldn't give me your dad's cell number. She said you'd call when you got back. You could have been killed."

Lucy's fierce devotion made me smile, and I held out a hand in a playful manner. "I'm very much alive. Want to pinch me to make sure you're not dreaming?"

We both thought about the last time he'd touched me in his car. He scowled and took a step back. "That's not funny, Remy. I was at the airport trying to get to you when Gabe heard you were on your way back."

He'd been coming to the rescue, my very own damaged knight in shining armor. An extreme reaction for an enemy. I exhaled and my breath puffed out in a white cloud.

"Why would you do that, Asher? And what are you do-ing out here? I wouldn't have pegged you for a stalker, and you obviously knew I was back in town, alive and kick-ing."

"I was worried."

Circling around him, I swiped a mound of snow off one of the stone benches so I could sit. The seat felt like a slab of ice, but my body protested standing.

"Were you now? Well, that's . . . confusing. One

minute you're threatening to attack me, and the next you're worried about someone else attacking me. Maybe you should stop playing games with me and find the guts to finish the job yourself. At least Dean is consistent."

Asher's body tensed and his head whipped toward me. I'd expected it, had provoked it, but couldn't help gasping at the fury that ignited in his eyes.

"If I thought you meant that, I'd be pissed off. Stop antagonizing me, Remy, and say what's on your mind."

"You first," I challenged.

"Fine." He stalked several feet away and glared at an innocent sapling that had bowed beneath the ivy creeping up its side. I almost missed his whisper.

"It was my fault."

"What?"

Louder, through his teeth, he said, "It was my fault."

"What are you talking about?" Maybe I'd hit my head harder than I'd thought because he made no sense.

His hands balled into fists when he faced me. "What I did to you was a warning. To make it easy for you to stay away from me." The sound of his bitter laugh startled a bird from a nearby bush, and we watched it flit to a tree branch. "It worked, all right. You didn't tell me when you left. I could've protected you if I'd been there, but I couldn't even get a phone number to reach you. My brother found out you were coming home when he called your mom on fake PTA business. The PTA, damn it."

I stood and approached him. "Wait a minute. Forgetting for a second that Gabe is involved with the PTA, let's focus on the important thing. You think it's your fault Dean got to me?"

Asher nodded, and my temper flared. When I shoved him in the chest with my good hand, he cursed. Even as I savored the heat that came with touching him, I gave him another shove. This time he didn't budge an inch, though

I'd put some effort behind the push. He grabbed my hand, holding it between his warmer ones with a gentle grip, and the fight left me as green fire sparked between us.

We stared at our joined hands, and I told him without anger, "You're an idiot."

As if my skin scorched him, he dropped my hand. "You're right. I shouldn't be here."

Asher could exasperate me like no other person I'd met. "Not about that. You're an idiot for thinking you're responsible for me. What makes you think I would've invited you? Who asked you to save me? I've been taking care of myself for a long time. What happened a couple of days ago . . . Well, it wasn't the first time. Dean, my stepfather, was hitting me years before you knew I existed. Hitting my mother, too."

At the mention of Anna, I retreated to the bench and huddled in my jacket.

"If it was anyone's fault, it was mine. I knew he'd kill Anna if I left her without protection, but being here . . . Well, it's been a long time since I felt safe."

My words trailed off, and I squeezed my eyes shut to hide from any pity in his eyes. The air shifted as Asher kneeled on the ground at my feet. He didn't touch me, but I wished he would.

He groaned, and his hand slipped to the back of my neck, urging me to look at him. His mental wall had gone up, proof that he wasn't taking any chances, and a wise action since I hadn't bothered with my own defenses.

"She was your mother. She should've protected you. Not the other way around."

The severity of his gaze willed me to believe him. "You're right, of course. What kind of mother lets her husband do the things Dean did to me?" The dour Officer Kazinski's horror at seeing the cigarette burn on my arm appeared in my mind. Anna had watched Dean brand me like cattle. My hatred for both of them mingled with sorrow because Anna and I would never have a chance to start over without the lies between us.

"Asher, I couldn't heal her. I tried, but I couldn't. She woke up for a few minutes, but . . ."

He grimaced in pain, and I wondered if he guessed what I'd risked to bring her out of the coma. It had been impossible to tell my father any of this, and now the words rushed out of me in a quiet confession. "I was so angry. She died because of Dean, and they hadn't arrested him. He had an *alibi*. He didn't even bother to come to her funeral. I *hate* him."

Asher squeezed my hand. "What happened?"

I described how Dean had shown up in the apartment and the fight that followed. "He wanted revenge. He knows what I can do, how I can hurt people. Last time I saw him, he was unconscious with two broken ribs, among other injuries."

I heard the satisfaction in my voice as I replayed that moment in my head when I'd transferred my pain and Anna's to Dean. I'd been sure I would die, and instead, I'd incapacitated him. A mere girl had flattened a grown man twice her size. That must have infuriated him.

"He wanted to kill me. I saw it in his eyes," I added, with a shudder.

I'd left a lot out to spare Asher. Like Dean knocking me to the floor and wrenching my shoulder. How he'd thrown me into the entryway table and the mirror hanging above it. And the moment when he'd known he'd won and intended to kill me, before I'd loosed my pain on him.

"I'd like to kill him," he said, his deep voice raw with emotion.

My urge to do the same frightened me because I knew I could do it with my new power. Shivering, I said, "I want to forget him."

Asher's expression softened as he brushed a gentle finger over my split lip. "Why haven't you healed yourself?"

"Too many people have seen the wounds. It would cause a lot of questions."

"Has he told anyone about you?"

"Not that I know of. At least, not anyone who would believe him."

Asher leaned forward until his forehead rested on my knees. "I give in. It doesn't seem to matter if I stay away, Remy. You need a bodyguard."

My uninjured hand slipped from his to stroke his unruly hair, and my fingers sifted through the dark, silky strands. It felt softer than I had imagined. "Don't you mean a Protector?"

The woods stopped breathing. When Asher's head came up, my hand fell away, and I let him read the truth on my face. He sat back on his heels with a blank expression.

"How did you find out?"

"My mother. Last night, I discovered some audio tracks she recorded and left on my iPod."

"What did she tell you?" he asked, in a flat voice.

"Enough for me to figure out who you were. At least, she gave me a name for what you are. I mean, it's not like I didn't know you were different the first time I scanned you when you'd burned your hand."

His lips quirked in a half-smile. "You never said anything. I thought maybe you hadn't noticed."

"Not likely. Hypothetically, say a normal human body is working at 60 percent efficiency. Your body is working at about 210 percent efficiency. Definitely not normal. Besides, did you think I didn't see how fast you move when we're alone? Or how strong you are? Give me a break.

You pulled Brandon and me out of the deep end of the pool like we weighed ten pounds each."

"I knew I wasn't careful enough around you, but I couldn't seem to—"

By rising to his feet and moving several feet away to stare into the wilderness, he shut me out. Mentally, his wall increased the distance between us.

"What does your family think about having a Healer living in town?"

He shot me an unfathomable glance before answering. "Scared and pissed off."

"All that, huh?"

Asher spun to face me and peered at me with obvious disbelief. "Why don't you sound afraid, Remy? Didn't your mother tell you how dangerous we are to you?"

Adjusting my sling to find a more comfortable position, I returned his look with considerable calm. "I've been in Blackwell Falls for weeks. They would've hurt me by now if they were going to. Why are they scared and pissed off?"

With his hands tucked in his pockets, he shook his head. "Don't think that. Don't ever forget you're in danger while Protectors are around." I nodded to placate him, and he continued with a wry twist of his full lips. "Lottie is afraid. She's worried about what will happen if others come for you, and they think we've been hiding you."

They called Charlotte "Lottie." As intense as our conversations had been, we didn't know much about each other. He didn't say it, but I knew she worried about him, not me.

Curious, I asked, "What about Gabe? Is he the pissed-off one?"

His eyes met mine, and he frowned. "It's complicated."

He didn't expand. There was some conflict there, and I wondered what it could be.

"Asher, my mother said something." I was taking a huge

chance telling him, but I'd come this far. "A theory the Healers have."

Asher's tone bristled with a challenge. "They think they have the answer to stopping the Protectors. A Healer with the ability to cure immortality."

The statement was a test to see what I knew, and I didn't blink. "And that's what you want? To be mortal again?"

He stared into the fog with fierce longing. "Almost more than anything."

I wondered about that *almost*. What did he want more than to be mortal? "Why?" I asked.

His tired sigh sounded loud in the silent clearing. "I never wanted to be immortal in the first place. What do you know about the War?"

I tried to remember my mother's words. "Anna said the Healers were greedy and kept all the profit from the healing to themselves. And the Protectors used it as an excuse to go to war. In the end, though, they killed the Healers to become immortal. Only it backfired because they lost the use of most of their senses." What had Anna said? *Can you imagine living forever and never being able to feel another person's touch?*

Asher leaned against a nearby oak tree, and his enigmatic expression gave no hint of his feelings. "She's right. It backfired big-time. The first Protectors to kill discovered their mistake, but by then it was too late. We were at war. You have to understand, Remy, it was more of a class war than anything else."

That wasn't how Anna had told it. "What do you mean?"

"The Healers treated us like servants, not partners. They used our energy for healing and our bodies to protect them. We were expendable, and they didn't give a

damn about us once they started charging for their serv-
ices."

The explanation made perfect sense. I could see how it
would have happened. The Healers got all the glory, while
the Protectors took a lot of the risk. I would have been
bitter, too, in their shoes.

Full lips tilted in a small smile, he crouched down on his
heels, absently fiddling with a stick he picked up. "You
would see our side." Before I could comment on his odd
remark, he continued. "My oldest brother, Sam, worked
with a powerful Healer. A lot of wealthy people sought
out Elizabeth, but no Healer was infallible, despite the
promises she made. With the kinds of stakes she played at,
failure wasn't an option. When she couldn't keep her end
of the bargain, Sam had to protect her from the angry,
very powerful people she'd duped."

With a slight flick of his fingers, the branch snapped in
two, making me jump. Asher didn't notice and brushed
the dust from his hands. His accent thickened as he spoke
until he sounded more British than American.

"Elizabeth took stupid chances to feed her affection for
gold coin. We tried to warn Sam, but he was loyal to a
fault. I wish you could've met him. You remind me of him
in a lot of ways."

He gave me a tender sideways glance that disappeared a
moment later. "When Elizabeth failed to heal the beloved
son of a particularly cruel merchant, he hired mercenaries
to execute her. Sam died saving her."

I shivered as I listened. This was the most I'd heard
Asher talk at one time, and it seemed impossible to believe
he'd actually lived through it.

"You could say Sam's death was the catalyst that started
the War. The Healers wouldn't take responsibility for what
happened. So many of my kind died during that time. . . ."

The words broke off, and he picked up a small rock, tossing it from hand to hand.

They'd been friends of his, too, from the shadows that crossed his face. It must have been hard to watch his brother die and the persons responsible walk away unscathed. It's how I felt about Dean.

"Anyway, the Protectors decided to go after the worst of the Healers as a warning to all. Without weapons against our kind, it was over for the Healers before it had begun. By accident, those Protectors discovered that they could steal a dying Healer's energy to become immortal. At least, we think it was an accident."

I had to ask. "Were you there, Asher?"

Absently rolling the rock in his palm, he shook his head. "No. Elizabeth had been targeted in that first wave of killing. To honor Sam, my father wanted to protect her. We didn't know what kind of woman she was."

The stone exploded into dust when it hit the trunk of a nearby tree, but Asher betrayed no sign of having moved.

"My father sent word ahead that the Protectors were coming for her, and we went to head them off. When we tracked her down, along with the other Healers she traveled with, she'd hired her own human mercenaries for protection. We told her why we'd come, and she *laughed*. Sam's sacrifice meant nothing to her, and she insulted him like he was a dog."

His eyes lit with a fury I understood. "You fought with her?"

Rising to his full height, he took a menacing step toward me, letting his guard drop. "No, Remy. I killed her."

Asher purposely frightened me, and a tremor chased its way down my spine, despite the fact that I knew he wouldn't hurt me. "Tell me what happened."

Sorrow weighed his shoulders down. "Her human mercenaries captured Lottie. My sister was young, you see, very sheltered. Elizabeth could train her, use her more easily than a male Protector. When reason failed to sway Elizabeth, my family fought. Elizabeth held a knife to Lottie's throat, and I attacked. When I tried to get the knife away, I stabbed her. It was an accident, but it didn't matter. Gabe and Lottie both wounded and killed two of the Healers protecting themselves. But my parents . . . At the end of that day, what remained of my family had lost our humanity."

He stopped speaking, lost in a past I couldn't begin to understand. With dread, I asked, "How old were you, Asher?"

Body rigid with anger, he focused on me. "Eighteen. Don't defend me, Remy. You're not going to tell me I was too young to understand what I was doing."

My solemn gaze met his furious one, and I shook my head. "No. No, I'm not going to say that. We're different, you and I. I don't think either of us has had the luxury of being young. Circumstance forced us to grow up faster than we should have."

I thought of Dean. My actions could have killed him, and I'm not sure I would have felt the regret that resonated in Asher's tortured eyes.

He returned to kneel at my feet. "What happened with Dean is different. You're a Healer, not a murderer."

When I grabbed for his hand, his face twisted in a grimace of pain. I'd forgotten I was poison to him and hurried to turn him loose, while raising my mental wall to shield him.

Asher wove his fingers through mine and stared up at me. "You're killing me here, Remy. It's my job to protect you. Not the other way around."

Startled by his insight, I shifted on the bench, distracted

by the heat of his hand in mine. Sometimes it seemed like Asher could read my mind. "I told you before, I can take care of myself."

He smiled and glanced at my sling. "Yes, I can see that." The smile faded and disappeared altogether. "I don't know what to do with you. I should hate you for being one of them."

"Why don't you?" I asked, holding my breath.

"You're different. I can't stand the idea of you hurting. And yet, I think I might be the greatest danger to you."

Strands of wavy hair fell in my eyes, and he smoothed it away with one hand. My heart beat a thundering pace in my chest until his hand dropped away.

The sharp angles of his face tautened, and he seemed to make a decision. "Remy, it's up to you. I know I scared you that last night we saw each other. I'll stay away if that's what you want."

At my unladylike snort, he looked confused. "Asher, what are you afraid of? That you'll suck out all my energy in a crazed desire to be human again?"

The color fled his face, and he backed away. That was precisely what he feared.

"You wouldn't do that." The finality in my tone couldn't be misread.

Asher shook his head. "Remy, you don't understand."

"Then tell me."

"I may not have a choice in the matter. With Elizabeth, I didn't seek to steal her energy or even know it was possible. It happened, and choice never factored into it. Can't the same be said for you? You told me yourself that your body started healing Brandon as soon as you touched him. It didn't matter that you were drowning. You didn't *decide* to heal him."

"So? You're healthy. Eternally so, according to you. That wouldn't happen with you."

One brow raised in disbelief. "Wouldn't it? Your body senses mine is not . . . right. Your energy comes at me, and it takes everything I have to stay in control. You make me feel alive, and I ache for more. Long to steal more, even when I know it could kill you. For reasons I don't understand, you're not like other Healers. I don't know how to protect you. Your instinct is to heal. Mine is to take. What if we both let our guard down at the wrong time?"

"And what?" I mocked him. "Our bodies take over?"

He stood and distanced himself from me. Ice dripped from his words. "You think I'm overreacting? You're very naïve sometimes, Remy. Do you think I can't sense how weak you are right now? I could take what I wanted, and you wouldn't be able to stop me."

The threat was real. I felt his energy drifting in the air as a deliberate warning. Rising to my feet, I squared my shoulders as best as I could in the sling. "You're wrong. I'm not naïve in the least. Wide-eyed innocence was beaten out of me a long time ago."

When he winced and would have apologized, I cut him off. "It's my turn to talk now. You listen. I understand you could hurt me. You're stronger and faster and you can steal my energy. Physically, you could kill me. I get that. You should understand something about me, though. This new power I have to hurt people? It's not always something I can control. My body senses I'm in danger and reacts. I'm not the only one who would get hurt if you lose control. Because if you harm me to the point my body turns on you, you better believe I'm not going to heal any damage I inflict."

We glared at each other for a long moment. The sound of a car starting in the distance distracted me. The sun had come out, and I had no idea how long I'd been outside. I sighed and scooted around Asher heading for the path that would take me back to my house.

Before I'd taken three steps, he caught my jacket. "Don't go."

"I have to. My family is probably looking for me."

He frowned. "I didn't think of that. I've kept you out here too long in the cold. You're too weak as it is."

I rolled my eyes. "Asher, do you hear yourself? You're angry at me, and you're still worried I'll catch a cold. That's my point. You have the ability to hurt me, but you never will. For the same reason I won't ever hurt you."

At his doubtful expression, I stepped close enough to feel his warm breath on my face and slid one palm along his whisker-rough cheek. Even as his body froze, he refortified his defenses, and his wall slammed upward. He hadn't grasped yet that all his defenses were too little, too late. It was time to let him in on the realization I'd come to during the night.

My voice sounded soft with affection. "You're *my* Protector, Asher."

His eyes widened with comprehension as he grasped what I was trying to tell him. He staggered back against the nearest tree, and I strode out of the woods to catch up with my father.

CHAPTER THIRTEEN

I caught up with Ben as he backed the car out of the driveway. He and Laura were upset I'd gone out walking without telling anyone. They both acted embarrassed because they hadn't bothered to look for the note on the fridge before jumping right into panic mode.

After apologizing, I plodded upstairs to bed, my feet dragging with exhaustion.

Lucy came in through our bathroom as I shrugged off my jacket.

"Well, if it isn't our resident runaway," she said, in a singsong voice.

"Could you be useful and help me with this thing? I'm dying to take a shower."

She ignored my glare when she walked over to help me remove the sling. "Oh, someone's touchy. Didn't the walk in the woods with Asher Blackwell cure your case of the grumps?"

From behind me, she worked the strap of the sling off my shoulder, and I twisted around in time to see her innocent smile. She walked away to close my bedroom door and the door to the bathroom before turning on me with curiosity.

"Remy, you tell me what you were doing in the park right now or else."

I raised one eyebrow. "Or else what?"

"Or else I will make you laugh, which we both know is the worst kind of torture in your current state."

She held both hands in the air as if threatening to tickle me. Lucy looked so ridiculous with her heart-shaped face scowling, I laughed anyway, and then winced in pain. Immediately remorseful, she rushed to finish helping me out of the sling. When I sat on the bed, she settled cross-legged next to me with an expectant stare.

I sighed and studied the ceiling. "He's a friend."

That earned me a poke in the leg. "Are you sure that's it? He called while you were in New York. He sounded so worried, I guessed something was up. What's with the early morning rendezvous?"

She sounded scandalized, and I grinned. "Get your mind out of the gutter, Luce. He heard about my mom. He *was* worried. We talked. That's it. As if I could get up to anything. Seriously, have you taken a good look at me this morning?"

Examining my tangled bed hair and ratty sweats, she gave a dramatic sigh. "What a waste!"

I giggled because I'd thought the same thing, and then groaned at the jarring aches. I moaned, "Uncle!"

Lucy laughed, too, and crawled off the bed. "Okay, I'll let you off easy this time. Word of advice? Be friends with Asher, but leave it at that. He's the kind of guy that leaves scars."

She left, and I drifted off to sleep wishing everyone would stop warning me to keep my distance from Asher Blackwell, including the boy himself.

I managed to sleep away most of the weekend. Suffering new pangs of regret, I wished I could heal myself when I had to get ready for school. After ten minutes of trying to button my jeans, I stood half-dressed and my shoulder ached from jostling it. Lucy came to my rescue with a loose skirt and a wraparound sweater that belted around my midriff—no buttons. She zipped me into my knee-high boots, fastened my hair in a loose braid, and helped me back into my sling.

On the ride to school, she shared how concerned our friends had been. They'd all called in the last couple of days to check on me. Lucy had told them what had happened with my mother and Dean so I wouldn't have to spend all day explaining my latest injuries. She described how Brandon had returned to school after nearly drowning. I hadn't said anything about the incident to Ben and hoped he didn't find out from some well-meaning parent. It had been bad enough when Lucy berated me for not telling anyone. Of course, I'd had other things on my mind at the time, which she thought excused me.

When we drove into the parking lot, I didn't see Asher's motorcycle and felt relieved to put off the inevitable confrontation. My friends presented a different story. Susan, Greg, and Brandon waited for us. Brandon opened my door to help me out of the car and stole my book bag before I could reach it.

He slung it over his own shoulder and leered at me. "How did you know I find a woman in a sling sexy?"

I rolled my eyes. "Greg, can you hit him upside the head for me?"

Greg did and I laughed as Brandon grumbled. I hadn't realized how I'd missed them all.

When we separated from the others, I asked, "How're you feeling, Brand? I'm sorry I didn't call."

He waved one large hand. "No reason you should've. I was perfectly healthy, and you had enough going on 'Sides, the EMTs couldn't find a thing wrong with me, except that I'd inhaled a bunch of water." He frowned.

"You know, I could've sworn I hit my head on the rim of the pool, but they didn't even find a bump. We checked the edge for blood, but there wasn't any."

Asher, I realized. He must have rinsed it off to cover my tracks when he went to check on Brandon.

I smiled. "I'm glad you're okay."

"Ditto." The leer resurfaced. "By the way, you look hot in a skirt."

Laughing, I shoved him in the side.

After third period ended, Brandon led me to the cafeteria, telling me a joke along the way. I laughed as I settled in my seat next to Lucy at our table and glanced up into Asher's forceful stare. My body froze. He must have arrived late to school. Sitting with his sister and their usual admirers, he looked beautiful as ever. He also appeared a man on a mission as he rose and stalked toward our table, his gaze never straying from me.

Lucy whispered, "Uh-oh. Did you guys fight?"

"Not really."

Asher arrived, greeted everyone with a friendly wave, and slid my chair back with easy familiarity.

"You guys don't mind if I steal Remy, do you?" he said, in a low voice full of polite charm.

He didn't wait for their objections. "Remy?" He waited with raised brows until I stood. When he turned to walk out of the cafeteria as if he expected me to follow, I veered off to the food line instead. We hadn't spoken yesterday and a lot needed to be said. He'd called while I'd slept and probably thought I'd been avoiding him, which was only a little true. Now, in this mood, I preferred witnesses around to keep him in check.

He appeared at my side, took my tray from me, and piled enough food for three on it. I raised an eyebrow but didn't say a word when he paid. He carried the tray to an empty table and held a chair out for me. When we were both sitting, I said nothing. Some stubborn part of me insisted that he should be the one to speak first.

He watched me, his expression impossible to read, as I picked up a donut and took a huge bite. I sensed his steely control, and it frustrated me since he'd been the flustered one the last time we spoke. Usually, I'd been off kilter because he'd known what was happening, while I'd been in the dark.

He studied my face while I ate, and I barely held my irritation in check. When I wiped my fingers on a napkin, he still hadn't said a word.

Pushing my chair back, I got to my feet. "Well, the conversation's been interesting. If you're finished . . ."

His eyes narrowed. "Sit down, Remy."

I looked down my nose at him.

"Please."

I sat, crossed my legs, and leaned back in an imitation of his relaxed pose, trying to appear as casual as possible while wearing a ridiculous sling. With a hint of boredom, I asked, "You wanted to talk?"

Something warm flashed in his eyes, and the distance dissipated as if it'd never been. He laughed, and my stomach flipped at the deep rumble of his voice. "You are amazing, you know that?" He glanced at the sling. "How are you feeling? I called yesterday, and your dad said you were sleeping. I thought maybe you were hurting."

"Not hurt. Just tired. It was a long week. What's with your sister?" I nodded over his shoulder to where Lottie glared at Asher's back. Lottie flicked a confused glance at my sling.

Asher didn't turn. "She's wondering why a Healer isn't healing her injuries. And she's angry at me for going and bonding myself to you."

My lungs seized, refusing to inflate. It was one thing to know the truth, and another to hear him say it.

Satisfaction gleamed through his slow smile. "Breathe, Remy."

He leaned both elbows on the table as I sucked in air.

Asher lowered his voice when the two girls at the next table shot curious glances in our direction. "After you dropped your bombshell Saturday, I did a lot of thinking. I couldn't believe I'd missed all the signs. The connection I feel to you, what happened the first time we touched."

His eyes darkened with some emotion I didn't understand. "I'm sorry about what happened before in my car. I wanted to warn you off. I thought you would be safer without me, but I can see now that there's no escaping this. You're *my* Healer."

My mouth dropped open. I hadn't expected him to admit so much. Even though I'd been the one to claim him as my Protector, I couldn't help the rebellion that shot through me at his words. His serious gaze left his intention to protect me unmistakable.

Not a chance, I thought. *I don't belong to anyone. I take care of myself.*

The rough edge to Asher's tone scraped along my nerve endings. "Like you took care of yourself with Dean? He almost killed you."

My protest died away when I realized I hadn't spoken my thoughts aloud, but he'd responded to them as if I had. It couldn't be. It wasn't possible.

I stared at Asher and waited. *Are you reading my mind?*

He hesitated and then nodded.

I sagged in my seat as I remembered the night at the pool and the times before that when my thoughts had focused on him. On my growing feelings for him. Horror had me cringing at the idea that he'd heard it all.

How long? How long have you been listening?

"Off and on since you healed me," he admitted.

Humiliation flooded through me, and my thoughts should have set him on fire.

He held up a hand after a moment to halt the mental onslaught.

"Remy." He closed his eyes and rubbed his forehead as if he had a headache. "I didn't choose this. You know I didn't. We're changing the longer we're near each other. I know you feel it."

I couldn't disagree. My mental walls had grown tougher and more flexible after his continuous prodding and that other ability—the frightening ability to twist pain and energy back on another—had grown stronger, too. Undeniably, he'd changed me. Still, I sensed he meant something more.

With effort, I made my mind a blank wasteland to shut him out.

His eyes focused, and he smiled. "You don't give an inch, do you?"

"What are you trying to tell me?"

"It's only a matter of time before other Protectors find out about you. It's a miracle you've lasted alone this long. I didn't want to feel anything for you, but we're past that now. I'm a Protector, Remy. You're a Healer. You could be the one we've heard rumors about, the one who could make us mortal again. I give you fair warning that I intend to take my duty very seriously."

Whether I want you to or not. I could hear the promise implied in his tone.

"I'm sorry, but yes."

"Get out of my head!" I said, in a fierce whisper.

He shrugged in apology, but his voice had an edge of humor. "I'm not sure I can. Honestly, I'm not sure I would even if I knew how. This link could be the most powerful asset I have, since I suspect you won't be talking to me for a while."

He betrayed me by invading my mind. Knowing it would irritate him, I thought, *Enemy,* and he scowled.

At this further evidence of treachery, I sent my shield soaring upward higher and more fortified than I'd ever done before. He winced as if he sensed the rage behind the gesture.

"I don't hear you all the time, especially when your walls are up," he said, when I stood. "I don't really understand it yet, but I suspect I hear you best when we touch. Or when your emotions are particularly strong."

Somehow, that didn't make me feel better. I felt too much when I was with him. He would know my secrets, the things I'd kept from everyone, including Anna. My nose almost touched his when I leaned forward and lowered my guard long enough to shout one thought.

Back off!

Asher didn't stop me when I retreated back to my friends.

CHAPTER FOURTEEN

*A*fter school, I headed to the Clover Café to study and sighed with relief when I didn't see Asher. He'd been reading my mind for weeks since I'd healed his hand at the bonfire. Obviously, not everything since I'd had to tell him I knew he was a Protector, but definitely enough to be humiliating. I remembered the night he'd loosed his power on me in the car. What had he said? *Damn you, Remy, for making me do this.* I'd been confused and too upset to realize his comment made no sense. Unless he'd been trying his hardest to warn me of how dangerous he was to me and had just heard me thinking how he'd never hurt me in a million years. Not exactly the kind of thing an enemy would do.

After ordering a drink, I headed to the restroom that sat in a corridor off the main café. Exiting, I discovered Gabe leaning against the wall in the dim hallway. Nervous, I tried to walk by him, but his voice stopped me short.

"Let's talk, Healer."

His tone didn't allow for a protest. He guided me down the hall with a hand near my lower back, not quite touching me. I shifted away, uncomfortable with the possibility of his touch, and wasn't surprised when he steered me toward a storage room. If he'd closed the door behind us, I would have screamed bloody murder, but he left it open as he retreated to one side of the closet.

"I'm getting really tired of the Blackwells manhandling me."

He didn't answer.

The café owner, a woman in her forties, happened by and glanced in the room. "What are you kids doing in here? This room is off limits."

She sounded irritated and overworked. I started forward, relieved to escape Gabe, but he blocked my retreat. I watched as he used his handsome face to charm her into believing that he was in love with me. He simply needed five minutes alone to convince me to believe him and could he please stay in the room if he promised we wouldn't touch anything. He flirted outrageously until she walked away with a blush and a swing to her hips.

"That was truly impressive, you know. What are you, half her age?"

He wasn't disturbed by my disgust. "On the contrary, I'm decades older than she is."

We stood across from each other and squared off like the wary enemies we were.

I shook my head, irritated at his arrogance. "What do you want?"

He folded his arms and managed to look relaxed and menacing at once. He leveled a steady stare at me. "I want to know what the hell you're doing to my brother, Healer."

"You're kidding me, right?"

The hair on the back of my neck rose when he didn't blink, and I guessed Gabe could be dangerous. A shadow passed through his eyes when he reached out to touch my arm. My walls slammed up in response.

"Asher's right," he observed, studying the green sparks

coming from my skin as he dropped his hand. "That hurts like hell."

He suffered the same side effects Asher did when my defenses were down. Apparently, my energy was poison to all the Blackwells. The knowledge I'd hurt him gave me confidence. "Sucks to feel human again, doesn't it?"

Those dangerous eyes of his glittered, and I shivered. I didn't know what Asher had shared about me and had to tread with care. "What exactly do you think I've done to your brother?"

He seemed to consider me. "Are you that naïve, girl? Do you know what it means that he's decided to bond with you?"

That was the second time a Blackwell had called me naïve. My voice remained calm, despite my anger. "As far as I know, neither of us had a choice in the matter."

Gabe's smile appeared grim. "Yet, here you are, fighting him every step of the way. Seems like it's a one-sided bond to me."

I thought of Asher's ability to read my mind and glowered, unwilling to share that revelation with Gabe if his brother hadn't.

Gabe stretched an arm across the shelf nearest him. The move made him look bigger, more formidable. It was a deliberate action and left me wondering how this manipulative man could be related to Asher. "You know he's in agony every time he touches you, every time you drop your guard. You may have bonded unintentionally, but make no mistake that he's choosing to put himself at risk to be with you. Now that I've felt a fraction of what he's going through, I can see he's a fool."

I hadn't realized it was that bad. I remembered now how Asher had winced in pain when we touched. Maybe he felt more alive, but if the radiation theory held, he felt extraordinary pain, too. Living without all their senses must have driven the Protectors mad if they were willing to kill Hunters to feel that. What were Asher's reasons?

A cloud of unfamiliar energy drifted toward me, seeking a way around my walls. It didn't have the control or finesse of Asher's energy, and I understood it came from Gabe. He meant to intimidate me, and I fought to stave off my panic.

He slanted a disparaging glance at my sling. "Your kind has brought us nothing but pain." His voice sounded silky with threat. "My brother would die for you. Are you worth it, Healer?"

I restrained my urge to kick him. Fleeing was the smarter course of action than an outright attack. He let me go when I sprinted for the door. And why wouldn't he? I ran like a coward.

When I sat next to Lucy, I pretended nothing had happened. Moments later, I saw Gabe return to his own table. He had no problem ignoring me as he turned his attention to one of his Sorori-toys, but I couldn't concentrate.

Asher and Gabe were both convinced that other Protectors would find me soon, and Gabe wouldn't be sorry to see me at their mercy. Comparisons of the two brothers kept running through my head. Gabe's icy energy could be cruel, unlike the comforting heat of Asher's power. I wondered why Gabe hadn't threatened me before, but guessed it had something to do with Asher. There was no doubt he would do me harm if Asher was hurt because of me.

The next day, I got to English before Asher and waited outside the classroom for Lucy to bring me my book bag. Ben had dropped me off at school midday after a visit to the doctor's to get the go-ahead to remove my sling. As I waited, Gabe's question from the day before replayed in my mind over and over again. I could trust Asher, but was I worth the sacrifices he would make every time he was near me? If the other Protectors came for me, would I be worth dying for? My eyes shut and I wrapped an arm around my burning stomach.

"Yes."

Somehow, I wasn't surprised to hear his low voice. I opened my eyes, and Asher's fierce, unblinking stare held me captive. I couldn't think while trapped by the power of that intent look.

"Yes, what?"

"Yes, you're worth dying for."

His certainty left no room for doubt, but he would learn I'd done nothing to be worthy of his sacrifice. Better he find out sooner, rather than when his life was in danger. I would do whatever it took to keep my family and this boy safe.

Asher smiled as if at a private joke and held out his hand. He had his guard up, and I slid my palm into his to savor the comforting heat of his touch. For the first time, I noticed that classmates wading in the halls on the way to class surrounded us. A few tossed curious glances our way, but I ignored these and wondered where Lucy was.

"She was here. I told her I'd give you your bag." He lifted one shoulder, and I noticed he carried my bag and his.

My displeasure at his easy answer to my thoughts must have shown on my face. He frowned as he pulled me into the river of students. "I'm sorry, Remy. I can't help it. I swear I'm not doing it on purpose."

Still uneasy, I nodded. "I get that, but I can't help feeling you're trespassing."

He looked grim. "I guess it's not very fair to you."

I sighed. "Neither is the pain you're in when we're together."

He looked around, and we both realized the hall had emptied. He stepped forward to hold open the door to our English class, and as I walked past him he whispered, "Can I drive you home? We can talk."

The butterflies took flight in my stomach at the idea of being alone with him, but I nodded. We made it into our seats as the bell rang. We didn't have a chance to talk, as the teacher began her discussion on *The Picture of Dorian Gray*. I picked up my copy of the novel and studied the picture on the cover. The cruel, handsome face of the immortal Dorian Gray reminded me of Gabe's face as he spoke to me in the storage room yesterday.

Asher tensed in the desk next to me, and I looked around to find out what had upset him. Nothing seemed out of place as Mrs. Welles continued her lecture on the book. He scowled at me, and I stared back in bewilderment until I realized he eavesdropped again.

I glared. *I realize you can't help it, but could you at least try?*

He picked up a piece of paper and wrote one word in an imperious slant. *Gabe?*

With a shrug, I ignored him, trying to think of nothing.

He tapped his pen on the desk to get my attention and pointed at Gabe's name. One eyebrow rose, demanding an answer.

Perhaps I would have told him about my discussion with Gabe later, but his arrogance brought out the worst in me. My eyelashes fluttered as I pictured Gabe's handsome face creased in a flirtatious smile, as he told the café owner he loved me. I had no idea if Asher could see a mental picture but figured he could when he glowered, folded his arms, and turned to face the front of the class looking a lot like a petulant child. He shot me a dirty look from the corner of his eye, and I guessed he'd heard my last observation. He seemed jealous.

Could there be an advantage to Asher reading my

mind? I pretended to listen to Mrs. Welles, but instead concentrated on mentally telling a joke Brandon had told me once, adding visual cues to make it funnier. When I got to the punch line, Asher slanted a smirk at me, and I knew he'd been listening.

He picked up his pen and wrote on the paper. *Brandon?*

I nodded to answer his question.

With a satisfied smile, he nodded. *Tell me a story.*

About what?

He scrawled another note. *You choose.*

Storytelling had never been my thing. You had to talk to tell stories, and I'd made a habit of keeping to myself for too long. Instead of a story, I settled on a memory that had come to me the night before.

I was eight and my mother had taken me to Rockaway Beach. Our ice cream cones melted faster than we could eat them—chocolate for me and plain vanilla for her. We sat on a long stretch of sand, squinting in the hot sun with the bite of salty air filling our lungs. We'd built a sandcastle using mixing bowls and pans borrowed from our kitchen and played tag with the waves. Then we'd collapsed in an exhausted heap of limbs on an old sheet instead of the towels we couldn't afford. Anna turned her face to the sun and laughed at some silly thing I'd said. That nine-year-old memory was the best I had of her, and that seemed too tragic for words.

A sudden, desperate desire for privacy had me raising my walls to try to block Asher out, and he gave me the distance I needed. We didn't look at each other the rest of the class. When the bell rang, I glanced over and found him watching me with an expression I didn't understand.

His low voice sounded tender. "Thank you for letting me see that."

I tipped my head to acknowledge his gratitude.

He took my bag again and we left the class. In the hall,

I stopped Susan to ask her to let Lucy know that Asher would take me home. Her eyes looked huge behind her glasses as she promised to pass the message along, and I figured Lucy wouldn't be the only one receiving the message. Asher's car was the same one he'd driven me home from the pool in. Daylight revealed a sporty, expensive Audi. I froze and stared at it in awestruck appreciation. Asher touched my arm in concern, but I was too busy falling in love with his car to notice. Ben would know exactly how I felt. Asher's gorgeous, sleek car looked like it would go very, very fast while hugging the road on every corner. My eyes glazed over. I really, really wanted to drive that car.

Asher's loud burst of laughter startled me back to awareness, and I looked into his smiling eyes. He knew I lusted after his car.

He held up the keys and shook them with one eyebrow raised in invitation. I was tempted, oh, so tempted, but I shook my head. "I can't. No license, remember?"

He opened the passenger door for me. When he sat in the driver's seat, he promised, "You have an open invitation to drive my car as soon as you have a license."

A promise I would hold him to, I decided, when he started the engine and it came to life with a quiet, powerful purr. I stroked the warm buttery leather seat and almost purred myself. The car had heated seats, and my body shivered in appreciation. I seriously loved this car.

I glanced up when Asher sighed. "What?"

He pulled the car onto the road. "Hearing your reaction to things, I can almost remember what it's like."

When I looked perplexed, he continued. "Tasting ice cream. Smelling the sea air. Feeling the sun on my skin. Your memories are so vivid, it's like I'm there with you."

"But I thought you felt more . . . human when you're

with me?" I wondered if he could feel my skin when he touched me.

His smile appeared sad. "Yes. When I'm with you, I feel pain like any other human."

The idea horrified me. "Do you mean you feel *only* pain?"

He shook his head. "I feel *mostly* pain."

The difference between only and mostly was lost on me, and disappointment swamped me. Maybe Gabe had been right to want to protect his brother from me.

Asher parked, and I stared out the window at my home. He touched my cheek and urged me to face him. "What did my brother say to you, Remy?"

I had to swallow the lump in my throat to speak as I remembered Gabe's warning. "I don't want to hurt you."

He dropped his hand and cursed. At least, I thought he cursed. He spoke rapidly in another language. I blinked, waiting for him to lose steam and was impressed by how long it took for him to run out of words.

"I'm going to kill Gabe."

I didn't realize he'd switched to English for a moment. A smile lifted the corners of my lips against my will. "What language was that?"

His voice had tightened with anger. "Welsh, French, and Spanish."

I whistled. "Not enough curses in one language?"

He looked sheepish. "Sorry."

My smile turned to a grin when his tension receded. "It's okay. I didn't understand any of it anyway, but I got the gist. I'd bet money Gabe's ears are burning right now."

"He shouldn't have interfered. He doesn't know what he's talking about."

"Is he wrong? I mean it, Asher. I don't want to hurt you. I'm not worth it."

His eyes burned with a green fire. "You're worth that and more. I'd withstand ten times the pain to touch you."

It became a struggle to answer when the air left my lungs. I felt the same way.

I knew he'd heard me when he took a deep breath that mirrored mine. He brushed my hair from my face and wrapped a curl around one finger. The low cadence of his voice cajoled me to play along. "Let's pretend you're not a Healer, and I'm not a Protector for a day. Come to the beach with me tomorrow after school. We'll talk about ordinary things and bore each other silly."

It would be impossible for him to bore me. I wanted to know everything about him. We both knew it was dangerous for us to pretend we were anything other than what we were. There were a million reasons not to go.

He tugged on the curl and I heard myself say, "Okay."

CHAPTER FIFTEEN

*A*t school the next day, Asher kept his distance. Neither of us wanted to broadcast that something was going on between us. My feelings towards him proved difficult to pin down, though I experienced a pang of pleasure when he ignored the girls at his table. As for Asher, aside from an infuriating desire to protect me, I hadn't a clue to what he felt.

"You know, if you continue to stare at each other like that, you're not going to fool anyone into thinking you're just friends," Lucy said.

"I have no idea what you're talking about."

It was such an outright fib I bit my lip to keep a straight face. She grinned at me, but worry remained in her eyes. Asher was the penultimate person I should be dating according to her, with only Gabe somehow managing to top Lucy's do-not-date, do-not-pass-go list.

She rolled her eyes and wiped her fingers on a napkin. "Sure, you don't. Be careful with that one, okay?" She inclined her head toward Asher's table. "Remember Dad's heart."

"Hey, Luce, don't worry. If it makes you feel any better, he has a car."

She frowned. "What does that have to do with anything?"

My shrug radiated innocence. "Nothing, I guess. It's just that I know your objection to boys who ride motorcycles."

Lucy threw her balled-up napkin at me. My nose crinkled as I picked it up between two fingers. "Eww. Can you be any more childish?"

Several minutes later, the bell rang. When I glanced at Asher's table, he grinned my way, and I returned his look with a smile of my own. His expression stood in sharp contrast to Lottie's, who appeared to have swallowed a lemon as she stared me down.

When our impossibly long English class ended, Asher and I let the other students file out first. He picked up my bag, careful not to brush my skin, though my guard was up. We walked in silence to his car where he opened the door for me and stowed my bag at my feet.

We made nervous small talk as he drove north. A short time later, he drove through the gated entrance to Fort Rowden State Park. I'd heard some kids at school talking about the old fort, but I hadn't been there yet. It wasn't really a military fort anymore, but a place to go camping, hit the beach, or hang out. One of the two-story rectangular white buildings had been turned into a hostel with dorms on the second floor and private rooms on the lower floor, but tourists tended to desert the Falls during the colder months.

Asher turned onto a road that ran parallel to the shore. The water and clouds danced together in fluid shades of gray and blue. Where the sky managed to part them, it showed itself in a flamboyant aqua. We rounded a corner, and a white lighthouse dominated the view, jutting out into the water on a shelf of sand.

Asher parked at the end of the road and shut off the engine. "No, let me," he said, when I moved to open my door.

He was out of the car and at my door before I could re-spond. He watched with impatience as I clambered out, still sore from my fight with Dean. Acting on a suspicion, I warned, "If you try to pick me up, I'll slug you."

With a rueful smile, he backed away. "Now who's the mind reader?" He gestured to the sandy lane that led to the beach. "Will you be okay navigating the path? I worried it'd be a rough go for you."

"My feet work just fine. Let's go."

We hiked side by side along the roped walkway bordered by sea grass until several larger pieces of driftwood blocked the way. I would have climbed over them, but Asher placed both large hands under my arms and easily lifted me over the debris with a cheeky grin before turning me loose again. I rolled my eyes at him and couldn't help it when my lips twitched. Some dormant girly part of me liked it when his strength made me feel small next to him.

"Tell me what you're thinking, Remy," Asher implored in a cajoling tone.

I glanced up at him through my eyelashes as we fell in step together on the empty stretch of beach. The salty wind blew colder and stronger in the open, and I tucked my hands into my coat pockets with a shiver. "I thought you could read my mind, Protector," I teased.

Frustrated, Asher ran a hand through his wind-tossed hair. "I told you I can't hear you when your walls are up."

I grinned, relieved. "Just checking."

We came upon an overturned tree that had washed ashore during a storm. Sitting, I patted the space next to me, and Asher sank down with all the grace I'd grown accustomed to. He glanced at my hand on the log next to his leg with a speculative gleam in his eyes, and I remembered what he'd said yesterday—he could hear my thoughts best when we touched.

I snorted and shifted out of his reach. "Okay, let's get something straight. You may be able to read my mind because of some crazy Protector-Healer bond we can't control, but that doesn't mean you have an open invitation to do so whenever you please. Consider this an invitation-only zone." I waved a wide circle around my head with both arms.

Asher shrugged, not ashamed in the least to have been caught out, and straddled the log to face me. "I guess that's fair. I'll do my best to abide by your rule, unless, of course, I feel it's in your best interest not to."

He seemed adept at finding loopholes when he wanted something. Thinking on my feet had become a necessity around him. "And what would constitute 'not in my best interest'?"

"Your right to privacy becomes secondary to your safety. If I perceive you are in danger, I won't hesitate to do what I think is necessary."

I shivered as I considered the sculpted lines of his face. A dark shadow of whiskers on the hollows of his cheeks and the wide curve of his jaw made him look dangerous.

"I warned you before, Remy. I will protect you."

There was no give in his stony expression: He meant what he said and I could do nothing about it. I didn't need him to protect me: I could protect myself. I dropped my wall to let him hear one thought. *Arrogant, obstinate jerk!*

He had the nerve to laugh when he heard me. "Come on. Don't be mad. Let's shake hands as friends."

One strong hand was held out for me to shake, and he smirked when I ignored it. It shouldn't have been charming, but I had to stifle my answering smile.

"Asher, my mom likened my energy to a kind of poison for your kind. Why would you risk touching me? Why would any of the Protectors risk that? The pain can't be worth it." I shook my head, trying to understand him. My teeth chattered as I huddled in my coat.

Asher stripped off his own coat and wrapped it around my shoulders, pulling the lapels together under my chin. Even as he backed away, the heat of his body sank into my bones and I shuddered. The cold wind didn't bother him in the least.

"I can't answer for the others, but for me . . . You know I lost some of my senses after the War. My other senses, though . . . Well, they were strengthened. We think they evolved to make up for the lack of taste, smell, or touch, like a blind person who has excellent hearing."

My curiosity about him had been eating at me for weeks. "How superior? Are we talking twenty-ten or X-ray vision?"

Asher flicked an uncertain look my way to see if I was joking and gave me a bemused smile. "Somewhere in between, I guess. I don't need lights to see in the dark, and I can hear sounds from miles away you would be hard-pressed to hear from ten feet away."

I whistled. "Impressive. What about food? You said you were hungry that night at Rosy's, and I've seen you eat plenty of times."

"Of course. My body isn't so different from a human's. We need food to fuel our bodies, too. If anything, we need more of it since our bodies run at 210 percent efficiency, like you guessed. We simply can't taste any of it."

"That's awful!"

He grimaced. "The best I can explain it is to say it's like we're sleepwalking. There were so many things in my old life that I took for granted. I want to smell things, taste things, *feel* things. It's one reason I don't mind the pain when I touch you. To *feel* pain. It's a gift, Remy, to someone who's been asleep for over a century."

His eyes burned with naked honesty. My breath caught until a seagull screeched in the distance and he glanced away. The moment was broken, and I sucked in air, trying for the umpteenth time to imagine what it would be like to be deprived of my senses. Even now, sensory information inundated me. True, he saw and heard the beauty, but he missed more.

The immensity of it all made my voice sound hushed. "I'm sorry, Asher. I wish I could help you."

He leaned forward with sudden urgency. "But you do. "

"By hurting you? I hate this!" I would have stood, but he gave a slight jerk on his jacket.

"No, Remy! You don't understand. When I hear your thoughts, it's like I'm reliving your memories. I'm not really feeling, smelling, tasting, but it's the next best thing. I've never tasted ice cream, but when you thought about eating it at the beach . . ." His eyes closed in remembered pleasure . . . my remembered pleasure. Then, he sighed as the memory faded, and his gaze focused on me again. A gentle smile flitted across his mouth. "It was heaven."

"How is that possible?" I asked.

"How is any of this possible? I don't have the answers." He frowned, and his hands fisted at his side. "You should know my desire to feel human isn't the only reason I want to hear your thoughts."

"Right. You want to *protect* me," I said, with a heavy dose of sarcasm.

He slid across the log until he rested a breath away, invading my space. Startled, I tried to move back, but he held on to the lapels of his coat. Both of his thumbs pushed under the collar and used the material to tip my chin back to meet his eyes. While his skin wasn't brushing mine, his warm gaze felt like a touch.

Passion roughened his voice. "True, but you're missing the point. You're unique, Remy. I've known dozens of

Healers in my life, and you're different. I want to know everything about you, and I have to fight the temptation to cheat when I can't hear you."

A strand of hair escaped my braid as I stared at him, half-afraid and half-thrilled to know my fascination wasn't one-sided. He wrapped my hair around his finger and continued, "One brush of my fingers against your skin, and your secrets are mine. The thing is, I don't want to take them. You've been through hell, and now you find yourself trapped into a bond with your enemy. You deserve a better man than me. It's wrong. It goes against everything we know, but I want you to *choose* to trust me."

My heart pounded in my chest as our breath heated the small space between us. My voice came out in a husky whisper. "And what if I want the same thing? What if I want you to trust me with all your secrets?"

His eyes lit with hope. "All you have to do is ask."

A long, tense moment stretched out between us as we thought about what that kind of intimacy could mean—he wanted open access to my soul, but it wasn't always a pleasant place to be. My thoughts could be ugly and mean, especially when it came to Dean. My memories weren't sunshine and roses, either, but dark and depressing. He didn't know what he asked of me because, if I invited him in, he'd find the nearest exit. I was the type of person who'd abandon her mother to a beast, and I didn't want him to know this person I was inside and hate me.

Asher must have seen some of what I felt on my face. His smile looked sad as he unwound my hair from his finger. "It's okay, Remy. Forgive me for pushing."

I couldn't trust him with my deepest thoughts, but I could give him something. When he backed away, I grabbed hold of his hand in a tight grip. Closing my eyes, I emptied my mind and let my senses overpower me.

My nose burned as I inhaled the briny air and a light

mist dampened my face. I could taste salt on the tip of my tongue as a strong breeze whipped loose strands of my hair into a frenzy and chilled my exposed flesh. The sole exceptions were where his coat engulfed me and where the low fire that always burned under Asher's skin warmed my hand. I concentrated on the rough skin of his palm and how it felt against the smoother flesh of mine as I slid my hand from his, breaking the connection and raising my walls again.

The air stilled between us, except for our loud breathing. Green sparks were fading when I opened my eyes, and I discovered his had closed as if he savored the memory of what I'd shared. He looked . . . overwhelmed and touched. I wondered what those sparks meant. They were not the blue of healing normal people, or the red that happened when I attacked. The green had to mean something.

Asher cleared his throat and glanced at the setting sun with amazement. "I've tried to hold on to the memory of what certain things felt like. I thought I remembered what the sea air felt and tasted like. I was wrong. My memories are mere shadows. I'd given up hope of feeling anything again. Until you."

My voice sounded choked with emotion, and I couldn't look at him. "Is this why the Protectors hunt Healers? To remember?"

"No!" He looked horrified at the suggestion. "We're nothing like them. They use Healers like a drug, but that kind of pain—most Healers don't last more than a few days."

I let that implication sink in. The brutality of those Protectors killing my kind for a quick injection of sensation terrified me.

"I shouldn't be able to sit near you, Remy. Not this long and not with my defenses down. But it gets easier every day. I told you, you're unique." His voice held a fierce promise. "I'll take whatever danger comes with this. You're worth the risk."

His words cut me with a new pain. What if he didn't feel the way I did? Maybe this was really about my power. I rose to my feet. "So, what now?"

He stood, too, and we faced each other. "We spend time together. Get to know each other."

I nodded, knowing there wasn't another option, as we walked toward the car. Too much was left for us to discover about each other, too many questions we had yet to answer. By a strange accident of fate, we'd bonded as Protector and Healer. Asher vowed to protect me with his life. Part of me felt glad to have someone watching over me, but I refused to play the weak damsel in distress.

He cared about me to some extent: His actions made that clear. Still, I wondered if his craving to be human lay at the heart of his desire to be near me. The possibility terrified me because the real reason I didn't want him in my head and in my heart had come to me when I considered losing him: I was falling in love with my enemy.

"Asher?"

"Hmm?"

He sounded distracted as he steered the car toward my home. The sun had set and left the car's interior dark, or I never would have found the nerve to ask my question.

"Can you feel me?"

"Of course. I can always feel when your walls are up. You know, you're the first Healer I've ever met who had defenses. Apparently, you even impressed Gabe with your ability. I know you don't care for him, but I wondered if you'd come to my house for dinner anyway?"

Caught up in my embarrassment at his misunderstanding my question, I nearly missed the anxiety in his question. "I'd love to." I would love to question his family. Anna had said I could cure Protectors of their immortality, but she hadn't given any details on how it worked. Maybe I could learn more if I spent time with the Blackwells.

Then, Asher's other words registered. He'd never met a Healer with defenses, which only reinforced what Anna had said. "Asher, you've said before that I'm unique. What did you mean? Is it because I have the ability to block you?"

A passing streetlight revealed his thoughtful frown. "No, though you having that ability is amazing in itself. All Protectors have mental shields and are taught to strengthen them as children to better help Healers—to keep our energy separate from theirs during the healing process."

"The mental prods." At his confused look, I added, "The way you send your energy at me sometimes. It feels like someone is poking me in the head."

He grinned at my description. "Yeah. That's how our parents train us to strengthen our shields. When it became clear you didn't know what a Protector was, I thought it would be a good idea to help you strengthen yours."

I smirked as I shifted in my seat to face him. "Plus, you wanted to annoy me."

"That was just a bonus." He didn't bother to hide his smug satisfaction.

Leaning over, I smacked him in the arm. My casual, affectionate gesture surprised us both, and it brought me back to the question I'd asked earlier. I didn't have the nerve to ask again if he could feel my skin the way I felt his when we touched. What if the same touch that gave me pleasure only brought him pain?

"The way you heal people is different, too," he continued. "I've never heard of a Healer who absorbed the injuries of the people they healed or had mild hypothermia afterward. Not to mention how you can push your own injuries off on others. Somehow, you're able to manipulate energy in ways I've never seen."

"Hypothermia?" Skepticism filled my voice.

He chided me. "Remy, your lips turned blue, you shivered like crazy, and you were so distracted you didn't notice I read your mind."

I grimaced at him. "Don't remind me. I'll get mad again."

"Do you always lose body heat like that after a healing?"

"Only with serious injuries, especially head wounds. It never happens when I heal myself."

He absorbed this in silence. We'd almost arrived at my house and disappointment set in again.

"You were cold after you healed my hand. Why weren't you able to heal yourself right away?"

I hesitated to tell the truth knowing how upset it would make him, and he smiled to encourage me. "I promise I can take it. I already know what kind of pain you were in."

"Okay. After I healed you, the pain was so intense I couldn't think. I couldn't heal myself."

"But you did something. I know you did because your body relaxed after I started talking to you." He pulled the car onto my street and parked in front of our driveway, switching on the interior light so he could see my face.

"Well, I couldn't concentrate enough to heal myself, but I couldn't let the pain continue. It's hard to explain, but basically, I killed the nerves in my hand so my brain couldn't register the pain."

The anguish on his face said he hadn't been prepared for my answer.

"Don't look like that, Asher." I ran a hand across his cheek to comfort him. "There was no risk. I've done it before."

"When Dean burned you with his cigarettes?" he said, in a hard tone.

I looked at him in surprise. The morning I'd met Asher in Townsend Park he'd been listening in when I remembered Dean's attack and my visit to the hospital. His anger that morning made more sense. At my nod, Asher reached for my arm, brushing away his jacket. "Show me," he asked.

I tried to pull away from his grasp. "Asher, don't. It won't do any good."

His expression didn't soften, but his voice held a plea. "It matters to me, Remy. I saw what he did in your thoughts. Please show me."

A beseeching Asher proved impossible to resist. Under his watchful gaze, I pulled off my jacket and the cardigan I wore underneath. I twisted my arm around so he could see the ugly scar peeking from under my short-sleeve shirt. Asher's jaw tightened, and I looked away in shame.

"He's a monster. What kind of man does this to a child?"

His fingers brushed the mark in a delicate whisper of a touch. My voice sounded flat when I answered his question. "Dean didn't know what I could do, but he suspected. No matter how quickly I could heal myself, he wanted me to know that he had the capacity to give more pain because I was his to do with as he pleased. Now, it's a reminder that I can survive anything, and I belong to no one except myself."

I knew I sounded defiant, but I couldn't take pity from Asher.

He met my rebellious look with a direct stare, while his hands gripped my arms. "I don't pity you, Remy. What Dean did to you . . . It would've broken a lot of people, made them hard like he is, but you're strong. You're good inside, and he could never touch that. Don't ever be ashamed of surviving a bastard like that."

Dampness clouded my vision, and I blinked to force it away. My jaw hurt from clenching it against the tears I refused to let fall. Asher seemed to understand I needed distance to pull myself together and let me go. I used the time to pull my sweater and coat back on.

My eyes didn't quite meet Asher's when I said, "See you tomorrow?"

He nodded and I climbed out of the car. Before I could slam the door closed, he called my name and I ducked my head back in. I wasn't prepared for the heat blazing from his eyes.

"There's another way you're unique that I haven't told you about."

"What's that?"

"I haven't known the touch of another human being in over a century. I feel you, Remy. Every touch, every look. I feel you. Go inside. I'll see you at school."

Stupefied, I stepped back and closed the car door. The car didn't pull away until I stumbled into the house on unsteady legs and closed the front door behind me with a tiny smile.

CHAPTER SIXTEEN

*A*sher waited in the school parking lot the next morning, and I moved towards him like a pigeon to a homing beacon. He straightened with a sweet smile that warmed me from the inside out. As he took my book bag, his hand reached for mine, giving me ample time to reinforce my defenses before he folded my small, mitten-covered hand into his larger one. A million reasons existed why we shouldn't do this, but not one of them mattered as we stood there smiling at each other.

He nodded toward my friends. "Would your friends mind if I walked you to class?"

"Probably." Absolutely, if Lucy had anything to say about it. She'd given me an earful the night before when I told her I intended to see Asher. She'd warned me he would break my heart and assured me she'd be there to pick up the pieces because that's what "loving sisters did when their idiot siblings made a huge, frickin' mistake." The short ride to school this morning had been a silent, awkward one.

Sure the hole I felt being bored into my back was accomplished by Lucy's angry glare, I shrugged. "Let's do it anyway."

Asher's forehead wrinkled in concern, but I distracted him by tugging his hand. Of course, he wasn't pulled off balance. He merely tugged back, and I was thrown against his chest. He grinned down at me and teased, "I'm stronger, remember? Me, Protector. You, Healer."

I gave him an innocent smile. "You're lucky I'm wearing mittens right now, or I'd make you pay for that."

His lips curved in a smirk as if he doubted my ability to do so.

Still smiling, I eased my walls down and created a very vivid mental picture of a video game version of me flexing bulging arm muscles in a threatening manner.

Laughter bubbled out of Asher, loud enough to draw stares, and I imagined what the others saw. Like me, they had to have noticed that popular Asher Blackwell kept himself from them. Always in control, always in check. The Asher before me was a different one from the boy I'd met on the beach—still beautiful, but somehow more relaxed. More touchable. In fact, my fingers itched to trace the scar that slashed through his eyebrow.

He stripped off my mitten, lifted our joined hands to his face, and folded my palm along the curve of his cheek with the tip of my finger near his brow. The remnants of a smile lingered at the corners of his mouth. "You have an odd fascination with my scar."

I'd forgotten to raise my guard again, distracted by his easy laugh, and he'd read my mind. Worried my touch hurt him, I tried to pull away, but he held tightly. He pleaded, "Don't go," and I knew he wasn't referring to my hand in his. "Trust me, Remy," he whispered. "I won't hurt you."

For a long moment, I stared into his eyes, wavering. It wasn't him I didn't trust, and I raised my shield, hoping no one noticed the green sparks shooting from my skin to his. "I can't."

Asher turned his head and pressed soft lips into the palm of my hand in a movement so quick I would have thought I imagined it, except for the heat radiating from the spot he'd kissed. He started walking toward the main building, and I stumbled along at his side. Everywhere, eyes followed us, gawking at Asher Blackwell holding the new girl's hand. He didn't seem to notice and said in a conversational tone, "Did you know you have a freckle right there at the corner of your mouth?" He gestured to the right corner of his own mouth.

I stopped walking to gape at him, but he tugged me along in his wake. Yes, I knew I had a freckle. It taunted me every time I looked at myself in the mirror.

In the same tone, he continued, "*Peter Pan* is a favorite story in my family. Not the cartoon version, but the real J. M. Barrie version. He's the boy that never grew up. We went to the play when it opened in the early 1900s. Have you read it?"

We had neared my class, and he pulled me out of the crowded hallway to a spot near the wall where he shielded me with his body. He didn't wait for me to answer his question.

"In the story, Mrs. Darling—Wendy's mother—has a kiss hidden in the right-hand corner of her mouth. No matter how hard her children or her husband try, they can never capture that kiss. It mocks them and puzzles them. Your freckle is like that kiss. It's hidden just there in plain view and teases me.

"I tell you so you'll know I understand about your interest in this." As he said "this," he traced the scar on his face. "You can trust me. I won't hurt you."

Warm fingers brushed that freckle as he watched me with gentle eyes. My defenses crumbled under that tender look, and I watched helplessly when he handed me my bag and walked away.

When the lunch bell rang, I rushed out of calculus to find Asher waiting in the hall. He'd managed to get from his class to mine quicker than it should have taken him, and I bet he'd used his Protector abilities to do it.

He reached for my hand with a comfortable familiarity, and we walked to the cafeteria. I glanced at him from the corner of my eye and found him doing the same thing. We both looked away sheepishly. I'd never had a boyfriend—my secrets hadn't been conducive to a relationship—and I wasn't sure how I should act. Would we eat with his friends or mine?

He seemed stumped by that problem, too, when we stepped into the cafeteria and the occupants of both tables eyed us with an air of expectation. Asher turned to me. "How about we find a new table to sit at today? Maybe one where there aren't so many ears eavesdropping on us?"

"You read my mind."

I winced when I heard my words. He laughed at my expression and the awkward moment passed. Carrying two trays through the line, he piled food on both, and I followed him to an empty table, eying the food he'd collected as we sat down.

"Pizza? A Twinkie? Are you kidding me? I can't subsist on junk food alone."

He looked sheepish again, and I had a sneaking suspicion I knew why. "You've never had any of these things, have you? You want to know what they taste like."

Suddenly, he sounded very polite. "I have to admit, I'm a bit curious."

I snorted and pulled the tray closer. "You want to satisfy your curiosity at the expense of my waistline."

An edge of excitement entered his voice. "American pizza and Twinkies were inventions that came after the War. I've eaten them since, of course, but they have no flavor. Are they as good as they look?"

His boyish anticipation had me grinning. It was comforting to discover he was like any other male, at least where his stomach was concerned. "Time to find out. Are you sure you want to do this? Your illusions may be forever shattered."

For a moment his eyes turned serious. "Do you mind, Remy? I'm being entirely selfish here. Please don't feel like you have to appease me."

I rolled my eyes and let my guard down. "Give me a break, Asher. There's no harm, as long as you're okay to touch me?"

He nodded and watched in anticipation as I picked up the Twinkie and took a huge bite. I tapped my finger against his hand under the table—in case those damn sparks made an appearance—as I chewed on the yellow sponge cake and its sugary white filling. He closed his eyes, while I chewed. After a moment, his eyes popped open and he sent me a disappointed frown.

"You don't like them, do you?"

I laughed and tossed the leftover cake back on the tray. "No. I got sick from eating too many of them when I was a kid. How did you know?"

He shrugged. "I'm not sure. I could just tell. It felt different from your memory of ice cream."

Picking up the slice of pizza, I took a bite. Again, I touched his hand as mozzarella, tomato sauce, and sourdough crust mingled with the spice of pepperoni. This time, a smile curved his lips as he watched me. He said, "You definitely like pizza."

Pulling my hand from his, I grinned. "Wait until you try a café mocha."

His eyebrow rose. "Your favorite, I take it?"

"Chocolate and espresso blended into caffeinated perfection. What's not to like?"

He leaned forward, placing both elbows on the table as he studied me intently. "What else do you like?"

"The list is too long to go over at lunch." I patted my

flat stomach. I'd put on some weight since moving to Blackwell Falls and my hip bones no longer jutted out the way they had before. Laura put huge helpings on my plate at mealtimes in her attempt to fatten me, as Lucy had warned me she intended to do. "Contrary to popular opinion in my home, I am a girl who likes to eat. I think healing burns off a lot of calories."

"Let's start with your favorites, then."

The serious look on his face said he wasn't kidding. I took a moment to think about my answer. "Okay, let's see." I ticked my answers off on my fingers. "Café mochas. Macaroni and cheese. French fries with tons of ketchup. A juicy hamburger smothered in bleu cheese. Coffee ice cream swirled with fudge."

Asher's eyes crinkled at the corners as he listened. "I see a theme of coffee and chocolate in your list."

I grinned without apology. "What about you? What were your favorites?"

He didn't even have to think about his answer and rattled them off in rapid fire. "Roast turkey with dressing. Bread pudding. Beefsteak pie. Scones with thick clotted cream and loads of gooseberry jam. And tea, of course."

For some reason, the last answers made me giggle. I could imagine him as a teenage boy in a very proper tuxedo sipping tea from fancy china and eating scones in a formal Victorian drawing room, while the ladies around him embroidered his handkerchiefs. When he raised his eyebrows at my laughter, I touched his hand to let him in on the scene I pictured.

He grinned when he saw my mental image of him. "The clothing is off by a decade, but you've got the rest of it about right."

Curious, I leaned forward. "How old are you, Asher?"

Before answering, he gave me a long, considering look. "I was born in 1868."

I quickly did the math. I'd known approximately how old he was based on what he'd told me, but knowing the exact number stunned me. I tried to process the information, but the hilarity of the entire situation struck me. My head dropped to the table as I collapsed in gales of laughter.

"Remy?" Asher sounded worried.

When I looked his way, he glanced around awkwardly at all the stares my outburst had drawn. That only made me laugh harder, and I couldn't answer him. When he appeared offended, I held up a hand as I tried to sober.

"What is so funny?"

Able to speak at last, I whispered, "You and me. Lucy warned me not to date you because you're a player. What would she say if she found out I was dating an older man?"

His eyes gleamed with some emotion I couldn't name. "And you? What do you think?"

I sobered entirely at his serious tone. "I won't say it's normal, but nothing about us is. I think I understand why I feel so comfortable with you when I've never fit in with people my own age."

My answer pleased him, and he slid his hand across the table to clasp mine. He spent the rest of lunch grilling me on my "favorites" while we pretended no one watched.

English continued in the same vein.

He quizzed me on any question that popped into his head, only now his questions were written on a piece of paper, while my answers appeared in my head. It grew easier for Asher to see inside my mind when my defenses were down, even without touching me. As long as I knew he listened, I could censor myself somewhat on the things I'd think about, though it wasn't foolproof by any means.

I found this out when he scrawled in his bold print, *Where do you see yourself in five years?*

It was a standard question on the college applications I'd filled out months ago when I could only dream of escaping Brooklyn. Instead of my standard response of graduating from a top university with degree in hand, an unbidden image of the two of us popped into my mind. In the mental vision, Asher had his arms wrapped around my waist, and we were obviously a couple. Horrified, I shut down the link between us and couldn't bring myself to look at him.

When I ignored his mental prods, he tapped his pen against his desk so insistently Mrs. Welles frowned at us. I lowered my guard and thought, *Cut it out! You're going to get us both in trouble.*

He tapped his paper again, and I read *Why you are embarrassed?*

Duh! You have to ask? I didn't plan on thinking that. It popped into my head.

He wrote again. *Ask me where I see myself in five years.*

There was a definite edge to my mental voice when I complied. *Fine. Where do you see yourself in five years?*

When he lifted his pen a long moment later, I stared at what he'd drawn. I thought it was supposed to be the two of us, holding hands. It could also have been an elephant grazing in the grasslands. I couldn't be sure because he was one of the worst artists I'd ever seen in my life. Looking up into his amused gaze, I realized he'd exposed this weakness on purpose.

I shook my head at him but didn't put my guard back up. When his pen tapped again, I smiled at what he'd written.

Trust me with your heart, Remy.

CHAPTER SEVENTEEN

*A*sher drove me home again after school. He pulled onto my street but didn't turn off the engine. Ben was waiting to give me a driving lesson, so I couldn't linger.

"So, I'll see you tomorrow?" I hoped it wasn't too obvious that I didn't want to leave him yet.

He grinned and handed me my book bag from the backseat. "Yes, if you survive your driving lesson. Be careful."

I protested with a laugh. "Hey, you haven't seen me drive. You don't know that I'm a bad driver."

"Yes, but I've seen the way you look at my car, and I've heard about your nickname."

Still laughing, I promised to be careful and reached for the door handle. He stopped me with a hand on my arm and I looked up to find his expression had turned somber.

"We've said it, but we haven't really *said* it. You and I— we're together. Not because of some Protector-Healer bond we have no control over, or any ability you may have to cure us. I care about you, and I think you care about me."

His tone sounded so emphatic, I didn't realize he wanted—no, needed—me to say something. When it occurred to me that he wanted my agreement, I nodded slowly. His square jaw unclenched as if he'd been nervous that my answer would differ from his.

In a calmer voice, he continued, "I'd like to take you out on Saturday. There's a place I think you'd like to see."

The idea of telling Ben about us had me grimacing.

"What's wrong?" he asked.

"I can't keep sneaking around. It's not fair to Ben. I'm not sure how this is going to go over."

Asher smiled. "I don't want to hide us. We have too many secrets as it is."

I promised to tell my father about us that night.

As I suspected, it didn't go well.

Ben had me drive out to the fort to practice three-point turns in the deserted parking lot in front of Paley Pavilion, a popular location for local events. Officially, Fort Rowden closed at sundown, but the gate was left open for guests at the hostel, campers, and those travelers with RVs enjoying a night on the town.

When I successfully completed parallel parking, three-point turns, and hand signals, Ben applauded me with a huge grin. He beamed with pride when he directed me to drive us home.

I decided to tell him now or never.

"Ben, I wanted to ask you something."

A quick glance at Ben in the passenger seat found him looking at me with a curious expression, probably because I hadn't asked for much since he'd brought me here. Hopefully, that would play in my favor.

"Sure. What's up?"

"Well, there's this boy . . ." Ben's expression turned cautious, and I hurried to get the rest of the words out. "I really like him, and we're kind of seeing each other. He wants to take me out on Saturday. On a date."

"Absolutely not," he said, his tone ringing with finality.

"You don't even intend to discuss this, do you?"

He folded his arms and glared at the windshield. "No."

For the first time since Ben had brought me to live with him, my temper flared at him. I drove out of the park, fuming. The moon had disappeared behind clouds, and the road appeared black with groupings of tall fir trees separating houses. Unlike in New York, streetlights were sparse, leaving long expanses of gloom on the road, like Morse code. Deer made a habit of grazing in front yards, which made me nervous when they could run out into the street at any time.

If my speed hadn't slowed to a crawl, I probably wouldn't have seen him in my rearview mirror. Dean. He stood in the shadows near the park entrance. The brakes screamed when I slammed on the pedal, bringing the car to a skidding halt. It took only an instant to unbuckle my seatbelt and climb out of the car, but he'd disappeared.

"Remy! What's wrong?" Ben opened his door and peered into the shadows.

Either I'd imagined seeing Dean or he'd managed to disappear into the trees in the park. Since Dean was in Brooklyn, I didn't want to worry Ben about my state of mind.

"Nothing. I thought I saw a deer in the road. I'm sorry if I scared you." Even I could hear how shaken I sounded.

"Want me to drive?" Ben offered.

At my nod, we switched seats and drove home in silence.

I waited until the front door closed behind us before I picked up the thread of our discussion. "Mind telling me why you're against me going on a date? It can't be the guy since you don't even know who it is."

Laura looked up with raised brows when I entered the living room on Ben's heels. Lucy was nowhere in sight.

Ben turned to me with a stiff expression as he stripped

off his coat and gloves. "Remy, we're not discussing this. It's too soon. Your mother died last week."

I froze in the act of removing my scarf and coat. "You think you have to remind me?"

He folded his arms over his chest. "Laura and I have been talking about this. We think you need to see a counselor. I don't think you're dealing with your grief."

"How would you know? You don't even know me."

His blue eyes hardened. "I know what I've seen. You haven't cried once. Not even at the funeral."

The rage I'd been holding in each time I saw how perfect his life had been here—without me—boiled to the surface like poison. "And you think you have the right to judge me for that, don't you? I've been here a month, and suddenly you know what's best for me. Who do you think you are?"

Laura stood and placed a cautionary hand against Ben's chest, but he ignored her. "I'm your father, Remy."

With a humorless laugh, I pulled off the sweater I wore over my tee and flung it at the couch. "You're not my father. If you were, you would *never* have left me in that hellhole with Anna, no matter what she told you."

Ben's voice stiffened with defensiveness. "I didn't know what was happening, Remy. I can't make up for that, but I'm doing my best."

The poison didn't just boil; it foamed and spilled over the edge. "How can you make up for it when you don't even know what happened? Oh, you think you know because of the abbreviated version you heard me tell the officers, but what do you really know? That Dean knocked me around a little from time to time?"

Laura stepped toward me now. "Remy, let's calm down before you two say something you'll regret. You have a right to be angry—"

"No offense, Laura, but do you know how many people have told me I have a right to be angry or sad or hurt? Usually when they want to shut me up. Ben wants me to talk to someone, so let's talk. I think you owe me." My gaze impaled Ben. "Do you have the courage to hear what I have to say?"

"I'll listen to whatever you have to tell me." The grief in his voice didn't stop me.

"Glad to hear it, *Dad*! Where to begin? How about we start with the first time Dean hit me when I was eleven? To be fair, it was an accident—he was punching Anna's face when I stepped between them—but that didn't stop him from hitting me a second time to teach me a lesson."

I couldn't stand still, pacing as I talked. "Apparently, I didn't learn the lesson well enough because he taught it to me over and over again for the next couple of years. It took eight broken bones and two concussions, but I finally got it. This?" I lifted my shirt and twisted to display the football-sized bruise that had turned my hip and lower back an ugly mix of blue, purple, and green. Laura's gasp sounded loud in the room as she glimpsed the injury for the first time. "This is nothing. Something this small happened when I merely looked at him the wrong way. You should see the lesson he taught me when I didn't get him his beer fast enough.

"My voice? All the guys seem to like it, but it didn't always sound like this. It was a parting gift from Dean."

My words came out harder now, with equal scorn for Dean the abuser and Ben the abandoner.

Laura touched her own neck, her eyes wide with horror. "The bruises on your neck?"

"I'm pretty sure he meant to kill me that last night. Who knows?"

She choked on a sob. Ben cried now, too, silent tears tracking down his cheeks. I couldn't make myself stop.

"You know, I didn't learn the lesson Dean meant to

teach me, but he taught me another entirely by accident. See, it was the tears Dean got off on. He liked hurting us and loved to make us cry. So, when I turned thirteen, I refused to shed even one more tear—my pathetic way of telling him to go to hell. Do you want to know how he retaliated?"

Within a few steps, I stood in front of Ben and shoved my exposed arm under his nose. "You saw it at the hospital. The officers and doctor guessed what it was from. Did you? A year of Dean putting out his cigarette in the same spot, burn on top of burn on top of burn on top of . . . You get the picture, right? He was pissed because he couldn't make me cry. And Anna watched the whole thing and did nothing. *Nothing!*" I shoved my face in his and my shout echoed off the walls. "Do you want to tell me again how I should cry for her?"

Ben's hand came up in a sudden movement. Years of habit had me flinching away from him and raising my arms to cover my face from the oncoming blow.

Everything stopped. My shouting. Laura's sobbing. My heavy breathing and Ben's filled the quiet room.

"Remy, sweetheart. It's okay. You're safe."

Laura's gentle voice finally reached me through the nightmare I'd fallen into. My arms lowered and revealed Ben's destroyed expression. He'd been reaching out to comfort me, and now he looked horrified, as if he really had struck me. A switch flipped inside me, and shame replaced anger. I felt sick when he took several swift steps away from me and put his hands behind his back to appear less threatening. As if Ben would ever threaten me. He was nothing like Dean.

Instinct had me wrapping my arms around his waist to comfort him, healing his skipping heartbeat out of habit and penance. "I'm sorry, Ben. I'm sorry, I'm sorry, I'm sorry." His heartbeat sounded strong beneath my cheek, and he nearly cut off my air supply when he returned my hug, carefully avoiding the bruise on my back. "I didn't mean it. I'm sorry."

His breath ruffled my hair. "You meant every word. I swear to you, Remy, I'd never hurt you."

I had to get away from him and the intense emotions in the room. Ben let me go with reluctance when I pushed against his chest. "I trust you not to hit me, but you could hurt me."

When he started to protest, I held up a hand. "I'm not Lucy. I didn't grow up in your safe home with a kiss good night and a story before you tucked me in bed. I love Lucy, but sometimes I hate you for loving her more. Because you can't tell me that there is anything on this earth that could take her from you. And you let me go."

Ben swallowed and said nothing.

A headache threatened, and I rubbed my forehead. "I'm sorry, Ben. I'm not trying to hurt you, but I've been taking care of myself for a long time. I learned how to survive without you, and I can't change that to make you feel better."

"What do you want from me?"

"I want . . . I want what you offered before. Be my friend. No counselors and no telling me you know what's best for me. Trust me."

Ben stepped forward. "I can do that, but we need something from you, too. For good or bad, I'm your guardian now. There have to be rules."

"That's fair." In an attempt to put things back on normal, even ground, I smiled, though it felt plastic. "What are your rules on dating?"

It was Laura who stepped forward this time, taking Ben's hand. "Dating is a privilege. If your grades suffer, the privilege is revoked. Ten o'clock curfew on school days and midnight on weekends. You tell us where you'll be at all times, and we meet the boy first."

Her no-nonsense speech sounded rehearsed, as if she'd told the same thing to Lucy. "I can live with that. Asher Blackwell will be here in the morning to pick me up for school. You can meet him then."

Ben's eyes lit with recognition at Asher's name, and he nodded. "Good."

We eyed each other across the room, having come to an understanding. Spent, I turned to leave the room. Laura touched my arm when I passed, and I squeezed her hand in apology. I'd never meant for things to go so far tonight and wanted to crawl into a hole to hide. I ran up the stairs and was at the top of the landing when Ben called my name. He stood at the bottom of the staircase with one hand on the railing.

"You were wrong about one thing. I don't love Lucy more."

I didn't know how to respond to the honesty in his voice. I nodded, turning toward my room, and he said to my back, "'Night, Remy."

CHAPTER EIGHTEEN

*S*leep eluded me.

I couldn't believe how I'd unloaded on Ben. The rage I'd felt had taken me by storm, and I'd meant to draw blood with my words. That I could treat someone I loved like that shocked me, and I could hardly look at myself in the mirror the next morning.

A knock sounded on the front door as I left my room. From the top of the stairs I heard Ben open the door and greet Asher in a cordial tone. "Hey, Asher. Come on in. Remy's not down yet."

Asher responded in the charming, proper voice he reserved for adults. "Mr. O'Malley. It's good to see you again."

Despite everything I knew about the evils of eavesdropping, I couldn't face Ben yet and couldn't bring myself to walk away. I sank down on the top stair and listened as they moved into the living room. From the shifting of fabric, it sounded like Ben had invited Asher to sit. Their familiarity reminded me of something Lucy had said my first day of school, something about Asher and Gabe buying sailboats from Ben's company that they'd later wrecked while racing. Ben wouldn't know they were immortal. Perhaps he thought he had reason to worry if I dated Asher.

Ben cleared his throat. "Remy mentioned last night that the two of you are seeing each other."

Asher picked up on something in Ben's voice. "And you're not happy about that?"

"To be honest, I'm worried. Your behavior has proved a little reckless in the past, and I'm not sure that's what she needs right now."

"Mr. O'Malley, Remy's not like anyone I've ever met. I won't let anyone hurt her, including me." A fervent promise infused his words that I recognized from all the times he'd sworn he would protect me.

My father sounded surprised. "You care about her."

It wasn't a question, but Asher answered anyway. "Yes, sir."

"Has she told you anything about her past?" Ben's palpable tension had me clasping my knees to my chest to calm myself.

Now, Asher sounded cautious. "Some. She's grieving for her mother right now. She blames herself for Anna's death."

"She told you that?" Again, the surprise in Ben's voice mingled with hurt, and I knew it was because I hadn't shared that information with him myself. He didn't understand how hard it was for me to talk to him, how my emotions for him were a tangle of newfound love and old, sour disappointment. I used to have fantasies about making Ben sorry he'd abandoned me. An amazing thing had happened since I grew to care for him. When I hurt him, it hurt me, too. My guard was already lowered, and I had a feeling Asher had been listening to me since entering the house. My head rested on my knees, and I whispered a thought to him that I hadn't been able to say aloud last night.

Asher, please make him understand that I love him.

"Yes, sir. When you brought her here, you made her feel safe for the first time in her life. Your family means the world to her, but she feels guilty for choosing you over protecting her mother."

Ben reacted to Asher's solemn assertion the way I always did—he believed him without question. "She should never have been put in that position in the first place. I should've been there."

Asher said again, "Yes, sir," and I knew he included himself in that statement.

A long moment later, Ben said, "Thanks for not lying, Asher. People have said that I couldn't have known what was happening to her, and I've even said the same thing myself. But damn it, I should've known!" I strained to hear his low words when he added in a quiet tone, "She's my daughter. I should've known."

There was another long silence before Ben spoke. "Remy says you want to take her out this weekend. I'd like it if you'd have dinner with our family tomorrow night so we can get to know you a little better. Remy can make her own choice, but I'd feel better if you agreed."

It sounded like they were getting to their feet, and I did the same.

"That sounds fair, Mr. O'Malley."

"Let me check to see if Remy is ready to go."

Ben's footsteps grew louder, and he came into sight as he neared the staircase. He paused and turned when Asher called, "Sir? She loves you, and you know how loyal she is to the people she loves. The two of you will figure it out."

Scrambling to get out of sight on the landing, I almost missed the shattered expression on Ben's face.

When Asher joined me in his car, I leaned over to brush a kiss on his smooth shaved cheek. The frozen expression on his face when I pulled away said I'd stunned him into silence. He remained quiet so long I worried I'd made a mistake and began to think of ways to laugh off the awkward moment, while my cheeks burned with humiliation.

My mind spun through the dreary possibilities until Asher stopped it cold with the simple act of running his fingers along my cheek in a tender gesture. His eyes warmed with affection when he smiled down at me. "You're welcome."

Of course, he knew my kiss had been one of thanks for the way he'd talked with my father. With a small smile of apology, I raised my defenses to reclaim some privacy.

"You didn't sleep well," he said, touching the black smudge under my eye.

"No. Rough night. I lost my temper with Ben and nearly wore out my welcome."

He shook his head. "Not possible. How can you not know that your dad loves you?"

This time the distance I put between us was physical as well as mental. "You weren't there last night." My tone made it clear I didn't intend to replay the scene for him, either.

Instead of backing off, Asher tucked my hand in his while he pulled the car out of the driveway. "You're too hard on yourself. Maybe your dad needed to hear the things you said, as much as you needed to say them."

I doubted Ben would think the same thing.

Dinner with Asher and my family was not nearly as painful as I thought it would be. I spent two days stressing over it and within ten minutes of his arrival, Asher somehow managed to bridge the uncomfortable gap that had sprung up between Ben, Laura, and me. Lucy seemed oblivious to the whole thing since she'd been out the night of the fight. She was becoming pro-Asher since he'd eaten lunch at our table the last two days. He'd put a lot of effort into charming her, and it had worked.

Through dinner, he did the same charm-boy act, until I realized it wasn't an act at all. Asher shone when a situation demanded the most proper kind of behavior, whether opening a door for me or carrying my bag whenever we walked together. When he held my chair at the table, he earned an approving glance from Laura. During dinner, he impressed Ben with his knowledge about current events — he'd lived in more countries during his lifetime than I could count on both hands. When I mentioned that I'd heard Asher speak fluently in multiple languages (leaving out that he'd been cursing at the time), he sent me a small smile that promised retribution.

After dinner, I helped Lucy clear the dishes, while Ben and Laura took Asher into the living room. Even without prior dating experience, I could tell this was the moment when Ben would give his blessing—or not—for Asher to take me out. Lucy, being the best sister in the whole world, ducked out on dish duty to eavesdrop on them. According to her, she simply looked out for my best interests. After eavesdropping the morning before, I felt too embarrassed to do it again and remained in the kitchen scraping dishes.

A few minutes later, Lucy returned, shaking her head and wearing a wide grin.

"What? What's going on?"

She took a stack of plates from me. "He told Dad where he's planning to take you tomorrow. I hate to admit when I'm wrong, but I think this guy has a serious thing for you. Go forth and date a Blackwell with my blessing, Sis."

"Seriously? Just like that?"

She flicked dirty dishwater at me. "What can I say? The guy knows you."

Curiosity set in, and I asked, "Where is—"

Laura bumped the kitchen door open with her hip. "Remy, Asher's waiting to say good night. He's outside

with Ben. You better go save him before your father bores
him to death with the facts about his car."

Ben could tire even the most enthusiastic car aficionado
when he got on a roll. I wiped my wet hands on a towel
and hurried past Laura. It was worse than she'd predicted.
Asher stood alone in the driveway, and his Audi had disappeared.

He grinned when I joined him. I hadn't paused to
throw on my coat, and he wrapped his jacket around my
shoulders. He tugged the lapels together under my chin
and used them to pull me closer to his warmth, winding
his arms around my waist.

"What happened? Did Ben carjack you?"

Asher laughed one of his rare open laughs that I felt all
the way down to my toes. "He's taking it for a spin around
the block."

I pressed my nose to his chest and the wool of his
sweater felt rough against my cheek. "Was it blackmail or
bribery?"

His chin rested on the top of my head, and his breath
ruffled my hair. "Neither. He had that same look on his
face you did when you saw my car for the first time. I had
to convince him to take it, although, if I'm truthful, it
didn't take a lot of persuasion on my part."

I imagined the look Ben must have had on his face spying Asher's sleek performance car—a kid in a candy
shop—and laughed, tilting my head back to see Asher's
face. He smiled down at me and I blurted out, "I like
you."

His smile widened and, in a lighthearted tone, he said,
"I like you, too."

It seemed very important all of sudden that he not misunderstand me. Maybe it was my fight with Ben or thinking I'd seen Dean a couple of nights ago, but I wanted him
to know I cared. I shook him, as much as I could consid-

ering his size and strength, but it got his attention. "No, Asher. I mean, I really like you. Apart from all the Protector-Healer mess and all the rest of what's happened and what could happen, I like you."

He didn't react in any of the ways I'd expected. A ferocious frown darkened his face as he looked down at me. My heart dropped to my stomach because clearly he didn't feel even a tenth of what I felt. I stared at the design on his sweater until he squeezed me lightly. "Stop it, Remy. You know I feel the same way. When did you see Dean?"

I gasped and tried to pull away, but his arms had become steel bands. "You were listening? My guard is up, damn it!"

Asher shrugged. "I told you, I can't control when it happens."

He didn't seem upset about it, and I scowled. My bad mood didn't make a dent in his arrogance. He'd launched into full Protector-mode.

"Dean?" he demanded.

He looked like he could stand there all night holding me hostage until I answered him. Disgruntled, I said. "I thought I saw him out at Fort Rowden a couple of nights ago." I explained about stopping the car and finding no trace of Dean. "He's in New York. There's no reason for him to come here, especially with the restraining order Ben took out against him. My eyes had to be playing tricks on me. That's why I didn't mention it."

Asher's expression had grown blacker as I spoke of the incident, but he looked thoughtful when I mentioned New York. Ben saved me from answering more questions when he whipped Asher's Audi S6 around the corner and into the driveway with a squeal of the brakes. He slid out of the driver's seat with his face flushed with boyish delight. I'd known driving Asher's car would be exhilarating, and Ben confirmed my prediction when I rushed forward to meet him.

"Well?" My voice sounded breathless with anticipation.

Ben could barely contain himself and threw an arm around me. His heart skipped, and my body healed him the way it always did when he touched me. I noticed Asher toss a curious look at Ben. "Handles like a dream. A 5.2 liter V10 with 435 horsepower. Be still, my heart! I hear it goes from zero to sixty in five seconds. I'd love to get it out on a track." His eyes took on a speculative gleam.

Asher grinned. "Name the day and time."

Ben shook his head, looking tempted. "Laura would kill me. I may have to get one when I retire, though. Thanks for letting me drive it." He tossed the keys to Asher and realized his arm rested around me. He dropped it and shook Asher's hand. "You have my blessing to take Remy out tomorrow. Just don't let this one drive. She has a tendency to put the pedal to the metal."

The last was said with a knowing look in my direction. I stuck my tongue out at him, and he floated toward the house on ten feet of air. I turned back to Asher. "See you in the morning?"

He tapped a finger on my nose. "See you in the morning. Wear something warm."

Something about the look in his eyes told me we weren't finished talking about Dean, but thinking about a full day spent in Asher's company, I suddenly didn't care.

CHAPTER NINETEEN

*H*e picked me up early the next morning and drove straight to the harbor. We quizzed each other on everything from my plans for college to my favorite songs. He didn't tease me when I admitted I had a perfect GPA and had applied to a few pre-med programs. I wanted to be a doctor—my abilities made it a natural career choice. In turn, I asked him why he and Lottie attended high school, while Gabe acted as guardian.

"It helps us to fit in better. Gabe refuses to go to high school again. He says four times was enough. Acting as our guardian stops people from questioning us about our parents."

"How did Blackwell Falls end up being named after you?"

"After the war, none of us wanted to go back to England. We came here instead, looking for a new beginning. When we arrived, there was nothing but trees and beaches for miles. We loved how peaceful and secluded it was. Then, Gabe opened a mill to keep busy, and people came from all over to work for us. Before we knew it, we were a town, and Gabe was mayor. You should see his portrait in town hall."

"You make it sound easy."

He smiled. "No. But money moves mountains, and we have it to burn."

My own smile was wry. I'd guessed as much. "Didn't people notice when you didn't age?"

Asher sighed. "We leave before that becomes a problem."

Lucy had said that this group of Blackwells was the latest heirs. "How many times have you returned here?"

"A few. We have to wait a couple of decades between visits. That way, we can return as the long-lost cousins, brothers, sons, etc. of the last Blackwells. We will the house to ourselves each time we leave."

I struggled to understand the reality the Blackwells lived with. "Why return here? What's so special about this place?"

"At first, it was a place to escape to. To forget the past and deal with who we'd become. Then, it became home. One of them, anyway." He shot me a sweet smile. "And now, there's you."

Before I could respond, he pulled the Audi into a line of cars waiting to drive onto the Cooper Island ferry. I didn't know a lot about the island, except that it had salt marshes and another of Maine's famous lighthouses. As we waited, he switched the discussion back to me and asked about my favorite books.

"That easy. *Gray's Anatomy.*" I laughed at the doubt in his expression. I couldn't blame him considering how dry the book was. "No, really. I have to picture people's injuries to heal them. I would've been lost without it."

Fascinated, Asher turned in his seat to face me. "You have to picture injuries to heal them?"

"Yes. How do the other Healers do it?" I asked.

"I'm not sure. I was never curious enough to ask before you." His answer made me squirm a little in my seat. It warmed me to know he felt as curious about me as I did about him.

"Is something wrong with your dad?" he asked.

"What do you mean?" I asked.

"Last night, I thought I sensed you healing him."

That's why he'd shot Ben that odd look. I nodded. "He has some kind of heart condition. It doesn't seem to give him any problems, but it keeps coming back. It kind of bothers me, actually. That's never happened before."

Asher's thoughtful silence ended when we were at last given the go-ahead to drive onto the ferry. As soon as we parked, we climbed out of the car and headed up to the passenger deck. The engines rumbled and the ferry motored along, leaving the Falls behind. I followed Asher to the front of the boat and onto a deserted U-shaped deck with green hand rails that resembled a forked tongue. A freezing wind nearly knocked me over as Asher informed me that the deck was fondly referred to as a "pickle fork" and not a "forked tongue."

He grinned, mischievously, when I glanced up. "You know, Asher, you seem to be in my head a lot these days."

His laugh sounded freer than usual. "That sounds like the beginning of a really bad pickup line. Are you going to tell me that I must be tired because I've been running in your dreams all night?"

He leaned against the railing with casual grace, while the wind tossed his long hair into a gorgeous tangle of chocolate waves. It wasn't fair that he could look so delicious standing in the elements, while I bore a strong likeness to a Q-tip—tall and skinny with a mass of curls frizzing out in the wind.

Asher reached into his coat pocket, whipped out a baseball cap, and waved it at me. With a smirk, he held it out. I elbowed him in the ribs when I took it from him and pulled it on, twisting my hair up under it. "Keep it up, buddy. I'm going to start thinking about how I'd like to throw you over the side."

With a tug on the bill of the cap, he merely laughed. "I can't help it, beautiful. You don't seem to be offering up any roadblocks today."

He was right, I realized, with surprise. My walls had been down all morning.

He grimaced. "I shouldn't have said anything. You're going to block me out now, aren't you?"

I considered him for a long time before shaking my head. It was time to take a chance, and if the shy, pleased light in his eyes brought on the butterflies, I could deal. Besides, his ability to read my mind could be a defense against danger.

"Will you be okay?" I asked. "It doesn't seem to bother you as much when we touch."

He looked surprised, as if he'd realized his own walls were down. "You know, you're right. I haven't been in pain at all this morning. Maybe I'm getting used to you."

I could only hope that was true. I wanted him to feel more than pain when we touched.

A half hour later, the ferry docked at the small harbor on Cooper Island. Few people lived on the three-mile-wide landmass, but some summer homes clung to the rocky cliffs. Asher drove off the boat and within minutes we'd parked in front of a tiny café, the lone business in sight. He swung my hand between us, his touch a test—one that obviously didn't pain him. He glanced at me out of the corner of his eye with barely suppressed excitement and nodded to the café.

"This is my surprise?" The dilapidated diner had seen better days. The faded white building needed a serious paint job. Better yet, someone needed to demolish it. It leaned to one side as if a storm had depleted its ability to stand upright.

Asher grinned at my obvious disbelief and shook his head. "I know it doesn't look like much. Your first surprise is waiting inside."

"First surprise? There's more than one?" Surprises had been few and far between in my life, and most of those had been bad. "You do realize it's not my birthday?"

"Something tells me you've missed out on a lot of presents. I hope you're hungry. Come on." An aging man stood behind the counter when we entered the café, and I was surprised to find the four tables in the space-challenged room all occupied. An incredible aroma of spices and . . . cheese? . . . filled the air. Asher waited for me to grasp what the surprise was, but I was at a loss until I spotted a sign above the counter on which the chef boasted they had the WORLD'S BEST MAC AND CHEESE. Asher's face blossomed into a pleased grin at my laugh.

"Seriously? World's best?" My teasing tone had a hint of skepticism.

"We won't know until you try it." Asher paid for a large to-go carton of the infamous pasta, and we headed back to the car. When I made a swipe for it, he proceeded to hold the carton out of reach. "Patience, woman! There's another surprise to be had."

He drove away from the harbor to the opposite side of the island that faced the open ocean. We arrived at a small cottage—a real one this time, unlike Ben's—and Asher shut off the engine. Reaching behind my seat, he retrieved a closed box.

"What's this?"

"Your second surprise. No peeking."

I trailed after him into the cottage. It was maybe four hundred square feet. The kitchen and living area were one room. I could see a bathroom and a bedroom to one side. Cramped and tiny, the space had room for a few pieces of furniture and little else. "What is this place, Asher?"

"My home," he answered, with simple satisfaction.

"This is yours?"

"I built it a long time ago, so I'd have a place to go to be alone."

He didn't say it, but I knew I was the first person he'd brought here. He set the box on the counter and built a fire in an old-fashioned wood-burning stove. I felt him studying me as I wandered around the room. Asher didn't have a TV, but shelves of books lined one wall. I trailed a hand along the back of the overstuffed couch, until I came to the end table with its black-and-white photo of Lottie wearing her usual bobbed hair, red lipstick, and a flapper dress. Another reality to face. The Blackwells had lived during the Roarin' Twenties.

I looked up at Asher. "I love it."

Something in him relaxed, and he smiled. "I'm glad."

He began unpacking the box: an espresso machine, milk, cocoa, and a packet of coffee beans.

"You're making me a café mocha?" I asked, stunned.

He mock-scowled at me and crossed his arms. "Not just any café mocha. I'll have you know I flew this particular blend in from Italy. This is going to be *the* café mocha of your life."

I giggled at the idea of him working the espresso machine in an apron like my neighborhood barista.

One eyebrow rose at me as if in disappointment. "Your mockery wounds me. I have half a mind to deny you your second surprise."

When I stepped up to him, his eyes lit with amusement. The look faded when I gave in to the impulse I'd had since the first day we'd met and ran my fingers along the scar that slashed through one of his brows. Smooth skin warmed me where we touched, and the butterflies I'd feared began to flit about my insides. Intent eyes watched me, hardly breathing, or even blinking when I stood on my tiptoes to kiss the scar. Strong arms wound around my waist holding me off balance, poised on my toes, when I would have pulled away. His eyes flashed with lightning, like the green sparks that lit between us, as his face lowered to mine, his breath touching my lips.

The fire popped behind him, and it felt like coming out of a powerful healing. Asher released me with a shaken look. Steady on my feet now, I felt more off balance than ever.

Asher loved pasta. Apparently, he'd thought me crazy to hold mac and cheese among my favorite foods, but he ate his words when I took my first bite and tapped his hand. I couldn't tell which of us enjoyed it more, but we both agreed the café had earned their "World's Best" title. The café mocha was lost on him, though, and I scoffed at him, "Tea lover."

After the impromptu living room picnic, I helped him wash the dishes at the sink, our hips bumping as he washed and I dried.

He tweaked my nose with soapy fingers. "Caffeine addict."

My lips twitched as I ducked away. "You know, you may have ruined me for all future surprises. I don't think anyone will ever be able to top today. The 'World's Best' mac and cheese and a homemade café mocha. Impressive, Blackwell."

"The day's not over, O'Malley. I have one more surprise."

My last surprise turned out to be a walk to the top of the island's lighthouse. A thrill sped down my spine when I stepped outside onto the deck and looked down to the ocean crashing against the rocks below. "Asher, you've got to see this!" I breathed.

He didn't join me, and I turned in surprise to find him

several feet behind me away from the rail that enclosed the deck. "Asher?"

A wry smile lifted one side of his full lips. "Did I happen to mention I hate heights?" He gestured to the scar above his eyebrow and tucked both hands in his coat pockets. I rested against the rail facing him, and he grimaced. "Do you have to do that?"

"It's completely safe. There's no way I could go over the side." I turned and leaned forward to take in the view. Two large hands suddenly grasped my hips, and I was lifted off my feet and yanked back several feet from the edge into Asher's chest. Both of his arms wrapped around my waist to keep me still, creating a warm, comfortable embrace I didn't want to escape from. His chin rested on the top of my head. A cold breeze buffeted us, but his body sheltered me.

"You're right. The view is better from back here."

I'd given him his cap back and felt his smile in my loose hair. "Sorry. My heart nearly stopped when you leaned over the edge."

"Did you fall before? Is that how you got the scar?"

"Hmm . . . Right after the War."

He sounded hesitant, and I wondered how he'd been hurt. "I thought the Protectors were invincible, outside our unusual circumstances."

"No. Not invincible. We can get hurt and even die, but it takes a lot of effort."

His tone sounded thoughtful, and I frowned. "That makes it sound like you've tried."

I twisted in his embrace when he remained silent. His expression was carefully blank. "Asher, what happened?"

He tucked a wayward piece of hair behind my ear. "It was a long time ago, Remy."

The finality of his tone made it clear he didn't want to

talk about it, and it hurt more than I would have expected. He wanted everything from me but wasn't willing to give the same. Taking a step back, I raised my mental walls.

Asher reached for me. "Remy, don't. It's not what you think."

I gave a nonchalant wave. "Don't stress about it." Asher wasn't fooled by my dismissive tone.

"I hurt your feelings, and I didn't mean to. I'm ashamed of what happened and worried you'll think less of me when you know the truth. It was a gut reaction."

"You don't have to explain. I really do get it." I aimed a tight smile in his direction.

"No, I don't think you do." The soft words whispered into my ear as he turned me to face him again. Embarrassed that my feelings had been so transparent, I stared down at my feet. "You let me in your head and in your memories, but your walls are up higher than ever. You're still guarding your heart, and I'm terrified I'm going to say the wrong thing, do the wrong thing, and you'll shut me out entirely. Because eventually you're going to realize a Healer shouldn't trust a Protector." He gave me a slight shake, and I raised startled eyes to his stare. "I'd given up on wanting more. You make me want more."

Not one word formed on my paralyzed lips. None. When I needed it most, my brain shut down. Asher's intensity stopped my breath, and I gazed back like the mute, mindless idiot I'd suddenly become. Hurt shadowed his face when I didn't respond. He turned me loose, and the moment ended.

His expression closed, and he said with a distant civility, "You mind if we head back now? I promised your father I'd get you home before it got too late."

The short, silent drive to the ferry dock turned out to be the longest ride of my life. Even if I'd been able to speak, Asher had shut down. It seemed to be a running theme with me to hurt the people I cared about most. He drove the Audi into the hollow belly of the ferry, set the parking brake, and left the car, striding away without another look. I trailed after him between the rows of mostly empty vehicles to the opposite end of the boat facing the retreating island. He stood framed against the cavernous opening with his hands on his hips and only a long net between him and the frothing waves. He muttered to himself in yet another unfamiliar language. He heard me approaching and whipped around.

"Remy, I'm sorry." He sounded frustrated. "I shouldn't have said anything. I knew you didn't feel the same way, but I—"

Words still wouldn't form, so I dropped my guard and hoped he'd find what he sought in my mind. When my walls lowered, he stopped speaking with a bleak expression that said it all. My feelings were a mystery to him, one he couldn't solve by reaching into my head.

He didn't back away when I stepped close and tangled my hands in the collar of his coat, using the material to tug his face down to mine. Some of the darkness left his tortured eyes to be replaced by surprise when he heard my intent seconds before I pressed my lips to his.

Asher's response was slow in coming, and I knew I'd shocked him. When I pulled away, his hands spread across my back to press me close. Against my cheek, he whispered, "Don't go."

The familiar plea loosened the knot of fear inside me. I wasn't going anywhere because there was nowhere in the world I'd rather be than with him.

Asher's arms tightened around me and his guard dropped. "You're everything to me," he said.

I feel the same, Asher.

The words popped into my head, and I knew they were true. I'd tried not to care about him, but it had been a futile effort. I remembered him telling me that the freckle at the right-hand corner of my mouth fascinated him, how that hidden kiss taunted him. My lips curved in a smile when he kissed that spot.

Neither of us was prepared for the crippling pain when my body began to heal his.

CHAPTER TWENTY

*A*n electric current of energy exploded between us. It reminded me of the night I'd nearly drowned and he'd used his power on me, stretching the tendrils of his energy throughout my limbs, weakening me while he grew stronger. Only this time my energy took over his body, and I couldn't pull away. Against my will, my body worked to heal another. Except Asher wasn't sick or injured. He was immortal.

Oh, Remy, you have the power to make them mortal again.

A memory of Anna's voice played through my mind, and I realized what was happening. I had no way of knowing if the cure meant instant death for him. I tried to pull away and sensed him doing the same, but we both failed. I'd lost control of my power and put Asher in danger. Somehow I needed to break the connection between us, to force my body to stop its course before it killed him. An idea formed, born out of desperation. If I could picture bones mending, then maybe . . .

Asher knew what I would do before the thought fully formed. He fought back, trying to put his guard up in a desperate attempt to protect me. "Remy, no!"

With a silent lament for the pain to come, I gathered the heat and the energy and pictured a perfect, healthy rib *snapping* in a clean break. We stumbled away from each other as my body released him, and green sparks sizzled from my skin to his.

"Remy!" The panic in his voice cut through the buzzing in my ears.

Our walls went up, and I hunched over to try to inhale a breath that didn't feel like it shredded my insides. Asher kept his distance, but his eyes burned with the ferocious desire to protect. When he stepped toward me, I knew he was willing to chance getting killed to help me.

"No! Stay back!"

He froze as if my frantic words sliced into him. In a softer tone, I explained between gasps. "Asher, it's me. My powers took over and started to work on you. Just give me a minute, and keep your guard up."

Closing my eyes, I concentrated on healing the rib I'd snapped. Nothing happened. I'd never caused an injury to myself like this, but it seemed I'd shorted out my ability to heal myself. Gasping in pain, I focused on Asher, while taking small, shallow breaths.

Worried eyes met mine, and his hands formed fists at his sides. "What happened?"

"You don't know? You didn't hear my thoughts?"

"No."

"It's true, Asher, what Anna said. I think my body tried to cure you."

He frowned. "Are you okay?"

Air flowed less freely with each passing second, and my chest hurt like hell. Something was wrong. It hadn't felt like this when my ribs had broken before. My face must have revealed my rising alarm because Asher stepped forward, ignoring my raised hand.

His deep voice sounded deadly calm. "Remy? I'm going to touch you. Our guard is up so we should be okay. The boat is docking, and I need to get you back to the car before people start asking questions. Can you walk?"

Nothing could have made me move at that moment but fear of discovery. We had to go, and I couldn't make it to the car on my own. I gave a brief nod, and he slid his arm around me to offer support. When my feet wouldn't go any farther, Asher picked me up and carried me the last ten feet. Somehow he managed to open the car door without putting me down and laid me across the backseat. I heard the car starting and Asher's curse when he had to wait on the cars in front of him to disembark.

Then the pain swept me away until the car stopped and Asher's face appeared upside-down above mine. He leaned in the door opening behind me, placed his head on my chest, and listened for a moment before pulling back. "Remy, do you trust me?"

My answer came out on a wheeze. "Yes."

"I think you punctured a lung when you broke your rib, and your lung is filling with fluid. I need you to let me help you." In a steady voice, he instructed me to lower my defenses, and I shook my head. "Trust me."

His solemn eyes promised everything would be okay. I let my guard down.

"Good. You're going to feel my energy coming at you, filling you, but don't panic. I want you to use it to heal yourself the same way you'd use your own. Do you understand?"

I nodded and wheezed, feeling cold. Asher's mouth tightened into a white line, and he placed a warm palm on my forehead. The heat comforted me, and my eyes closed to concentrate on it, but Asher's stern voice wouldn't let me be.

"Remy, focus."

A momentary blast of intense heat hit me before his energy unfurled and stretched through my body. I tried to remember what to focus on, but my chest hurt. *Right, my chest.* I gathered his energy as if it was my own, and the *humming* jump-started. His power felt intoxicating, different and exotic. This time, when I scanned my body, I discovered my left lung had been punctured by my broken rib. Able to picture the injury now, I used Asher's energy to heal the wound. The bone reset with a sickening *crunch,* and the hole in my lung mended. Slowly, I imagined the pressure on my lung dissipating and the organ expanding within my chest. Considering the extent of the injury, I'd never healed an injury so fast and knew I had Asher's power to thank for it.

Long minutes later, I took a soothing breath, and it flowed with ease.

Asher's hand fell away from my forehead, and I felt his sigh of relief when he rested his forehead on my shoulder, his energy fading from me. Tired and feverish, I noticed that an upside-down Asher looked as beautiful as a right-side-up one.

He ran his fingers through his tangled hair and gave me a weak smile. "Now, you're just giddy. I can't tell you how good it is to hear your thoughts again. You kind of disappeared there for a minute."

You saved my life. Thank you.

Asher's voice dropped to a hoarse whisper, and his eyes were fierce. "What are we doing? We have no idea what we're playing at. We could've killed each other. You nearly killed yourself to protect me!"

I grimaced at the memory. "That wasn't really my intention. My body kind of took over, and it seemed the best thing to do was distract it. This keeps getting better, you know? Apparently, I have a new ability to wreak havoc, in addition to healing its aftermath. Yea, me!" My weak attempt at humor fell flat, and Asher didn't lose his freaked-out expression. "Why am I so hot? My skin feels like it's on fire."

Gentle fingers brushed across my cheek, and for once, his skin didn't feel warmer than mine. "It's a side effect of tapping into my power to heal yourself. It'll fade in a little while. Can you sit up? I need to get us back on the road."

With his help, I moved to the front passenger seat. My injuries were completely healed, but the long day had drained me. My head turned as if drawn by magnetic force to watch Asher's profile in the shadowed sunlight as he drove.

"What was that?" I asked. "What did you do?"

His distant expression reminded me of when we'd first met. "What I'm supposed to. Helped you use my energy to heal yourself."

My mother had said that was how it worked. Before the War. "But how? I thought you had to fight not to attack me?"

"Well, that's not really a problem now, is it? Not when you've shorted out your power trying to save me." A pulse beat in his temple, and his voice was laced with tension.

"It wasn't your fault, Asher."

He didn't show any sign of having heard me, but I knew he listened.

"This one was all me. I lost control. Something happened—I don't know . . . I did what I had to."

His jaw worked, and his hands tightened on the steering wheel, the knuckles turning white. "I didn't think. I saw you hurt and reacted. Your guard was down. What if I hadn't been able to control myself? I could've killed you."

I didn't have to read his mind to know where this would end. No matter what I'd said, he blamed himself for what I'd done to protect him. He retreated from me to keep me safe. "I think I proved that I can protect myself."

Asher shot a piercing look my way. "Why is it that every time you protect yourself, you end up hurt or almost dying?" he asked.

His anger surprised me. "You're mad at me? Because I saved you?"

"You could've killed yourself to protect me, Remy!" Asher had never yelled at me, and it took me aback.

"So?"

My stubborn answer enraged him further. "So?" he repeated. I was glad when he switched to another language because I had a feeling he wasn't saying anything I'd want to hear. He shot me a frustrated glance. "How can you possibly think I'd want you to sacrifice yourself to save me? As if there wasn't enough danger, now I have to worry you'll take a bullet for me."

My arms crossed as his anger ignited my own. "As if, you jerk. You can take your own stupid bullet."

"That's all I'm asking. Promise me you won't do that again. Swear it, Remy."

I was frustrated, and my arms uncrossed. I had no idea what my body would have done to him today if I hadn't interfered. Hell, I didn't even know why my body had chosen today to go on the blink. What if I'd killed him? I wouldn't be able to live with myself.

"I can't promise you that." If it came down to it, I'd break every bone in my body before I caused him harm. "What about you? Today, I was the dangerous one. We don't know what would've happened if I hadn't stopped myself. Will you promise to defend yourself the next time I lose control?"

"No!" He sounded as horrified as I did at the prospect of hurting him.

At a stalemate, we stared out the windshield until he reached into his coat pocket and tossed an object into my lap: his cell phone.

"Call Ben. Tell him we'll be back in Blackwell Falls in thirty minutes so he doesn't worry, and let him know I'm taking you to dinner. I need to show you something."

His commanding tone allowed no room for argument. Normally, this irritated me, but he'd piqued my curiosity. Ben had no problem with Asher taking me to dinner if I arrived home by curfew. His happy tone as he asked about my surprises reminded me that today had started off perfectly. Now, Asher took the cell back from me in angry silence. I refused to apologize for protecting him.

He drove through town and parked at the cliff near where we'd had the bonfire a lifetime ago. For once, he didn't open my car door but waited for me to follow him down the path to the waterfall. It had grown progressively colder as the sun began its descent in the sky, and I trailed after him through the deserted wilderness, feeling hesitant as shadows claimed the last of the light.

No longer frozen, the waterfall tumbled into a creek that had morphed into a small pond. Asher stopped when he reached a small incline by the waterfall, picked me up with an arm around my waist, and shot up the small slope in a dizzying blur of movement until we stood on the hill above the water. I was dropped back on my feet next to a bench made of the rough, angular pieces of a broken rock.

Asher's open demonstration of speed and strength shocked me. I understood why the Protectors had won the War: The Healers would never have seen them coming.

Striding several steps away in the space of a heartbeat, Asher watched me and listened to my thoughts. Barren leafless trees surrounded us, while behind us and to the sides a slant of earth hid us from the view of anyone who ventured to the waterfall. In front of us, a twisted tree trunk framed the blue axis of ocean and sky. We were isolated in the growing darkness, and for some reason that fact made me nervous enough to raise my defenses.

"Finally, you show some sense."

Asher's voice resonated with anger and something more—despair. I could feel a chasm opening between us. My voice broke when I asked, "Why did you bring me here?"

His eyes looked almost black in the shadows. "Few people come here after sunset, and we needed a private place to talk."

"About?"

"You. You seem to think you're invincible because you have this ability to heal yourself. You haven't grasped how dangerous Protectors are, how easily we could kill you. That's my fault because my feelings clouded my judgment. I didn't want you to be afraid of me, but it's time I make you understand."

Another test, I realized. "I already know what you can do with your energy. I'm not an idiot."

He looked larger, his shoulders wider, when he stood with his feet braced apart and his hands loose at his side. The danger I sensed reminded me of my encounter with Gabe, and I grasped what Asher had been suppressing around me. "Healers didn't lose the War because Protectors stole their energy. That was a lucky windfall for those of us who desired immortality," he taunted, as if he included himself in that number.

He wanted to scare me, but I'd learned never to show fear. I stepped toward him, and Asher's eyes narrowed in warning. "I don't believe you. You already told me how you became immortal. It was an accident."

"Accident or not, I killed one of your kind, Healer." His voice sounded silky with threat and the hair on the back of my neck rose. "Or maybe it wasn't an accident at all. Maybe I lied to get close to you, to feel human again."

Knowing what my fears were, he could twist them. "I get what you're trying to do, but it won't work." I heard the uncertainty in my tone when he began to circle me as if considering the best angle of attack. "Asher, stop it. This isn't funny. You're mad because you want me to be some meek girl waiting around for a man to save her. Been there, done that. Never again."

He shook his head and hissed in frustration. "We're not playing games here. This isn't about you being female, and God knows, I'd never call you meek. Your life is at stake, though, and you're up against an enemy you can't possibly beat alone."

"I'm not defenseless like the other Healers. You know I can hurt people with my power."

An uncharacteristic sneer curled his lips. "Your power won't matter because you have to be in pain for it to work, and if you're hurt, you've already lost. You are the Protectors' dream come true or worst nightmare, any way you look at it—pain and mortality. When they come for you, they won't come alone. Do you think you can take more than one at a time? And what about Ben, Laura, and Lucy? Can you save them, too?"

"Leave them out of this!" Remembering how my grandmother died made my stomach lurch.

"Why? The Protectors won't. You can bet on that. Don't you see? There's a reason the Healers worked with Protectors. You need me, but I can't protect you from yourself. I don't know how else to make you see. This isn't about pride—yours or mine. You can't do this alone."

"You don't know that." My hoarse whisper betrayed my fear.

"I'm one Protector," he warned in a silky voice. "See if you can stop me, Healer."

Chapter Twenty-one

*A*sher crouched down, and a moment later an arm wrapped around my neck from behind and yanked me off my feet. I never saw him move, but he had me in an unbreakable hold, cutting off my air supply for a heartbeat before the heat of his body vanished.

My lungs rushed to suck in air, while adrenaline and fear kicked in when I twisted about to find empty space where he'd been seconds before. Memories of Dean stalking me mixed with the threat of Protectors attacking my family.

"Too slow, Healer. You're looking in the wrong place."

I turned towards his voice, but only a small breeze stirred the air where he'd been. His speed made it impossible to track him through the shadows.

"I could kill you. It would be so easy to take what I want." Raw emotion infused his guttural words as if he spoke his darkest fear.

A hand brushed my arm and retreated with my scarf. On his next pass, the scarf looped around my waist, binding my arms to my side until the material fell to the ground. Reason fought with panic, and one thought surfaced. This was Asher, my Protector.

"You're wrong. You wouldn't hurt me." The conviction in my voice didn't slow my galloping heartbeat. If he wanted to attack, I'd be powerless to stop him.

"Wouldn't I?"

Fingers sifted through my hair, and I shivered. Again, the air stirred where he should have stood when I swung around. He stalked me, forcing me to play prey to his predator, to demonstrate the superior strength and speed of Protectors. Fear threatened to overwhelm me. I'd be useless to protect myself, let alone my family.

Asher appeared in front of me, a fierce expression tightening his features. "No, Remy. Not useless. You have to be smart. Don't use your powers unless it's as a last defense. You have senses we don't. Use them!"

I heard the desperation and grief in his voice and realized he'd heard me, even through my guard. His thoughts appeared transparent, too, though I couldn't read his mind. It killed him to know he frightened me. Always he fought his desire to be near me, worried he'd hurt me with his hunger to feel more, to be more *human*. My sacrifice on the ferry had terrified him, and he risked everything to show me I couldn't stick my head in the sand.

I would need more than my powers to stay alive if the Protectors came for me. When they came for me. I had to stop reacting and start thinking. My shoulders squared, and I blocked him out of my mind. Knowing the truth helped me regain a measure of calm to fight back—to fight *for* him because I could feel him slipping away, distancing himself to protect me.

Closing my eyes, I took a deep breath and stood very still. Only an immortal could have heard my soft whisper. "Come and get me, Protector." Then I waited.

Seconds later, a breeze tousled my hair, and my nostrils filled with Asher's woodsy scent. Warm breath fanned my face, and whatever he'd been about to do was stalled when

I closed the space between my breath and his to brush a gentle kiss on his mouth.

A stirring reminder that I knew he had feelings for me.

A soothing reassurance of my feelings for him.

He disappeared in an instant with a gasp of shocked fury. Too late. He'd betrayed his feelings when his hard lips had softened against mine for a millisecond.

"What are you doing, Remy? Fight back!"

"I am." I lowered my guard, leaving myself wide open to his attack.

You won't hurt me.

A tree shook as if he'd struck it in rage.

You won't hurt me.

The ground trembled when he threw a massive rock, and it shattered into bits of stone and dust.

You won't hurt me.

His cry of outrage served as my lone warning before he tackled me, knocking me to the ground. My mind registered that Asher tempered his strength and cushioned the fall with his body, rolling us so he landed on top. My body registered that a man larger and stronger than me pinned me to the grass, and I was caught between instinct and reason. A week ago, a day ago, five minutes ago, terror would have won, and I would have fought my attacker in a red haze of fury and fear. A scream bubbled up in my chest fighting to claw its way out of my throat, and it took everything I had to remember Asher held me.

You won't hurt me.

"No, I could never hurt you," an unsteady voice murmured in my ear.

His weight disappeared as he rolled us until my softer curves rested on top of his harder muscles, but he made no other move to touch me. Every breath he took lifted me, and his rapid heartbeat slowed to its abnormal pace beneath my ear. I'd never felt closer to another person.

Asher's arms closed about me in a tight embrace, and I tangled my fingers in his hair.

When my pulse slowed, I lifted my head to peer down at his tortured expression. Then, I punched him in the arm as hard as I could.

"Damn it, Remy!"

He rubbed his arm under my glare. "Don't you ever do that to me again. *Not ever.*"

"I won't. I'm sorry. I shouldn't have scared you like that. I didn't know how else to make you see . . ."

"Not that. I'm in danger, and you showed me what I didn't want to see. Next time, try talking to me. I'm a fairly reasonable person."

He frowned in confusion. "Then what?"

I placed a hand on each of his sandpaper cheeks and framed his face. "Try to scare me away. I don't care if you think I'm safer without you, you jerk. We're in this messed-up situation together. If you want out, say so and we'll end this right now." The hard edge to my words dared him to lie and say he didn't care for me.

His eyes shadowed with familiar pain at my unguarded nearness, but his arms didn't release me. The night air felt cool on my back, and I savored the heat that sank into me from chest to feet where we touched. "I know this is a mistake, Remy, but I don't think I could leave you now if I tried. God help us both, I'm in love with you."

His words eased the knot of tension that had formed inside me. I wasn't in this alone.

"A Protector and a Healer. Can you imagine what they'd say if they knew?" We both mused on that in silence for a moment, and then our soft laughter filled the air.

My head dropped to his shoulder, and my eyes grew heavy when Asher's fingers tugged through my hair, brushing away bits of grass. "I'm sorry I scared you. When

you acted as if the danger to your life was nothing, I reacted without thinking."

"Why?" My voice sounded huskier than usual to my
own ears.

"You terrify me," he said in a fervent whisper. "For the
last century, there hasn't been a single person who's
touched me. When I learned I'd never age, I convinced
myself that my heart had been cut out along with my
senses."

"I don't understand. Most people want to be young forever." My fingers traced from his chin to his Adam's apple,
and his words vibrated through my chest, my fingers, and
my mind.

"They're wrong. Immortality is a curse. Humans are
supposed to die. It's the fear of death that gives meaning to
our lives—knowing that what's precious to you could be
taken away at any time makes every minute, every *thing*
mean more. When every day is the same, you become
numb."

"But you must've experienced amazing things!"

"I have, but knowledge and experience don't make up
for what I lost. A century ago, any hope I had of a normal
life—marriage, children, a future—went up in smoke.
Protectors can't stay in one place too long. We don't form
attachments outside the family because it would be too
dangerous. We're ghosts living a shadow of a life."

Attachments, he'd said. He meant love. I couldn't imagine living as long as he had without human affection.
These last hellish years of my life had been a drop of water in a pond compared to his life. "There must've been
people you loved." It wasn't an accusation, but a fact. You
couldn't live in Blackwell Falls without knowing that
Asher had dated more than his share of girls. And those
were only the ones I knew about.

I felt more than saw his smile. "That's part of the lie. A

way we fit in. We decide what they gossip about, the questions they ask. In the beginning, I had mortal friends and family, but I learned that loving a human means watching them die, while I have all the time in the world to grieve for them. You're the first I've loved."

Neither of us said what we thought. If there wasn't a cure for immortality, Asher would one day watch me die. Sooner rather than later, if the Protectors came for me.

Asher pushed me up to face him. "You need tools to protect yourself. I'm not saying I'm backing off, but you should know how to handle yourself in a fight. I'll teach you, if you like."

I nodded because I couldn't question his logic. If I'd been able to protect myself before now, maybe I could have stopped Dean.

His soft laugh raised goose bumps on my skin. "Today didn't exactly go how I planned."

The wool of his sweater felt pleasantly rough against my cheek. "Yeah, it was great until my powers freaked out on you."

He sighed. "I've been thinking about that. I don't understand why it happened now."

"Like you said, we're changing each other. We've been using our defenses less and less. Hardly at all today, and this was the longest we've been together."

"We need to set some rules about touching."

"Like?" The idea of restrictions between us irritated me.

"We can touch, but . . . nothing else . . . when we both have our guard down." When I raised my head to protest, he curved a hand around my neck to force my gaze to meet his direct stare. "I mean it, Remy. If you don't agree, I'll walk away right now. I'll do whatever it takes to keep you from hurting yourself to protect me. Even if it kills me to stay away."

He meant it. He would leave me if I didn't agree to his

terms. "But what if you're hurt? We both have to have our guard down for me to heal you."

"My injuries heal on their own. It takes longer than with help from your powers, but it's a side effect of being near you. Even my burned hand would've healed on its own. I didn't know at the time how your powers worked, or I never would've let you heal me." Strong arms shook me a little. "You don't have to save me. I'm not Anna. I can take care of myself."

The words echoed mine. It wasn't fair to insist he respect my ability to defend myself when I wouldn't give him the same courtesy. "Okay. So what now? Where do we go from here?"

He twined his fingers through mine. "I'd like you to come to my house tomorrow. We can start your training. And maybe Gabe and Lottie will have an idea about what's happening between us. Will you come?"

I already knew Gabe and Lottie didn't like me. Asher picked up on my trepidation and misunderstood the reason. "They won't hurt you. They know how I feel about you."

Embarrassed by my fear, I didn't correct him. "I trust you. I'll come."

His lips moved in my hair, and silence reigned for a long moment. "I need to get you home."

I turned my nose into his chest and breathed him in one last time before letting him go. "You're right. Ben was great today, and I don't want to push my luck."

With his help I stood, and he put a hand on my lower back to guide me down the incline. One of his brows rose when I shot him a nervous glance. "I can't believe you carried me up here. You've been holding out on how strong you are."

Asher's grin held a hint of superiority. "You don't know the half of it."

Without warning, he bent and threw me over his shoulder and shot down the hill. In seconds, we arrived at the car and he set me on my feet next to the open passenger door. An amused grin tilted his lips as he waited for my reaction, and his nearness undid me, stealing my breath away. His smile faded, replaced by intense longing.

With one step forward, he crowded me into the "V" of the opened car door with his body, blocking my exit with one hand on the door and the other on the roof of the car, not quite touching me. He leaned forward and caressed my cheek with his own, whispering in my ear, "Keep your guard up, okay?"

It was nearly impossible to speak, but I managed to whisper back, "Yes."

Asher's breath trailed along my jaw to my neck. He placed one sweet kiss on my collarbone, and his mouth found its way back to my lips. This time when he kissed me there was only the heat of his skin against mine. Sparks flared, but they had nothing to do with my being a Healer or him a Protector. These flashes were little explosions under my skin wherever he touched me. I took the single step forward that brought my body flush with his and slid my arms around his neck. My stomach clenched, my pulse quickened, and for a moment his lips hardened against mine.

When he grabbed my hands and set me away from him, it took a long moment for the fog to clear from my mind. I thought I imagined the green shocks of light shooting between our hands until I glimpsed the wince of pain on Asher's face. My confusion disappeared, and I realized my walls had slipped. I tried to pull my hands from his to ease his pain, but he wouldn't let me go.

His eyes blazed at me with a power that had me yearning to step into the fire again.

"Your defenses, Remy."

I grimaced and reinforced them. "Sorry about that."

His forehead dropped to mine again. "It wasn't that. Remember when I told you that I could hear your thoughts when you were feeling particularly strong about something—even when your barricade is up?"

My face warmed as embarrassment flooded through me. I cleared my throat. "Yes, well, sorry about that, too."

A corner of his full lips tilted up. "Are you kidding? Knowing I affect you the same way you do me? I wouldn't give that up for anything."

"Then why?" I indicated his fingers still wrapped around my wrists with confusion.

"My control was slipping, too. Green sparks, remember?"

"Oh."

Asher backed away, letting me go. "Yeah. Oh. Get in the car, O'Malley. I need to get you home before your dad flays me alive." Circling around the hood of the Audi, he opened the driver's door, resting his elbows on the roof of the car with the keys dangling from his hands. "You know, if you keep this up, you won't have any secrets from me."

I grinned at him. "Bet I have a few you haven't heard."

He laughed and got in the car. A short time later, he stopped the car at my house and escorted me to the front door. We were both aware of eyes watching from behind the curtains as we hugged good-bye. It wasn't until he walked away that I dropped my guard and called his name. He turned with a questioning smile.

I love you.

His stunned expression was the last thing I saw before I pushed the front door closed. That was definitely one secret he hadn't heard.

CHAPTER TWENTY-TWO

*A*sher picked me up early the next morning.
Luckily, Ben and Laura had left early to go sailing because I wasn't too sure how my father would have reacted to Asher's motorcycle. I shot a doubtful glance at the red helmet he handed me, thinking it wouldn't be much help in a crash. Asher responded with a challenging arch of one brow, as if I'd insulted him. Recalling his reflexes of the night before, I had to admit I'd be insulted in his shoes. I put the helmet on, straddled the seat behind him, and wrapped my arms around his waist in a death grip.

The engine started with a throaty roar, and my eyes squeezed shut. Asher took off and cold wind rushed past me, filling my nostrils with the salty scent of the ocean and the boy I loved. I braved opening my eyes and the world sped past without the barrier of windows or steel doors. Houses, water, and the green-brown blur of earth and trees swirled together, and a thrill of excitement shot from my spine to my toes as I leaned with Asher's body into a turn. The freedom intoxicated me. Asher's hand squeezed mine at his waist when I laughed.

He drove toward Fort Rowden State Park, but headed farther west down a road I'd never been on before, passing a wetlands reserve Ben had mentioned. He turned north on a street that dead-ended at a cement barrier like those that separated the lanes of the highway. Asher parked the bike on a plot of dirt at the side of the road. Cutting the engine, he pulled off his matching helmet and twisted to face me. "Good morning."

"Hi." I smiled, feeling shy after exposing myself so completely the night before. "Is something wrong with your car?"

He grasped my arm to save me from a face-plant when I slid off the bike. His dismount was ten times more graceful, and he placed our helmets on the seat before guiding me around the cement barrier. With a sheepish grin, he admitted, "No. I wanted the excuse to touch you."

My skin warmed, and I blurted out, "Where are we?" I looked about with curiosity. A worn dirt path rounded a bend ahead, and the ocean lay in front of us.

Asher's expression lit with excitement. "The locals call it the Edge of the World."

He tugged me around the corner. The view took my breath away, and I settled against Asher's chest to take it in. We stood a hundred feet over the beach at the edge of a cliff. Everywhere I looked an infinite fabric of turquoise sky was sewn to blue ocean. With no fence to bar us from stepping right up to the edge, it felt like the very end of the world.

"Remy?"

"Hmm?" I rolled my head against his shoulder to meet his gaze.

"I love you."

My breath hitched at the intensity in his deep voice. With our guards up, he pressed soft lips to my forehead and then the corner of my mouth. Remembering the hidden kiss meant only for him—I smiled and threw my arms around him. I kissed him back and thought, *I love you.*

The embrace changed when he heard me, and he gripped me tighter. His guard slipped and his energy swirled in the air around us. I worried he was in pain, but he merely slipped a hand into my hair and spread his fingers over my scalp in a gentle caress. The heat spread through me, and my own guard slipped. The knowledge that my touch could hurt him enabled me to pull away. He couldn't hide his wince when he strengthened his own defenses. He dropped his forehead against mine and gave a soft laugh that sent a shiver through me. "Rule number two. You can't think things like that when I'm kissing you. It makes me forget rule number one."

I sighed. "I hate how it hurts you to touch me."

"It doesn't matter. I'm grateful that I can feel you at all." His lips pressed a sweet kiss into my open palm.

"What does it feel like to you?" I wondered if he felt the heat I did.

"Hmm . . . Let's see. Your skin is like the satin ribbons my sister wore in her hair as a child." The fingers of his free hand whispered across my cheek until he captured a long curl. "Your hair is soft as the silk handkerchiefs my mother embroidered for my father."

His face slipped to the curve of my neck, and his breath stirred the exposed skin there until I shivered again. "And sometimes, I can almost imagine you smell like lemons and vanilla."

My body froze, and Asher lifted his head to eye me with curiosity. "Did I do something wrong?"

I studied his sculpted features. "Laura bought me a lemon-vanilla-scented lotion in South Portland. I've been wearing it for weeks."

"You must've been thinking about it," he said, with a frown.

"Or maybe your sense of smell is coming back."

Long, elegant fingers wove through mine, and he shook his head. "Not likely. I don't smell anything now."

Disappointed, I let the matter drop, but wasn't convinced. If he could feel me, maybe his other senses could return, too.

Asher sank to the ground and tugged me down by his side a few feet from the ledge. "I wanted a chance to talk alone before we went to my house."

"Is something wrong?"

His smile appeared slightly crooked "No, but you should know what to expect."

"You mean Lottie? I'm guessing I know where I stand with Gabe."

Asher glanced away, looking distinctly uncomfortable. "Not quite. Your mother left out some important details about the bonding process."

My skin suddenly turned ice cold. "You're not telling me I'm going to bond to him, too?"

Asher swung around in shock. "No! No, we form one bond at a time. Usually between the oldest daughter and the eldest son."

A long pause stretched out as he waited for me to grasp what he was saying. "But we . . . You're not the eldest."

"Right. In the natural course of things, you should've bonded to Gabe."

I thought of bonding to Gabe with his scary energy and menacing looks. The idea of him in my head was so repugnant that I shuddered. "Like hell!"

My fierce tone made Asher grin. "I agree wholeheartedly. Gabe, on the other hand, is not too pleased with the situation."

The scene at Rosy's when I'd first met Gabe suddenly made sense. He'd been testing my connection to Asher. I shuddered again.

Asher laughed. "You don't have to worry. I thought you should know in case the subject came up. We've never known a bond to skip the eldest."

I gave him a smug smile. "Maybe that means you're the

weird one this time. What about Lottie? How much does she hate me?"

He grimaced. "Not hate exactly. More like fear. Lottie doesn't react well to change. She likes things the way they are, and knowing how you've affected me and Gabe, she's scared."

Rising to his feet, he reached down to help me up. Gripping his hands, I asked, "Are you sure this is a good idea? What if my being there hurts your family?"

Asher tugged me close and wrapped his arms around me. "Don't worry. I've warned them to keep their guard up. Ready?"

I nodded and we walked back to the bike.

"One more thing. I checked on Dean's whereabouts. According to his credit card statements, he's still in New York. You don't have to worry about him."

A wave of relief went through me that I hadn't really seen my stepfather that night. My mind must have played tricks on me. "Thanks for checking. How were you able to get that kind of info?"

An enigmatic smile lit his features. *Money*, I guessed. He'd said it could move mountains. "You didn't have to do that."

"Yes, I did. One day you'll believe me that you're not alone in this."

Settled on the motorcycle behind him, I hugged him tight. *I already do.*

Even knowing how rich he was, Asher's house was nothing like I expected. Possessions meant little to Asher in the way of those who'd always had money. His house was a mansion—a grandiose, gaudy Victorian that watched over the harbor and the town below. As long as I'd been in Blackwell Falls, I'd seen the building adorning the hilltop with its fanciful, old-fashioned rose gardens, pastel yellow paint, wraparound porch, and fancy turrets. I'd thought the house was a hotel and nobody had told me any different, probably assuming I knew it was Asher's home.

I lost it. When Asher sent me a questioning look, I said through my giggles, "You live in a wedding cake."

He didn't take offense but reached over to tickle my ribs as we climbed the stairs to the front porch. I shrieked and twisted away from him. His eyebrows shot up as he realized how ticklish I was. Then, without me seeing him move, he'd swept me off my feet with both arms wrapped around my waist, and his fingers playing over my sides. He smirked at me squirming above his head. "Say uncle."

Helplessly laughing, I leaned down instead to touch my lips to his. When his arms loosened at my touch, I wriggled away. Before I could get entirely free, he grasped my hand and spun me back into his arms. Our laughter faded as he bent to kiss me.

A throat cleared nearby, and I would have sprung away if not for Asher pinning me to his side. I peered around him and saw Gabe watching us from the open front door. He looked mildly curious at finding us embracing on the front porch. I had to fight the urge to hide behind Asher. "Let me go!" I whispered.

He merely dropped a kiss on my forehead and faced his brother with me tucked under his arm. He ignored my subtle shove in his side. "Remy, you've met my brother."

"Hi, Gabe." This time Asher let me go when I shoved him.

Gabe inclined his head toward me with the barest hint of civility. "Healer. You might as well come in now that you're here."

With an uncertain look at Asher, I grasped his hand and followed his brother through the front door. The rooms I could see had been painted warm creams, soft yellows, and cool sage greens with comfortable furniture in darker woods and jewel-toned plush velvets. Framed photographs hung on every wall, most in black and white, and the lilting voice of a French café singer crooned softly in the background.

For a family that lacked the use of many of their senses, an abundance of sensation could be found in their home. The antique vases of crimson and pink roses decorating every surface brought the perfume of a summer garden indoors.

"So that's what it smells like."

Gabe turned to look at Asher, but I knew what he'd sensed through his hand on mine.

He tilted his head at a vase on an entryway table. "Our home. Remy smelled the roses."

Gabe's eyes lit with interest. "You smell them, too?"

Asher shook his head. "No. Her touch is the only thing I feel for myself. With scent and taste, it's more that I sense what Remy thinks things smell and taste like." He smiled down at me and shrugged. "She loves roses."

Gabe's eyes gleamed with speculation, and I wondered if it was a mistake to raise false hopes when we had no idea what could come of this. *Asher, are you sure this won't make things worse?*

A hand soothed along my back. "It's okay, Remy. Gabe doesn't expect anything."

Gabe leaned forward, dropping all pretense of formality. "You're reading her mind now?"

Lottie slipped into the room behind him, the same intent look lighting her delicate features. "How is this possible? I've never heard of a Protector able to read a Healer. Not even when a bond existed."

Gabe studied me, and I felt hunted again. "I'd say we've moved beyond what was possible. Remy is unlike any Healer we've met. Can't you feel it?"

Lottie paused a moment, seeming to concentrate, and her eyes opened wide in surprise, her red lips pursing. Whatever she felt, she did not look happy about it.

I sensed nothing unusual and turned to Asher. "Feel what?"

He tucked a hair behind my ear. "You're humming."

I blinked in surprise. As usual, when I touched another, my body gathered energy in preparation for scanning and healing. I'd thought that if I didn't send my energy outward, Asher couldn't sense the hum of electricity tripping under my skin. "You can feel that?"

His mouth quirked in a wry smile. "Always. At first, only when we touched, but now it's all the time. It seems to be getting stronger the longer you're around Protectors. Gabe even noticed it when you met the first time."

Glancing around the room, I noticed that all three Blackwells looked slightly off balance as if they had migraines. My *humming* hurt them, I realized. It was the reason Asher always felt pain when near me. With my guard lowered and surrounded by Protectors, my body went on high alert, and it wasn't something I could shut off. I raised my barricade, and a moment later, their expressions eased.

"I'm so sorry. I didn't know."

Lottie frowned. "Do we really need to do this? She's Asher's problem. I don't understand why I have to be here."

Asher started to say something, but Gabe spoke up first. "We've talked about this, Lottie. This affects us all. If the Healers are changing, we need to know how."

Gabe waved me into the living room. He wasted no time and proceeded to grill me about my abilities for the next hour. He wanted to know what the bonding felt like, what it felt like to heal, and what I knew about my family history. Like Asher, he'd never heard of a Healer with a shield or one who absorbed the wounds of the person they'd healed. He listened, his emotions impossible to decipher.

"You know, Asher," Gabe finally said. "In many ways, her energy works like ours. A Healer's power should be limited to manipulating her energy in the body of the person she heals. This one absorbs and controls energy in ways unique to both Healers and Protectors."

Gabe's eyes dropped to the small cuts on my arms from my fight with Dean that I'd neglected healing out of fear of discovery. His hand grasped mine, flipping it over to get a better look at the wounds. His eyes burned like my father's had at the hospital, but he didn't mention them.

"Regardless of how her powers work, she doesn't stand a chance, Asher. She's defenseless against our kind." His sister didn't sound unhappy about this fact.

"Not defenseless, Lottie," Asher inserted in a quiet tone.

"You want us to risk our lives on that?"

"I refuse to let Asher be harmed because of me." My words held a fierce promise.

Gabe's smile wasn't friendly. "You sound like a Protector."

"I don't believe in letting someone else take all the risks for me."

A shadow passed through Gabe's eyes, and I don't think he realized that he still touched my hand, squeezing it in a grip that was almost painful. "If there had been more Healers who believed that, maybe there never would've been a War."

Lottie came forward and pressed a hand to her brother's shoulder in wordless comfort, and I wondered what it would be like not to feel such a gesture. My heart ached for this family, despite their surliness. I couldn't imagine being unable to *feel* Asher. An overwhelming desire to help them filled me. I didn't realize my guard had lowered or that I'd focused my energy at Lottie's hand, until a loud gasp and green sparks breached my concentration.

Lottie had a fist to her mouth and looked as if she would cry. Somehow I'd hurt her, and I wasn't sure what I'd done. My guard blasted up and I stood, seeking the nearest exit. Asher was so stunned watching Lottie, he didn't stop me right away. I almost made it out of the living room, but a large mass blocked the doorway.

Gabe glared down at me. "What did you do, Healer?"

"Let me go." My voice barely reached a whisper. I glanced away and saw a frightened Lottie still standing where we'd left her.

Gabe's energy surged at me, but Asher suddenly stood between us. "Back off, Gabe. You don't understand."

Gabe didn't leave the doorway, but his energy retreated. "I understand our sister is in pain and your little Healer is responsible. You should never have brought her here, Asher."

The two of them glowered, and the hair rose on the back of my neck at the way Gabe and Asher squared off against each other, powerful muscles flexing as they readied for battle.

Chapter Twenty-three

*G*abe launched himself forward, and Asher met him halfway to protect me. They fell to the ground with a thud that shook the house. Trying to become invisible, I slid sideways and backed into the wall with my heart pounding because I stood in a room with angry Protectors.

Asher grappled with Gabe, defending me against his family. I shouldn't have come here. Gabe landed a punch on Asher's chin, and I winced when Asher's neck snapped back. Asher merely regrouped and shoved his brother away, a table breaking beneath Gabe's weight. They both rolled to their feet in a blur, circling each other.

"Lottie, tell him!" Asher's deep roar had me jumping out of my skin. "Tell the truth, Lottie, before we can't take this back!"

Lottie turned away, crying openly now. Gabe paused, staring at her, and Asher used his distraction, pinning him to the wall. "Now, Charlotte! I was in Remy's head. I know that she didn't hurt you. She would never hurt any of us."

"Lottie?" Gabe asked, confused.

"I felt you, Gabe," she bit out. "My hand on your shoulder. She did that. She's making us human again."

Asher had been wrong. There was no mistaking the hate in his sister's eyes as she swung toward me.

Asher slowly loosened his hold on Gabe. "I told you before. She's not like the others."

Gabe watched Lottie race out of the room in tears, his expression thoughtful.

"Remy? You okay?" Asher touched my arm, and I observed it shook.

"I'm sorry," I blurted out. "I didn't mean to do it. I thought how awful it would be never to feel you, and I wished I could help somehow."

He pressed his hands to my cheeks. "You did nothing wrong."

"Asher." For the first time since I'd met him, Gabe's voice thickened with emotion. "Your Healer has powers she hasn't even tapped into yet. If the others find out what she can do, there will be no protecting her."

Asher looked more determined than ever. "We'd better find a way. Remy is our best hope for a cure."

We left Gabe in the living room, and I followed Asher up the stairs, leading me to the room the family used as a gym to begin my training. On the second floor, I trailed behind peering through doorways. My attention caught on a large, framed black-and-white photo that hung on the far wall of a masculine bedroom. Asher followed slowly when I moved inside the room to get a better look.

It was me, sitting on a log the first day I'd met Asher at the beach. Except it wasn't a me that I recognized. Sadness lingered in the clear eyes of the girl who stared off into the distance and frailty settled about the shoulders that hunched against the cold. What surprised me was the strength in her features, the firm resolve in the set of the jaw. This girl—this woman—was a survivor. My fingers traced the long strands of hair that danced in the wind. Unbeknownst to him, Asher had captured the moment I'd

decided to stay in Blackwell Falls instead of returning to
New York, a decision that had most likely saved my life
and had brought me to him.

"I'm beautiful," I whispered in shock. "You made me
look beautiful."

"You *are* beautiful." Asher's voice sounded reverent, and
I tore my gaze from the photo. He stared at me and not
the picture. "I've been dying to take your picture again
since that day, but I didn't dare ask after what happened."

I smiled, remembering. "You mean when I tried to destroy your camera? I told you why I was upset. I thought
you were taking pictures of the poor little abused girl."

He whistled. "Yeah. You should see those pictures."

Curious, I asked, "Where are they?"

He pointed to another wall where three smaller color
photos were framed together in a series. I had always
thought myself a gawky, awkward girl who'd never grown
into her height, but as I studied his pictures, I saw myself
as Asher did. In each one, the sky shrank and I grew larger
as I stormed closer, intent on taking the camera from
Asher. True, I looked tall, but in the midst of my passion,
I was a confident warrior.

"Wow. I'm amazed you didn't drop the camera and run
screaming." I tossed a rueful glance his way, and then
turned in a slow circle. This had to be Asher's bedroom.
There were few furnishings aside from the massive bed
with a dark wooden headboard, stretching halfway up the
wall, carved with intricate designs. With heat flushing my
cheeks, I scanned the rest of the walls and discovered
dozens of photos, some of his family, but most of strangers
in foreign, exotic places I'd never been. I remembered
someone saying on my first day of school that Asher was a
talented photographer. It was easy to see why. "These are
really good, Asher."

He shrugged. "I've had decades to refine my skills. It's one of the few pleasures left open to us. To be able to appreciate the beauty in the world. For Lottie, it's music. Gabe likes books and poetry. We've studied under some amazing teachers through the years, though never with the same one for too long."

"It must be hard to start over so often."

Asher gave a slow nod. "I've come to accept it over time. Shall we?" I followed him from his room and down the hall to the gym. Expensive equipment lined the walls, but the center of the room held only a large, blue mat.

Asher grinned. "Gabe and I like to spar to stay loose. Take off your shoes."

I pulled off my boots and socks and tossed them aside, while he did the same. Rising, I faced a barefoot Asher, both of us in jeans and tees. He circled me, and I spun on the balls of my feet to keep him in sight.

"What happens now?"

His eyes narrowed. "I attack, and you defend yourself."

With no more warning than that, he sprang at me, too fast to evade. My single other option to defend myself would be to use my ability to hurt him, and I couldn't do that. I let myself fall with him to the mat where he cushioned my body.

Flat on our backs and out of breath, we stared at each other, knowing this was a futile exercise.

Gabe seconded our thoughts from where he leaned against the wall watching us. "It won't work. You're trying too hard to protect her and she's unwilling to hurt you to protect herself."

Asher helped me up. "Go away, Gabe."

Something had changed downstairs with Lottie's confession. For once, Gabe didn't look quite so evil. I heard myself asking him, "What do you suggest?"

He pushed away from the wall. "Train with me. Asher

can watch and give you tips. That way you'll know what a real attack will be like."

Asher's protest went ignored as I stared at his brother. "And what if I hurt you defending myself?"

Gabe's eyes flashed with arrogance, and he shrugged. "I'll take that chance."

I studied his handsome face and didn't see another option. Asher had convinced me I needed to know how to defend myself, and Gabe appeared willing to teach me. "Fine. Let's do it."

Asher stepped between us, his jaw tight with anger. "No. You could get hurt, Remy."

My fingers traced his lips. "That's kind of the idea, Asher. You know this is the right thing to do. This will never work if you're going easy on me." Asher wavered, and I went in for the kill with a teasing smile. "Besides, Gabe knows you'll rip him apart if he does any permanent damage."

Gabe's brows rose at the last, but Asher finally smiled. He turned to his brother, and a dark warning passed between them before Asher stepped to the side of the room. Gabe took his place at my side. He didn't circle me like Asher had, but stared at me with a blank expression. The next instant I lay flat on my back, and the air had been forced from my lungs as he pinned me to the floor.

I felt his energy coming at me, but my walls held strong. Before I could retaliate, Gabe's weight disappeared. Gasping, I rolled to my side to see Asher lifting Gabe off his feet with a fist gripping his shirt, while his brother readied himself to fight back.

"Asher, stop!"

Through gritted teeth, he asked, "Are you okay?"

In a stronger voice, I insisted, "Yes! Let him go. He was only doing what we asked." I stood and went into a crouch. "I'm ready to go again."

Asher loosened his hold and faced me with a desperate expression, his hands balled in fists. "I can't, Remy. I can't watch this."

"You were the one who told me I needed to be prepared. This is me preparing. Now tell me what I did wrong."

He took a deep breath and finally said, "You were only using your eyes. We move too quickly for sight to be of use to you. You need to open your other senses."

I remembered the night at the waterfall when I'd felt the air shift and smelled Asher's scent when he closed in. I faced Gabe and braced myself. His face remained expressionless when I ordered, "Again."

Seconds later, I lay flat on my back when Gabe knocked my legs out from under me. He didn't help me up, but eyed me from several feet away, while I gasped and struggled to regain my feet. Determined, I glared at him. "Again."

For the next half hour, Gabe attacked wordlessly, and I tried to find a weakness. Asher offered advice through gritted teeth, and I could tell it killed him to watch Gabe striking at me. Sometimes, Gabe would land a blow to my ribs or back instead of knocking me to the ground, but he always danced out of reach before I could retaliate. He simply moved too fast.

Then he began to taunt me.

"Why don't you stay down, Healer? We all know you're dead the second a Protector gets his hands on you."

Another blow.

"I thought you were going to hurt me. You're the only one in pain here."

An arm struck me across the middle and sent me flying backwards. I hit the ground with a jarring thump that made me see stars. This time, Gabe gave me no time to recover. He flipped me on my stomach and twisted my arm behind me, while he kneeled with his knee in my lower back. It took everything I had not to cry out when he pulled my arm up higher.

"Enough, Gabe."

Gabe ignored Asher's warning as he leaned forward to whisper in my ear. "You're weak, Healer. Incapable of fighting back. You're going to get my brother killed for nothing."

With a sickening pop, my shoulder slipped from its socket in a familiar explosion of pain. It was the moment I'd been waiting for. Rage consumed me, and I lowered my shield to strike back at Gabe with everything I had. He dropped to the mat beside me, clutching his shoulder. His beautiful face contorted in pain, and I experienced a surge of grim satisfaction to find all traces of arrogance erased.

Asher rushed forward to help me sit up. His eyes looked bleak, and I reassured him, "I'm okay. We're both okay."

I crawled over to Gabe. He glared at me, and I smiled back, feeling mean. "Hurts like hell, doesn't it?" He didn't answer, but his energy swirled as if to protect himself from another attack. I rolled my eyes. "Cut it out. I know what you were trying to do, Gabe. I get it, okay? Now, let me help you."

"Don't bother. It'll heal on its own." His cold tone had no give.

"You mean in a few days? Shut up, you ungrateful jerk, and be still. Pain makes me irritable, and I might decide to break something while I'm in there." I turned to Asher who looked ready to carry me out of the room. "If you feel his energy come at me, you have my permission to give his shoulder a good yank."

Asher's voice sounded grim. "I don't like this."

"Gabe won't hurt me. He was trying to help me, even

though he does a great impression of an evil jackass." I twisted back to Gabe and placed my good hand on his cheek. He froze at my touch, and I closed my eyes to lose myself in the healing. It was difficult to ignore my own pain, but soon the *humming* took over. Gabe's internal workings resembled Asher's, and it took a concerted effort to heal his dislocated shoulder. Out of spite for the numerous times he'd thrown me to the ground, I considered leaving the bruises covering his arms, back, and side, but healed those, too. Green sparks lit between us when I pulled away.

I sank to the floor beside him, beads of sweat forming on my forehead.

Gabe studied me with a bemused expression. "You're not very smart, are you? Now you're weak and injured. You couldn't hurt me if you tried."

I raised one brow. "Couldn't I?"

His glance strayed to my dislocated shoulder and he grimaced. "Stupid, Healer!" he spat.

"Shark!" I stuck my tongue out at him and smirked. He was in a snit because I'd managed to beat him.

In a single fluid movement, he stood. "You waited too long to defend yourself. Next time we train, be prepared to take me out sooner. Now that I know what you can do, I won't make it so easy for you."

He walked out of the room without a backward glance.

"I really dislike your brother, Asher, but I have to admit he's growing on me."

"I think he likes you, too. He's not usually that nice." Asher's hand stroked my back, and he stretched out beside me with his face inches from mine. "You ready?"

I nodded and felt Asher's energy spreading through me. As I had in the car, I used his energy to aid me in healing myself when I found my own energy depleted. Long minutes later, I sighed as the pain disappeared. Feeling a thousand times better, I sprawled on his chest while he ran a hand from my shoulder to my hip, leaving little sparks of heat behind with each pass.

"He's not wrong, you know. I'm afraid of my new power. I wasn't willing to use it on him until he pissed me off."

Asher kissed my forehead. "I figured that out, or I wouldn't have been able to watch without beating him to a pulp. He was right to step in. I couldn't have pushed you that far."

"I know. Gabe's smarter than I gave him credit for."

Asher's laugh nearly toppled me off him. "Please don't tell him that. His ego is swelled enough already from the world telling him he's beautiful."

I snorted. "Ha. He's got nothing on you."

"You just like me for my scar," he teased.

"Hmm. You never told me how you got that scar."

He slid me off him, and we faced each other on our sides with his arm cradling my head. After a long hesitation, he said, "It was a long time ago. After the War, we returned to our home. It took a while for us to realize we would have to leave everything we knew behind or risk discovery."

"Every few years—when people might notice we never aged—we moved, changed our names, and set up a new home. Made new friends. But when you watch everyone around you die year after year, something inside you dies, too."

He paused and his memories filled the silence. "It killed me a little at a time, the numbness and the death and watching every dream I'd had die. This"—his finger traced the scar on his temple—"was a mistake. I jumped off a cliff, almost decapitating myself on the way down. I wanted to feel anything, even pain, but in the end . . . nothing. Six months to heal all the injuries and broken bones, but I didn't feel a thing."

"Is it so bad?" I whispered.

A corner of his mouth lifted. "I wouldn't wish it on my worst enemy."

His words acted as a vise constricting my heart. We'd never be normal, never be free to dream like everyone else. "What if I can heal you? You don't have to fight so hard to be around me anymore. What if you could be mortal again?"

Asher's arm curled under me, hooking around my neck to pull me closer. "Not while there's a chance you could be hurt."

I couldn't let go of the idea. My body had already tried to heal him. Neither of us knew what would have happened if I hadn't stopped it. My mother said the possibility existed. Maybe . . .

"No."

"But—"

He touched the corner of my mouth with a gentle finger. "I'll give you anything you want. My heart is yours as long as you want me, but don't ask me to risk losing you."

Words disappeared again. I placed his hand over my heart, and we stared at each other, falling more into each other. I would stop fighting him for now, but I wasn't giving up. There had to be a way to make him mortal again because if there wasn't, he'd lose me anyway. There was one thing we could all agree on.

Healers had a short lifespan once Protectors discovered their existence.

CHAPTER TWENTY-FOUR

*E*verything I'd learned about Protectors had made one fact undeniable: My abilities put everyone I cared about at risk. Being a Healer wasn't something I could shut off, so training with Gabe and Asher became my top priority. Over the next couple of weeks, my life settled into a new routine. School, homework, dinner with the family, and when I could get away, evenings spent in the Blackwells' gym getting thrown to the mat by Gabe. The abuse continued until he wore me down, and I retaliated by wounding him.

Patience developed into one of my greatest assets—I only needed to touch him once to end the fight, but it grew difficult to take blow after blow while I waited for my chance. The pain made me ill-tempered, but we all knew it would be my prime weapon.

Asher gritted his teeth through the whole process and helped me understand more about how the Protectors moved (fast) and what to expect when they came for me (death, unless I managed to get away). He and his brother drew up multiple escape plans with various rendezvous points to meet up in case an attack came while I was at school, at home, en route from school to home, at the pool. . . . The list went on and every strategy had a contingency plan. I had no illusions that Gabe helped me out of the goodness of his heart or a newfound liking for Healers. I'd accepted that, if the Protectors showed up, I'd need any help the Blackwells were willing to give. My life wasn't the only one at stake anymore.

Despite our preparations for danger, I think we all sensed a storm brewing. It festered in the rare glimpses of worry on Asher's face, and the militant way Lottie avoided any contact with me, keeping to her room when I visited. It lingered in Gabe's tense voice when he snarled at me during training, cursing me for my weakness that could destroy his family.

Then Gabe heard a rumor that some Protectors were planning on visiting.

"Visiting? Are you kidding me? I'm going through all of this, and you're inviting them to town for a slumber party?"

Gabe had made his announcement after knocking me flat on my back and promptly left the training room, not caring in the least how his announcement affected me. Asher touched my arm, drawing my attention away from staring daggers into Gabe's retreating figure.

"Remy, look at me. It's the way things work in our world. If we turned them away, there would be questions."

Crouching on his heels at my side, Asher's solemn gaze begged me to believe him. I ignored his outstretched hand and rose to my feet without his help. "You could have told me you were BFFs with the enemy," I accused.

Asher stood and tossed me a towel. "Remy, I *am* the enemy."

I grabbed the towel, hanging it around my neck, and considered shoving him. He sounded as irritable as I did.

"I hate this," he continued, crowding me. He wrapped a fistful of my towel around each of his hands to pull me closer, his knuckles brushing my collarbones in a whispery caress. "I hate it that I can't ask them not to come. And I hate it that I know you won't go while they're here."

He was right. I wouldn't leave my family. Sighing, I turned away from the heat in his narrowed eyes. "Why are they coming here? Why now?"

Asher slipped his hands in his pockets. "It's our fault. Mine and Gabe's. Protectors are a tight community. When you don't check in, they notice. We've been distracted."

By me, he meant. "But why come here? Why not pick up the phone and say 'hey'?"

Asher smiled. "Spencer and Miranda are friends, Remy. They helped us get out of Italy when our parents died. Like I said, we're a tight community."

It didn't escape my notice that Spencer and Miranda were also immortal, which meant at least two more Healers had died. I wasn't naïve enough to believe that every Protector achieved immortality by an accident of fate.

"No, you're right." Asher's eyes didn't leave mine. "They were bitter and angry at the way the Healers had treated them. It was no accident, but it was war, Remy. I won't make excuses, but mistakes were made on both sides."

I didn't know how I felt about that. I had never met another Healer. Was I supposed to feel an instant loyalty to their kind because their power ran through my veins? Could I ignore the things they'd done to the Protectors that had driven Asher's people to fight back? I only knew what Asher and my mother had told me.

"That's not true. You know who I am."

I nodded, and it was a long moment before I broke the silence. "If Spencer and Miranda are your friends, can't you trust them?"

Asher shook his head. "I trust them with our lives, but not yours. They don't hunt Healers, but that doesn't mean they'd resist the temptation of you in the same room."

"I get it. I'm catnip for Protectors." With a wry smile, I picked up my bag. "So, what's the plan?"

The plan was for me to stay out of sight while the Protectors were in town. Asher and Lottie skipped school most of the week, presumably to visit with their friends. I'd promised Asher to steer clear of anyplace in town outside home and school to avoid any possibility of chance meetings. I didn't realize how accustomed I'd become to seeing Asher until I went a few days without.

To keep my promise, I stayed at the school library to catch up on my studies instead of joining my friends at the Clover Café. I'd kept my end of the bargain with Ben and Laura, keeping my grades up. When my brain threatened to implode, I set aside the equations I'd been working on for math and decided to head home on foot. Unlike New York, Blackwell Falls was a safe place to walk the streets, unless you counted all the Protectors running about.

A full moon lit the evening sky and cast shadows on the thick clouds when I left campus. An unexpected alarm raised goose bumps on my skin. The air felt pregnant with danger, like those seconds before Gabe would attack. Footsteps sounded behind me, and I twisted around, crouched and ready to defend myself as Asher and Gabe had taught me. The parking lot was empty. Convinced someone watched me, I scrutinized the school's main building and saw the outline of someone passing by an upstairs window. My laugh sounded loud in the quiet night, and I felt foolish for getting spooked. Asher would have called if I had something to worry about. Still, I raced home and didn't breathe easily until I'd locked myself in the house.

I would have dismissed the incident, except the same thing happened later that evening when I helped Ben take the trash out after dinner. He'd gone back in the house ahead of me, and I had the strange sensation that someone watched me from the shadows in Townsend Park. I peered into the trees, half hoping to see someone. At least then I'd know I wasn't going crazy. The other half of me dreaded the discovery of what I'd find. I didn't see anyone, but I couldn't shake the notion that someone stalked me. I longed to call Asher, but he was off limits so long as his friends were in town. Determined not to worry my family until I had proof, I said nothing and kept my eyes open.

The calls started two nights later.

Ben and Laura had gone to meet friends for dinner, leaving Lucy and me to fend for ourselves. After a quick meal of leftover spaghetti, Lucy beat me upstairs to steal the shower, leaving me to clean our few dishes. I was about to yell after her when the kitchen phone rang, and I answered it. Whoever it was didn't speak. Assuming the person had dialed the wrong number, I hung up.

Less than thirty seconds later, the phone rang again. Heavy breathing sounded on the other end of the line, and it felt like the person lingered behind me the way the hair on the back of my neck rose.

"Listen, if you're a prank caller, we get the message. Time to move on and irritate someone else." When the person didn't respond, I hung up again. Immediately, the handset sounded under my hand, and I nearly jumped out of my skin.

Tired of the game, I yanked the receiver to my ear with an impatient movement. "Who is this?"

The distinct *snick* of a lighter flaring to life echoed on the other end of the line.

Dean. The phone dropped from my limp fingers and hit the floor with a *crack,* spinning across the tiled floor to come to rest under the small kitchen table. Dropping to my knees, I scrambled to grab the phone and checked the caller ID for the last call received.

A local number was listed, and praying an innocent

prankster would answer, I dialed. It rang six times before a woman answered in a breathless voice, a tourist strolling down on Beech Street who had heard the pay phone ringing. Her friends had dared her to answer it when they'd seen no one about.

I dropped the phone back in its cradle and sank into a chair at the table. Asher had reassured me that Dean remained in New York, but what if he'd made it to Blackwell Falls? Few people knew how the sound of a lighter could terrify me, and I didn't know anyone who would play such a prank on me. It had to be Dean.

"Remy, you okay? Who was that on the phone?"

Lucy stood in the doorway in a robe. Her eyes narrowed in concern, and I pulled myself together, keeping my tone light for her benefit. "Prank callers. They freaked me out a little."

She wrinkled her nose in distaste. "It was probably Brandon or Greg trying to get a rise out of you."

My sister looked so innocent standing there barefoot with her hair wet—so unprepared to protect herself—that I decided to tell Lucy at least a little of the truth so she'd be on her guard. "I don't think so. The caller pretended to be Dean. The boys would never be that cruel. You mind if I call Asher and ask him to stay with us until Ben and Laura get home?"

My fear registered, and she sat across from me, touching my hand. "They really rattled you, didn't they? Go ahead and call him. To be honest, I'd feel better having him here, too."

Asher answered his cell on the first ring.

My voice sounded hesitant. "I'm sorry to call you. I know you said not to, but—"

"They're gone, Remy. I was just about to call you. What's wrong?"

I told him what had happened.

He said, "I'm on my way," before I could even get my request out. Lucy tossed me a confused look when I hung up until I relayed his brief end of the conversation. She laughed and squeezed my hand again. Less than ten minutes later, Asher called to let me know he'd arrived at the front door.

Relief flooded through me, and I nearly jumped into his arms. Instead, I stepped back to allow him to enter. My brows rose when I glimpsed Gabe at the edge of the front yard, circling the house. "What's he doing?"

Asher closed the door and braced his hands on his hips. "Checking to see if anyone is out there. Tell me what happened."

I relayed the calls in the kitchen, and his expression tightened. "Stay here," he said. "I want to check the locks and windows."

Lucy and I waited in the living room, and he returned a few minutes later. Lucy seemed surprised at his quick reappearance, but didn't mention it. When a knock sounded on the front door, he answered it and spoke in quiet tones to Gabe. I heard him tell his brother good-bye, and then he returned to the living room.

"Nothing. No tracks and no evidence that anyone has been hanging around."

Asher and I eyed each other. He really meant that the caller wasn't a Protector.

"Remy thinks it was Dean," Lucy said, tucking her hair behind her ear in a nervous gesture.

Asher suggested, "Maybe Ben can have someone check on his whereabouts. For tonight, I'll stay until your parents get home." Translated, that meant he already had his brother checking on Dean.

Lucy nodded and yawned, her jaw cracking. "Thanks,

Asher. Tell your brother I said thanks, too. I wouldn't have thought he would do something nice like that. No offense."

His smile had a wry edge. "None taken."

Before I could disillusion her on Gabe's motives—which had more to do with his brother and nothing at all to do with us—Lucy said good night and headed up the stairs. Asher and I stood rooted where she'd left us in the living room and stared at each other.

Asher moved suddenly, his arms winding around me, yanking me into his body, so I had to lean against him on my tiptoes. Both his palms flattened against the middle of my back, and I felt safe for the first time in days. Relieved to be touching him, I hugged him close and breathed his scent in. I don't know how long we stood like that, but it was like coming home.

Eventually, he pulled away and studied my face. "Gabe is checking on Dean. We'll know more soon." He swallowed. "Spencer and Miranda had just left when you called, and I was sure we'd given something away somehow. I've never been so scared."

I brushed his hair off his forehead. "I'm sorry. I didn't want to take any chances with Lucy."

When I hesitated, he shot me a suspicious look. "What are you not telling me?"

I sighed. "I think someone's been following me the last couple of days. Nothing I can pinpoint, and there's never anyone there when I turn around. Still, I'd swear I was being watched."

He listened silently as I explained the creeped-out feeling I'd had at school and when I'd been taking the trash out. When I finished, he stepped back, sank down on the couch with his elbows on his knees, and passed a weary hand over his face.

"You should've told me. We've made plans to help you, but they're useless if you keep secrets. It's not only your life at stake in this. Your family, my family. We're all in danger."

Regret instantly filled me. A lifetime of taking care of myself had overpowered common sense. I sat beside him, not quite touching him. "I'm sorry. I don't know what I was thinking."

"You were thinking you could take care of everyone and everything. You weren't thinking about what we'd all do if something happened to you. Do you have a death wish?"

"No! I knew you would've called if you thought I was in danger from your friends."

Asher's hands hung limply between his knees, and he gazed at me with bleak eyes. "They're not the only threat out there. What will it take for you to understand? If something happens to you, there's no coming back from this for me."

Tears pricked at the corners of my eyes, and I wished I could cry for once. Words always seemed to fail me when it came to Asher. Years of being told I wasn't good enough had worn me down, and I didn't know how to tell him that I felt the same way.

We'd always communicated best when he heard my thoughts. Acting on instinct, I scooted across the couch to sit on Asher's lap, pressing my nose against his neck. After a long moment, he wrapped one hand around my bare feet to warm them and the other around my shoulder to secure me against his chest.

My fingers rasped against the whiskers darkening his jaw. "I'm sorry. I can't seem to get the words out. To tell you what I feel. I wish you knew."

His chin rubbed against the top of my head, and he sighed.

On impulse, I looked up into his tired eyes and asked, "Asher, do you trust me?"

"Of course."

"Keep your guard lowered."

He frowned. "Why?"

"Please."

He stared down at me for a long moment, and finally nodded. My hand curved to his cheek, and I focused all my energy on him. The idea had occurred to me sometime after I'd managed to exert my power on Lottie, allowing her to feel Gabe. That day, there'd been no side effects to what I'd done, and I guessed it was because I hadn't truly healed her. The sensation had been temporary, lasting only as long as Gabe held my hand. I'd wondered ever since if I could do the same thing for Asher. My powers had worked with his siblings when my intense desire to help them had kicked in. I hoped it worked the same way a second time and concentrated on how I knew he missed the scent of the sea and the world around him.

"Remy? What are you—" His words cut off abruptly, and he inhaled a deep breath. "Tell me I'm not imagining this."

"Tell me what you're experiencing."

His eyes stayed closed as he moved his head from side to side, trying to take in everything at once. "Flowers. Wildflowers, though, not roses like my house. Earth. Sea air. I can smell." His eyes opened, and he looked around the room, spying the vase of flowers on the side table. A wide smile lit up his face. "I can smell!"

Suddenly, Asher's nose burrowed in my hair. I giggled when his breath tickled my neck, and he gave a loud sniff.

"Lemons and vanilla. Delicious enough to eat." He nibbled at my neck, and I laughed again. He stilled and sat in silence, a peaceful calm settling on his face.

A minute later, he inhaled once more and dropped a kiss on my chin. "It's fading. Suddenly, I'm the one without words."

He turned his head abruptly as if listening to something in the distance. I waited a moment and finally heard it, too, about twenty seconds later. A car was pulling into the drive. Ben and Laura were home, and explanations would be required.

With a great deal of reluctance, I scrambled to my feet and whispered one thought. *I love you.*

He reached for my hand and intertwined his fingers with mine. "One day I hope to hear you say that out loud." When I opened my mouth to speak, his fingers settled on my lips. "No. Not now. When you say it, it should be because you want to say it, not because I want to hear it. I've waited for you a long time. I can wait until you're ready."

I hadn't said "I love you" to anyone since I was a child. The last person I'd said it to was Anna. I hoped Asher was right that someday I could tell him what I felt without my vocal cords freezing up. Letting down my mental shield was far easier than breaking down the walls around my heart.

CHAPTER TWENTY-FIVE

*B*en took me to the BMV the next morning to get my license. Throughout the night, the calls had continued to our house from various pay phones in the area. Ben had finally taken the phone off the hook until morning when he'd changed our number. An alarm system would also be installed right away.

Trying to set aside my worry, I passed both the written and driving tests with flying colors. A proud Ben caught my attention when he waved the keys to my Mustang under my nose. He grinned with delight. "Ready to take your car for a celebratory spin?"

"Oh, yeah!" Barely containing my excitement, I snatched the keys out of his hand. He laughed and watched as I unlocked the driver's door. He made no move to join me, and I raised a brow at him.

"What're you waiting for, old man? Scared to get in a car with me now that I have my license?"

My father snorted and almost ran to the passenger door. I realized he'd been waiting for an invitation. When we were seated, I started the car and we listened with reverence to the roar of the engine. With care, I backed the Mustang out of the driveway and onto the road. My fear that I would stall the car faded when I shifted smoothly from first to second gear. Ben grinned at me, and I knew he understood what discipline it took not to stomp on the gas to see what my baby could do.

Avoiding Fort Rowden, I headed out of town. We rolled down the windows and turned up the radio. It didn't matter that the air was freezing cold or that the music was Ben's favorite—the Bee Gees—and he shamelessly sang along at the top of his lungs in falsetto. What mattered was that this moment couldn't be more perfect, and I wished I could tell Ben how I felt.

My heart tripped over the words coming out of my mouth, but I did the best I could. "The car is unbelievable! Thanks, Dad."

Ben cleared his throat as if a sudden lump had formed. "You deserve it. I love you, Remy."

Out of the corner of my eye, I saw Ben's lips tip into a grin that mirrored my own.

Later, Gabe acted irritable when he couldn't get a rise out of me. Spencer and Miranda had suspected nothing. In fact, they knew nothing about my existence. Still, their visit had made our danger a reality. Despite this, my euphoric mood couldn't be affected by a blow to the ribs.

Gabe growled when I smiled up at him from the mat where he'd knocked me flat.

"Oh, quit being such a bully and help me up," I coaxed him. He stalked away, cursing me as he went.

Asher rolled his eyes at me in warning to stop poking at his brother. "Why don't we call it quits for the day? You're not concentrating."

I shrugged as he helped me to my feet, holding my hand in his. "Can't help it. The world is suddenly not such a bad place." A wicked idea formed, and I glanced between him and the impractical vase of flowers Lottie always put in the gym because she liked the way they looked. "Things are coming up roses."

At the lame joke, I dropped my guard and concentrated as I had the night before. His mouth dropped open, and I knew he smelled the roses in the room.

Wrapped in each other, neither of us saw Gabe coming. He launched himself at Asher with a force that sent them both flying backwards. Asher's head hit the wall with a loud *crack*. With a fist grasping Asher's shirt, Gabe held him in place with predatory strength and glared back at me over his shoulder.

"Do you think this is a game, Healer? Do you want to watch my brother die at the hands of those coming for you? Maybe I should take care of him now so no one else is hurt because of your carelessness. Better Asher than the whole family, right?"

I didn't think or plan my next move. To hurt Gabe by touching him might mean transferring that pain to Asher if I touched him, too. With cold fury, I gathered my energy and sent it at Gabe across ten feet of space. Red sparks lit, and his face turned white when I snapped a bone in his forearm.

It took real effort to control my rage, but I managed to cut off my energy and put my defenses in place. Asher and Gabe both dropped to the floor staring at me, and the edge of fear on their faces twisted a knife in my gut. I turned to find a furious Lottie standing behind me. I ignored her and went to kneel at Gabe's hip.

"Can I touch you?"

He gave a hesitant nod, and I placed a hand on his broken arm. He winced, but didn't move. Several minutes later, when the green sparks had faded, he stretched the arm with relief while mine throbbed. I scanned myself and was relieved when I healed my broken arm without Asher's help.

Gabe stood and regarded me with approval. "Good

work today, Remy. You may not be completely useless, after all."

It was the first time Asher's brother had called me by my
name since I'd learned he was a Protector.

He ignored my shock and turned to Asher, who had
climbed to his feet, uninjured. "Sorry, bro, but it was necessary. Your girl has a hair trigger where you're concerned.
You might want to have a talk with her. I don't think she
grasps that you're the Protector." His head tilted and he
glanced around, slightly bemused. "I think I'm losing it. I
could've sworn I smelled roses in here."

I looked anywhere but at Asher, not wanting to see his
fear again. My gaze landed on Lottie. I'd had little interac-
tion with her since I'd begun training at the Blackwells'.
She left or holed up in her room to avoid me, and I
couldn't blame her for hating me when I'd injured her
brother.

She took a threatening step forward. "Why don't you
leave, Healer? Haven't you done enough harm for one
day?"

Gabe placed a restraining hand on her shoulder.
"Enough, Charlotte. I provoked her. She protected Asher,
the same as you would."

Lottie knocked her brother's hand away and departed
with another glower in my direction. "Don't compare me
to *her*. *I* would never do anything to put my family in
danger."

Gabe and Asher remained in the gym, and their stares
weighed on me. Angry now, I wanted to go home to get
away from Asher and the look of fear that I'd seen on his
face.

"Damn it, Remy! I wasn't afraid of you."

Reinforcing my shield, I spared him a disdainful look.
"Right. Could've fooled me." He betrayed me to think I

could hurt him. Even Gabe knew I'd do anything to protect Asher.

"I didn't betray you!" He leaned down to help me up
and ground his teeth when I ignored his outstretched
hand.

"Get out of my head, Asher!"

His arms crossed over his chest, and he glared down at
me. "Try turning down the volume. It's hard to ignore
you when you're shouting."

If I didn't leave, I'd end up punching him in his handsome face. I rose to my feet too quickly and suffered a
bout of light-headedness that had me swaying. The floor
rose up to meet me until Gabe steadied me with a hand
on my shoulder.

Asher rushed over in concern, but I glowered at him
until he backed off. He didn't seem upset at my rejection,
but shot me a triumphant glance. "You know, threats
strung with compliments aren't very effective."

I stared at him in confusion until I realized the jerk had
heard me thinking he was handsome. With a mean smile,
I pictured Gabe's beautiful face and his bracing hand, filling my mind with him until Asher would see nothing else.
Asher's smug look faded into a dark scowl, and he stepped
forward with his hands in fists at his side.

Gabe heard only one side of our conversation, but he'd
got the gist. He steered me away from an enraged Asher.
"Hey, focus." He sighed when we didn't say anything.
"Either of you notice how easy it was for me to pin
Asher?"

It occurred to me that it shouldn't have been possible.
Asher should have heard him coming, unless . . . We both
turned to stare at Gabe, and he confirmed what I'd been
thinking for some time. "He's becoming human."

Gabe's expression hardened, and he gripped my arm
with a new desperation. I felt a tiny shiver of fear, know-

ing he could kill me before I could choke out a scream. "Don't lie to me, Healer. Are you the cure?"

My eyes met Asher's. He looked terrified. As if he were scared to believe.

"Yes," I finally answered. "I think I am."

We moved to the garden, and Gabe served tea like we were having an ordinary conversation about everyday matters. He had a million questions, and I couldn't answer any of them. I didn't know why I'd been able to attack Gabe without touching him. I didn't know what set me apart from other Healers. My mother had been powerless, and I sensed nothing different about my father, aside from his irregular heartbeat. What else could there be? Gabe left me alone with Asher, his dissatisfaction evident.

I tried to gauge Asher's mood as he sat in the lounge chair next to me. He hadn't said anything while Gabe quizzed me. When he lifted a teacup to his lips to take a sip, I impulsively directed my energy at him, trying to use my power without touch. Asher's lips curved on the rim of the delicate china, and I knew he'd tasted the tea.

"Remy," he sighed.

Rising, I went to curl up next to him on his chair, my head resting on his shoulder so I could see his face. "What are you thinking?"

He dropped a kiss on my nose. "I'm frightened about what happens if others discover your abilities, *mo chridhe*."

I'd never heard the endearment and wondered what it meant. My heart flipped at the tenderness in his eyes, and I smoothed the worry lines on his forehead. "And what will you do if you're too human to protect me?"

Asher's jaw worked as he turned to study the rose garden in the distance. "It's happening when you're not around now," he admitted. "This morning I bumped into Lottie in the kitchen, and I felt her. A few minutes ago, I smelled the ocean. And earlier, I was too busy smelling roses to hear Gabe coming. What if I can't keep you safe?"

"Aren't you the one who's been trying to convince me that we're in this together? We keep each other safe, you idiot."

He finally smiled. "You say the sweetest things to me."

Asher's eyes fixed on my curved mouth. He pulled me to my feet, and I leaned into him. He put his hands up, palms facing me, and I rested mine flat against them. My smaller hands looked fragile next to his, and the heat I always felt when we touched spread from our hands through my body like tiny prickles of fire.

A peaceful serenity settled over me. Suddenly, the fear disappeared as if it had never been, and the words came with ease.

"I love you, Asher."

His guard slipped, and he stared at me with an intensity that crackled in the air between us. "Say it again."

"I love you."

His fingers wove through mine, using them to drag me closer, and he kissed me. My thoughts shattered in a million different directions, and then coalesced into one word—*Asher*. His lips softened against mine. The heat radiating from his hands intensified, and I clutched him tighter until my hands began to tingle.

"Remy?" Something in his tone alerted me.

We pulled away and stared down in awe. Small sparks of green light shot from our joined hands, dancing along both his skin and mine. For the first time, they felt . . . pleasant and warm. It reminded me of the sparklers children played with on the Fourth of July, drawing lazy circles in the sky with traces of light.

Asher smiled, obviously experiencing the same sensation. "This is new," he said, softly.

"But kind of cool, huh? Any pain?" My own voice sounded reverent.

"None. It's . . . nice."

We watched in silence as the flickers of light made the cool night air glow. Too soon the flames faded away.

"Let's do it again," I said.

Asher shook his head. "I don't think so. I didn't notice it before, but I should've. Your humming is fading. Are you feeling okay?"

Now that I thought about it, I hadn't been feeling normal since I'd used my power on Gabe. My body felt tired and achy, as if I'd run ten miles.

Asher studied me with concern. "You have a tiny bruise on your neck where Gabe clipped you. Can you heal it?"

I tried to gather my energy. Sparks sizzled from the tips of my fingers, but nothing more happened. "I think I shorted out my powers when I hurt Gabe and healed my arm. Otherwise, I feel fine."

I punctuated the statement with a sneeze. Asher put a hand to my forehead and grimaced. "You're burning up."

"That's you. Your skin is always hot." My voice sounded grouchy to my own ears.

He smiled. "No, *mo chridhe*. It's definitely you. How long has it been since you had the flu?"

"I haven't been sick since I got my powers." I sneezed again.

"I think I'd better get you home. You need to get some rest."

I protested all the way home. It was not possible that I was sick. I couldn't be coming down with something, not when I couldn't heal myself. I was still objecting when Ben dosed me with flu medication and ordered me to bed. I fell asleep as soon as my head hit the pillow, dreaming about sparklers and what *mo chridhe* might mean.

CHAPTER TWENTY-SIX

*B*y morning, the flu had arrived full blown, and I grew irritable on top of being miserable when I couldn't heal myself. Laura and Ben left to go sailing and—to my thinking—to escape my evil mood. Even showering exhausted me, and I was sprawled on my bed with wet hair when Asher arrived to check on me.

"You can't go to bed with wet hair."

He went into the bathroom to retrieve a hair dryer and returned to help me into the chair by the window, tucking a blanket around me and draping my hair over the back of the chair.

"Go ahead and sleep, *mo chridhe*. I'll take care of you."

The hair dryer flicked on and his fingers tugged the long curls, separating them to let the air hit them. I half-dozed as he dried my hair, enjoying his light touch. I woke when he lifted me and sat in the chair with me curled on his lap, tucking a blanket around both of us. His heat comforted me, and I settled against him, drifting.

My voice sounded thick with sleep when I asked, "What is mow-cry-uh?"

"It's a Gaelic endearment my father called my mother."

That didn't seem to be an answer, but I lost my train of thought. "Hmm."

"I've been thinking." He rested his chin on the top of my head.

"Hmm?"

His laugh rumbled under my ear. "Are you awake?"

My words slurred. "Barely. Your fault. You're a human electric blanket. What're you thinking?"

"We've done nothing the normal way. The way we met and everything that's happened since. We've skipped a few steps. I want to take you on a date. Multiple dates."

He sounded nervous, and I frowned. "We've been on dates. The island. Your house. The beach."

"I mean a real date."

"But I like our dates." The petulance had returned to my voice.

"You mean when you broke your rib to save me on the ferry or when I'm forced to watch you spar with Gabe?"

"Well, when you put it like that . . ." I grumbled.

He blew out a breath, mussing my hair. "I grew up in a different time, Remy. If I'd met you then, I would've called on you for tea. I would've courted you with carriage rides through the park and candy and flowers and poetry."

My head rolled against his shoulder so I could see his face, as I struggled to piece together what he was saying. "You want to court me?"

Raw emotion burned in his voice. "You *deserve* poetry."

I studied the soft full lips that could kiss me into oblivion, and his eyes that could see into me. I'd never wanted anyone to pursue me—the idea sounded archaic—but Asher changed everything. In truth, he already owned my heart. My head dropped back to his chest, and I breathed in his woodsy scent mixed with my clean one. "Okay," I said.

"Okay?"

"Hmm. I like daisies."

"Daisies." He sounded bemused.

"Yes. And peanut M&Ms."

"Good to know. I would've guessed chocolate-covered espresso beans."

"Mmm, those, too. Oh, and I'd rather you recited *Peter Pan* than poetry."

"I'll remember that."

I fell asleep listening to the rapid, irregular beat of his heart under my ear, wondering why it made me think of Ben.

By Tuesday morning, I felt human again. My powers had returned, and I'd eradicated the flu. I rushed out the door to drive myself to school in my Mustang for the first time. When I opened the driver's door, a huge bouquet of cheerful daisies sat on the passenger seat. Lifting them to my face, I inhaled their earthy, green scent. Then, anxious to see Asher, I started the car and jumped when a narrator's voice blasted from the stereo reading an excerpt from *Peter Pan*. Somehow Asher had snuck the flowers and CD into my car.

He waited for me in the school parking lot and opened my car door. I stuttered, thanking him for the flowers, and he grinned. As had become our routine, he took my bag and walked me to class. He left me at the door with a gentle kiss on my lips.

His courtship continued at lunch when a café mocha waited for me at our table. Asher wore an enigmatic smile and refused to tell me how he'd managed to get the drink from off-campus during school hours. He touched me constantly during the day with a hand in mine, his arm around my shoulders as we walked, or a quick brush of his lips on my cheek. My friends looked shocked to see the unattainable Asher Blackwell smitten, and Lucy shook her head at us with a happy grin. Money traded hands between Brandon and Greg, and I suspected another wager had been placed.

The rest of the week passed in a whirlwind of gifts as Asher wooed me. Peanut M&Ms *and* espresso beans made it onto my lunch tray. Tiny, square love notes hid in secret places for me to discover, including coat pockets, tucked between the pages of my books, and in my locker. A first edition of *Peter Pan* appeared gift-wrapped on my bed— Lucy admitted Asher had drafted her to help deliver that present. I melted each time I read where he'd underlined the description of Mrs. Darling's hidden kiss.

My phone rang Thursday night while I got ready for bed. There had been no further crank calls since Ben had changed our home number and he'd given me a cell to keep on me at all times. Asher had saved all the Blackwells' phone numbers in the memory, and I resisted the temptation to leave Lottie a piece of my mind. The more time Asher devoted to me, the ruder she'd become. Instead of sticking to her bedroom during my visits, she now followed Asher and me around like a demented chaperone, never leaving us alone for more than two minutes at a time.

A smile curved my mouth when I remembered Asher's solution to escaping her earlier that evening. He'd sent Lottie on a made-up errand and tugged me into the pantry off the kitchen. Lottie had found us a couple of minutes later just as the green sparks faded. We'd learned that the sparks sporadically happened with more frequency, even when one or both of us had our guards up. We couldn't predict when they'd happen, and we'd had to make up odd excuses a couple of times when someone noticed them. We suspected they were connected to the changes in Asher's body as he became more human. It seemed that my body healed him of his immortality a little at a time, though no one could explain why or how. I sensed Asher felt torn between his desire to be mortal and his need to protect me, but neither of us felt willing to separate to slow the process.

At my breathy hello, Asher said, "Did you find it?"

Laughing at his eagerness, I settled on the bed and asked, "Find what?"

"Check under your pillow."

Reaching behind me, I shoved aside a mountain of pillows and found a small wrapped box. "Another present? You don't have to give me gifts, Asher."

"I'm making up for lost time. Besides, you love them."

I fingered the black ribbon on the box. I liked that he hadn't used pink since I'd never been a girly girl. "You see too much."

"Only what matters, *mo chridhe*." His deep voice rumbled through the phone. "Did you open it?"

"Just a sec." I untied the bow and lifted the lid off. Inside was nestled a long silver chain with several charms. Holding it up to the light, I twisted the necklace to study the different trinkets. He'd chosen each one with care. A sister charm for Lucy. A tiny car for my father. A lighthouse for the place we'd had our first date and a little ferryboat for where we'd shared our first kiss. The small ice cream cone reminded me of my mother. My favorite, though, was the tiny thimble like the one Peter Pan had given Wendy when she asked for a kiss.

"Oh, Asher. I love it!" I said, around the lump in my throat.

"Go out with me tomorrow night? We could go to dinner and a movie. Maybe even double-date with Lucy and Tim like normal people."

Turning the chain in the light again to watch the charms dangle and gleam in the light, I beamed. "I would love to go on a date with you."

On Friday morning, Ben and Laura met Lucy and me in the kitchen. Weeks ago, a friend had offered them a cabin on Cutter Island to use for a second honeymoon. I'd completely forgotten Ben and Laura's anniversary and felt like a heel. They planned to hit the road before breakfast and wouldn't be back until Sunday night. On their way out the door, Laura gave us a list of emergency phone numbers and ran through the house rules—no parties, no drinking, no drugs, and no boys in the house. Ben seconded the no-boys-in-the-house rule as the door slammed shut behind them.

Lucy and I rolled our eyes at each other. When the door opened unexpectedly, Ben found us doing a celebration dance in the entryway. He looked worried. "Maybe we shouldn't go. With the crank calls, I don't feel right leaving you girls alone."

Looping an arm around his waist, I reassured him. "Dad, go. Have fun. We haven't had a single call since you changed our number. Lucy and I will be fine."

Lucy gave him a cheeky grin. "Besides, Remy and I will be heartbroken if you back out. It's not often we get the run of the house. You know you can trust us."

He nodded and we pushed him out the door. "Keep the doors locked and the alarm on. Call us when you get home tonight. If you need anything, we're less than two hours away." Finally, he left, and Lucy and I waved until the car disappeared around a corner before resuming our celebration dance.

Later that night, I proudly wore my necklace and let Lucy dress me up, even going so far as to wear heels with my red skirt. We had dinner at La Fleur. Tim seemed pleasant enough, and he obviously cared about Lucy. She practically glowed sitting next to him, and I could have liked him for that alone. After dinner, we all headed next door to the Broderick Theater, the only movie theater in town. The scent of buttered popcorn wafted through the building, making my mouth water. I couldn't concentrate on the screen with Asher sitting next to me.

We didn't dare touch in the dark in case sparks flew. It would have been impossible to explain a sudden flare of green light that originated from us. The air between us almost sizzled anyway. At one point he turned to stare at me with the light from the movie screen flickering over his face. He took a deep breath before facing forward, the taut line of his unmoving body belying his tension. I followed his example and hoped the movie wasn't an epic.

A long time later, the lights came up in the theater. Asher's hand slipped into mine, and green sparks lit across our skin.

Lucy caught the glow out of the corner of her eye and gasped. "What was that?"

"Static electricity. Asher shocked me. I heard there was a storm coming."

Lucy and Tim walked out ahead of us, and Asher glanced sideways at me. "Static electricity? That's the best you can do?"

I rolled my eyes. "I didn't hear you offering up an explanation."

"Fourth of July came early?" His lips quirked.

I snickered. "You really light up my life, Asher."

He laughed and tossed an arm around my shoulders. "That was awful."

Lucy turned and shouted, "Hey, you two. Catch up already. Let no man—or sister—get between me and ice cream."

We walked to Heavenly Ice Cream. Asher ordered me a scoop of Espresso Chip and a Triple Citrus Italian ice for himself. He grinned when I touched his hand so he could taste the dessert. His spoon dipped into my bowl so he could try mine, too.

"Hey! No cross-contamination. Keep your citrus out of my espresso."

He grinned without apology. In retaliation, I dipped a finger in my ice cream and tapped the tip of his nose, leaving behind a smudge of tan cream. His eyes promised retribution. It wasn't fair that he could look so gorgeous when anyone else would have looked silly.

Asher leaned forward so only I could hear his whisper. "You've got that look you always do when you're thinking about how handsome I am."

I scowled at him. "Ego much?"

"Never before you. How can I help liking that you find me attractive? Especially when it's mutual. Have I told you how beautiful you are in red? Honestly, I don't think I can stop myself from kissing you."

I held my breath as he came closer. Instead of aiming for my lips, his nose brushed mine. Amused, I pulled away to wipe the ice cream off my face with a napkin. I swiped it across his face, too, and he laughed, ducking away.

Tim shook his head with a rueful smile. "I thought Lucy and I were bad."

Lucy smirked. "Told you so. I am a diehard romantic, and Remy and Asher even manage to make me blush."

Asher and I both threw our napkins at her.

"Says the sister who bet on when we wouldn't be able to stay away from each other any longer," I said.

Lucy shrugged. "I seem to remember winning that bet and giving you half the pool the day you two caved."

Asher's eyebrows rose as he pieced together what we were talking about. He looked at Lucy with new respect. "Smart woman. Remind me never to bet against you."

I spent the next ten minutes trying to puncture Lucy's inflated ego until Asher's sneeze distracted me. It took a full minute for it to register that Asher didn't sneeze, shouldn't sneeze, hadn't sneezed in over a century. I twisted in my seat, and we stared at each other in shock while Tim continued to tease Lucy. As I watched, he grabbed a napkin and sneezed again.

His tone sounded a comical mixture of incredulity and misery. "You've got to be kidding me."

I would never have wished the misery on him, but I couldn't help it when my lips twitched.

He glared at me. "Don't you dare laugh."

Lucy shot us a curious look. "What's so funny?"

"I think Asher's coming down with something." There was no way I could explain that my immortal boyfriend hadn't been sick in over a century, but I'd managed to give him the flu.

Tim grimaced. "Oh, man. That sucks."

I touched Asher's forehead and noticed the skin felt hotter than usual. "You have a fever. We should go. You're going to need a lot of rest and fluids if you have what I did."

As we left the ice cream shop, Asher's cell rang, and he held back to answer it. His miserable expression transformed from concerned to furious in an instant as he listened to the person on the other end. When he hung up and rejoined us, I was terrified I knew what he would say.

"I have to head home to take care of some family stuff. Would you guys mind taking Remy home?"

Tim nodded and Lucy asked, "Is everything okay?"

Asher rolled his shoulders and gave her a distracted smile. "Yes. Just the usual family drama."

The usual family drama didn't exist as far as the Blackwells were concerned. Asher stepped close and pulled the edge of my jacket closed against the cold. Too low for Lucy and Tim to hear, he said, "Something's up with Lottie. Gabe wouldn't tell me over the phone, but they need me to come home." Asher sighed. "I'm sorry, Remy. I wanted this to be a normal date. If this is another of Lottie's attempts to keep us apart, I'm going to throttle her."

I stroked a hand over his shadowed jaw. "Don't worry about it. Go take care of your family."

"I'll call you as soon as I can." He sighed in frustration and dropped a kiss on my lips.

CHAPTER TWENTY-SEVEN

*T*im dropped us off at the house, and I waited impatiently for Asher to call. Two hours passed without news, and I knew something was wrong. I double-checked the alarm and door locks, trying not to worry Lucy. We called Ben and Laura to reassure them that we'd returned home safe and sound from our date. It sounded like they were having a blast, and I felt guilty for wishing them home.

Lucy headed upstairs, and I paced restlessly through the living room. Finally, a knock sounded, and I peeked through the curtain to see Asher. I yanked open the front door, and he entered with Gabe on his heels.

"Asher? What's going on?"

He didn't speak right away, and fear skittered along my nerves. "It's my sister, Remy. She's betrayed us. She's the one who's been stalking you. The phone calls and the person you felt following you. She did it."

Shocked, I stared between him and Gabe. "Why would she—?"

Asher touched my hand. "It gets worse. She called Spencer and Miranda and told where to find you. They're on their way."

My knees buckled, and I sank down on the stairs. Lottie had looked at me like she hated my guts. I should have expected this. "When will they get here?" I said in a flat tone.

"Tomorrow, we think. We haven't been able to reach them." He kneeled down in front of me, bringing his eyes level with mine. He looked tired and worried and feverish. "I'm sorry, Remy. She was scared, and she convinced herself she was protecting our family. She knew it was wrong as soon as she did it."

Gabe leaned against the closed front door watching us. "It wasn't just Asher's senses returning. Having you around has affected us all, and Lottie never wanted to be mortal again." He shrugged as if he didn't care one way or the other about his own mortality.

Asher hit the wall. "I should've seen this coming!"

"How could you have?" Gabe asked.

I'd made Lottie vulnerable, and she'd hated me for it. I dropped my head into my hands, bracing my elbows on my knees. She must have been terrified when she began to feel things. At least Asher and I had been going through everything together. "Is she okay?"

Asher's laugh sounded bitter. "How can you even ask? We were supposed to protect you, not bring more danger into your life."

At least I knew my stalker's identity. Dean could be discounted from the equation. I took a deep breath. "Do Spencer and Miranda know where I live?"

Asher stood with his hands in fists at his side. "No. She told them she suspected a Healer lived in Blackwell Falls. That's enough to bring them here to investigate. And if they come, they'll find you."

"I thought they were family. Can't you explain . . . ?"

Gabe broke in. "If they're coming to kill you, our ties won't stop them. They'll think we betrayed them by keeping you a secret."

"Right. I'm the enemy."

In a tortured voice, Asher continued, "Lottie called them today. They planned to catch the first flight from England in the morning. We're leaving right now to cut them off in Portland."

I rose to my feet and wrapped my arms around myself. "My parents are gone, Asher. I'm responsible for Lucy. I can't leave her alone."

Asher's eyes took on a desolate look. "I know. Gabe and I are going alone. We're going to head them off tomorrow afternoon when they get off the plane. We'll tell them we found the Healer and killed her. Killed *you*. Whatever it takes to make them leave. I swear to you, Remy, I'll fix this."

I scrubbed a hand over my face. "What if you can't? What if they insist on coming here to see the proof? Oh, God. My family, Asher. I can't . . . I wouldn't be able to live . . ." I pictured Anna watching her home burn with her mother's body inside.

He cut me off. "Don't go there. I'll take care of it. I won't let anything happen to you. I told you, I'll do whatever it takes."

Acid churned in my stomach. I believed he would do everything in his power to keep us safe. The Protectors were coming to kill me, and he would try to stop them, while I waited here in agony. All my training had been for nothing because Asher would go in my place. I suddenly couldn't drag enough air into my lungs.

His arms engulfed me. "I promise everything will be okay. You can believe me," he whispered.

I didn't believe in vows, but I heard myself asking for one, anyway. "This isn't fair. I need you, Asher. Please, please promise you'll come back."

He tugged me into the living room out of Gabe's sight and trapped my face between his hands. "Nothing on this earth could keep me from you. Don't you know? This isn't a tragedy we're in, *mo chridhe*. We get to live happily ever after."

"I love you." My voice barely reached a whisper.

He pulled me close in a desperate embrace. He'd never kissed me like this, with total abandon, not even the first time on the ferry. Like that time, though, my body began to heal him, and I tried to pull away. Asher wouldn't let me go. His hands fisted in my hair, his lips pressed hard against mine, and I couldn't get close enough to him. Too soon, he set me away from him, pain clear in his eyes. Green sparks sizzled between us as we separated.

"I'll come back, *mo chridhe*." He backed away as if it took all his strength to walk away and disappeared out the front door past his brother.

"Gabe?" He paused in the act of following Asher and looked at me. "What does mow-cry-uh mean?"

The hardness in Gabe's eyes softened. "It's Gaelic for 'my heart.' My father started calling my mother that when he met her. He said his heart didn't truly beat until he met her."

I grasped the doorway to stay upright when my legs threatened to crumple. Gabe met my harsh stare with cool eyes. "Return without him, and I'll break every bone in your body."

He nodded. "And you remember your training, Healer. You brought my brother back to life. I'm rethinking my idea that the only good Healer is a dead Healer. Don't make me wrong."

The door slammed closed behind him, and I prepared to live out the longest night and day of my life.

Left on my own to guard Lucy, I sat in my room, jumping at shadows and listening for any weird noises. Despite Asher's reassurances that Lottie was the stalker, I couldn't shake the notion that something dark and twisted lurked outside, anticipating an opportunity to slither in.

Asher called once during the night to let me know he'd reached Portland. He sounded miserable with the flu, and I wished I'd healed him before he left. He didn't complain, but Gabe grumbled in the background that all bets were off if Asher got him sick and his threat almost made me smile.

After we hung up, it was back to waiting. Morning brought a relief and dread. Lucy noticed my quiet mood and left me to my thoughts. When she mentioned going out with Tim for the day, I snapped to attention. I convinced her I had a sudden desire to drown in chick flicks, and she stayed home to keep me company. The day dissolved in a blur of microwave popcorn and pedicures. In the end, I didn't fool Lucy.

"What's up with you and Asher?" she asked. "I heard his voice last night. Everything okay?"

It occurred to me that Lucy had canceled her plans with Tim to stay home and cheer me up. My stilted smile folded under her concerned gaze, and I wondered if I'd be able to protect my sister when the chips were down.

"Whoa. You didn't break up or anything, did you? That would be really stupid of you. He's different than I thought he'd be. It's obvious to anyone with eyes in their head that you belong together."

I tried to regain control of my runaway emotions. "No. He's going through some stuff with his family. He had to go to Portland last night. I'm worried about him, that's all. He's supposed to call soon."

She smiled and looped an arm around my shoulder. "Give him some time. He'll call."

By six in the evening, I'd given up pretending interest in the movies and paced in front of the living room window. My phone rang, and I took it into the hallway for privacy.

"Asher?"

"It's me. Everything's okay, Remy. It went better than we could have hoped!" He sounded relieved and exhausted.

"We're safe?" It couldn't have been that easy.

"Yes. I saw them back on the plane myself. We convinced them that Lottie has been acting oddly. We told them we'd hunted for a Healer in town and hadn't found one. They believed us. They had no reason not to when we've never lied to them before." Regret roughened his voice. "To be safe, we're going to wait until the plane takes off, and then we'll be on our way back."

I slid down the wall until I sat on the floor. The bad feeling I'd had all night lingered. "Are you sure?"

His voice caressed my raw nerves through the phone. "I'm sure. They'll be back in a couple of months to visit, to check on Lottie. We'll need to keep a low profile, so we don't draw attention to ourselves, but we're safe for now."

I tried to shake off the lingering sense of doom. "How long until you're back?"

"A few hours, at most." He sneezed on the other end of the line.

"I should've healed you before you left. You should go home to rest when you get back. We'll see each other tomorrow. It's been a long day for everyone."

His voice dropped low. "I'll sleep while Gabe drives. You okay?"

Apparently, I wasn't fooling anyone today. "Yeah. Just tired. I didn't sleep last night. See you tomorrow?"

"Yes. I love you."

"I love you, too. And Asher? Thank you."

"You have nothing to thank me for. We're in this together, remember?"

We hung up, and Lucy poked her head in the hall. I wondered what she'd heard. "Everything okay, now?"

I clambered to my feet. "Sure. Want to get out of here and get some dinner? I'm going stir crazy."

She gave me a wicked smile. "Only if we can get Greek pizza with extra olives."

At my nod, she raced upstairs to dress, and I followed. My rotten mood faded as relief stole in. If Asher said the Protectors were leaving, I believed him. We were back at square one. With a lighter heart, I determined to have fun tonight with my sister to make up for my distraction today. When we'd bundled up in jeans, sweaters, and our coats, we headed down to Beachfront Pizza and shared an overloaded, salty pizza with sourdough crust while sitting in the crowded upstairs dining room overlooking Main Street.

Eventually, we ate our fill and stopped in at Heavenly to take some Espresso Chip ice cream home for dessert. I pulled the Mustang into the garage, and Lucy raced ahead of me to the house. The alarm was off, and I wondered if I'd turned it on before we'd left. I almost bumped into my sister when I stepped into the kitchen behind her.

"Lucy? What are you—?"

My question halted when I felt her trembling. I glanced around her and saw my nightmares brought back to life.

Dean sat at my family's kitchen table with a gun in his hand.

CHAPTER TWENTY-EIGHT

"*C*ome in, ladies."

Dean pitched his voice low and friendly as he sprawled in a chair, tipping it back on two legs. It was the slick tone he used when he wanted something. He looked as if he'd been roughing it recently with streaks of dirt smeared on his face and his blond curls greasy. His flannel shirt and jeans were filthy, as if he'd been tramping through the woods.

Lucy had no idea what my stepfather looked like, but she understood the danger of the stranger before her. My sister clutched the forgotten bag of ice cream, like an animal caught in the sights of a snake about to strike.

Dean's smile sharpened, his hand tightening on the weapon. He motioned at Lucy with a lazy wave of the gun, and my heart threatened to stop. "Why don't you both toss me your phones?"

We slid them across the floor, and he pocketed them.

"What are you doing here, Dean? We don't have any money. At least not enough to matter once the cops find out where you are. You must've set off the alarm, and I'd say you've violated the restraining order we took out against you."

He laughed. "You forget. I installed alarms for a living once. The police aren't coming."

I had forgotten that. At one time I'd suspected him of using his skills to break into those homes, but he'd been fired from that job before he got caught.

"As for the money," he continued. "I have another reason for being here."

"Revenge," I said, with flat certainty.

The chair legs hit the floor, and Dean dropped the relaxed façade. "Oh, yeah. Revenge," he said, softly. "Six hours in a jail cell with a dislocated shoulder. You did that. I lost everything because of you, bitch. Want to know how I got through it? I imagined wrapping my fingers around your throat and squeezing."

His eyes closed as if he were lost in the memory, and his lips curved in a smile. Lucy began crying, and he continued, "Shh . . . this is my favorite part when I stare into your pretty blue eyes, princess, and you realize you're gonna die."

Lucy whimpered, and I considered striking him down right then. It would be so easy to break his neck. Except he had the gun and my new powers were unpredictable, at best. I'd get one shot to hurt him, and if I failed, I'd be too weak to protect Lucy. Asher's voice shouted in my head for me to be smart and wait for an opening. Dean's eyes snapped open, narrowing to dangerous slits when I moved a few inches away from Lucy to divide his attention. The rage in his voice was a riptide towing me under an ocean of fear.

"Of course, it'd never work. You'd just turn the pain back on me and heal yourself. That's when it occurred to me." He tapped a finger to his head like a lightbulb had gone off. "People'd pay for your talents."

"Remy, what's he talking about?" Lucy's voice quivered.

"Nothing." I'd been so desperate to keep the truth from my family. It killed me to have Dean spill my secrets. Everything I'd done, all the lies I'd told, hadn't kept Lucy safe.

Dean grinned. "You didn't tell them you're a mutant?" He turned to Lucy. "Your sister, here, can do real special things. Like heal broken bones with her mind. Or break them."

I ignored Lucy's confusion and stared at Dean with hatred. "Why don't we test that theory on you, Dean?"

He whistled through his teeth. "Aren't you the brave one?"

"Why don't you get to the point?" I said, bitterly.

"What's your hurry, Remy? We've got all night with your parents out of town. They left you a real sweet message on the machine to tell you they'd check in with you tomorrow."

He'd been watching and waiting for a chance to strike. "I saw you," I said. "I saw you out at Fort Rowden."

"Mmm. I nearly took you then. I thought about killing your daddy in front of you."

More likely he'd been intimidated by the size of my father and slunk away in the dark. "You could've gotten to me a thousand times in these last weeks. What were you waiting for?"

"This." He held up an object I hadn't noticed on the table. My iPod. "Your mother interrupted me before I could listen to the whole thing, and I think it's time we got to know each other better, girl."

Dean rose and motioned to us with the gun. "Into the living room. We're gonna do a little show-and-tell."

Lucy didn't move, and I shook her until she dropped the bag of ice cream. Her shocked eyes met mine. "You'll be okay. I'll get you out of this. Trust me, all right?"

She gave a tiny nod, and I tugged her by the hand to the living room, placing my body between her and Dean as he followed. He purposely stayed out of reach, I noted with growing anxiety. In the living room, he motioned for Lucy and me to sit on the couch while he moved toward

the cabinet that held Ben's sound system. Dean popped the
mp3 player into its slot on the stereo, fiddled with some
buttons, and Anna's voice filled the room.

*"Remy. Hi, baby. You probably wondered why you got an
iPod . . ."*

Dean searched out Ben's liquor cabinet next, holding up
a bottle of tequila in triumph. He uncapped the bottle and
took a huge swig as Anna explained that she'd made the
recording to tell me the truth about who I was. I understood Dean's motive. The secret to controlling me hid in
my mother's stories, and I was suddenly glad my mother
hadn't known everything about me.

"Enough. This isn't an apology."

Dean grinned with enjoyment and swilled another
ounce of my father's liquor. "That must've burned."

He knew the anger and hurt I'd felt listening to Anna.
A master manipulator, he understood what her silence had
done to me. My stomach burned watching him take pleasure in another of Anna's betrayals.

She got to the part about how my powers had developed,
recapturing his attention, and Lucy squeezed my hand. Disbelief colored her features. She thought Dean and Anna
were crazy for believing this magical nonsense. She desper-
ately needed to think that this was all a bad dream, and I
could only squeeze her hand back in weak reassurance.

Dean listened to my mother talk about how she'd loved
the popular Tom, and he shook his head with a mocking
laugh. "Geez, your mother was pathetic, even back then."

"And yet you married her. What does that make you?"
I said.

Dean's lip curled in warning, the way it did when he
would hit me. "Smart. Why do you think I married her
when she had a brat in tow? She did whatever I told her
to, and the generous checks from your daddy kept on
rolling in, princess."

". . . rumors spread like wildfire in our small town. It was just a matter of time before the Protectors heard them and hunted us."

Dean frowned at this new piece of information. He almost growled, "What the hell are Protectors?"

Misdirection seemed to be my only option, and I shrugged. "Got me. Anna was obviously insane. She called me a Healer." I said the last word with my fingers hooked in exaggerated quotes, mocking both Anna and Dean with the gesture. "And you're just as bad. The things you think I can do are impossible. Any sane person would know that."

Dean took a threatening step toward me, amber liquid sloshing in the bottle in his hand. "I know you healed your mother all those years. You broke my ribs and dislocated my shoulder. Lying isn't going to save you."

Refusing to show fear, I met Dean's glare with a cool stare and swallowed the bile rising in my throat. "Who's lying? We fought, a mirror shattered, and you hit the floor, landing on your shoulder. You seriously need a reality check."

Anna's voice filled the tense silence.

"Two men—Protectors—had come to our home because of rumors they'd heard. They suspected my mother was a Healer and hurt my father to force my mother to choose between betraying her secret and watching him die. When she healed him, they murdered her. . . ."

A smile twisted Dean's lips. The gun swerved toward Lucy.

"No!"

The shot left me no time to react. One moment Lucy sat next to me, clutching my hand in a death grip. In the next she'd fallen sideways with a red stain blooming at the waist across the thin cotton of her tee. Her guttural scream nearly broke the hold I had on my control. Dean waved the gun when I would have reached for her.

"I want to see what you can do, but I'm not stupid. Try to touch me, and I'll shoot her again. Only next time it will be in the head. Got it?"

My choppy nod satisfied him, and he waved me on. I sank down on my knees next to the couch, and Lucy's hand clawed at mine, her brown eyes latching on to me in pain. Blood oozed from a hole the size of a nickel in her side. Lifting her shirt out of the way, I pressed my free hand to the wound to slow the bleeding while I scanned her. The bullet had gone through her side, missing her organs, but she was losing too much blood, too fast. If I didn't close the wound, she'd die.

She moaned when I put more pressure on her side. "Please, don't. It hurts."

"Hold on, Luce," I breathed. "I'm going to help you."

Stripping off my jacket, I balled it up under my sister to slow the blood flow leaking from the exit wound and placed my other hand on her stomach. My first priority had to be sanitizing the injury. Otherwise, I could close the skin with the ingredients for an infection brewing inside her.

I snarled at Dean. "Give me the bottle! I need to clean the wound before I can heal it."

Instead of handing the tequila to me, he chose another bottle from the cabinet and sent it rolling across the floor with a shove of his boot. Grabbing it, I poured the fiery liquid over the burnt holes. Lucy sobbed, and I wanted to cry right along with her as I held her down. I tossed the empty bottle away and placed my hand back on her stomach.

Closing my eyes, I concentrated on sending my energy into her body. The bullet had torn through skin, tissue, and muscle. All repairable, but the blood . . . It was hard to focus when my sister lay dying under my hand. I took a deep, calming breath. As fast as I could, I repaired the torn tissues and muscle, beginning on the damaged inside and working my way outward. It took a few minutes, but the bleeding stopped.

"Son of a bitch." Dean's amazed whisper barely registered as Lucy's skin pulled together at the rough edges of the bullet entry. The gaping wound disappeared and all that remained was gunpowder residue and blood. The exit wound had closed, too, but she looked so pale.

Lucy's eyes flickered open. "Remy?" Her voice sounded stronger, and relief flooded through me.

Shoving back from my awkward position suspended over Lucy, I glared at Dean. "You want me alive to make your fortune? You better get ready to play doctor, you bastard, because I don't know that I'll have the strength to stop the bleeding."

Dean frowned at Lucy's stomach. "What the hell are you talking about? You can't even tell I shot her."

Taking a deep breath for strength, I lifted my hands from Lucy. Blue sparks arced between us, and she gasped. Then, my awareness narrowed to gut-tearing pain as my flesh tore open and hot liquid pooled at my side. Collapsing on the floor, my vision narrowed to Lucy's face as she hovered over me. A high-pitched sound reached me, and I realized she cried with fear. It hurt to bring myself back to awareness, but I couldn't leave her alone with Dean.

"Remy? Oh, please, please. I don't know what to do. Tell me what to do!"

"Towels . . . stop bleeding."

Lucy jumped to her feet and froze when Dean trained the weapon on her again. He threatened, "You're not back in twenty seconds, I kill her. And then I come looking for you."

She must have nodded because he let her go, the soles of her shoes squeaking across the wood floor. Dean kneeled nearby just out of my reach, surveying the damage to my body.

"You kept a few secrets of your own, didn't you, girl? I can see I'll have to rethink my plans. Profits go down if you die the first time out."

My lips pressed together to restrain my furious response, and I shivered with the aftermath of healing. Lucy returned with the towels, and I instructed her through chattering teeth to compress them against my side as hard as she could. Gray spots pressed on my eyes, and I struggled to stay conscious. When I was able, I focused my energy on stemming the loss of blood. Too weak to heal the twin holes in my side, I slowed the flow of blood until it congealed.

Lucy hiccupped. "Remy?"

My eyes caught on her, and I did my best to assure her. " 'M okay, Luce. Just weak. Is how my 'bilities work."

She choked on a sob. "What he said is true. You have powers."

I winced. "Yeah, Luce."

Dean interrupted us by shoving Lucy aside. "Why aren't you healing yourself? If this is a trick—"

I glared at him. "Need . . . time to rest."

The wheels turned in his mind, and a light came on. His eyes raked over Lucy's body, as if considering ways to fill the time. "You know, I was going to kill your sister, but maybe I'll just shoot her every so often to keep you in check."

He leered at her the way he'd stared at me, making me feel unclean each time his eyes had roved over me. Lucy's arms crossed over her body protectively.

"Dean?" I whispered. He looked down at me, and I enunciated each word, glancing between him and Lucy. "I'll. Kill. You."

He grinned. "Easy, princess." He rose to his feet. "Time to go, ladies."

"Where are you taking us?" Lucy asked.

"Does it matter? Move."

Dean unhooked the iPod from the stereo, and I worried what might be on the third track that I'd ignored. Anna had said it contained instructions to find my grandfather, and I'd had enough to deal with at the time, having just realized Asher was a Protector and I'd bonded to him. Now I regretted that I hadn't found the strength to listen to my mother's voice since.

Lucy helped me up, and I swayed against her when the light-headedness hit. She wrapped an arm around my waist to hold a towel against my side. "Be ready to run," I whispered.

She gave a tiny nod.

I couldn't let Dean take her with us. The terrible things he'd do to Lucy to control me would destroy us both. My body was too weakened to do much damage, but a small distraction would give her a chance to escape. I prepared to gather my energy when my cell phone rang in Dean's pocket. The shrill sound filled the room, followed by the beep indicating I had a message.

I told Dean my pass code through gritted teeth, and he played the message on speaker phone. Asher's voice was laced with tension. "Remy, we're on our way back. Listen, I just spoke to Lottie and she confessed she only called you once. The other calls had to be Dean. Take Lucy and get out of the house. I'll be there as soon as I can. I love you, sweetheart."

The phone disconnected, and some of my strength returned at hearing Asher's voice. I couldn't stop the smile that curved my lips.

Dean glared at me. "Who was that?"

"That was someone who will hunt you down when he finds out what you've done. If you want any chance of escaping, you'd better leave now."

"Why is that?" he asked.

"Asher knows all about you. He would've called the police by now. They'll be here soon."

He frowned. "You're lying."

"Look at me." I stared into his eyes letting him see my grim satisfaction. "Tell me I'm lying again."

He recognized the truth on my face and grimaced. I hoped we'd ruined his plans, and he'd run back to the sewer he'd crawled out of.

I should have known that was too much to ask for.

Dean grabbed Lucy, wrapping one arm around her neck with bruising strength while digging the gun into her temple. Without Lucy's support I wavered and barely managed to stay on my feet.

"We're all going. You, me, and Lucy, here," he demanded.

He motioned for me to walk ahead of them out of the living room, and I staggered to emphasize my weakness. Dean snarled when I fell over at the foot of the staircase, crumpling to the floor as I pretended to black out.

"Get up!" If he hadn't been afraid of touching me, he would have kicked me when I failed to respond. "Get up, damn it! I will shoot your sister."

With a silent apology to Lucy, I prayed she'd forgive me for my silence. As I'd expected, he did something to hurt her, and she screamed. When I remained still, he told Lucy, "See what's wrong with her."

His fear of touching me worked in our favor. Lucy shuffled forward and leaned over me. She touched my fingers, and I squeezed her hand to signal her to be ready. Her forefinger rested on my throat, and I forced myself not to scan her, to see how he'd hurt her.

In a shaky voice, Lucy told Dean, "I can't find a pulse. I think she's dead. You killed her!"

My sister put on an incredible performance for Dean, then. She sobbed and fell over me, clutching at my body with desperate strength. And he believed her.

He cursed, seeing his money stream dry up. Something crashed nearby, and Lucy's jump covered my startled reaction as Dean began to tear apart the entryway. Lucy moaned in real horror. When faced with a hysterical fe male, Dean did what he'd always done. He struck out. He charged at us to take out his frustrated rage on Lucy.

The air shifted as he came closer, and my nostrils filled with the acrid scent of smoke mixed with alcohol and sweat. In my attempt to wait for my one perfect shot, I almost waited too long. He stood over us when I opened my eyes. His widened in shock to see me alive, but it was too late. I touched him and managed one feeble blast of energy. It didn't transfer my injuries, but it sent a shock wave of pain into his body. He fell backwards into the front door and slid to the floor with a groan, barely conscious.

"Run, Lucy!" I croaked.

She ignored my demand and hauled me to my feet.

When I told her to forget me, she shouted, "Are you crazy? Get up!"

She wouldn't leave without me, and I did my best to help her. I would never make it out of the house with Dean blocking the front door and the garage so far away. Our only chance was to hole up on the second floor until help came. "Upstairs. Hurry!"

Lucy half shoved, half heaved me up the stairs. The door to my room had closed behind us, and we heard Dean's boots hit the bottom step, his roar of fury echoing through the house. Lucy propped me up against the wall, locked the door, and then ran to lock the bathroom door that opened onto her bedroom. She returned with a towel, and I grimaced when she replaced the bloody one at my side with the fresh one. The bleeding had started again.

"What now?" she asked.

"Try the phone."

Lucy flung herself on the bed, reaching for my phone on the far nightstand. She picked up the receiver and shook her head. "No dial tone." She pulled the phone closer, and it came away with a stripped wire. Dean must have disabled all the phones before we got home.

"We'll wait for help. Someone had to have heard the shot. Can you move my desk in front of the door?"

She had just finished moving it when a scratch sounded on the other side. Dean's voice coaxed, "Right about now you're figuring out you can't call for help. Why don't you give up, Remy, before you get your sister killed? Like you did your mother."

His whisper insinuated itself into my head, as I tried to focus. "Lucy, open the window. If Dean gets through the door, we'll need to jump." Without a tree or lattice to climb down, we risked getting injured, but staying meant death.

She ran to do as I asked and came back frowning. "You're never going to believe this, but I think Charlotte Blackwell is down there."

"Actually, I'm right here."

Lottie hopped down from the windowsill with a light jump. Asher had been holding back if he could make a leap like that through a second-story window. With a rush of adrenaline, I shoved Lucy behind me and gathered the remnants of my energy to defend her.

Lottie raised both hands. "Whoa. Asher sent me. I'm here to help." Her eyes took in the blood covering me and Lucy with repressed horror.

I glared at her. "And I should believe you, why?"

Her face contorted. "You have no reason to believe me, but I'm sorry. I was stupid and scared and selfish."

"Are you expecting me to disagree? You little—"

She cut me off. "Please, Remy. There's no time for this.

I have to get you out of here. I promised my brother. I *can't* break that promise."

I really looked at her for the first time. The mask of hatred Lottie always wore had melted away, replaced by guilt and grief. She didn't like me and wouldn't protect my family. But she loved her brother. Asher wasn't here because of her, and he would blame her. The only person he would blame more was himself, and she knew it.

The door shook on its hinges as Dean pummeled it, and I made a quick decision. "Take Lucy first."

Both of them shouted, "No!"

Lucy insisted, "You're hurt. I'm not leaving you behind."

I ignored my sister and told Lottie, "Lucy goes first. I won't argue with you about this."

Lottie looked frantic. We both knew there was only time to get one person out at the rate Dean would come through the door. "Asher will kill me. Don't make me do this."

"I'll kill you if you don't."

She didn't move, and I could tell she considered taking me against my will. I played the one card I had.

"You owe me, Lottie. You brought the Protectors down on my family. I won't go with you, and I won't leave her here."

My energy swirled in the air between us, making it clear I'd put up a fight. She didn't know how frail I was, and I hoped my threat was convincing because I didn't have the strength to stop her if she forced me to go with her.

Lottie's shoulders curled with defeat.

The door shuddered, and Dean shouted, enraged.

"Go, now," I begged.

Before Lucy could protest, Lottie shot across the room and picked her up, tossing her over one shoulder in a fireman's hold. She jumped onto the windowsill and they vanished. I limped to the window and watched them disappear into Townsend Park. A wave of relief whispered through me. My sister would be safe.

Behind me, the door splintered beneath Dean's boot. His face appeared in a crack, and he smiled.

"You're dead," he said, with an eerie calm.

While he pulled at the pieces of the door to get at the desk, I stumbled into the bathroom, throwing the lock as the desk scraped across the bedroom floor. In seconds, the bathroom door shook as Dean worked to kick it in, too. I considered trying to get away through Lucy's bedroom, but I'd used up my reserves of energy. My body caved on itself, and I sank to the floor, curling on my side with a desperate desire to sleep. From a distance, my mind recognized the evidence of shock.

The banging on the door faded away as I balanced on the edge of consciousness.

Asher met me there.

He'd blame himself for not getting to me in time, for leaving me in the first place. I wished I had two minutes to comfort him, to say good-bye. I'd been so stupid, so sure I needed to protect my heart from him. I hadn't understood that it had been too late from the instant I'd met him. I'd loved him forever and that wouldn't change even if he disappointed me, rejected me, and broke my heart into a million pieces. It was a pointless effort, but I hoped Asher could hear me anyway.

Asher, I love you.

The door snapped in two.

Dean loomed over me. He spotted me lying there, bleeding and useless. His triumphant stare was the last thing I saw before he kicked me in the head.

CHAPTER TWENTY-NINE

*S*omeone woke me by pounding nails into my temple with a blunt hammer. At least that's the way it felt. I opened my eyes to find myself alone in a tiny, square room. In the dim light shining through the blinds at the single window, I could make out my prison's yellow walls, queen-sized bed, nightstand, and the wooden chair Dean had tied me to. He'd bound my hands behind me and tied my ankles to the seat's legs. A foul-smelling cloth filled my mouth, imparting a salty taste of sweat and blood.

Daylight meant I'd been missing for hours. Asher and my family would be freaking out, but they would never find us so long as Dean had me holed up somewhere. Escape seemed impossible until I heard footsteps creaking on a wood floor above me. The gag muffled my screams, and Dean had secured my chair to the bed to make it impossible to raise an alarm by rocking it.

After a quick inventory, I discovered he'd wrapped a makeshift bandage around my middle to keep pressure on the injuries. The holes must have started bleeding again at some point during the night when he'd moved me. Dean hadn't let me die, which meant he still had a use for me.

Taking advantage of his absence, I gathered my energy to heal myself. I made progress on my the gash on my head, but was still too weak to heal the bullet wounds.

The healing left me exhausted—but it was entirely worth it when the pounding eased and the small slant of light in the room stopped burrowing itself into the back of my eyeballs. Then, I discovered a sudden longing for a bathroom.

The longing had grown to desperation by the time Dean returned. The door swung open enough for me to see a narrow hallway with more doors leading off of it like a hotel hallway, except the building didn't feel like a hotel with its musty furnishings. Dean closed the door, flipping the lock. He'd cleaned up at some point, pulled a baseball cap down low on his head to cover his blond curls, and exchanged his stained flannel for a thick wool coat. He gripped a paper bag in one hand, its contents easily identified as a bottle of alcohol, and he tossed it on the bed.

He studied me as he tugged off his cap and lobbed it at the bed, too. "I see you've been busy. The cuts on your head are gone. Feeling better?"

A calm, solicitous Dean terrified me more than an angry one. At least when he raged, I knew what to expect.

"I'm guessing you need a bathroom," he continued. "That means you're gonna be smart and not give me a reason to kill you." He leaned forward until his breath brushed my face. "I've got nothing to lose now. Got me?"

At my stiff nod, he circled around to loosen the bindings on my hands. Before the ropes had dropped to the floor, he scuttled away and pointed the gun at me. "Untie your legs, but leave the gag in."

It took several tries to unknot the rope because I'd lost all feeling in my hands. When I rose, my legs gave out, and I collapsed back in the chair. It took a minute to rub sensation into my limbs. Unfortunately, the return of feeling brought pain.

Only my need for the bathroom enabled me to drag myself up on my third attempt. I stood hunched over to ease the dull ache in my side. Dean opened the door to the hall, checked for people, and backed out of the room as I shuffled toward him. The empty hallway reminded me of an abandoned dorm with its impersonal white walls and multiple closed doors. Next door, the utilitarian bathroom featured a shower, toilet, sink, and small window. Dean refused to let me close the door all the way.

Dried blood had crusted on my jeans and tee, and the water ran red with Lucy's blood when I scrubbed my hands in the sink. In the small mirror above the sink, I caught my first glimpse of my face. More red smeared from my temple to my chin, but its source—the cut from Dean's boot—had disappeared as he'd noted, a tactical error on my part since he knew my powers were returning.

After rinsing off what I could with the paper towels, I used the toilet, humiliated to know he listened on the other side of the half-open door. Washing my hands again, I noticed a small paper taped to the mirror—a list of rules and regulations for guests staying at the hostel at Fort Rowden State Park. Immediately, I recalled the long, rectangular building with its communal upstairs dorms and private rooms below. Ben had mentioned in passing that the hostel emptied out in the winter as fewer tourists visited Blackwell Falls during the colder months. There had been no sounds coming from the other downstairs rooms, but voices now accompanied the footsteps overhead.

Help could be a scream away. I was two seconds from pulling off my gag when Dean pushed the door open and ordered me back to the bedroom.

Dean remained unruffled, almost pleasant, when he instructed me to tie up my feet and put my hands back behind me. While holding the gun to my head, he retied my hands, his fingers never brushing my skin. Instead of rising, he lingered, kneeling at my back.

The hair on the back of my neck rose at his soft voice.

"How does it work, Remy? Your mother obviously didn't know what you could do. Explain it to me. I hurt you, and you one-eighty the pain back on me? Is that it?"

Cold metal—the barrel of the gun—traced from my shoulder down my bare arm in a gentle caress, and I shuddered. An answer wasn't required with my mouth covered, and I kept my eyes trained on the far wall.

Rounding the chair, he retrieved the paper bag from the bed, pulled the top off the bottle, and took a thirsty swig. Pale blue eyes studied me as he dragged the back of his hand across his mouth. "So what do I do with you? Nobody saw me bring you in last night, but it's only so long before the people who checked me in realize who I am from the radio and TV alerts. The police are looking for us. We can't stay, and we can't go. So tell me . . . What the hell do I do with you?"

He shook his head as if the conclusion he'd reached saddened him. "Maybe I should turn you over to the Protectors since they seem so anxious to get their hands on you. They might even pay a hefty sum for you."

He'd listened to the rest of the recording, I realized. I made a guttural noise in the back of my throat, and he whipped the gag from my mouth. My tongue felt huge, and it took two tries to force words through my dry, swollen lips.

"You can't do that!"

"Can't I?" A smile quirked one side of his mouth.

"They wouldn't just kill me, you idiot! They'll kill everyone related to me, including you."

My cheekbone exploded when Dean backhanded me. My teeth sliced the inside of my cheek, and I tasted iron. The temptation to spit blood on his shiny, new clothes almost overcame me. The threat of his immediate and vicious retaliation stopped me, and I ducked my head to hide my expression.

Every fiber of me wanted to fight back. I yearned to snap, to break free, so that he would know I did not belong to him. He did not own me, and I wouldn't swallow one more humiliation at his hands. My fear of him disappeared as rage consumed me, leaving no room for other emotions. If my power had been stronger, I would have stopped his heart mid-beat.

Then, I heard Asher's voice in my head, a memory of him telling me to be smarter than my opponent. My breath hitched, and I subdued the wild animal inside. *Think, Remy!*

Dean hated anyone who stood up to him. For years, my refusal to cry had eaten away at him. Every cruel act sought to break my will: beating my mother, the constant abuse, shooting Lucy, and now threatening to bring the Protectors down on my family. He wanted to strip away everything I cared about, so I'd submit to his control like a meek mouse.

Well, I could cower like Anna. If he wanted a show of fear, I'd give him one.

When he raised his hand to hit me again, I fought against the ropes binding me. Whimpering, I struggled until my eyes filled with tears of pain. Then, I begged, "Don't hit me. Please don't hurt me anymore."

Dean froze for one second, and then slapped me hard across one cheek.

He shoved the gag back in my mouth with his eyes focused on the ceiling as he listened for a sign that someone had heard my hysterics. Of course, no one came to investigate. The few guests above had no idea what happened beneath them, and the pitiful amount of noise I'd made wouldn't have raised an alarm.

Dean's attention swung back to me. My upper body swayed in the chair as if I comforted myself with the rocking motion.

"You're only good to me if we both get out of here."
He used the gun to tip my chin up so he could see my
eyes.

I thought of Asher and Lucy and Ben and Laura. What
if I never saw them again? Dean nodded, as if he could
read my fear.

"We're leaving tonight, and you'll behave like a good
little princess, won't you, Remy? No more using your
powers unless I tell you to. You know why?"

Temper flared at anyone telling me when I could use
my abilities, but I stuffed it down beneath a guise of sub-
missiveness. My fast breathing, stifled by the gag, sounded
loud in the room.

"Two reasons. First, I know how to find the Protectors
thanks to your mother's helpful recordings and will gladly
tell them where to find daddy dearest. And we both know
what Protectors do to innocents, don't we?"

It wasn't necessary to fake my shiver of fear.

"Second . . ."

He stepped behind me, grasped my hand and jerked it
until the tiny, delicate bones in my wrist gave way, snapping beneath the pressure. The dirty gag absorbed my
scream of pain.

Dean's body engulfed and hovered over mine when he
bent to whisper in my ear. "I can tell you're faking, Remy.
You can't hide the rebellion in your eyes. But I'm going
to make you afraid. We've got some time to kill, and I'm
gonna remind you what happens when you defy me."

Blunt fingers stroked my cheek, the gesture a horrify-
ing parody of Asher's sweeter caress. Then, the pressure
increased on my broken wrist, and I wished death would
come fast to stop the pain.

My stifled cries had faded to soft moans hours ago. Dean
had taunted and hurt me. In between blows, he'd forced

me to heal my injuries so he could study how my abilities worked. Too soon, my powers had faded, but the pain didn't stop. When it became too intense, my mind had disconnected from body and place. Without a response to feed on, Dean had finally grown bored and left me bound to the chair while he went outside to investigate the cars parked behind the hostel, looking for the perfect one to steal for our getaway.

As soon as he left, I scanned myself, battling the despair that choked me. Three broken bones—the wrist and two fingers on my right hand—and a series of burns trailing from my left elbow to my shoulder, plus a nasty one on my neck—punishment for passing out. Everything ached, including my head. My vision blurred, and I suspected I had a concussion from Dean's repeated blows.

I was too weak to heal myself, exactly as he'd been counting on. The torture ensured no retaliation against him during our escape. He wanted me subdued and shaking with terror because he could provide a bottomless well of pain. His intent to break me down a little at a time, to bend me to his will, would be successful. Shame burned behind my eyes, and I squeezed them shut.

Oh, Asher. Please help me. I can't do this alone.

As I'd expected, he didn't answer.

The door opened, and Dean entered with urgency in his movements. The light peeking through the blinds had disappeared long ago.

"Time to go, princess."

He stooped to untie my hands and feet since my wrist made the latter task impossible. A thousand fire ants crawled over me as blood rushed back into my limbs. When I could stand, I wavered like a drunk. I was almost too weak to walk, let alone attack him.

Cursing, he waited while I shuffled ahead of him to the bathroom, where he forced me to remove the gag and clean the new layer of blood off my face. He tossed me a sweatshirt to put on over my ruined clothes and to hide the burn marks on my arms. When I couldn't raise my arms over my head, he yanked the garment down with a rough jerk that left me reeling. Satisfied at last, Dean ordered me into the hall. Without the gag, I considered yelling, but it seemed pointless when Dean would be on me before I could get more than a whisper out.

We left the hostel through a side door and climbed a small slope to a row of cars parked along an access road that doubled as a parking lot behind the building. The forest butted up against the edge of the hill, and below a light shone from the second-floor window of the hostel. A couple of people moved about, but judging by the number of cars around, they were probably the only ones. Somehow Dean had managed to get a private room on the isolated lower floor.

I shivered in the damp cold as I waited for him to knock out a window in an older Chevy Malibu that had no alarm. He'd acquired a flathead screwdriver from somewhere and jammed it in the ignition to start the engine. The clever rat had no end to his survival skills. Once the car ran, he ordered me into the driver's seat while he climbed in the back. The entire time he managed to keep the gun between us.

With difficulty, I buckled my seatbelt and put the car in gear with my left hand—my broken wrist made my right hand useless—and checked all the mirrors for pedestrians. I had a sudden urge to laugh. Wasn't it perfect that I'd recently received my license? I could be the driver in my own kidnapping without getting a ticket. On some level, I knew my giddiness signaled that I wasn't thinking clearly.

Dean directed me to drive the car off the park grounds. Instead of taking the direct route into town, he ordered me to turn right onto a course that would circumvent the more populated neighborhoods. In the backseat, he swilled tequila and sang along to the rock song on the radio.

"Hey, princess. Want a drink?" he asked as he rested his arms on the back of the passenger seat. The bottle hit me in the shoulder and I jumped, my reaction making him laugh.

"No? You think you're better than me, don't you? You and your rich daddy. At least I'm not a freak."

He laughed again, and the sound sent shivers up my spine. We passed the lagoon, the moonlight shimmering on the surface of the small body of water, and I remembered Asher had brought me this way on his motorcycle to show me the "Edge of the World."

I didn't plan what I did next. My body took over, and my foot stepped harder on the gas. The tires squealed when I took a fast right turn onto the street that led to the viewpoint.

Dean shouted, "Stop the car!"

I did the opposite. I stomped on the gas pedal until it pressed to the floorboard.

The gun was pressed to my head, the cold steel digging into my temple. It was a useless threat since he would kill himself if he shot me, forcing me to lose control of the car. He cursed as trees rushed past, and it registered that he wasn't wearing his seatbelt.

The car's headlights picked up the cement barrier at the end of the deserted road. The tires chewed up the distance between us, and I took a deep breath and never took my foot off the gas. The peaceful night splintered as metal screamed and buckled. Glass shattered, and my body was thrown forward against the seatbelt. Then, silence reigned again, and the pungent scent of the gases from my deployed airbag filled the car.

A surge of adrenaline coursed through my body. My

ears rang, but as far as I could tell, I felt no worse than before the impact. No movement came from the backseat, and I undid my seatbelt as fast as I could with my left hand. My door wouldn't budge more than a few inches. Twisting in my seat, I placed both feet on the side panel and shoved, gritting my teeth against the pain. Finally, it opened wide enough for me to slither out.

I was almost free when a hand gripped the back of my sweatshirt. Panicked, I fell back and the door closed on Dean's arm. He yelped and let me go so abruptly, my momentum carried me to my hands and knees. My broken wrist collapsed under my weight, and I cried out. Dean moved about in the car, and I dragged myself up. Ahead of me the dirt path led to the cliff with trees and thick shrubs to either side. Behind me lay the road I'd driven down. Not a soul in sight in any direction. *Hide, Remy! Get a move on, girl!*

Turning, I stumbled onto the dirt path. When I rounded the bend, the edge of the cliff dropped a hundred feet to the ocean below. The path continued to the left along the edge of the cliff, and I followed it a ways before weaving my way into the shrubs and trees. I'd only gone a small distance when a bout of faintness forced me to lean against a tree for support.

My hand went to my side and came away stained with blood. The wounds at my waist had reopened. Sliding to the ground, a small opening appeared in the brambles just big enough for a body to crawl into, and I inched my way in. Collapsing flat on my back, I stared up at the night sky, framed by a bleak canopy of stripped branches and snarled ivy. I couldn't fight any more. *I give up.*

In the distance, footsteps stomped along the path. It seemed so far away as the stars spun above me in dizzying patterns, and my body shut down. Cold, exhausted, beaten.

No more running. No escape. Hopeless, hopeless, hopeless.

"Hey, Remy . . ."

I would die.

"Come out, come out."

I was dying.

"Give up, princess. Nobody cares about you. This is over."

I am dead.

"Found you."

Asher, forgive me. I love you.

CHAPTER THIRTY

*D*ean dragged me out of the brush and dropped me at the cliff's edge. His sideways glance made his intention clear: He would throw me over the side. His smile scraped along exposed nerves, until one solid, blunt realization cut away from the others.

I don't want to die.

Some last reserve of strength I didn't know I had surfaced. I morphed into a wild animal, kicking and clawing at him, as I tried to escape his grasp. Fingernails scraped across his face and came away with skin. A fist bounced off his chin, one heel landed a sharp blow to his thigh, and he cursed. Screams pierced the night air as we struggled.

"Shut up!"

Grabbing my arms, he jerked me up. The top of my head collided with his chin, and he stumbled back, his hands loosening their grip. Freed from his control, I rolled several feet away and rose to my knees.

Dean's eyes clouded with murderous wrath, and steel flashed in moonlight as he aimed the gun. My eyes squeezed shut, my arms rose to cover my head as if to deflect a bullet, and the gun fired, the shot exploding over and over again in a discordant echo.

"What the . . . Where did you come from?" Dean sputtered.

Asher's energy burned strong and brilliant. Terrified I was hallucinating, I peered up at him standing over me with a curious half-smile on his beautiful face.

I wanted to shout, "He's behind you!" Even as the words formed on my lips, Asher collapsed, folding to his knees mere inches from me with pain tightening his features. The heat wave of energy waned, the warmth of it shimmering like a mirage, and I understood.

Asher had stepped in front of the bullet.

His brow furrowed, and his skin paled. When he bowed forward, I caught him against me with one hand, staggering beneath his weight as my broken wrist bent between us. Warm liquid seeped through the back of his shirt, dampening my fingers. His forehead rested against mine, his heart skipping against my chest at its familiar abnormal pace.

"Run," he begged, in a hoarse whisper. "Remy, run!"

Leave him behind, he meant. Sacrifice his life for mine. As if I could. As if my body would obey such a command. "Never." *Not without you.*

Warm fingers wound through my hair, and Asher's eyes stared into mine, anchoring me. "I heard you calling to me, love. I'm sorry it took me so long to get here."

Dean's angry threats drifted away on the wind as Asher's energy surrounded me in swirling invitation. "Take it, Remy," he demanded. "Save yourself."

"Asher!" He fell sideways to the ground, and I didn't have the strength to hold him upright. A bullet wound to an immortal should have been all fireworks and no pain. What happened when that immortal had been made more human through bonding with a Healer like me? Asher's heart stuttered and slowed as he fought to stay conscious long enough to help me heal myself using his power. He could die because of me. Because of Dean.

Rage scorched a vicious, boiling path through me. Without hesitation, I plucked Asher's energy from the air with his help, taking what he willingly offered, praying it wouldn't kill him.

We'd only guessed at what happened when we both lost control. We knew his body hungered for the human sensation mine brought when I died. We'd thought mine sought to cure his immortality. *Oh, Asher, we were wrong. So wrong.*

The devastating current of Asher's power met no resistance in my weakened body. The weeks of using Asher's energy to heal myself, the times he'd demonstrated his power, the way he'd held my ability hostage—none of those moments prepared me for the full force of his energy scorching through me. Suddenly I understood how he'd tempered his strength to protect me, and the steely control it must have taken to fight his instinct to overpower me.

I had no such control, and like a Protector, I absorbed all he had to give, and the implosion of his energy felt like the sun had risen inside my body. Blistering, sweltering pain as my body lashed his power to the exhausted remnants of my own, transforming me. My heart sped up as I became something new—unstoppable, indestructible, invincible.

Immortal. This is what it felt like to become immortal, I realized.

It shouldn't have been possible. Only Protectors could become immortal. Still, Asher unknowingly sacrificed his immortality for my mortality, and the mystery of me, of what I was, snapped into focus.

As the seconds ticked by, Dean grew impatient. His flighty eyes gave evidence of his desire to escape. Killing us would be the easiest way to get away clean. No witnesses to hinder his getaway, plus the added bonus of revenge against me for humiliating him.

In an instant, I thought of six ways to kill him. With the power surging through me, I could move as fast as Asher, and Dean's weaker human body couldn't stop me. I could snap his neck before he took his next breath, and it took everything I had to remain still, to stop myself from murdering him. *I won't be him.*

My hands flexed at my side and I rose to my feet so quickly, Dean blinked in confusion.

Before me, Asher lay dying. The air buzzed and crack led, electrified by the *hum* of my latent rage toward a man who'd stolen everything from me. *Leave, you fool. Before it's too late.*

Struggling for control, I took a step forward, and Dean's finger nudged the trigger.

"No," I said.

A red bolt of lightning struck him, and every bone in his hand snapped with a sickening *crunch*. The weapon dropped from his useless fingers, and Dean clutched his arm in startled agony, his mouth forming a surprised "O." Cruel eyes landed on me and took in the calm certainty in mine.

"You don't ever get to hurt me again."

An incensed howl escaped his throat, and he reached for the gun at his feet. He fired off a shot, shock flitting across his features when I disappeared and reappeared unharmed six feet to the right of where the bullet bounced off a large rock. Frustrated, Dean corrected his aim, the crack of successive shots punching empty air as I sped through the clearing until I stood three feet in front of him, ready to take him down.

In the distance, two sets of feet crunched over rock and loose dirt, moving too fast to be human. *Protectors.* Distracted for a moment, I turned to see Lottie and Gabe Blackwell entering the clearing at full speed. Even as they skidded to a stop, Dean's arm wrapped around my neck, yanking me backwards, and the gun pressed to my temple. For one instant, habitual fear crept back in and my limbs froze, paralyzed by terror.

"Stay back!" Dean shouted as the Blackwells crept forward. Confusion and fear had his arm tensing around my neck so I strained on my tiptoes against him. Lottie's face collapsed when she realized her brother lay dying. *My fault, my fault.* I considered flinging myself over the edge of the cliff with Dean to stop him from hurting anyone else.

"Remy, no!" Asher fought to sit up. Intense and low, his voice strummed my raw nerves. "Please, stay. I need you. This isn't a tragedy, *mo chridhe,* remember?"

Somehow, Asher knew my thoughts, even without his power, and that gave me hope. Behind me, Dean tensed with indecision and fury at finding himself surrounded.

"You must be Dean," Gabe said.

"Who the hell are you?" Dean snarled.

"I'm the one who's going to help you get away," Gabe answered, smoothly.

A light clicked on for Dean. "You're Protectors."

Gabe gave an elegant nod.

"Why would you help me?"

"Because you're going to do something for me." He flicked a casual glance my way.

Dean barked a laugh as he grasped Gabe's meaning. "That's priceless! You want me to kill her for you? Consider it done."

"No!" Asher shouted. "Gabe, what are you—?"

Gabe didn't look at his brother. "You misunderstand me, human. See what she's done to my brother? In love with a human!" he spat. "She's made him weak, an albatross around our necks."

Dean shot him a calculating glance. "You want me to kill your brother?"

"It shouldn't be too difficult. Afterward, you can leave and take that with you." He gestured toward me with a wave of his hand.

Asher and Lottie both looked shocked, but Gabe ignored them to stare at me.

"The only good Healer is a dead Healer, right, Gabe?"
I asked, bitterly.

"I told you where I stood the last time we spoke,
Remy," he answered in the same careless tone.

Two things caught my attention. He called me Remy,
and the last time we spoke he'd told me not to forget my
training.

Then, Dean said, "You've got yourself a deal," and swung
the gun toward Asher, his finger nudging the trigger.

Everyone's reactions registered in slow motion. Asher's
eyes met mine with a good-bye. Lottie moved to shield
her brother. Gabe raced toward Dean, ready to free me
because he knew what I'd do. He'd often accused me of
forgetting who was Protector and who was Healer in my
training. He knew nothing could incite my powers like
my desire to protect Asher.

He was right.

The bullet never left the chamber. All movement stopped
when a second blast of red lightning slammed into Dean.
He screamed when his body absorbed every wound he'd
inflicted on me. Twin bullet holes, broken wrist and fingers, burns, bruises—they struck him at once and he released me. Twisting out of his reach, I met his anguished
stare emotionlessly.

In mindless terror, he scrambled backwards, far too
close to the cliff's edge. Arms windmilled when his foot
met air, and he lost his balance. With Asher's power flow-
ing through me, I could have stopped it from happening.
I could have reached him in time, but I did nothing.

Dean's face contorted, and his hands clawed air, seeking
purchase in a void, and I watched him disappear over the
edge, his eerie shout echoing.

In the stark silence that followed, Asher's labored

breathing sounded loud. Recalled to myself, I forced the power down, trying to regain control. I dropped to my knees at an unconscious Asher's side a second before Gabe. I saw Lottie's fist swing before Gabe did and caught it in my hand an inch from Gabe's nose. Both Protectors stared at me in shock, but my attention had snagged on the fact that I couldn't feel Lottie's skin against mine. Already I was losing myself. Time was running out.

To Lottie I said, "It's not what you think. Gabe would never betray Asher. He knew I'd do whatever it took to save Asher. You know that's true."

She glanced at her brother, and I dismissed her, releasing her fist to face Gabe who crouched a short distance away. "Thank you."

Suspicious green eyes studied me. "You're different, Healer. I'd say you were like us if I didn't know that was impossible." He looked scared for the first time when he glanced at his brother. "What's going on here? Why isn't Asher healing?"

"He's dying. He sacrificed his power to help me, but I can save him if you'll both trust me."

"Are you strong enough?" Lottie took in the blood seeping through the sweatshirt and the wounds on my face.

"Yes," I lied without an ounce of guilt.

Gabe wasn't convinced so easily. "If you die saving him, we lose him just the same." His soft words made his decision clear. He would not help me if it put my life at risk.

It was easy to lie with Asher's life hanging in the balance. "I'll be fine, Gabe."

My answer convinced Gabe and he went to stand with his sister. Leaning over Asher, I watched until they stood several feet out of reach before I whispered, "Tell Asher I loved him. I'm so sorry."

"No!" Gabe sprang forward to stop me, but it was too late.

My lips brushed Asher's, and I loosed his power with a sigh, the vines of our energy spreading and unfurling through his body as I healed him. His power had blended with mine until the bifocal line separating them had disappeared. Immortality was mine, but I'd never wanted it, especially without Asher at my side.

I knew he'd make it when I felt his mouth moving against mine in a sweet kiss and his arms closing around me. Full, hard lips formed to my softer mouth, and our breath mingled in a relieved sigh. This kiss was different than all the others. I'd always wanted to kiss him like this, without one of us having to worry about staying in control. When my fingers traced his face, I knew he felt me. Then my body took over, and I let it happen without a fight.

To save him, I made him immortal again. My life was the cost we'd both pay when my body absorbed his wound on top of the injuries I already had.

He jerked in my arms. *Too late, love. Don't hate me.*

His injury cut through me, and he transformed once more into the powerful one, the immortal one. As I'd known they would, his Protector instincts took over, sensing a dying Healer nearby. Without his volition, his body stole my energy, absorbing it. This was the one thing he'd feared most. *Forgive me.* I felt Asher go to war inside himself, battling to stop his body's reaction. Willing himself to die to save me.

Asher, let me go.

For one moment, I thought he'd acquiesce, that he'd accept there was no other way. His power shimmered in the air, stronger than I'd ever felt it.

I love you.

Almost immediately, the connection between us broke off as Asher sprang away from me, forcing a physical separation. Green sparks exploded in the air, and I collapsed into Gabe's waiting arms. A moan reached my ears, but it was my voice—a guttural acknowledgment of pain as I returned to my body, once more a wrecked mortal too weak to heal myself. My power had gone, along with the *humming*.

Gabe's gentle voice sounded in my ear. "Easy, Remy. I've got you."

Asher crawled forward, taking me from his brother. He flinched when his hand touched the new blood spreading across my back. "Why, *mo chridhe*? Why did you do it?" he whispered. "You should've let me die."

"I'm sorry, Asher," I gasped. "Please, don't hate me."

"Hate you? How can you even think that?" he said, tortured.

You wanted to be mortal.

Strong arms tightened around me. "Yes. To have a future with you." He leaned his forehead against mine, and his eyes filled with tears. "I could've borne living through ten centuries knowing I'd discover you at the end of them. But all of this means nothing without you. Don't leave me when I just found you."

Gabe placed a hand on Asher's shoulder. "There's still a chance. Humans have survived worse, and Remy is not a normal human. She needs a hospital. I'll go get her family. She'll need them."

The sky danced in a dizzying circle when Asher stood with me in his arms.

Urgency fueled Gabe's words. "Asher, go now!"

Asher sprang forward from a crouch, holding me against his chest. The stars streaked as he ran, and my world narrowed to his rigid face, the sole steady object against the blurred backdrop of the passing scenery. I felt like I floated in the deep end of the pool as Brandon had taught me. My eyes shuttered, but Asher shook me until I stared up at him.

"Don't sleep, Remy. We've a ways to go yet."

There was no reason to pretend. "You came for me, Asher. I pictured you a thousand times, and you came."

"Of course, *mo chridhe*. You showed me where to find you."

The sound of my own voice distracted me as it came in gasps. "I waited, but I thought you wouldn't get there in time. I tried to be strong, but he kept hurting me. Oh, God, Lucy! He shot Lucy!"

"She's safe," he promised, grim-faced. "You saved her, remember?"

I didn't remember. Confused, I wondered when I'd saved her. A memory flashed of her going out a window, but that didn't seem right. Suddenly, I couldn't remember where I was, except that Asher held me. Unable to fight any longer, my eyes flickered closed again, seeking the abyss of sleep.

"Remy! Wake up!"

I blinked, focusing on his mouth as he continued to yell at me until the floodlights outside the Emergency Room blinded me.

"Help! Somebody help me!" Asher shouted.

New arms lifted me away from him, placing me flat on a hard surface. Strident voices arrowed over my head. Strange hands touched my wrecked body as they poked and prodded. An oxygen mask covered my mouth and nose, and a needle pierced my arm. A rubber band of time stretched taut until Ben's relieved voice snapped me back to awareness.

"You're safe now, baby."

His rough hand squeezed mine for a brief second, and my body jump-started, *humming* with relief. Knowing my father and Asher watched over me, I let go of consciousness.

CHAPTER THIRTY-ONE

A nurse jarred my broken wrist checking the burns on my arm. She smiled when she saw my eyes fixed on her face and left me alone. Eyes closed, I returned to my body with a shattering reminder of the pain my stepfather had inflicted. The familiar loneliness of the impersonal yellow walls and white hospital linens weighed on my chest, causing an ache that had nothing to do with my injuries.

Stale air shifted as someone slid noiselessly to the room. Instead of Asher, Gabe braced himself at the foot of the bed, grasping the metal frame in both hands with a forbidding expression on his perfect face. Instantly fearful, I whispered, "Gabe? Is Asher . . . ?"

"He's fine. Anxious about you. He's down the hall with the police and didn't want to leave you alone. They're questioning him about how he found you." Lips pressed into a thin line, he studied me. "You look like a horse dragged you through a field of glass, by the way."

I blinked at the colorful description.

"Well? How do you feel?" he asked.

"Like a horse dragged me through a field of glass," I choked out.

He snorted and slipped his hands in his back pockets, rocking on his heels. "A Healer with a sense of humor.

Who knew they existed?" The small smile disappeared, and his brows rose in surprise. "Your power is back."

He winced, and I raised my defenses, ignoring his unasked question. The time would come for explanations, but not until I'd listened to the last of my mother's recordings and had confirmation of what I suspected. I could only hope my iPod had survived the car crash.

Gabe didn't press the issue. "We need to get our stories straight before the police question you."

"How long have I been out?" I asked.

"Two days."

Another two days of my life lost, thanks to Dean. My anger reignited, and I snuffed it to smoke and ashes. "Where is everyone?"

"Your dad has scarcely left your side since they brought you out of recovery. They operated to fix the damaged tissue from the gunshot wounds to your side and back. Your father donated blood, I believe."

Gabe explained that Asher had told everyone he'd been driving out near the fort when he saw me driving off the grounds with a man in the backseat. He followed me and arrived in time to see Dean run away, leaving me wounded at the side of the cliff. No one knew Asher had carried me to the hospital instead of driving me there in a car.

The Blackwells had recovered Dean's body from the beach and buried it where it would never be found. There was no way to explain why he had wounds that exactly mirrored mine and a close examination by the police would have brought the Protectors back to Blackwell Falls. It was best for everyone if Dean simply disappeared off the face of the earth. With my mother gone, no one would miss him.

"How did you find me?" I asked at one point.

"Asher heard you calling him. We should've been look-

ing for you outside of town like everyone else, but he insisted Dean held you somewhere nearby. I thought he'd
lost it when he said you showed him where to find you,
but then we missed you at the hostel by minutes. The
bond you two have . . ." Wide shoulders lifted in a graceful shrug. "Nothing could've kept him from finding you."

He gazed at me with an odd expression. Frustrated, I
blurted out, "What?"

Strong hands gripped the railing again, threatening to
bend it. "I don't understand you, Healer. You changed. I'd
guess you were like us on that cliff, if that were possible."
Gabe's penetrating stare held less animosity than before. In
a quiet tone, he asked, "You made him immortal again
knowing it might kill you. Why?"

"You ask the wrong questions, Protector."

"What do you mean?"

"You once asked if I was worth dying for," I answered.
"Not what I would sacrifice to keep him safe."

With a slow nod, his hands relaxed their hold on the
bed. "You're not like the others, Healer. You almost make
me wish that I . . . Never mind. I hope for everyone's sake
the others never find out about you." Hardness infiltrated
his eyes again, and he added in a smooth, uncaring tone,
"They always do in the end, though."

Gabe disappeared through the doorway. He didn't know
how dead-on he was. I truly was unique in the world of
Protectors and Healers. Amazingly enough, Dean had
started me on the path to comprehension. *You think you're
better than me, don't you? You and your rich daddy, but you're
both the same. At least I'm not a freak.* No one could have
guessed at the reason I could cure immortality, and the answer lay in the fact that I could become an immortal myself. *When* the Protectors found out the truth, my life in
Blackwell Falls would end because they'd never stop hunting me or my family.

"You're awake!"

Ben stepped into the room, rushing to my side. Under the fluorescent lights, his face appeared gray with worry and grief when he stroked the tangled hair from my face. Absently, I noted the return of his heart arrhythmia—I'd healed it time and again in the last weeks and never saw it for the clue it was. "Hey, kiddo."

"Hey."

"You gave us one helluva scare. How're you feeling?"

I considered repeating my response to Gabe, but only said, "Alive. Lucy?"

"Bruised from jumping out a second-story window, but otherwise okay. She wanted to be here, but we thought she should rest." His gentle touch unsettled me because it was the opposite of what I'd been expecting. "She says you're a hero. That Dean shot you when you tried to protect her."

A hero. That was laughable. Dean had shot her *because* of me. She would be better off if I left. They all would. My father felt responsible for me and guilty for leaving me. It would make it that much harder to convince him I needed to go.

"Ben, I want to leave Blackwell Falls."

Hurt clouded eyes like mine. "What?"

"Dean came here because of me. There's a chance he'll come back." The lie nearly choked me, but I reminded myself it would keep them safe. "Lucy got hurt in my place, and it could be worse next time."

Everyone around me got hurt. The really unlucky ones died, and it would only get worse from here on out with the threat of the Protectors hanging over our heads. If I left now, Ben could go on blissfully unaware of the truth my mother had kept from him.

White lines stood out around Ben's mouth. "Remy, what are you talking about?"

"Mr. O'Malley?" A polite voice interrupted Ben's staccato words.

We both turned to see the newcomer—an officer in uniform—hesitating in the doorway, tapping a notepad against his leg. Asher stood behind him, his eyes roving over me with worry and love.

"Sorry to barge in on you folks," the officer continued. "Mind if I come in? We need to get your daughter's statement."

"Can't this wait, Murphy? She's not in the best shape. How did you even know she was awake?" Ben asked, frowning. The officer must have questioned my family already, or Murphy was one of Ben's poker buddies. I'd miss the seven degrees of separation in Blackwell Falls when I left. Asher's brows rose, and I ignored him. Barricade or not, I couldn't keep him out of my head with the intensity of my emotions.

"We asked the hospital to call when it looked like she was coming 'round. It's best if we do this now while your daughter's memory is fresh." Peppered, caterpillar brows rose when he took in my discolored face, and added, "You okay with that, Remy?"

I nodded because the questions would put off the inevitable with Ben. *Coward.*

When Murphy turned to close the door on Asher, I said, "No, I want him to stay." I needed the strength his presence offered.

Ben's breath huffed out, but he didn't argue. He surprised me by scraping a chair closer and holding my uninjured hand, avoiding the IV line and my feeble attempt to pull away. Asher settled into a chair by the window, watching in silence.

Wiry, silver sideburns blended into unruly gray hair as Murphy pulled a sharpened yellow Number 2 from behind his ear. Despite the color of his hair, I guessed he must be in his early forties since his skin appeared smooth with a few wrinkles about the eyes and lips, a telltale sign he smoked or used to smoke.

Pencil at the ready, he studied me with tireless patience. "Your sister tells us that you went out to dinner and when you got home your stepfather was waiting in your kitchen."

I nodded.

"What happened next?"

I hid every detail that would have revealed me as a Healer but, unlike the last time Dean had put me in the hospital, this time I didn't skip over the uglier facts. The more Ben knew, the easier it would be for him to send me away. If he imagined these things happening to Lucy or Laura, I could convince him to let me go.

Dry-eyed, I described the events at the house, except in this fictionalized version I'd been shot in place of Lucy and Lucy escaped without Lottie's help. When I told Murphy how Dean had discovered me in the bathroom and kicked me in the head, I felt Ben's shudder through his fingertips. As if I discussed a stranger, I described everything, each horror related in the same dead voice. Hurt piled on top of hurt like the burn scar Dean had branded me with so that I became numb to all but the shame because he *had* broken me in the end. I'd given up before Asher arrived.

His energy swirled in the air as if to comfort me without a touch. My father looked up as if he felt it, and I saw Asher glance at him with curiosity.

"Any idea why your stepfather kidnapped you?" Murphy inquired.

Bitterness infused my voice with a harsher edge, and I told the truth. "As far as Dean is concerned, he owns me. It's not kidnapping to take back what belongs to you."

When I finished, Murphy made a last notation, closed his notebook, and tucked the pencil away in a shirt pocket. "That should do it. We'll let you know if we have any other questions. Your dad has my card if you need anything. In the meantime, we'll continue searching for him."

Before he left, serene brown eyes fixed on me. "You're stronger than you think, Remy. I've met his kind before. Don't let him get in your head when you've survived this far."

Alone with Ben again, I wondered how Murphy guessed I teetered so close to the edge, full of self-loathing and guilt. More than my body had broken. I felt turned inside out, wanting things I couldn't have, and yearning for more than I had a right to ask for. I didn't want to leave.

"Asher, I'll never be able to thank you enough for find-ing Remy." Ben shook Asher's hand and laid a hand on his shoulder. "Right now, I need to have a long overdue conversation with my daughter. You mind giving us a minute?"

"No, sir." In front of my father, he stepped close and leaned over to kiss my cheek. In my ear, he whispered, "I'll be in the hall if you need me." He tapped a gentle fin-ger to my head, reminding me he could hear me without words, and left. Silence reigned for a long moment, and I waited for Ben to agree to my leaving Blackwell Falls.

"Okay, enough!"

Ben's heated outburst startled me, and he swooped in to scoop me out of the bed, sheets and all. He eased back in his chair, not disturbing my IV line as he held me.

A passing nurse ran into the room when she saw him. "Mr. O'Malley! You can't—"

Ben glared at her. "The hell I can't. She's my daughter. Get out!"

She turned on her heel, and I suspected she intended to

find someone bigger and meaner to threaten Ben. My father's blue eyes lasered mine.

"You're not responsible for everyone and everything, Remy. You didn't bring Dean here, and you did everything you could to protect your sister. More than anyone could've asked of you. And before her, you protected your mother. We should've been there. Me, your mother. We should've been there because it's the parents' job to keep you safe. You're a kid, Remy. A wise, beautiful kid who didn't deserve any of this. Are you listening? This wasn't your fault!"

He looked like he wanted to shake me, but his hands remained gentle.

"I'm never sending you away. If you try to go, I'll fight you. Blame me for leaving you to deal with that bastard on your own. Hate me and rage at me and try to shut me out, but I'm not going anywhere. You're not alone anymore. I'm here, Remy."

My dad wanted me to stay. Dams fractured inside me, and Ben's features blurred. Embarrassed, I ducked my head to wipe the tears on the sheet. Salty and hot on my tongue, they flowed harder. Appalled, I listened to my breath hitch on a sob as control escaped me. The fear, worry, and sorrow I'd bottled ruptured. *My dad wanted me to stay.*

Ben's grip tightened. "Cry, sweetheart," he whispered. "For you."

My voice broke on another sob, and I buried my face in Ben's neck. I sensed Asher retreating from my thoughts as my father rocked me like a child, murmuring nonsensical words as I cried out five years of grief for all I'd lost.

Later that night, Lucy and Laura came to visit.

My eyes were swollen from crying, and my throat raw. I'd eventually fallen asleep in Ben's arms, hiccupping and sniffling. The nurse returned with a doctor, but Ben said something to them and they left us undisturbed. Asher's lips had brushed my forehead before he left to check in with his family.

When Laura walked in, she immediately fussed over me, driving the nurses crazy as she chased after them to check my bandages. Her cool hand soothed an imaginary line across my forehead, easing the headache that centered there.

She listed my injuries in a shaky voice—concussion, gunshot wounds at my waist and back, burns up my left arm and on my neck, two broken fingers and broken wrist on my right hand, plus the rope burns on both wrists and my ankles—but it was Lucy who passed me a compact mirror under Laura's disapproving stare when I asked for one. My reflection shocked me. Bruises and scratches covered my face, most likely from Dean dragging me from the shrubs. No wonder everyone looked at me with horror. I watched, distressed, as my blue eyes filled with tears again.

Laura tucked a thin blanket around me. "Asher's a good boy. We're so lucky he got you here when he did. The doctors are amazed you're doing so well already. They said a few of the burns might leave scars, but the scratches aren't deep. The bruises will heal, you'll see."

Lucy pulled herself up on the bed to sit next to my legs and casually added, "Hey, everybody's wearing them this season. We have matching shiners, Sis."

Ben and Laura had similar worried expressions when I burst out laughing, grasping my side, but Lucy grinned, unrepentant. Her face did sport a bruise similar to my own, and I spied other bruises under the neckline of her blouse.

"Move over, Remy. Give a girl a little room. We can

compare war wounds." She shoved my leg until I scooted over an inch, and she curled up next to me, her hand resting lightly on my arm.

A nurse—a male nurse, this time—walked in and frowned when he saw her. "That's against hospital rules."

Laura's voice could have blistered rock. "Sue us."

Ben and Laura pushed the nurse ahead of them out of the room. Ben called over his shoulder that they'd be back as soon as they found a decent cup of coffee. He winked at me, and I knew he intended to sneak one back to me. I smiled and the door closed behind them. Lucy lay next to me in silence, and I could almost feel her thinking.

"When are you coming home, Remy? I hate the house without you there."

The nightmares that had plagued me for years had found her. I heard them in her tense, tired voice. She'd been protected her entire life, and in one night, Dean had changed everything, leaving scars that would never go away completely.

"Couple of days, I think. Longer, if Dad has anything to say about it. How're you doing, Luce?"

She rubbed her eyes. "I should be asking you that. You sound like crap, by the way."

My voice did sound awful, husky and thick from crying. "Thanks for that. I can always count on you for honesty."

"You can always count on me, period, stupid." With solemn eyes, she glanced up at me. "You could've told me the truth. It wouldn't have changed anything. It doesn't change anything."

I stared back with disbelief. "You say that now, but you don't know everything."

A frown twisted her lips. "You mean about the Protectors? Actually, I do. The Blackwells told me whatever I hadn't figured out when Lottie dropped me at their house. I know about you and Asher bonding and how you've been training with his family. I almost beat the crap out of Lottie when she confessed how she betrayed you. Nobody messes with my family."

Shocked by her calm acceptance, I asked, "How are you handling this so well? I've lived with my ability for years, and I still handled these past weeks poorly."

Lucy's smile bore a hint of smugness, and I glimpsed a small resemblance to me for the first time. "Oh, like it was hard. Sis, you had bruises appearing and disappearing like magic. Our parents may be oblivious, but I figured something was up with you. And any fool can tell the Blackwells are different. Why do you think I warned you away?"

Touching a button on the bed remote, I lowered the mattress so we could both rest more comfortably. "You objected to motorcycles?"

"I'd smack you in the head if you didn't have a concussion. Speaking of which, why haven't you healed yourself? Are your powers not working?"

"Too many questions. It's the first thing I learned when my powers developed. Imagine what would happen if word got out."

She pondered that for a moment. "Right, the Protectors. Not to mention the scientists who'd want to experiment on your skinny carcass."

If it wouldn't have hurt so much, I would have hit her in the face with my pillow.

"What about Mom and Dad? Will you tell them the truth?"

I sighed with regret. Ben would need to know the truth since I was staying. He deserved to know, considering the secrets Anna had kept from us both. "Not now. Maybe someday. Knowing the truth might put them in more danger. This has to be our secret for now—ours and the Blackwells'. Can you live with that?"

Making herself more comfortable, Lucy kicked her ballet flats off, and they dropped to the tiled floor with an uneven thud. "Are you kidding? I feel like Willow in season one of *Buffy the Vampire Slayer,* except Buffy is my sister."

My brows rose. "I'm nothing like Buffy."

Lucy's drowsy voice rang with unconcern. "You have an alter ego, and you have superpowers you use to save people, including me. Hence, Buffy. Don't argue with me. How many times do I have to tell you that I know everything?"

Of course, she had it all wrong.

Lucy sighed and her hand grew heavy on my arm. "You mind if I fall asleep? I haven't been able to close my eyes the last few nights with you gone and the house . . ."

Imagining what the house looked like, I grimaced. In a forced light tone, I said, "No. But if you try to steal my pillow, I'll knock you out of the bed."

She grumbled, "You're such a grouch."

"Lucy? Do me a favor?"

"Hmm?" She sounded half-asleep already.

My energy *hummed,* healing all but the telltale bruise on her face. She gasped when blue sparks lit the room.

"Wear something with a high collar for a couple of days so no one notices your bruises are gone."

"That is so cool." Her soft voice vibrated with awe.

Teetering on the edge of sleep myself, I heard her add with pride, "My sister, the Healer."

CHAPTER THIRTY-TWO

I felt Asher's presence before I saw him.

In the last two weeks since I'd awakened in the hospital we'd been careful with each other. Asher acted attentive, and we'd seen each other every day. He'd become a steady fixture at my home, with my family accepting his presence. It should have been perfect. And yet . . . There'd been no discussion of what I'd done to him by stealing his mortality or what the days ahead held.

My friends and family, and even his family, could be blamed for some of that. The door to my room had revolved as guests flowed in and out, bringing their worry and concern and leaving behind the solid belief that I belonged in Blackwell Falls.

Leaning back on the palm not encased in a cast, I raised my face to the stingy sun with my eyes closed. It cast a golden glow over the clearing at the center of Townsend Park's labyrinth. Earlier, when I'd stopped by Asher's house, I'd glanced out on the bay and discovered it transformed. Dozens of sailboats skimmed across the dark blue ocean, taking advantage of the surplus of good weather. My family sailed among them, the first time they'd left me alone for longer than a couple of hours since Dean had taken me.

Nightmares plagued our house now. An army of maids

had shown up on our doorstep shortly after I'd been admitted to the hospital, courtesy of the Blackwells. According to an astonished but grateful Laura, they'd kicked her out of the house, while they scoured every trace of Dean from our home. Carpets, furniture, wood floors. Everything stained by blood had disappeared and new furniture sat in its place. The Blackwells had refused payment from my father, insisting that they wanted to do what they could to ease my homecoming.

Laura and Ben weren't without their own nightmares. They worried Dean would return, and I hated the pretense we had to keep up. My parents—a thrill went through me whenever I thought that—watched Lucy and me for signs that we cracked under the pressure of all we'd been through.

I worried most about Lucy. She hardly slept, and rarely in her own room. Since I'd returned home, I often woke to find her curled beside me on my bed, her hand resting on my arm as if she sought comfort even in sleep. Dean had broken something inside her, too, and I cried for her when she couldn't see and waited for her to talk to me.

Of course, I cried at telephone commercials and sappy movies now, too. Once the floodgates opened, they couldn't be dammed again. After so many years of isolation, a place existed where I fit, the last piece in an ornate, complex, perfect puzzle. In this town on the edge of the world, I felt loved. *I am loved.*

"More than you'll ever know."

The rough timbre of Asher's voice soothed and warmed where the sun couldn't. He'd arrived on silent feet as usual, and happiness fluttered through me. *I love you.* Eyes closed, I smiled, and a moment later his lips touched mine in a gentle caress that said hello and good-bye all at once.

The time had come to clear the air, then.

Slowly, as if filled with regret, he pulled away, and I straightened, patting the seat next to me. My iPod had been recovered from the car wreck, and I moved it aside to make room for him. "Sit with me."

Asher sat as far away as he could while still resting on the stone bench. Not a good sign. His brother had warned me he'd be like this.

"When did you speak with my brother?"

"This morning. I went to find you, and we had an interesting conversation."

I played the scene through my mind.

Lottie had opened the door at my knock. We'd eyed each other with suspicion. Her hatred had dissipated, but she didn't like me any better than before. As for me, while I felt grateful she'd helped Lucy escape, I couldn't forget how she'd betrayed me. We both loved Asher, though, and that became the basis for a momentary truce. She apologized, and I forgave her with a fierce warning that if she ever betrayed anyone I cared about again, I'd ensure the sewer was the only thing she smelled for the rest of her miserable life.

Gabe had eavesdropped on our conversation from where he leaned against the doorway to the living room. "That was unexpected, Healer," he said, after Lottie left the room. "Forgiving her. Asher can hardly stand to be in the same room with her, and she knows it."

My brows rose in surprise. "Why are you telling me this?"

"Perhaps because I think you can convince my brother to forgive her, too," he said, in a hard tone. "We would not be in this situation, after all, if not for you, Healer."

I could see it pained Gabe to watch his family hurting, and I responded to that instead of the insult. "Are you implying that a Healer can do good while there's still breath in her body, Protector?" I asked with heavy sarcasm.

He understood the reference immediately. I stood in mute fas-

cination when he threw back his head and laughed his way out of the room. *Even going, Asher's brother truly was beautiful.*

"You know, you could edit that part out of your memory." Asher's wry tone made me laugh.

My lips twitched, and I shrugged. "Gabe is beautiful." At his scowl, I held up a hand. "But he's not you. Gabe is a pleasure to look at, like a marble sculpture. Cold and untouchable. But you . . . My hands itch to trace the scar on your face, to run through your hair, to feel your skin. And when you touch me, my heart leaps out of my chest. You stun me, Asher. You have since the first day I looked up and saw you standing on a beach."

My words silenced him. His jaw slackened, and he stared at me with wide eyes. I'd been fighting him and my instincts every step of the way. I had one thing to thank Dean for—I would not take one minute with Asher for granted.

"You need to forgive your sister, Asher. Eternity is a long time to hold a grudge, and she's your family."

His mouth snapped closed, and his eyes narrowed. "What's wrong, Remy?"

"What do you mean?" I asked, confused.

"This," he said, gesturing between us. "You don't do grand declarations. It feels like you're saying good-bye."

A smile twisted my mouth. "Funny. I thought the same thing about you when you kissed me a few minutes ago."

Color stained his cheeks, and he had the good grace to look away. So I'd been right. He couldn't forgive me for making him immortal again, and I couldn't be sorry when he sat in front of me, alive and more handsome than any man had a right to be.

"There's nothing to forgive!" Hard hands grasped my shoulders to force me to look at him. He didn't hurt me, but I couldn't glance away from the intensity in his expression. "I didn't want to leave you. I haven't had nearly long enough with you."

"How long will you want me?" I asked in a tremulous voice. "How long when I continue to grow old and you stay the same age? How long when the Protectors come hunting and your family is in danger again?"

He brushed a strand of hair from my face and stroked a finger down my cheek. "A lifetime should about do it, *mo chridhe*. You're so quick to abandon hope. Have you changed your mind about me?"

"Never!" I stood and his hands fell away from me as I paced a short distance. "But you may change yours. There are things you don't know, things I figured out when Dean had me."

Rising to his feet, Asher put his hands in his jeans pockets. "Does this have anything to do with your conversation with Gabe?"

I nodded. Closing my eyes, I recalled following Gabe to the living room.

"I need a favor, Gabe."

His brows rose. "You're more demanding than one of my Sorori-toys, you know."

I choked on a laugh, surprised, when he added, "Protector hearing powers, remember?"

My grin faded as I held up a small vial of red liquid. Gabe had the resources to see this done. "I need you to test this."

"Your blood?"

I nodded. "You said you felt I was different from other Healers. This will prove it."

Frustration marred the line of his brow into minute wrinkles. "Not likely. Without a sample from another Healer, I'm not sure what I'd be looking for."

I sensed disappointment and wondered if Gabe had wanted me to be the key to a cure. I was. I'd proved that with Asher. Yet, no one knew how or why or if the results could be duplicated without killing me. "There you go asking the wrong questions again, Protector."

Hearing something in my tone, he glanced up. "You know something." It wasn't a question.

"I suspect something," I corrected. I hadn't listened to the last of my mother's recordings yet. That was something I wanted to do with Asher since it would affect us both. "I think you should compare my blood to your own, Gabe."

"Tell me," he insisted.

"I'd rather let you do the tests and come to your own conclusions without my idea tainting the results."

Gabe sat back in his oversized chair, his large body making it appear small. "You really do suspect something. It must be one heck of an idea. Mind telling me how you came up with it?"

"Dean. He said something, and it got me to thinking."

Asher's brother scowled at the mention of Dean, and I was glad that his sudden anger was not directed at me. "What did he say?"

"Something about my father, actually. He meant to insult me at the time, but it had another effect entirely. Especially after what happened with Asher when Dean shot him."

I smiled with satisfaction when Gabe's mouth dropped open as I explained those moments after I'd stolen Asher's energy. No one, not even Asher, knew the impact that pivotal moment had on me. They knew I'd used his power to strike down Dean and to heal Asher. They knew I'd nearly died when I returned his power to him, making him immortal again. Gabe suspected I'd been "different." More "like them," but he didn't grasp the truth. How could they know I'd become immortal myself for a few brief moments?

My eyes opened suddenly when Asher's fingers traced my jaw.

"Explain, Remy," he demanded.

His tone brooked no argument, and I sighed. Time for

confessions. I hadn't meant to keep this from him, but there'd been few moments of privacy these last two weeks. In as few words as possible, I explained the change that had come over my body when his power had over-whelmed my defenseless system.

I finished, and he turned away with his hands clenched in fists at his side. "This is my fault, Remy. I'm so sorry. When Dean shot me, I felt human, weak, and I knew I couldn't protect you. I'd failed you. Being with you, I'd become too mortal to heal like I should've. That's why I told you to use my energy. If you could heal yourself, you stood a chance of getting away."

My hand trembled when I ran it over the muscles in his shoulder. "You didn't fail me. You took a bullet for me, Asher. I would be dead now if you hadn't shown up. I'd given up. On you. On myself."

The shame I still felt made tears come to my eyes. Arms wrapped around me tucking my face against a sturdy chest, and I settled against him, willing to be comforted by him for the rest of my life. His voice rumbled against my ear. "You didn't give up. When I arrived, you were fighting back. You were sure you were going to die, but I heard one thought surface above all the others. Do you remember?"

I don't want to die. That had been the only thing in my head when I knew Dean would kill me.

"You're braver than anyone I've ever met. I don't know another person who could've had the strength to make it through those hours with Dean."

I ducked my head into his shirt, my clunky cast resting at his waist. I hadn't felt brave or strong. I'd thought only of my family and of him. To distract him, I said, "Don't you want to know the rest of my conversation with your brother?"

I felt his nod as he rested his chin on the top of my head, and I fell back into the memory.

Gabe had put two and two together and made the leap to sixteen. The test I'd asked him to run, the way my power worked, and my ability to become immortal. He sat forward in his seat. "You understand what this means? If it's true . . ." His words trailed off, and we both considered what it meant for me to be the first and only of my kind, and the unique powers my makeup leant me.

Gabe's breath hissed out, and he whispered, "They'll want to use you, or they'll want you dead. The Protectors and Healers will both come after you. You don't stand a chance with ten Ashers at your side."

Slowly, I let the memory fade away, allowing Asher time to process the new information. Like a coward, I'd used the memories to make him understand the truth when I couldn't bear to say the words out loud. Neither Healer nor Protector, I was something else—something never before seen. Asher deserved to know what he faced if he stayed with me. I should leave to protect him, to protect them all, but I wasn't strong enough. I needed him, but if he chose to walk away, I'd do everything in my power to let him go.

"Ah, Remy," he breathed. And he laughed.

It was the last possible reaction I'd expected. I'd prepared myself for him to be cold or regretful. In my wildest imaginings, he'd been supportive. In none of the thousand conversations I'd had with him in my head did he laugh.

Asher leaned away and spied my expression. He laughed harder than before, gasping for air. Anger and hurt fought, and anger won out. Glaring at him, I turned and stalked away, picking the nearest path that would take me out of the park. I'd gone two feet when an arm clamped around my waist.

"You're beautiful when you're mad at me," he said, amusement still in his voice.

Tears blurred my vision, and I aimed an elbow into his stomach, attempting to get loose. I ended up hurting myself instead when the limb bounced off rock-hard muscles. I cried out, and Asher turned me in his arms with gentle, inescapable force. The laughter faded from his face as he checked my elbow and placed a soft kiss on the red skin.

My breath hitched, and my anger was forgotten beneath a wave of heat that started where his lips touched me. A tiny smile lifted the corner of his mouth, and I knew he heard me.

"I'm sorry I laughed," he said.

"Why did you?" His reaction made no sense.

"I've known how unique you were, Remy. What you suspect only confirms what I've believed from the first moment I saw you. I thought I knew the worst, but this . . ." One side of his mouth tilted up. "You took me by surprise when I thought there were no surprises left."

In a halting tone, I said, "I'll understand if you want to walk away. No sane person would volunteer for this."

Serious eyes fixed on me, and he said, "Come away with me."

Startled, I tugged on my arm, but he didn't let me go. "You are insane."

"Yes. Completely crazy about you."

"That's not funny." I pushed against him until he finally released me. I couldn't tear my eyes from his intent gaze and the seductive persuasion in his voice.

"Leave this place with me, Remy."

Scowling, I felt tempted to punch him again. "Be serious."

"I've never been more serious in my life. Say yes, and I'll go home now to pack my bags. We can be gone by nightfall."

He meant it. I stumbled back several steps. The stone

bench cut into my thighs and I sat, overwhelmed and tempted. "You know I can't leave. There's school and my friends. My family . . . I can't."

My voice sounded anguished to my own ears, and I felt torn in two. After so many years alone, I'd found a home and a family. I couldn't give that up, not when it might be taken away from me soon. But I loved Asher, and I wanted to be with him. Would I have to choose?

"No!" Asher knelt at my feet, pressing my hand to his face. "I would never make you choose. I know what family means to you."

"Then, why?" I asked, bewildered.

"My brother's right. They will come for you. When they find out . . ." He shuddered. "The longer you stay here, the more vulnerable you'll be. What if I can't protect you?"

The weeks we'd been together, I'd changed in so many ways, but so had he. The return of his mortality brought relief and fear. Relief that he could feel human again, and fear he'd be too human to save me. It would happen again if we stayed together.

My fingers trailed into his hair. "You make me stronger, Asher. I don't need you to be immortal to save me."

"I didn't save you when Dean showed up. I should've been there!"

I'd known he blamed himself for Dean kidnapping me, but I'd thought he understood. Pushing off the bench, I kneeled before him, remembering the last time we'd been in this position right after he sacrificed himself to save me.

His skin felt hot, and I gave in to the impulse to touch his scar. "You were. In my heart and in my head. You heard my thoughts, but I heard you, too. I heard you telling me to be strong, to remember my training. I felt you willing me to stay alive until you could find me. You never left me, Asher, not for one second."

Asher's eyes held the shattered look I knew I wore each time he told me he loved me. He didn't see himself through my eyes and didn't understand how I could love him in return. I could see that I'd have to remind him often. *I love you, I love you, I love you.*

"I love you, Asher."

"I'll never tire of hearing it."

Strong arms crushed me to his chest, mindful of my injuries, and one hand wound through my hair to angle my head. He kissed me until we were both breathless, and the heat of his energy scorched through me again. He reached for my uninjured hand, twining our fingers, and I held on to him with all my strength. Eventually, we eased apart and stared at the green sparks warming our joined hands.

When they faded, I raised uncertain eyes to his. "Are you sure, Asher? There's no way of knowing what will happen if we stay together. This could only be the beginning."

He grinned. "I wouldn't miss a minute of it. Besides, you need me," he added, smugly. "I heard you think so."

I didn't deny that it was true.

"What's next, sweetheart?" he asked.

"I want to find my grandfather. My mother believed he might be able to help us."

Asher threw a glance at the iPod still sitting on the stone bench. He knew the importance of that last recording. Rising to his feet with his usual grace, he bent to help me up.

"Are you ready to listen?"

Was I? Could I hear Anna's voice without the rage and bitterness I'd felt last time? I gauged my tangled feelings. Anger was there, but then so was love, the two emotions forever knotted together when it came to my mother.

"Yes," I whispered, then added with more certainty, "Yes."

"Shall we, *mo chridhe?*"

He scooped up the iPod and took my hand.

A pessimist most of my life, I believed that the worst could and did happen. Yet, standing in the sunny clearing with Asher loving me, possibilities unwound before me, painting a hazy but possible future. Maybe we would have the future I'd dreamed of yet.

A memory came to me unbidden of my mother, and it didn't hurt like before. She recited a line from an Emily Dickinson poem to me that she'd heard somewhere, and it had stuck with me.

> *"Hope" is the thing with feathers—*
> *That perches in the soul—*

"Emily Dickinson?" Asher said, surprised. "My sister loves that poem."

Facing him, I smiled. "You know, one of these days, your eavesdropping is going to get you in trouble."

He smirked. "Don't be mad because I've discovered all your secrets."

"You think I don't have any more secrets?" I said, amused.

"You don't." When my expression didn't change, doubt flitted across his features. "Do you?"

Silently, I strode to the head of the path leading back to my house.

"Remy?" he called after me. "You don't have any other secrets, do you, *mo chridhe?* I'm not sure my heart can take it."

Not all surprises were bad. It hadn't taken long for me to discover how those few minutes of immortality, of possessing Asher's power, had changed me in some small, physical ways. I couldn't wait to see Gabe's face the next time we trained.

Asher's confused gaze met mine. "Remy?"

"Catch me if you can, Protector," I called over my shoulder.

With a laugh, I sped out of the clearing with supernatural speed, my feet scarcely meeting the ground as I dodged trees. In the distance, I heard Asher's startled laughter as I disappeared, followed by the sound of his light footsteps chasing me.

Nearing the exit to the street, I slowed, entirely willing to be caught. Asher almost ran into me where I leaned against a tree under a canopy of branches sprouting new green leaves. The recording could wait.

"I love you, *mo chridhe.*"

His lips touched mine, and I felt his smile when I responded. *Always.*

EPILOGUE

So, that's it. You have the information you need to find your grandfather.

He'll help you if you ever need him.

One last detail . . . If you go to him, don't tell him who your father is. I kept his identity a secret from my family all these years to keep you both safe.

You've probably guessed why by now.

When we met, I knew instantly your father was different from any man I'd met. I loved him from the beginning with a passion that shocked me. A part of me recognized something in Ben and gravitated towards it. He became my magnetic North.

I'll always wonder what could've been if I'd stayed.

But it would've been impossible to protect you. It didn't matter that neither of us had the powers of our ancestors—our legacy flows through our blood, and you can't argue with blood. Healers and Protectors have a history of destroying each other, and I couldn't risk you getting caught in the middle of that, baby. And you would be tossed in the middle of that bitter War if they discovered you.

I never told Ben what I suspected. It was only when your powers developed that my suspicions about him were confirmed. I don't think your father even knows the truth about himself, and it will be up to you whether or not you tell him what he is.

You're special, baby. The first of your kind.

Half-Healer. Half-Protector. The best of both and more powerful than either could dream of.

Be safe, Remy, and remember, I love you. . . .

ACKNOWLEDGMENTS

This book was a long time in the making. It took a village, as they say.

A huge debt of gratitude is owed to my agent, Laura Bradford, who always believed in this book and these characters. You don't know how much that meant to me.

To my lovely editor, Megan Records, you gave me the opportunity to continue Remy's story. Consider my world changed forever—thank you for that and for everything that you give back to the book community. These other wonderful KTeen people contributed to this novel, including Alicia Condon, Craig Bentley, Arthur Maisel, and Alexandra Nicolajsen. Thanks for your hard work!

Kate Hart, you were my very first beta reader *ever,* and I owe you my everlasting gratitude for not mocking me for that early draft. I'm honored to call such a talented writer my friend.

I wrote this book in my first semester at Spalding University's MFA program under the tutelage of my faculty mentor, Ellie Bryant, and continued to edit it with my second semester faculty mentor, Eleanor Morse. I learned so much from each of you and owe you so much. Thanks also to the Spalding students who workshopped chapters of this novel in Barcelona, including Jackie Gorman, Jenny Barker, Kendra Sigafoos, Carmen Bryant, and Kristin Doherty.

I hardly would have dared to write this book if not for the encouragement of Virginia Gannaway, Roger Perez, and Laurie Wielenga urging me on chapter by chapter. You were my cheerleaders, from Chapter One until I typed THE END. Thank you.

Along the way, many readers offered comments on various versions, and I am indebted to them, especially Cindy Corpier, Debra Driza, Laura McMeeking, Kari Young, Krista Ashe, Holen Mathews, Kathy Bradey, Nicole Runyan, Stephanie Kuehn, and Trish Leaver.

I also owe a shout out to the Class of 2k12, Bookanistas, Apocalypsies, and YA Rebels groups. Thanks for being there with me every step of the way this last year.

And finally, to my family, thanks for being you. I love you more than Kraft Blue Box.

FOOD FOR THOUGHT

1. If you had the ability to heal people, how would you use your power? Would you keep it a secret, like Remy does, or would you tell the world? Why?

2. How does Remy's ability bring her and Asher closer together? How does it push them apart?

3. How would you handle living life as an immortal? Would you return to the same places, as Asher's family does, or would you use the opportunity to live in completely new areas? Why?

4. As a victim of domestic abuse, Remy endures a lot of pain and fear. In several ways, her situation is similar to what many kids face today at the hands of bullies. Have you ever dealt with a bully? Do you think Remy's way of dealing with Dean is effective? If not, what else could she try?

5. How does Anna's journal help Remy empathize with her mother? In what ways does it make Remy hate her mother even more?

CORRINE JACKSON

Don't get too close...

Touched

A Sense Thieves Novel